Praise for Jerri Corgiat's debut novel,
Sing Me Home

"A treasure . . . a tender, romantic story of a big-time musician and a small-town girl discovering the things that matter most."
—*USA Today* bestselling author Susan Wiggs

"A masterful blend of Nashville glitz and down-home simplicity that will touch any romance reader's heart. *Sing Me Home* strikes realistic chords, reaffirming for all of us that the most important things in life aren't money and fame, but love, devotion, and family."
—*New York Times* bestselling author Catherine Anderson

"The unforgettable characters resonate long after the last page is turned."
—Susan Mobley, *Romantic Times Book Club* magazine

"This heartwarming debut novel will renew hope in the midst of winter. . . . Like a country song, it's sad and happy in all the right places."
—Huntress Book Reviews

"An intriguing family drama." —The Best Reviews

"Fans of small-town romances and musicians as characters will love this book." —All About Romance

"Ms. Corgiat does a wonderful job of developing the relationship between Lil and Jon. . . . [They] change before our very eyes as the story unfolds."
—*A Romance Review*

FOLLOW ME HOME

Jerri Corgiat

AN ONYX BOOK

ONYX
Published by New American Library, a division of
Penguin Group (USA) Inc., 375 Hudson Street,
New York, New York 10014, USA
Penguin Group (Canada), 10 Alcorn Avenue, Toronto,
Ontario, M4V 3B2, Canada (a division of Pearson Penguin Canada Inc.)
Penguin Books Ltd., 80 Strand, London WC2R 0RL, England
Penguin Ireland, 25 St. Stephen's Green, Dublin 2,
Ireland (a division of Penguin Books Ltd.)
Penguin Group (Australia), 250 Camberwell Road, Camberwell, Victoria 3124,
Australia (a division of Pearson Australia Group Pty. Ltd.)
Penguin Books India Pvt. Ltd., 11 Community Centre, Panchsheel Park,
New Delhi - 110 017, India
Penguin Group (NZ), Cnr Airborne and Rosedale Roads, Albany,
Auckland 1310, New Zealand (a division of Pearson New Zealand Ltd.)
Penguin Books (South Africa) (Pty.) Ltd., 24 Sturdee Avenue,
Rosebank, Johannesburg 2196, South Africa

Penguin Books Ltd., Registered Offices:
80 Strand, London WC2R 0RL, England

First published by Onyx, an imprint of New American Library,
a division of Penguin Group (USA) Inc.

First Printing, November 2004
10 9 8 7 6 5 4 3 2 1

Printed in the United States of America

PUBLISHER'S NOTE
This is a work of fiction. Names, characters, places, and incidents either are the product of the author's imagination or are used fictitiously, and any resemblance to actual persons, living or dead, business establishments, events, or locales is entirely coincidental.

To Mike and Mac, my best guys,
who continue to teach me about love

ACKNOWLEDGMENTS

As always, thanks go to Marcy Posner for her advocacy, and to Claire Zion and the staff at New American Library for their support and direction. Also to my friends and family for their continuing encouragement, love . . . and high jinks. Where would I get my inspirations (especially the wacky ones!) if not for you?

Since my childhood, I've spent summers at the Lake of the Ozarks in Missouri, and have drawn on many of the wonderful people I've met and places I've visited to create my fictional corner of the state for both *Sing Me Home* and *Follow Me Home*—Cordelia, Lake Kesibwi, and points between—along with their colorful, friendly residents. Thank you, central Missouri, for your warmth, charm, foibles, and beauty—and for always welcoming a Kansas native into your midst!

Chapter 1

Stalking back up the sweeping driveway that led from her mailbox to her colonnaded home perched on a hilltop overlooking Cordelia, Missouri, Alcea O'Malley Addams saw him about a half an hour before she ran him off the road.

Well, she didn't exactly see *him*. What she saw was a plume of dust beyond the water tower, about an inch tall at this distance. Both the tower and St. Andrew's steeple in the heart of old Cordelia spiraled above the treetops. Around her, acres of pastureland rolled downhill to meet copses of oak, sycamore, and maple, as well as a new strip mall, housing development, and a complex of expensive retirement condos several miles away. On the horizon, the Ozark hills lay quiet, achingly green after last night's April rain.

Once upon a time, Alcea had boasted about the panorama to anyone who would listen. Now neither the small dirt tornado nor the view held her attention. As she stretched her stride to miss a puddle, her mind was focused on money. Always on money. She was surprised dollar signs weren't spilling out of her ears.

She clenched a letter in her hand, the one her postman Eddie or Freddie—like Tweedle-Dum and Tweedle-Dee, the old Steeplemier brothers looked exactly alike—had just handed over. The one that had arrived registered from Cordelia Bank, where her ex-husband, Stan, was president. The one that said, *In accordance with R. S. MO 443.25, request is hereby made of notice of sale . . .*

And just like that, her home was gone.

Okay, not *just* like that. It had taken her four years to run through the money markets, bonds, stocks, and most of the antique furniture that had been the bulk of her divorce settlement, a one-time payout she'd taken instead of alimony, in exchange for Stan's agreement to give up his claims on the house. She was a dummy. Now she was left with a small savings account that she hoarded jealously, much to her fourteen-year-old daughter's dismay, and child support payments that barely covered the utilities. She also had a living room that looked like a deep-piled football field, empty of all its furniture save a china cabinet that had belonged to Stan's parents.

She kicked a rock, annoyed at the sentiment—*his* sentiment—that made her keep it. Stan's father had died in a car accident when he was thirteen. His mother, Ellen, seven years ago. But now she wondered if she could sell it before Stan remembered she had it, whether the cabinet would bring enough for a payment. . . . Oh, balls. At the top of the drive, she halted next to her Taurus and chewed her lip. And then what? She and Kathleen could break up what was left of the dining room suite and use it for kindling when the heat was turned off in the fall?

She stared at her house, at the brick-fronted facade with its wide veranda and rows of green-shuttered windows. Rock music pounded through the open French doors on one of two balconies upstairs, keeping beat with the ache in her head. In her youth she'd sat atop the water tower and dreamed of owning this house. Now she did. And was about to lose it.

She pointed her chin toward the second story. "Kathleen!"

It was the finest house in Cordelia, if you didn't count her sister Lil's compound a mile distant, and she tried not to. In the summer, roses climbed trellises that her yard man, Erik Olausson, had installed for her when she'd been a new bride eighteen years ago, then had tended for another fifteen. Until she'd let the old Swede's services go along with her housekeeper's. Now she polished the windows and fussed with the roses and mowed the acreage herself, sitting atop a tractor clad in denim and one of her mother's old straw hats. Always early in the morning, when nobody could see she looked like a gapeseed.

She tried again to outstrip the bass player. "Kathleen!"

The doors to Kathleen's bedroom were flanked by Mexican urns foaming with pansies. She'd picked up those urns on one of those inane excursions she'd once taken regularly with friends from the country club. She snorted. Some friends. Where were they now? Still at the country club, whispering behind their hands whenever she entered on Kemp Runyon's arm or with her sister Lil and her famous country star husband Jonathan Van Castle.

"For God's sake . . . Kath-LEEN!"

She'd known the foreclosure could happen—known it *would* happen—but she'd acted like a dumb ostrich. Damn Serena Simpson. Compared to *her*, the affair with his assistant that had put an end to their marriage had been a walk in the park. Why did Serena, her ex-husband's latest, want *her* house? Hell, the airhead owned that entire complex of luxury condos.

It took two more tries, but Kathleen finally appeared, a cordless phone to her ear, a book in her hand. She draped herself over the railing, blond hair spilling forward to shade her face. Except for the voracious reading habit, everyone said Kathleen was a twin of Alcea when she'd neared fifteen, and she'd soon reach Alcea's five-foot-eleven. All of the O'Malley sisters were tall and bordered on skinny (her little sister, Mari, *was* skinny). Even though their mother, Zinnia, was not. Still, it was Zinnia who had always cast the longest shadow. Staring up at Kathleen, Alcea realized that she'd only been a year or so older than her daughter when she'd latched onto Stan, making a choice that had led her to this calamity.

Teenagers were dumb.

Kathleen twined a bare foot around her calf and continued her conversation despite Alcea's tapping high heel. "No, it's the *fire* that's the metaphor, not the lake. . . ."

Or maybe not so dumb. Kathleen was undoubtedly dissecting her book with Lil's stepdaughter Melanie. Their discussions on Things Literary flummoxed Alcea. She felt less stupid around Kathleen's other best friend, her cousin Daisy. Daisy's specialty was eye shadow, not Shakespeare. Eye shadow, Alcea could grasp.

Foot tapping turned to whacking the envelope on the palm of her hand.

"Back in a sec, Mel." Kathleen broke off and raised her brows at her mother. *"What?"*

She looked bored. Boredom was one of her two expressions. The other was disgruntlement. Oh, wait. And livid anger. But thinking of all the confusion she'd felt at Kathleen's age, Alcea suddenly wanted to hug her daughter and never let her go. Not that she would. Hugging was out. The confiding girl with the sweet kisses had disappeared over the last three years. Alcea frowned. Also gone was the roll of baby fat around that girl's middle, along with anything to cover it. Even though the temperature still hovered under seventy, Kathleen was dressed in short-shorts and a top that barely made it past her rib cage. Looking at her figure, Alcea bit back an aren't-you-cold comment, not wanting to spark an argument, and also willing to admit that if she looked like that, she'd probably wear next to nothing, too.

"I'm going into town." Well, she didn't look like *that*, but at thirty-six she was still proud of her figure, made more astounding by what she did for a living.

Snort. Some living. "I'm picking up Kemp for a late lunch at Peg O' My Heart, and—"

"He's letting *you* drive?"

Alcea ignored her. Kathleen thought Kemp was a throwback to the fifties. Which, nearing fifty himself, he was in a way. But he was also, well, sweet. Cordelia wasn't exactly a hotbed of eligible bachelors. Not that she was looking for hot. She was looking for faithful. Dependable. *And wealthy,* a sneaky little imp with clear eyes whispered.

"His car is at Cowboy's." Cowboy's Tow and Service was the local garage. "And I have to stop at the bank. I have some business to discuss with your dad." She had to talk to Stan. No, as much as she hated it, she had to *plead* with Stan. And if that didn't work, maybe she'd wrap one of those gold chains he liked to wear around his thick neck and choke him. She stooped to pick up the purse and keys she'd left on the veranda steps when she'd mustered the courage to collect her mail.

"Tell Dad I'm not seeing him Sunday."

Alcea sighed and opened her car door. The scent of cinnamon, cloves, and cocoa rolled out from the cakes she'd loaded in there earlier. "We've been over this before. You have to. Every other weekend. It's part of the custody agreement." Although she could sympathize with Kathleen—she didn't want to see Stan, either—she didn't need to give Kathleen's father an excuse to wrangle over child support payments.

"Who cares?" Here came disgruntlement. Kathleen's fine brows dipped over the liquid brown eyes that were so like Alcea's. "It's not like we've ever had *anything* to talk about, and since he moved into Serena's, she's always around, and he like acts like I'm not even *there*."

Alcea knew what Kathleen meant. She'd only seen Stan that besotted with one other woman: his mother. "At least it's only one day. He was supposed to have you both Saturday *and* Sunday. And your dad is your dad."

"He's never acted like a dad."

Livid anger wasn't too far off. Wistfully, Alcea thought of the days when Kathleen had caught every word she'd dropped like rare jewels spilled from her mouth. "And he's also the one paying for your dress to the spring dance."

"I don't even know if I'm going. Boys are so *lame.*" Alcea could second that. Kathleen's expression took on a calculating look. "But Serena said she'd take me shopping. . . . You know, sometimes, like, she's not too bad."

This brought Alcea up short, even though she knew Kathleen could be bought. Hadn't she bribed her enough times herself? "I thought you hated her." Serena was a topic Alcea allowed Kathleen to rant about without interruption.

"She's okay. I mean, you have Kemp"—Kathleen made him sound like a case of measles—"so why shouldn't Dad have someone?"

True. And she couldn't say she hadn't enjoyed seeing Lothario led around by the nose for the last six months. She almost voiced the words, then thought better of it. Nothing good ever came from sticking kids in the middle of parental battles. "Don't go anywhere while I'm gone."

"But—"

"And don't invite anyone over, either."

"But—"

"I'll be back around three." She'd learned to ride over the *but*s.

Alcea slid into the Taurus and, with an offhandedness she didn't feel, tossed the envelope next to two cake carriers. She'd traded in her BMW for the used Ford two years ago, explaining to anyone who'd asked (and even those who hadn't) that she was tired of taking the BMW all the way to Sedalia whenever it needed a repair. She lowered the visor and checked her appearance. The starched white collar with its ribbon of lace looked demure, elegant, and went with her white silk pants. She tucked a strand of gold hair back into her chignon. Her appearance would meet with Kemp's approval. Thinking of Kemp, she glanced at the envelope. Oh, balls. She worried too much. Something would save her. Stan would delay foreclosure, like he had before. Or there was Lil. Or Kemp. He was already halfway besotted, so . . .

That damn clear-eyed imp suddenly surfaced in her head again, as it had with increasing frequency over the last few years. *Your problems aren't Serena's fault. They aren't Stan's. And you're a worm to think anyone else should solve them.*

Suddenly sick of herself, of her whole damned life, she flipped up the mirror, revved the engine, and took off with a squeal of tires. She could think of a lot more things she liked better than introspection. She looked around. Like her acreage. Dang, but it looked just as good as when Erik Olausson had mowed it. Her mood lightened a tad until she passed Lil's house, gated and barely visible from the road. Along with Cordelia's premier home, Lil had a burgeoning business, a solid marriage, and two beautiful stepchildren, including Melanie, who never talked back. She looked around for something to distract her from thoughts of her perfect sister and her perfect life, and her gaze landed back on the water tower. The plume of dust had moved away.

As a teenager she'd made a regular habit of climbing the tower. In her bravest moments, she'd even swung down from a crab apple tree outside her window and made her way through darkened streets to sit on its railed ledge at night, searching out the moon-washed white of the colonnaded house. She'd always gone alone, except . . .

One night, she surprised a boy up there, a senior to her sophomore. She'd noticed him at school. With his sea-foam eyes a sharp contrast to his dark hair, who wouldn't? But she'd ignored him. Those translucent eyes were usually pinned to a book. And popular Alcea O'Malley didn't *do* books. But that night she'd seen him in a new light. Moonlight. Its glow had highlighted his cheekbones, shadowed the hollows of his face, and turned his clear eyes silver. Those eyes had stared right past the artifice of Alcea O'Malley and straight into her heart. He'd made her look at herself, even while she was busy staring at him. She'd returned home with her head in a whirl, had decided that she might even take up reading. Dakota Jones. Who could forget that name? Or the possibilities he'd raised?

She grimaced. Obviously she could. Within weeks of that night, she'd sported Stan's high school ring on her finger. Stan's mother had approved his choice of Miss Cordelia. And Miss Cordelia had thought exchanging that ring for a wedding band after they'd graduated was quite a coup. A much easier coup than relying on herself. And Dakota Jones had became just one of those silly romantic memories that shined brighter through the polish of time.

She braked at an intersection, and her car unexpectedly slid onto the highway before coming to a halt. Fortunately, no cars were coming. She slapped the steering wheel. Figured. Spongy brakes were cosmic payback for her continuing lie about the BMW. She sighed. She'd take the Ford to Cowboy's after she visited the bank. . . .

And pay for the repairs with what? Deciding that if one more thing went wrong she'd explode, she stabbed the accelerator and burned tire tracks into the road behind her. Looking ahead, she saw the plume of dust had disappeared.

Chapter 2

A cloud of dust followed Dakota Jones's Jeep down a back road into Cordelia. Open to the sky the way he liked it, the wind whistled past his ears, rattled the flaps of the cardboard boxes in the backseat, and wreaked havoc with his half sister's hairdo.

Hitching up his old army jacket with a shrug of his shoulders, Dak gazed over the landscape. "Things look different. I remember cattle and pastures here instead of a housing development. Still, it's good to see Cordelia isn't dying." Unlike a lot of the small towns he'd idled in over the years. He briefly tipped up his sunglasses and looked at Florida. "But what still blows my mind is how much you've changed."

A half an hour ago, picking her up at her apartment, he'd seen her for the first time in twenty years. She'd changed from the waif with overly large blue eyes that he remembered into a strawberry-blond bombshell whose e-mailed pictures didn't do her justice.

"Did y'all expect me to stay nine forever? If you'd come home once in a while, it wouldn't be such a shock." Florida tried to gather her windblown hair. "And can you slow this pup down? I'd like to get back to work without looking like I spent my lunch hour in a blender."

"Sorry." He grinned and ratcheted down the Jeep's speed as they approached the water tower. He wasn't accustomed to riding with a companion. "I hadn't planned to stay away—it just happened." He hadn't returned since he'd graduated from high school, even though he hadn't intended to stay away, either. Life just hadn't pushed him this direction again.

"Doesn't seem to me like you plan much at all."

Dak shrugged, flashed another smile. "I told you I'd pay the travel expenses if you and Cowboy ever wanted to join up with me."

"I had better things to do than visit those old backwaters where you stick yourself." Florida pushed her hair back and held it in a knot. "And Grandpa? Why, you couldn't have budged him out of this place with a crowbar."

"I wish you'd told me he was sick." He and their grandfather hadn't been close, but he would have liked to have said farewell to Cowboy in person, not over a burial plot.

"He wanted to keep it quiet except from me and Peg and Julius."

He smiled fondly, thinking of his grandfather's longtime paramour and longtime mechanic.

"The three of us shared his care," Florida continued. Her eyes dimmed to a shade of navy and the faux Southern accent fell from her voice. "He didn't suffer much, and he wasn't too drugged to enjoy your e-mails right up to the end." She smiled again, although her lips quivered. "He got a kick out of the Internet, although it took me forever to convince him it wouldn't bite after you sent him that computer."

Some uncharacteristic sense of familial obligation had at least led him to keep in electronic touch with the only relatives he had after his and Florida's mother had died.

They hit the shadow of the water tower. On impulse, he pulled to the side of the road and got out. Like nothing else had so far, the flattened blue orb with the catwalk ringing its underside struck him with an unfamiliar twinge of nostalgia. Sticking his hands in his khaki pockets, he studied it. For the almost four years he'd lived in Cordelia as a teenager, he'd loved that tower as much as he'd hated his grandfather's narrow, dark house. "I spent a lot of nights up there staring at the hills, wondering what burg Tamara had landed in and what my own future held." Sometimes he'd also get the glimmer for a new story.

Florida had alighted more slowly, encumbered by her spiked heels and the narrow turqoise skirt that matched her suit jacket. She moved up beside him. "I remember."

At the bitterness in her voice, he looked over. Her lips were tight. She'd had a worse time of it than he'd had after Tamara had left them here. She'd only been six, not old enough to understand their mother. Or him, for that matter.

She glanced at her watch, a platinum band that must have cost her a half-year's salary. He looked from it to the silk suit. "I take it the secretary job is going well."

"Managing assistant." She avoided his eyes. "And I need to get to the bank."

He followed her back to the Jeep, letting her evasion pass without comment. After she'd gotten her long legs tucked back in, he put the Jeep in gear, eying the water tower as it disappeared in the rearview mirror. Only once had his night musings been disturbed. What was that girl's name? He ran his hand through his hair, then shook his fingers loose from its tangles. Alice? Some beauty a couple years behind him in high school. She was a road not taken. One of many, but he'd still covered a lot of ground.

Florida knotted her hair back again. "So what will you do first?" Sapphire studs sparkled on her ears. They looked like the real McCoy.

"Take my gear to the house." He motioned in back to his duffel, boxes, and laptop. All his worldly possessions. "Then look over my inheritance." He paused. "Are you upset Cowboy left it all to me? If you are, you can have it."

"That ol' dog of a place? I told him I didn't want

it. Neither did Peg. She's got her own business to run. And even though Julius always talked about going partners with Grandpa, he never had the money. It'll take a fortune to fix it up, so good thing you have one."

"I thought old Julius and Cowboy still worked the garage."

"Julius still does, but he injured his hand way back and can't work fast anymore. The place barely made enough in the last years to keep Grandpa in chewing tobacco. And the house was crumblin' around his ears. That trailer in the back is still there, still an eyesore, and still grown over with Virginia creeper."

"Julius doesn't live there anymore?"

"He moved out after he finished off the rooms over the service garage. It's all yours, brother. Grandpa left me some cash and a pair of earrings our dear Grandmama didn't run off with." When he stopped at the intersection to Highway 52, Florida took advantage and dipped into her purse and withdrew a silver tube. Opening it, she put another coat of berry sheen on her full lips. "They're paste, which figures. Cold day in hell when I'll have diamonds."

He glanced at the suit, the watch, and thought of the earrings. Not funded by her job. Her fiancé? "Didn't you mention a wedding in your future a year or so ago? Sam somebody?" He turned toward town. In the summer, the highway was clogged by visitors headed toward the Ozark lakes. Today traffic was nonexistent.

"It— We hit a snag." Florida twisted the tube shut and grabbed once more at her hair, wiggling around in her tight skirt to smile at him. The smile looked like it took effort. "But that's neither here nor there. I'm really glad you're back. Are you . . . Will you stay?"

As the highway narrowed into Main Street, sturdy old farmhouses interspersed with newer tract homes and a brand-new high school gave way to broad airplane bungalows fronted by porches held down by pots that would burgeon with geraniums in another month. A few Victorian homes and more than a few trees grew tall among them.

"Florida . . ." He sighed at the hopeful look in her eyes. "I'm only staying until I can find a buyer for Cowboy's Tow and Service."

"Oh." She faced forward again. "I'd hoped you'd give a permanent address a try."

Even when she was small, she'd been needier than him. "But from what you've said, it will take a while for me to get the place fixed up. No problem. I don't have a schedule to keep."

"You never have a schedule. Just a permanent case of wanderlust." Her voice held acid. "Like Tamara." They never had called their mother *Mother*.

"I wish you'd known her like I did." He didn't try to defend his lifestyle.

"I don't." Florida's jaw was set.

"She tried. She did the best she knew for us."

"Right." Florida's voice was dry.

"She wasn't mother material. She was . . . what she was."

Florida opened her mouth, then snapped it shut, apparently realizing their minds wouldn't meet on this topic.

They neared the heart of town. His tires rubbed over some brick visible through worn concrete. St. Andrew's steeple came into view, then the bulk of the church, sitting pat in the center of the square, its rough, milky stone showing through a screen of trees budding with new leaves. Tulips nudged each other for space along the walks under their branches. If he remembered his town history, the church and state had battled for supremacy. Church had won in the 1840s, compliments of the first mayor, a hellfire-and-damnation minister. He eased to a stop at the four-way on Oak Haven Road. Next street parallel would be Maple Woods Drive. Just beyond that, Cowboy's service garage and the narrow gray house.

Florida finger combed and nodded to the right. "The bank's around the corner."

He ignored her hurry and leaned his forearms on the wheel. The square looked more spiffed up than when he'd known it, but some things didn't change. He still couldn't see through the steam on the windows of Up-in-the-Hair Beauty Salon. Midway down a row of two-story brick storefronts with white-trimmed windows, a cigar store Indian still sat in front of O'Neill's Emporium. "Is Paddy O'Neill still around?"

Florida snorted. "He'll last forever. He's probably in there"—she poked a polished nail at Peg O' My Heart Cafe on the corner opposite the beauty salon—"chewing the fat with the other old geezers."

"I'll look him up. As long as I'm here, I might as well do some writing and keep my editor happy." Paddy had once known everything about everything. He'd be a good place to start. "Do people around here know what I do?"

"Maybe Mr. Eagleton, but he keeps to himself." Eagleton was his old high school English teacher, likely long retired. "Grandpa bragged on you way back, but he was disappointed when you threw in the brass ring. From then on, your biggest accomplishment was having him for a grandfather. Doubtful anyone much remembers what he was yammering about over a decade ago. I barely remember myself. What's the name of those books? *One for the Road*?"

He glanced at her, amused. "Have you read any of them?"

"One." She darted a mischievous glance at him. "About bored the pants right off me."

He laughed. "Good thing not everybody feels that way."

"Still, it's too bad they aren't published under your own name so you could take credit."

"Credit's not all it's cracked up to be." His walk away from success didn't bother him any—but he didn't want to explain it. "I'd appreciate it if you'd keep what I do to yourself, but don't lie for me. If word gets out, it's not a big deal. It's just easier if people don't know."

Florida shrugged. "Makes no difference to me. How you live . . ." She shook her head. "Small town to small town. Sounds like a perfectly hideous way to spend your life."

"But you live in one," he pointed out.

"Cordelia's not all *that* small. Besides, unlike you, wherever Peg and Cowboy were was home for me. At least all the home I was likely to get." Resentment scraped her voice again.

He ignored it. "How is Peg holding up?" The diner's owner and Cowboy had been an item since long before he'd arrived in Cordelia. They'd never married, though. Maybe one marriage was all a Jones man could tolerate.

"She misses Grandpa like all get-out, but she's still rattling along." Florida sighed. "It must be something to have someone love you like that."

It was stifling. "What's that?" He pointed to an unlikely silhouette. The front half of an antique carousel horse protruded above the door of the building next to the Emporium.

"Merry-Go-Read. Remember? I e-mailed you about Lilac O'Malley starting a children's bookstore after she married Jonathan Van Castle four years ago. I think she owns three now."

"Ah, yes. The Cordelia Girl Made Good. Do she and the superstar live here?"

"During the school year. They mostly spend summers at Lake Kesibwi. Gawd, what I wouldn't give for her hunk of a husband and her piles of money. Although I wouldn't want her family. Or at least not her older sister. Alcea Addams is a bitch."

Alcea, not Alice. "Addams? Who did she marry?"

"My . . . Stanley Addams."

Stanley Addams III. Dak had wasted some time during his youth envying the kid with the shiny Corvette, the football trophies, the doting mother, and the golden-haired girl hanging on his arm during those last weeks before graduation. Alcea had latched on to Stan after Dak had humiliated her in the high school cafeteria. Good ol' Stan.

Stan, not Sam. He glanced at Florida. "Your—"

"My boss," she said firmly. "And they're divorced."

"How long?" He remembered Florida's e-mail messages about Stan dating back for about five years, but apparently she hadn't told him everything.

She pinked. "Long enough. We need to go or I'll be late."

He was curious in a detached way, but felt relief more than disgruntlement at her sealed lips. She hadn't told him everything, but then neither had he. Hypocritical to start pretending now that they'd ever had a close-knit family. Or that he'd ever wanted one, beyond a few fleeting moments on that water tower and a dumb decision he'd made in college.

He started the turn, not noticing a Taurus bearing down from the right until it skidded through the stop sign and barreled straight at them.

"Hang on!" Dak stomped the accelerator before the car rear-ended the Jeep. The Jeep bucked up against a curb to the left in front of the bank and came to a halt. The other driver swerved right, crossed the intersection, bumped over the sidewalk, and trundled through the wet grass in front of St. Andrew's. A few midday strollers sprang aside. A stand of tulips bit the dust. The car jounced a few more yards and crunched against a stand of blossoming lilacs. Good thing, because the next obstacle was a solid oak.

Dak looked at Florida. She'd tightened her arms around her waist. "You okay?"

"I am, but—" For whatever reason, a red flush suddenly joined the fluster on her face, but she waved him away. "I'm okay. You'd better check on the other driver." She looked over. "Oh, good God. It's Alcea."

Dak looked at the Taurus. It sat still and silent. Suddenly, the ignition ground, the motor whined, and mud flew as the driver threw the car in reverse—and went nowhere. He shook his head. "You have a cell?" Florida nodded. "Better call Julius at the garage. She'll need a tow."

"Idiot woman."

As he crossed the street, wheels spun, the ruts deepened, and Dak grinned. At this rate, she'd dig her way right through to China. Out of the corner of his eye, he saw a small crowd gathering outside of Peg's. At the forefront was a crooked figure, thumbs hooked in suspenders, grizzled face wreathed in pure enjoyment. Beside him, a short, heavy woman with a bushel of orange hair matching an orange uniform frowned at the car. Dak's grin widened. Even with the added years, he would have recognized them anywhere. Paddy O'Neill and Peg, not about to miss the show. Cell phone to her ear, Florida climbed out of the Jeep and leaned a hip against the rear.

When he was six feet from the Taurus, it roared again. He dodged a clump of sod. "Hey! Shut it off!" Obligingly, it fell silent. Slapping dirt off his leg, he approached the driver's side and tapped on the window.

For a moment, nothing happened, then the window purred down. "Yes?" The voice was chilled, but polite. The ear he could see was rosy.

He almost laughed. It *was* Alcea O'Malley. How could he have forgotten how she could hit that note of disdain? She'd used it on him repeatedly after he'd spurned her attentions. The memory stirred an unusual moment of regret.

Red stained her collar. Without thinking, he touched her neck. "You're hurt."

She jerked sideways. "I am not hurt."

He looked at the red goo on his finger and frowned.

Florida approached, picking her way carefully around puddles. "Julius is on his way."

Alcea glanced sideways, saw him still studying his hand. "It's raspberry glacé." The words were hissed. "I had a cake. Five of them, as a matter of fact. Three dark cocoa–buttermilk with raspberry glacé and two cranberry-pecan. Real butter, fresh buttermilk, specialty cocoa, and fresh fruit. They were expensive to make. And now they are *slime*." She flung open the door. It narrowly missed him. She swung out her legs, slender in white trousers spattered with red. "My brakes failed. And if you hadn't taken that turn like your pants were on fire—"

"Him?" Florida snorted. "I believe *you* were driving like a bat out of hell. Which figures."

"I beg your pardon." Alcea planted both feet and rose to what might have been an impressive height if the spikes on her shoes hadn't sunk in the mud. She teetered on the verge of falling backward but caught herself on the door frame. "I don't know why you feel compelled to offer an opinion, Florida. This doesn't concern you."

"Uh, ladies—" Dak pushed his sunglasses up on his head.

"It certainly does. Y'all almost broadsided me. I could have been killed!"

"And what a loss that would be." Alcea glared at Florida, then at him, and her eyes widened. They held the same dark depths he'd almost drowned in as a teen. "Aren't you—"

"Dakota Jones. I wasn't sure you'd remember."

"I, uh— Yes. I do." Her hand flew to smooth back the hair that had escaped from a knot, and only succeeded in smearing red jelly into the strands. "How are you, Dak?" She offered her hand with an air that made him unsure if he was supposed to shake it or bow and kiss it. Kissing it might be less of a mess, but he grasped it anyway. Their gazes locked—and their hands stuck together. Blushing furiously, she yanked back her hand.

Even in her confusion, she was still a beauty. The years sat easily on her, time honing her fine bone structure, experience sharpening the intelligence in her eyes. Her hair had deepened to the color of the sun just before it set. He'd liked it better when she'd let the nighttime breeze swirl it around her shoulders. With the remembered feel of it brushing his cheek, his mind sang with an echo of adolescent yearning.

"I'm, uh, sorry about all this." She nodded toward his Jeep. Florida smirked, and Alcea glared at her again before turning her attention back to him. "I hope it's not damaged."

"Another ding isn't going to hurt it. We took the liberty of calling for a tow."

"I can't af—" She looked at Florida, then at the people in front of Peg's. "I mean, I don't need a tow. Kemp"—she looked back at him, colored—"Kemp's a friend. He'll take care of it later."

"Why put Kemp to the trouble?" He paused. "On the house, of course."

"Oh, I couldn't—" A tow truck rumbled around the corner. COWBOY'S TOW AND SERVICE was visible through the rust on the door. She looked from the truck back at him. "That's right. I'd forgotten you're Cowboy's grandson. I'm sorry for your loss." After a beat, she nodded stiffly to include Florida.

"Touching." Florida tapped her watch. "But if y'all don't mind, I need to get to work."

Alcea's eyes narrowed on Florida's wrist. "Nice timepiece. TO MY DARLING on the back, if I remember correctly. I didn't care for that watch when Stan gave it to me. Such an unoriginal sentiment, why, it could have been meant for just about anybody. *Which figures.* That's who Stan used to bed when he was married to me. Anybody." The small crowd in front of Peg's edged closer.

Florida's lips trembled. "Shut up, Alcea. Just shut

up." She looked at Dak. "I get off at five." Without another word, she turned and stalked toward the bank.

The crowd heaved a sigh of disappointment. The tow truck angled closer to the car.

Frowning, Alcea's gaze followed Florida, then she glanced at him defensively. "She usually gives as good as she gets."

He shoved his hands in his pockets. "Whatever's between the two of you is your business, not mine."

Her frown deepened as if she wasn't sure she approved of his lack of chivalry. With a high-pitched *beep-beep,* the truck backed toward them.

Alcea ducked into the car and retrieved an envelope and her purse. The mud sucked at her heels. "Oh, balls," she muttered. She slipped off her shoes and nylons, and hurled them into the backseat.

He tried to keep a straight face. She watched the truck, but he could feel her sideways glance. He wasn't sure if the heady scent of vanilla and cinnamon that enveloped him was from her or from the mashed-up cakes in her car. "So you did become a baker."

She started, then stared. "I'm surprised you remember. . . ."

"Hey! *That merry wanderer of the night.*" Julius clambered down from the truck. He had the same broad smile Dak remembered, although his carrottop had faded to rust, his freckles into deep lines, and a few more pounds filled his coveralls.

"A Midsummer Night's Dream." Dak laughed at their old game and clasped Julius's left hand. He noted that the right one was contorted. "Sorry to hear about your hand."

"Eh, had a tussle with an engine block. Engine block won." He flexed the hand. "Doesn't bother me too much anymore. Can't write, but I can still find my way around a car, so—"

He was interrupted by a gasp.

"Well, for land's sakes, is that Dakota? *My* Dakota?" Peg waddled toward them, jowls quivering. An enamel butterfly poked into her hair bobbed agreeably. "Let me have at you." Before he could duck, Peg engulfed him in a hug that squeezed the air from his lungs. She held him at arm's length and beamed. "Oh, dear, oh, dear. You've got Cowboy's smile. Came and went like white lightning, and just about took my breath away every time." Her faded blue eyes teared and she swiped at them, smudging the circles of orange on her cheeks. "Oh, shoot. I didn't mean to get all soggy."

"Good to see you, Peg."

But Peg had already turned to Alcea. "Alcea O'Malley Addams, what do you think you're doing driving in here like a bat out of hell?"

Alcea winced. "My brakes—"

"And would you look at your car? It'll take a month of Sundays to get all that goop cleaned up. Too bad, too, as I already had two of those cakes sold." She *tsk*'d. "Julius, don't stand there gaping like a carp. Get yourself to work."

Grinning, Julius bobbed his head and hurried back to the truck.

"Alcea!" A willowy woman stepped out from Merry-Go-Read and headed toward them. Her cropped curls gleamed lemon in the sun above a swirling azure dress, giving her the look of a blue iris. A short woman with salt-and-pepper hair and a determined expression followed. Her violently flowered purple skirt whipped around plump legs. Both shared the same eyes, but different tints. One as clear as sky; the other foggy behind thick glasses. Alcea moaned.

Reaching them, the older woman gave Dakota a curious glance, but spoke to Alcea. "Honeybunch! Where in tarnation are your shoes?" She looked at the car. "You must have been driving like a bat out of hell!" Alcea sighed but kept her mouth shut, and the woman turned to him. "Why, I'll be. Thought I recognized you. It's Dakota Jones, isn't it? Been an age. Zinnia O'Malley, if you've forgotten." She pumped his hand. "And you remember Lil?" Alcea's mother and sister. He remembered.

"I used to baby-sit for your sister." Lil was lovely, but her older sister still outdid her. "We were so sorry about Cowboy." Lil's eyes were soft. She touched Alcea's arm with a look of concern. "Are you okay?"

"I'm fine," Alcea said, voice short.

Zinnia frowned at Alcea, then up at him. "Don't believe we saw you at the funeral."

He smiled at the unspoken rebuke. In small towns, some things Just Weren't Done. "I was sorry to miss it, but Florida couldn't reach me. My laptop was broken." And computer techs weren't behind every tree in the backwoods of Maine.

She still looked suspicious. "No cell phone?"

"Mother!" Alcea protested.

"No cell phone," he repeated agreeably. "I think they're intrusive."

"Well, can't say as I disagree with you there." Zinnia's face relaxed. "Still, too bad you missed it. We gave Cowboy quite the send-off, didn't we, Peg?" She gave Peg's shoulder a sympathetic pat but kept her eyes on Dak. "You travel a bit, don't you? Just like your mother. Every time I turned around, seemed Cowboy told me Tamara was off someplace else. I don't think he could keep up with her. I was sorry to hear she'd passed, by the way. Going on about fifteen years or so, isn't it? Lord love a duck, how time flies. You know, your mother and I were only a couple years apart in school. Didn't run with the same crowd, though." Her expression said she didn't think that was a bad thing.

Dak frowned, and Alcea interrupted. "Enough reminiscenses, Mother."

Zinnia lowered her brows at her oldest.

With a quick glance at their faces, Peg spoke up. "We can all go jaw in a minute, but right now we got to get this girl taken care of. How in Hades will she get back home?"

They all frowned at the Taurus. Julius had it almost hooked up.

"I can't give you my van. I need it for the business today," Zinnia said. "Lil?"

"Of course I can take her home, but I hate to think of her and Kathleen out there without transportation. It's so isolated." A pretty frown settled on Lil's brow. "Maybe Jon could—"

"I *can* figure this out for myself."

Dak glanced down. Alcea's toes had curled into the mud. She had beautiful feet, long and ivory with pink polished nails.

"I know!" Peg spoke like Alcea hadn't. She motioned to a neon-blue panel truck. It had wings of orange fire mixed with the rust along its sides. "She can take my truck. I don't need it until tomorrow afternoon."

Alcea looked at the truck, blanched, and opened her mouth, but her mother spoke first. "Well, that's settled. You're a generous person, Peg."

Peg beamed at Zinnia, Zinnia beamed back, and Lil smiled at them both.

"Keys are in it, Alcea." Peg started toward her diner. "Dak, let's go get a load off. We have some catching up to do."

Lil and Zinnia followed her, but Dak stayed where he was. Alcea hadn't moved. Fingering her envelope, she stared after the trio with a hopeless look on her face.

Dak touched her arm. She jumped. "I'll have Julius take a look at your brakes. If nothing's too wrong, I'm sure it will be ready tomorrow."

"I can't . . ." She broke off, chewing her lower lip. A nice, generous lip.

"It won't cost you anything," he said gently.

Her cheeks pinked again and she looked down at

the envelope. "Thank you." Her voice was small. "Really. Thank you." She rotated the envelope between her fingers, and her eyes finally focused. She cleared her throat. When she looked at him again, her eyes were still damp, but they also held steel. Now"—she glanced at the bank—"if you'll excuse me, I have some business to handle."

Dak watched her go. With every step, her back grew stiffer and her chin notched farther up. He smiled. Apparently, she chose to ignore the fact that she was barefoot and had raspberry jam in her hair. He admired her spirit. And he wondered how close a friend that Kemp fellow was.

Chapter 3

Smiling to himself at the memory of Alcea's queenly, raspberry-clad carriage as she'd walked away from him yesterday, Dak dragged a couple of aluminum lawn chairs out to the patio behind Cowboy's house. Dawn was just cracking the horizon. Settling into a chair, he kicked off his sandals and put his feet up on an upended bucket—one more piece of junk to match the junk in the house. Sighing, he reluctantly let go of Alcea's image and forced himself to think about the enormity of the task that faced him. He'd forgo his usual morning musings in his journal in favor of a list. It would be a long one. And it would start with *Lease another Dumpster.*

Before he'd met Florida for supper last night, he'd explored the thin two-story home where he'd spent his high school years. It was crammed to bursting with everything from trunks of books and papers in the cellar to an ancient bottle of Boone's Farm at the back of the fridge. A toilet was leaking, screens needed mending, the porch was rotting, the roof needed repairing, and the gray serrated shingles lapping the house didn't look like they'd seen a paintbrush since the one he'd wielded on it when he was sixteen. And that was the house. He hadn't taken a close look at the service garage that was connected to it by a breezeway.

While he'd rummaged around, he hadn't been

struck with any pangs of nostalgia. His brief years here weren't particularly memorable. Cowboy had done what he could to make things pleasant, but he'd been a taciturn man and his affection had been clumsy—especially around the quiet teenager Dak had been. His grandfather had experienced more success with Florida, who had clung to him like a castaway on a life raft.

Thinking of his half sister, he frowned. Last night, they'd met at the local hangout, the Rooster Bar & Grill. The place was like a million others of its ilk—neon beer signs glowing through a smoky haze, country twitter on the jukebox, waitresses with a sashay and a ribald wink—and some of the best food you could come by, although Florida had only picked at her grilled chicken sandwich. As he'd done better justice to a half-pounder, they'd chatted about her college years in Warrensburg and the places he'd traveled to over the years. And they'd avoided most things personal, like why his marriage had ended and why Florida sported dark crescents under her eyes. But then he'd mentioned all the crap strewn in and around his grandfather's three-acre property and suddenly they'd been discussing Tamara.

Tearing small pieces off her sandwich, Florida had smiled fondly. "Cowboy was always talking about how he'd get that messy yard all cleaned up, but he never did. It was always like that, remember? Y'all should. You spent more time out back than inside."

"The house was confining." He leaned back, abandoning his plate and feeling like he'd never be able to eat again. "And I liked looking at the view."

"And up until Tamara dumped us here, the entire country was pretty much our playground, huh?" Her voice was dry.

This afternoon he'd realized he'd soon grow tired of fencing over their mother, and he was. She was gone. There wasn't a point. "Tamara did love us, Florida. She sent us letters up until she died—remember those? And cards and presents on our birthdays."

"Big whoop." He felt his face darken. Florida looked up, and her voice softened. "I mean, if she loved us so danged much, Dak, then tell me why you think she didn't come back."

"Same reason I didn't. And it wasn't because I don't care about you." Not seeing his mother again had hurt—of course it had. But since he'd found himself with the same inclinations, he'd empathized. "Staying in one place would have killed her. It was her nature, that's all. She was just . . . Tamara."

Florida dropped her gaze again, but not before he saw she didn't accept his answer. Maybe someday she'd learn there weren't any easy ones. Sometimes you just had to take things as they were. "Let's not argue about her, Florida. Look, I can agree that Tamara probably shouldn't have had us in the first place. She wasn't cut out for motherhood, and maybe she didn't have normal maternal feelings. But maybe that's because her mother ran out on her. You can understand that, can't you?"

Florida nodded. "But—"

"So she put us with Cowboy because she thought we needed stability and a formal education. It was *because* she cared about us that she finally left us. She'd done her best, but she knew she wasn't making the grade." At least with Florida, he thought. With him, it had been different. "We have different memories because we had different experiences. I understand her because I'm like her."

"Maybe some of that's true, but—"

"I know you went through hell when she left us here. And I know I didn't." He shrugged. "Let's just agree to disagree on the subject. What do you say?"

Frowning, Florida crumbled the bread between her fingers. After a long moment, she finally said, "You're right. She's gone. And what I'm interested in now is having some kind of relationship with you. So . . . if that's the way you want it, I'll try to keep my mouth shut."

"And I'll appreciate the effort." He'd smiled. "Because I'm beginning to learn that could be a pretty tall order."

She'd laughed, and they'd finished their meal feeling pleased with each other.

He dispensed with last night's memory, adjusted his spiral notebook and jotted a few reminders about electricians, plumbers, and roofers. Then he once again eyed all the crap that had started the whole conversation with Florida.

The town had filled out in every direction but this one, likely due to low-lying areas farther on where septics wouldn't perk. Cowboy had taken advantage of the relative isolation to let his property go. But despite the weed-eaten, overgrown, junk-strewn yard, it *did* have a view going for it. To the right, Cowboy's acres skipped to a rusted wire fence, then the land fell into fields and pasture, swirls of cream and kelly punctuated by stands of trees. Beyond were the deep woods of the Ozark hills, rising into the morning mist. Soon the sun would flood the sky with pastel light, deepening the shadows in the valleys, turning the newly leafed oaks vivid green, and inflaming the redbud trees. Dogwood blossoms would flutter like white moths in the understory.

He pulled his gaze away from the hills and settled it on more practical matters. A lot of this stuff he could take care of himself. Some would require help. Far off to his left, beyond the edge of the service garage, was a row of white pines screening a delivery alley. One pine was dead. He scribbled *tree removal service,* then scanned the back half of the property. The deep yard ended in a crowd of trees that shielded the place from development to the north. And right in front of the trees was the trailer Julius had lived in before he'd moved over the garage. The trailer clung to its torn-skirted moorings amid a tangle of brush. Steps made a drunken walk up to a one-room addition tacked none too sturdily onto the front. He grimaced. It wasn't just ramshackle, either. It was pink. All pink. Like a sixty-five-foot roll of bubblegum. He studied it a moment, then shook his head and looked down at his list. Words failed him.

"Yoo-hoo." The screen door to the patio clattered open, and Florida stepped out, holding a StarMart cup with a straw poking out. She looked every inch the corporate professional in her red suit, high heels, and slash of matching lipstick. "I hope y'all don't mind, but Julius said he saw you out here. He's changing the oil on my Miata this afternoon, so I thought I'd see if you'd walk me to work."

He pushed aside his annoyance at being disturbed at his favorite time of the day and stood up, mustering a smile. She'd just lost her only family except for him. It was understandable she'd seek him out. "Isn't six thirty a little early for work?"

"I'm just putting in my share of overtime." She didn't sound happy about it.

He slipped on his sandals, wondering if work was the reason for how tired she looked. She'd started at the bank as soon as she had her business degree. In her e-mails, she'd breathlessly recited every detail as she'd worked her way up from teller to managing assistant. Now that he thought about it, she'd had less and less to say about work over the last six months. "Getting tired of your job?"

"Y'all know how it goes. Things change." She led the way on a dirt path that rounded the side of the house. "Oh, hell. Who am I trying to fool? After that encounter with Alcea, you must've guessed my boss and I weren't exactly platonic. *Things* didn't change. After their divorce four years ago, Stan changed."

And the e-mails that had mentioned Stan had started before that. He didn't comment.

She read his mind, though, and glanced over her

shoulder. "I know it sounds bad, but his marriage was awful. And we loved each other." Her voice grew muffled. "He would have left Alcea a long time before he met me, but his mother would have disinherited him, and S.R., his daddy, had raised him to run that bank. I guess Ellen Addams was a bulldog when it came to family values. Told him she'd seen the pain infidelity could cause. And he *did* follow the straight and narrow the whole time she was alive, even though it about drained the life out of him. All Alcea cared about was her daughter. And Stan's money."

They emerged at the front of the house and followed the walkway to the street.

"I suppose Stan told you all that." He tried to keep judgment out of his voice—the truth was always a matter of perception.

Florida frowned. "Of course he did. Who else was going to tell me? It's not like I took out a billboard advertising our affair. I wasn't exactly proud of it, you know."

"But you didn't marry him."

"Because he didn't ask." She turned up Main and he fell in beside her. Her head was up but tears glinted in her eyes. "It's all Alcea's fault. She bled him dry. It made him freak, the idea of getting married again. I was patient, knowing it was going to take him a while to get over that she-dog, and then six months ago Serena Simpson came to town."

They paused at the corner of Maple Woods Drive. On the opposite corner, Sin-Sational Ice Cream's green-and-white striped awning fluttered in the breeze. Florida's version of events didn't jive with Alcea's aging Taurus, and her near panic that she might have to pay for a tow. "Serena Simpson?"

"A ditz of a city transplant." They stepped off the curb and crossed to the square. The church's stone was mellow in the sunlight. Squirrels chattered over acorns, and birds twittered overhead. "She was married to some rich-as-Trump fellow three times her age who owned a bunch of those new condos they've put in for retired folks moving out here. When he died, she came to look them over, and she stayed. It didn't take her long to find another sugar daddy, and now she prances around like she owns the place. And Stan. She's gorgeous. She's an airhead." Florida sighed. "And, dammit, she's *nice*." She made *nice* sound like a dirty word.

"You're not so bad-looking yourself. But you're one up on her. You're also smart."

"I knew I'd like having y'all around." A smile tickled her lips, then disappeared. "But I'm not so sure about smart. Not anymore. I . . ." She glanced at him, then sipped from her straw. "Well, one good thing has come out of Serena Simpson. She's finally putting Alcea in her place. You should have seen the scene in the bank yesterday."

When the smile surfaced again, he wasn't too sure if *nice* applied to Florida, either. In his mind's eye, he saw that straight, proud back marching toward the entrance, remembered that fearful look of determination, and couldn't match Florida's amusement. "What happened?"

" 'May I see Stan Addams,' Alcea asks, as cool as you please, like she didn't have muddy bare feet and red gunk in her hair. I couldn't help it. I laughed out loud. And then in Stan's office . . ." Florida gurgled. "She started out calm and collected, oh-so-reasonable, but it wasn't long before she was yelling. Stan kept his cool and explained to her the bank could no longer carry her mortgage. You could have heard a pin drop when he referred to her as a deadbeat."

"She's in arrears and her ex-husband is foreclosing?"

"Don't look so disapproving. It's the board's decision. The bank has been carrying Alcea for months, and she doesn't need that big house, anyway. You should have heard her beg."

He gave her a sideways look. "How did *you* hear her?"

Florida sipped again. "Uh, he didn't shut the door." She handed him her cup. "Y'all want the rest of this? My stomach's queasy."

Stan hadn't shut the door? Or Florida had eavesdropped? He decided it was none of his business and glanced in the cup. "What in the hell is this?"

For some reason, she colored. "7UP. I told you I'm queasy."

"Ugh." He tossed the cup in a trash can. First thing in the morning, all he wanted was coffee. Black. They neared the far end of the square. Glancing across the street, he saw Julius wander into Peg O' My Heart Cafe. Even from here, he could hear the clank of silverware and a jumble of conversation.

They crossed Oak Haven and Florida stopped in front of the bank. "Thanks for the company. Where are you off to now?"

Over her shoulder, he saw a neon-blue panel truck pull up in front of the diner. "I think I'll grab some biscuits and gravy at Peg's."

"Yuck." Florida grimaced, then poked the ridges of his belly. "It's a wonder y'all stay slim, the way you eat. Speaking of eating . . . supper again tonight?"

"Sure." Out of the corner of his eye, he saw Alcea step out. She slammed the door and went around to the back of the truck. Paying attention with only half his mind, he made arrangements to meet Florida after she got off work, then loitered while she climbed the steps to the bank's entrance. Once she'd disappeared through its white-columned doorway, he turned and headed for Alcea.

Chapter 4

Alcea flung open the back doors on the truck, revealing a short row of white bakery boxes, and prayed her car would be ready later today. Kathleen had hidden in the backseat on the way to drill team practice this morning, then insisted Alcea drop her off more than two blocks away from school. Alcea had sighed, but couldn't say she blamed her. She slid her hands under two boxes, wondering why she'd bothered baking them at all.

Last night, still in a state of disbelief not only over Stan's refusal to extend the loan but also his refusal to lend her any money like he'd done on other occasions in the past four years, she'd whipped out four cakes in some kind of demented frenzy. The money they'd bring wouldn't buy a single brick on her house.

Stan's parents, the illustrious Addamses, were undoubtedly flopping around in their graves. His mother had ruled Stan with an iron hand, and from everything she'd heard about his father, he'd sown some oats, but ended up as much a prude as Ellen. They would have disowned a son who could treat her and Kathleen like this. But even evoking their names hadn't budged Stan. The home she'd dreamed about since childhood, and lavished with her attention since her marriage, was lost. She was rather surprised she didn't feel more pain now that she'd finally poked her head out of the sand. Maybe pain would hit her later, but right now stark fear was center stage.

Of course, she'd have to work. Like that was a new idea? While she'd waited for the cakes to cool, she'd looked at the want ads, just as she had with increasing frequency in the last couple of years. But this time, she'd *really* looked. Not that it had made a difference. PicNic Poultry Processing Plant was the only place an unskilled and uneducated worker was paid a reasonable salary, but that was out of the question. Becoming Kemp Runyon's employee would ruin her hopes where he was concerned. Not to mention she didn't want to smell like a chicken.

Not that smelling like a chicken wouldn't be appropriate, since she was acting like one. She hadn't mentioned anything to Kathleen about the house. Before she had to, she hoped she'd drum up some idea of where they could live that didn't involve the shanties on the edges of town, the trailer parks in North End, or the two small rooms over her sister's store.

She'd thought about Lil last night as she'd readied for bed. Her distaste for those two small rooms wasn't because she didn't want Lil's help. But her and Kathleen in two rooms? One of them would be dead within a week. She'd ask Lil for a loan instead. She'd only need a cushion until Kemp came through. Because the way he looked at her, undoubtedly he would, and not in the very far future.

She'd climbed between her sheets, thinking of Kemp. But somehow she couldn't keep his image fastened in front of her. He kept transfiguring into Dakota Jones, probably because Dak had hovered at the edge of her mind all afternoon. Why, she didn't know. Maybe because he was a poignant reminder of the dreams she'd held the last time she'd had a clean slate, a time before she'd realized it took more than dreams to create reality. Whatever the reason, she finally gave up on Kemp and let Dakota fill her head, dreamily recalling the face of the youth she'd briefly fallen for on the water tower and replacing it with the image of the man she'd seen this afternoon.

And what an image. Unlike Stan, whose similarly angled features had grown soft with overindulgence, or Kemp's, which had blurred together with age, time had honed Dak's face into a slash of high cheekbones, arced brows, and square jaw, split by a cleft. A crinkle of laugh lines saved his sun-swept features and his laser-sharp gaze from harshness. The color of his eyes helped, too. They were translucent gray washed with blue-green—chameleon eyes that changed color with the light.

Yearning grew again. Only this time not for houses and jobs. This time restlessness blossomed deep inside with the sweet heartache of youth remembered. A time when all things seemed fresh and possible. A time when romance lay in the touch of a hand, a sideways glance from smoky eyes, the fire of a smile in the moonlight. And a few glancing moments when soft lips on hers hinted at passion she didn't yet understand and had never found with Stan.

Rolling over, she touched herself in a way Stan never had, letting her fantasies of Dak overrun her worries. But like so many times during her marriage, her solitary climax only plunged her into a profound feeling of loneliness. Overwhelmed by her emotions, she clutched her pillow and wept out dashed hopes, time lost, and fell asleep under the exhaustion of sheer anxiety, holding on to her night dreams about Dakota Jones like a lifeline. And when she'd awakened this morning, she'd given herself a mental slap for her fantasies. Because fantasies they would remain. Dakota Jones in his decade-old Jeep and his army surplus jacket wasn't her idea of Prince Charming.

Balancing a cake on each palm, she nudged the truck's door with her shoulder. A hand reached out to catch it before it closed and she started, nearly dropping a box. "What the—?" She turned and met Dak's eyes, which were shimmering with a hue just this side of a pale blue dawn. And looking very Prince Charming-like. "Oh."

"Let me give you a hand." He reached in the back for the last two boxes.

She stood back and admired the roped tendons of the backs of his thighs. Her gaze moved up to a tight rear end that was better than Prince Charming's.

"So you did become a baker." He repeated his comment from yesterday, glancing back. The corners of his eyes crinkled when he caught her staring.

She colored. The crinkles and the offhand comment suddenly transported her back to the water tower and the things she'd spouted when he'd encouraged her silly dreams. "Uh-huh." Brilliant. If she remembered right, he'd gone off east somewhere to college, although the sandals, khaki shorts, and open-necked, untucked shirt didn't indicate he'd used his education. "I mean, it's something to keep me busy."

The look he gave her said, *Liar, liar, pants on fire.* Too late, she remembered he'd seen her turn white at the idea of paying for a tow truck, but he said nothing as he followed her to Peg's. From inside, the scent of bacon rolled out. He reached around her to open the screen door, and she noted the dark hair on his arm, and then the long, smooth muscles, and then she wondered at herself for noting. She averted her gaze to the HELP WANTED sign in the window. It was curled at the edges and yellowed from age. *No way.*

Taking a step up, she turned her head. "Will my car—?" He was so close, they almost bumped noses. She jerked, and the back of her head hit something hard. She heard a gasp of pain, and turned back around. "Kemp!"

Stumbling back in the doorway, Kemp was rubbing his nose. He had a lot of nose to rub. His pale eyes, an indiscrimate hazel, were watering. As usual, he was neatly dressed, today in a navy suit that squared his shoulders and a gold-and-navy striped tie that matched the short-cropped hair gone white at the temples.

"Kemp, I'm *so* sorry."

"Don't worry about it, Alcea." He didn't look at her, though. His normally friendly face with its slightly smeared features frowned at Dak. "Let me take those."

He reached for Dak's cake boxes. Dak stepped back. The territorial gesture gave her a bit of a thrill, but before they could start a cranberry-pecan tug-of-war, she thrust one of her boxes in Kemp's hands instead. "Thanks."

Kemp's frown deepened, but he turned and led the way into the diner. Half of Peg's tables were thronged by old-timers like Paddy O'Neill and her former yard man, Erik Olausson. They rooted here every morning. Others held farmers in overalls that had stopped in on their way to or from Beadler's Feed. Their work-hardened hands cupped mugs while they cursed the weather. Today it was too wet. It was always too something. A few suited young men from the bank were holding a meeting in a corner booth, papers spread out between juice glasses and oatmeal bowls. Another table sported tourists, garbed in resort wear and undoubtedly bound for the Lake of the Ozarks, or Lake Kesibwi a bit farther south. The latter picked at their pastries—which, to Alcea's critical eye, looked as appetizing as shredded wheat—and gaped at everyone else.

At the grill, Peg's fry cook, Tansy Eppelwaite, flipped eggs onto a plate, her shoulder blades moving like chicken wings. Smoke from the cigarette clenched between her teeth wreathed her gray sausage curls. She rasped out, "Order up!" and the whole diner paused. Taking her time, Tansy flexed, hitched up an apron that could wrap twice around her frame, and picked up the plate. She pivoted and, with a practiced flick, sent the dish sliding down the counter. With a leap over Eddie-or-Freddie Steeplemier's fat boots, Peg's waitress, Rosemary Butz, scooped up the platter, and the patrons broke into applause. A tuft of dandelion hair waving, Erik stuck gnarled fingers in his mouth and whistled. Rosemary bowed, apron bow twitching over a broad behind, her heart-shaped face pinking under a cloud of glossy brown curls. Tansy cackled, and the diners returned to their talk, papers, and sunny-side-ups.

Dak smiled and looked around approvingly. Alcea didn't know what there was to approve of. Peg's occupied a narrow space, fronted by windows, backed by a long mirror, and crisscrossed with black and red tiles that clashed with orange waitress uniforms. The last time she'd slid into a red vinyl booth, she'd snagged a filmy cotton skirt on a strip of duct tape. People around here would put up with new development all over the town, but change one thing about Peg's and there would be an insurrection.

Kemp spoke into her ear, voice low. He'd overapplied the aftershave. "I was disappointed you had to cancel lunch yesterday, but after I saw today's *Sun*, I understood."

"I—" She stopped. "What do you mean, after you saw the *Sun*?"

Kemp's face looked ponderous. At least she thought it did. It was hard to tell, since it was his normal expression. "Perfectly understandable you had other things that took priority."

Sheesh. The *Cordelia Daily Sun* must have reported her car accident. Silly old rag. She set her cake box between a postcard stand and the cash register on a display case that sat perpendicular to the door. Kemp followed suit. The high-backed stool behind the case where Peg normally reigned was empty.

"It was my fault." Dak set his boxes next to theirs. His fingernails were trimmed short, his hands long, lean, and sun seared like the rest of him. She gave a quick, veiled glance at that rest of him, and then gave herself a mental head thunk. She had to stop salivating over him like some hormone-addled teenager. All he'd done was pay for a tow . . . to the garage he now owned, so it couldn't have cost him much.

"Your fault?" Kemp studied Dak. "Kemp Runyon," he finally said. "And you are?"

"Dakota Jones."

The men shook hands. "And how do you know Alcea?" Kemp queried.

Sensing more testosterone on the rise, Alcea smiled at Kemp. "Dak and I went to high school together. He came back to town yesterday for the first time in twenty years." A mental kick joined the head thunk. Now Dak would think she'd *counted,* for Pete's sake. She had, but he didn't need to know it.

"And one of my first acts was to run Alcea off the road."

She looked at Dak, surprised he was taking the blame for what had clearly been her fault.

"You weren't hurt, were you?" Kemp looked at her, concerned.

"You mean the *Sun* left out a fact? What a surprise." Irritated at her irritation, Alcea managed another smile to try to soften the waspishness in her voice.

Kemp frowned. "The *Sun*? I don't understand—"

"Dak! Over here!" Julius's voice boomed from the back of the diner. He motioned to a seat beside him. *"Unquiet meals make ill digestions."*

Swinging through the kitchen doors to one side of the grill, Peg frowned at the mechanic.

Smiling, Dak shook his head. "Got me on that one, Julius," he called back.

"Comedy of Errors!" Julius boomed. "C'mon over here and set yourself down."

Dak nodded at Kemp, then Alcea, holding Alcea's gaze a little longer than was necessary. His eyes really were amazing. "If you'll excuse me . . ." He wove his way toward Julius, accepting handshakes and greetings.

When he was gone, Kemp twinkled at Alcea in that

rather awkward way he had when he tried to be jocular. "And what are you up to with these, m'dear?"

"Oh. Peg just asked if I'd mind baking her a few cakes. I love to bake, you know, so I—"

"That's nice." Kemp glanced at his watch. "I have a meeting in a few minutes, but I'm glad I ran into you. Listen, I know it's none of my concern, but if you need some assistance with that matter yesterday, I'd be happy to investigate options."

Alcea frowned, ticked that he'd interrupted her and puzzled by his remark. Did he think she planned to sue Dakota Jones? "Um, sure."

"I'll call you later, and try not to worry. Everything will be okay." He squeezed her arm. Perplexed, she watched him leave.

Peg bustled up behind the display case. The butterfly stuck in her hair whipped side to side. "My goodness, honey, you'd no need to bust your buns bringing these things in today. I would've understood."

Damn, it had only been a little fender bender. Why was everyone getting their undies in a knot? Still at the grill, Tansy gave Alcea a sideways glance and snickered. Alcea looked down at herself. Had she forgotten her pants or something?

Peg leaned closer. "Don't mind her. She'd never say it, but she's plum pleased you brought these in. Andy's birthday is today and Tansy can't bake worth savin' her life." Andy was Tansy's grandson—his name usually preceded by *No-Account*. If the pastries were any indication, Peg had nailed the extent of Tansy's way around an oven. "So, seeing I already got a full two of these sold, I'll get you a check right away—I can sure understand you're wantin' the money somethin' fierce."

Something fierce? Her confusion increased. She started to follow Peg to the back room but stopped. It seemed like when she'd emerged from behind the postcard rack, everyone in the place had quit chewing to stare. Rosemary Butz swiped at a table and glanced over, face sympathetic. What was going on? Alcea hesitated, uncertain whether to move through the sea of curious gazes or retreat back to obscurity on the other side of the postcards.

A hand gripped her wrist. "Have a seat." Before she could react, Dak pulled her down into his booth. Julius sat across, sipping his coffee and idly turning the pages of the newspaper.

"Good of you to ask, boy," Julius said, apparently concluding a conversation in progress. "But much as I'd like to, I don't have the funds for that old garage." He barked a laugh that made Alcea jump. "Sure hope the new owner'll want me to stay. I sure don't cotton to the idea of moving in with my sister."

"You know Alcea, don't you?" Dak still had hold of her, his fingers warm on her skin.

"O Beauty. Till now I never knew thee." Julius folded up the paper. Flustered, she squirmed, but Julius had turned his eyes back to Dak.

"Othello?" Dak released his grasp, and she was disappointed.

Julius shook his head, grin widening. He planted the newspaper under his elbows and waited.

Dak spread his hands. She could still feel the imprint of his fingers. "Got me."

"*Henry VIII,* by God." Julius slapped the booth beside him, and Alcea jumped again. "That's two!"

Dak flashed Alcea a crooked smile. Her heart did a little flutter until she dug her fingernails into her palm to stop the nonsense. "Julius has just about memorized everything Shakespeare ever wrote."

"My mama, may she rest in peace, may not have had much schooling, but she knew her Shakespeare, she did. Named me after the great Caesar."

What Julius Caesar had to do with Shakespeare, Alcea couldn't tell.

Dak smiled at Julius but tilted his head toward her,

his gaze holding her fast to her seat. "Fortunately, *my* mother didn't name me Brutus, even though she had a fondness for Shakespeare, too."

For some reason, Julius frowned, but Dak didn't appear to notice.

"We're named after flowers. My sisters and me," Alcea offered, not knowing what else to say. "Alcea, Lilac, Marigold."

Dak's eyes wandered over her face. "Pretty," he murmured. "Fitting."

She squirmed. The exchange was odd, as though he—and Julius, too—wanted to distract her, but she was still conscious of stares boring holes in her back. A few booths over, someone said something and Paddy O'Neill cackled. She reddened, although she didn't know what she had to be embarrassed about.

Dak took a look at her face, then twisted, looping an elbow over the back of his booth. "Hey, Paddy." He gave a nod out the window. "That your Indian getting bushwhacked?"

From across the aisle, Eddie-Freddie laughed. "Thar he blows!"

Alcea looked out and saw two children running at an awkward gait across the church green, the cigar store Indian balanced between them. For several decades, Swiping the Indian had been a Cordelia institution, high on the list of I-dare-yous. The Indian always turned up unscathed but smarting from the blow to its dignity. Part of the game was finding a new place to put it. One time, her youngest sister, Mari, and her friends had managed to get it all the way up to the St. Andrew's steeple, where it had leaned with its arms crossed, gazing over the gathering flock beneath it with an injured air. Usually, though, it was the prank of teens, not young kids like these. Alcea's gaze narrowed. She could swear that was her sister Lil's stepson, Michael, and her sister-in-law Patsy Lee's third child, Rose, up to no good before heading to Mrs. Carswell's fourth-grade class. Wherever one was, you'd find the other, Michael usually in the lead with Rose tagging behind in a giggling dither.

Paddy's chair scraped back, and he headed for the door. "Danged kids." But his voice lacked heat. If he'd really hated the routine, he would have stuck the Indian indoors long ago.

Peg trotted up, wisps of hair stuck to her cheeks and a piece of paper clenched in her hand. "Whew! With that kitchen, you got no need to pay for one of those fancy saunas." She nudged Julius's arm. "Scoot yourself on over, you old thing."

Julius obliged. The smile he directed at Peg was warmer than the red that remained in his hair, and Alcea wondered if they had something going on. Peg tried to slide her girth into the booth, got stuck part-way there, and settled for keeping half a haunch on the seat, feet stuck into the aisle.

"Here you go, sweetness." Peg slid the check to Alcea, and fanned her face.

Julius frowned. "Doc said you need to watch that heart." His gruff voice had softened.

"Oh, I am, I am. Old ticker's got a lot of miles left on it yet—you just wait and see."

Sweetness? Peg may use the occasional *honey*, but she'd never addressed Alcea with real affection. Of course, Alcea had never given her much of a reason to, either. Alcea started to fold the check, then stopped and studied the amount. She hesitated, then decided on honesty. "I think you made a mistake."

Peg waved a hand. "No, no mistake. I've been thinking the amount I pay you for those cakes is a mite too small. I just raised your prices. People will pay more than what I been charging. They're that good." She turned to the others. "Did I tell you I bought the empty space next door? City got it for back taxes owin' and has been pressing me for the last coupla years to take it on and fix it up. Got it dirt cheap, but don't know what to do with it 'cept add more seating. 'Course that'd mean I'd really need me another server."

Alcea was still staring at the check. "But—" Peg was not known for being loose fisted, and Alcea wasn't sure she liked the idea of being beholden, even if she could use the money.

"Don't you worry about that none, sweetness. I can afford it." The bells over the door sang. "Oops. Another customer. 'Scuse me." Peg heaved herself up and waddled off.

Alcea fingered the check. "I don't understand what's going on," she murmured, hardly realizing she'd spoken out loud.

Dak pulled the *Cordelia Daily Sun* out from under Julius's elbows and slid it over.

Alcea heard a familiar voice ring out. "Morning, Peg! I just had to stop in and get me one of those wonderful chocolate cakes. My customers just can't get enough of them, and I have a houseful this week."

"It's your mother," Julius said, as if she'd gone deaf. "That bed and breakfast your folks opened a couple years back sure keeps her jumping."

Her mother liked jumping. Zinnia was never happy unless she was in the center of things. Correction. Unless she *was* the center of things. And with her son deceased some time ago and her three daughters established, she hadn't had enough to meddle with so she'd badgered Pop into starting a business. Still, her *mother* was buying her cakes. For a moment, Alcea felt proud. There wasn't that much her mother had ever thought she was good for.

Dak pointed at a listing in the classified section.

In a voice loud enough to hear in Arkansas, her mother continued, "Better than I can make myself, I tell you."

Alcea frowned. Her mother always told her she used a touch too much cocoa. Alcea sniffed. That was because her mother used whatever she could glom onto at the store. *She* ordered hers from a specialty shop.

She tuned her mother out and scanned the classified

section Dak had fingered. Her eyeballs bulged. The looks, the snickers, and Peg's generosity suddenly made sense.

"Best cakes in the whole wide world." The voice rose and Alcea slid down in her seat. "Anyone who hasn't had one of these is sure missing out."

By the grill, Tansy snorted. For God's sake. Her mother was up there acting like her shill. Trying to look both dignified and collected when she really felt like screaming, Alcea pushed to her feet, knowing her face was flaming. "I'm over here, Mother."

Zinnia's face went rosy. "Why, so you are, honeybunch. I didn't see you."

Alcea fell back into her seat and ran a weary hand over her face. Dak looked grave, and Julius looked anywhere else besides at her, the relief on his face evident when the Steeplemier brothers asked him if he'd seen the pothole out on Bunker Road that had banged up their Chevy's oil pan.

Alcea dropped her head into her hands. "I didn't know Stan would do this."

Making the admission to Dak was easy. Just like that night on the water tower, there was something in his gaze that made evasion pointless.

"Required, I believe, to put a notice of sale in the paper." Dak's quick smile came and went, but it wasn't without sympathy. "It's not the end of the world."

"But to have everyone know." She spoke to the tabletop. "Oh, God. And Kathleen's friends have likely heard of this, and I haven't told her how bad things are."

"She'll live through it. So will you."

Alcea's temper flashed and she raised her head. "Easy for you to say."

"Maybe," he agreed equably. "What do you plan to do?"

"I suppose relying on the lottery doesn't count?"

"She's going to get herself to a family meeting this

weekend, that's what she's going to do." Zinnia stood at her elbow. Peg hovered behind. And all ears in the joint turned toward them like a bunch of homing satellites. "Lord love a duck, we'll figure the whole thing out, just like the O'Malleys have always done. When God gives you a lemon—"

"Mornin', Miz O'Malley." Eyes lit with curiosity, Rosemary bobbed her head at Zinnia and slipped coffee in front of Alcea, although she didn't remember asking for any. "Can I get you anything else, Alcea-doll? Tansy might not be too great with the fried eggs—I hate it when the edges get all brown and curly, don't you?—but she does serve up a fine plate of pancakes. Or if you think that might not set well—although Mama Butz used to say breakfast was the anchor to the whole day—the orange juice is fresh-squeezed and there's some oatmeal or whole wheat."

Alcea frowned. She and Rosemary hadn't been close enough in high school—or since—for terms of endearment. "No, thank you."

Rosemary looked disappointed, but when Alcea added a glare, she scampered off.

Alcea looked up at Zinnia. "Mother, would you please sit down and lower your voice? What family meeting?"

"What a heartfelt invitation, but I can't stay."

Alcea gave an inward sigh. She hadn't meant to hurt her mother's feelings.

"I have guests to attend to," Zinnia continued. "However, after our birthday celebration Saturday, we're having a family meeting and I'd appreciate it if you'd come off your high horse and join us, since you'll be the center of attention."

A family meeting sounded only a step up from the whole birthday shebang, and on Alcea's list both ranked just below putting bamboo shoots under her fingernails. Still, it was possible—probable—Lil would offer her a loan. She clenched her teeth. "I'll be there."

"Fine. I'll count on it." Zinnia looked at Dak and her face thawed. "Maybe you'd like to join us for the party, get reacquainted? Henry passed, you know. Five years back." Henry had been Alcea's brother, and Zinnia's oldest.

"I remember him from high school." Dak nodded. "I'm sorry."

Zinnia's eyes misted but she carried on. "Patsy Lee—Henry's wife, do you remember her?—will be there with her four kids. And Lil will be there, too." Zinnia ticked people off on her fingers. "And Lil's husband, Jon, and their two. Not sure if Mari will come down from Kansas City or not, but it's not likely you recall her, anyway. She's not married, but she's got quite a career for herself designing greeting cards or some such. I never did understand much about computers. My baby—Mari—would have been about kindergarten age when you left."

Dak looked bewildered, so Alcea intervened. "The family has four birthdays between mid-April and mid-June, so we celebrate them all at once to get them out of the way."

"That's not precisely true." Zinnia folded her arms. Alcea dodged to avoid the Dumpster-sized handbag hanging from her forearm. "May is just so full of soccer games and end-of-school activities, and June brings Little League and vacations, plus my Ladies' Auxiliary over at the church runs the Bible Camp, so—"

"We celebrate them early to get them out of the way," Alcea said.

Zinnia glared at her.

This time Dak intervened. "I'd enjoy that very much, Mrs. O'Malley." His eyes lingered on Alcea.

"Do call me Zinnia. No need to stand on formality, I always say. Around one, then. Family picnic in our backyard. Maple Woods Drive, just a hop and skip from here. It'll be nice to have the place to ourselves. No guests this weekend." She looked at Peg and Julius. "You all are welcome to come on over, too."

Both demurred. Peg had her diner, and Julius his garage to run. Alcea wished she could just run. After some more pleasantries, Zinnia took her leave, nodding at each person in turn, except for Alcea.

"There was no need for that sour attitude, sweetness." Peg chastised Alcea as she squeezed back in by Julius. "Zinnia's heart is in the right place, even if she can be a mite—"

"Bossy? Overbearing?"

Peg shot her a look, although Alcea noticed amusement behind the pale eyes. "I was going to say helpful. Still. I don't know what difference any meeting's gonna make. Plain as the nose on your face that what you need is a job. Doesn't take no meeting to figure that out."

Julius turned back to the Steeplemier brothers. Rosemary approached to refill their cups.

"You given that any thought?" Peg persisted.

Alcea glanced at Rosemary's bright eyes, Dak's interested face. She shrugged as though her options were many.

"I heard tell Ed Wilson needs a receptionist at the insurance company," Peg said.

"Ooo, that would be a funny one, wouldn't it?" Rosemary leaned across the table and snagged Julius's cup. "Remember typing class, Alcea? Miss Abernathy said Alcea must've been born all thumbs."

"But I can damn well answer a phone."

"But Louella says Ed needs someone who can type forms." Rosemary poured, replaced the cup, then picked up Dak's.

"Hmm," Peg said. "There's an opening at Sin-Sational."

Rosemary nodded. "That'd do, except Alcea made some loud comment last week about fleas in the ice cream, and I guess Old Ben was about fit to be tied. He said she scared two tourists right out of the place."

Alcea reddened. "I didn't say the chocolate chips

were fleas. I said they were tiny as fleas. And they were." She felt, rather than saw, Dak's quick grin.

"I think," Rosemary said, as though somebody had asked her, "she should go to work for Betty Bruell. Nothing wrong with being a shampoo assistant, and she could enroll in that beauty school over in Sedalia." Coffeepot empty, Rosemary touched her mop of curls, looking dreamy. "I always wanted to go to beauty school, but Mama Butz said she'd worry too much with me doing all that back-and-forth driving."

"Except Alcea stiffed Betty Bruell her tip last time she was at Up-in-the-Hair." Peg said. "Didn't you?"

"She poked me with the scissors!"

Peg gave her another look. "After you said it looked like Betty had cut Kathleen's hair with hedge clippers."

Alcea sat back with a thump. It wasn't her fault. If people like Old Ben and Betty expected people to shell out their hard-earned cash, they should provide value. If she owned a shop, *she* would.

"I know," Peg said. "Maybe she should work for me."

"Ooo," Rosemary let out a squeal. "That would be such fun. Do say yes, Alcea."

Julius abandoned his soybean discussion. *"The labor we delight in physics pain. Macbeth,"* he said before Dak could even guess.

"Here?" Alcea's voice squeaked. Pain didn't begin to describe it. Schlep eggs and toast to half Cordelia's population? Everyone she knew stopped by Peg's. "I, uh, I appreciate the offer, I really do, but, uh, there are a couple of other things I want to check into."

Peg's gaze was knowing. "This job is likely too much for you, anyway."

"Too much for me? How hard can it be, delivering food, cleaning off tables?"

Peg exchanged a look with Dak. Alcea fidgeted when they traded a smile. Some customers entered the diner, setting the chimes jangling. Saved by the bell.

Peg pushed to her feet. "You just check on those other things and let me know. I'll hold the job till, say, Monday?" She jogged Rosemary's elbow. "I think there's some other folks lookin' for refills."

Alcea watched Peg and Rosemary walk off. "Hold the job? Like applicants are swarming to this prime opportunity?" She grew aware of Dak and Julius sitting in silence. "Oh, come on. Waitressing isn't exactly brain surgery."

Julius's eyebrows rose, but he only scooted out of the booth. "I gotta run. I'll have your car ready by five, Miz Alcea, sure as shootin.' You coming, Dak, boy?"

"In a minute."

After Julius left, Dak slid sideways on his seat, one arm on the table, the other riding the back of the booth. She was conscious that if she leaned back, his fingers would brush her neck. She made herself sit forward, cupping her hands around her coffee.

"If you're looking for a place to live, I might be able to help."

"You?"

"There's a trailer on the back of Cowboy's property."

Somehow she managed to keep her jaw from dropping. Exchange her home for a trailer? Before she could blurt, "Not in this lifetime," a thought brought her up short: the two small rooms over Lil's store.

"It'd only be temporary until I sell the place, but I could rent it out cheap." Dak named a figure that was far below anything she'd seen in the paper yesterday.

She narrowed her eyes. "Deposit?" This *would* only be temporary, if it was even necessary. There was still Kemp.

"No deposit."

She'd better keep her options open. She eyed him from under her lids. He was looking at her with more than just a little appreciation. "Well, maybe. When can I see it?"

Maybe she could get him to come down even more

on the rent. She batted her eyes, feeling rusty for lack of practice. Still, surely the magic she'd felt when they'd kissed so many years ago hadn't been entirely one-sided. Dak's eyes registered delight, and she figured she'd made progress.

"I haven't been inside it since I got here," he said. "Why don't you give me the afternoon to get it cleaned up. Tomorrow morning, say, nine?"

"Tomorrow morning," she agreed, slowly sliding back in a languorous way until her neck rested on his hand.

The move didn't get quite the reaction she expected. He burst into laughter. And his laughter drew stares. Suddenly, she was sixteen again, sitting in the high school cafeteria, right next to him like this, her face burning with the same shame and embarrassment.

"I have to go." She scrambled to her feet.

Dak grabbed at her hand and missed. "I'm sorry. I didn't mean to laugh."

Sure he hadn't. She didn't give him the courtesy of a response. Careful to keep her head high, she walked out of Peg's, telling herself she'd never step foot in there again.

Through the rest of the day, her humiliation lingered, even though she knew it was overblown. The town had surely suspected her straits for a long time. And Dak's crowning whack to her ego was minor compared to that notice in the paper. But after she picked up Kathleen, her pique faded at the sight of Kathleen's obvious distress. All the way home, her daughter sat wrapped in sullens, hair hiding her face. There was no doubt the notice in the *Sun* had passed through the high school gossip chain.

When they got home, Alcea tentatively broached the topic. It was like poking a pin in a balloon. Kathleen vented for an hour, ignoring Alcea's attempts to insert a word. Alcea finally gave up and just let her rage. After Kathleen had run out of air, Alcea was too battered for any more tries at a reasonable discussion. Kathleen was beyond reasonable.

After she'd banged her bedroom door shut, Kathleen spent the rest of the night on the phone, pouring out her woes. To her cousins Melanie and Daisy, most likely. Great. Now the entire family would have a bird's-eye view into the emotional fallout of Alcea's bird-brained decisions. Alcea retaliated by immersing herself in baking six dozen chocolate chip (big chips, not like the ones at Sin-Sational) cookies, throwing in extra just to spite her mother.

Between Kathleen's calls, Kemp slipped one in. His tone was solicitous. He'd checked, and there was little she could do about the foreclosure. The news didn't surprise her. And he invited her to an early supper Monday night at the country club. Which also didn't surprise her. Kemp liked Discount Dinner night. That he wasn't willing to splurge on the Saturday-night prime rib disgruntled her, until he explained he'd be out of town this weekend. She accepted his offer and hung up, feeling like an ingrate. She should be glad he was still interested in her despite the unveiling of all her warts. But she'd found his kindness irritating. For some odd reason, Dak's matter-of-fact attitude about her situation was more . . . acceptable.

That evening, she left to pick up her car at Cowboy's. She'd dressed with care, telling herself her primping was only a confidence booster. But when she found only Julius at the garage, her disappointment was so sharp, she knew she'd lied to herself—damn those luminous eyes, anyway. What in the hell was wrong with her? She already knew the outcome of any advances she might make to Dakota Jones. The scene in the diner was almost a replay of the one they'd enacted in the cafeteria twenty years ago. Maybe this time he hadn't treated her like she had a fungus, but was mild amusement really that much better?

She collected her car from Julius and drove home, determined to put Dakota Jones out of her mind.

Chapter 5

Of course, putting Dakota Jones out of her mind was a silly exercise, since she had an appointment with him first thing the next morning.

After delivering Kathleen to school and the chocolate chip cookies to Peg, Alcea left her car in front of the diner, deciding a walk on a nice spring day was what she needed to clear her head. By nine on the nose, she stood on the front porch of Cowboy's gray-shingled house. The railing was rickety, the whole thing needed paint, and the floorboards creaked as she shifted from one foot to the other. The interior door was open, but she saw no movement. Taking a deep breath, she punched the doorbell. The buzzer sounded like an angry hornet.

She could at least congratulate herself for taking no time at all with her appearance. Not that she'd had a choice. After another restless night, she'd overslept. And Kathleen had seemed to delight in waking her with only twenty minutes left before they needed to leave. She shoveled her hair behind her ear. There'd been no time for the hair straightener or the smooth chignon. Without either, her natural waves pretty much made it look like she'd slapped a shrub on her head. A fitting crown, really, for the faded jeans and sandals she'd leaped into. At least Dak couldn't possibly think she was trying to impress him. Scare him, maybe, but not impress him.

Julius and a few oldsters sat on lawn chairs scattered in front of the garage next door. She gave Julius a nod and tried to ignore the others. Since the foreclosure notice had surfaced in the paper, she attracted stares with the same ease that Peg's Blue Monday special attracted flies. Well, she assured herself, juicier scandals would soon come along, and the old ones would be forgotten except in a few grizzled heads. She could weather it. Like she had a choice?

She jabbed the buzzer again, then cupped her hands to peer inside. Dim shadows; nothing else. Tapping her foot, she checked her watch. Seven after. The gawking eyes had grown annoying. Feigning a smile like she was greeting someone, she yanked on the screen door. Fortunately, it wasn't locked. Leaving the looks behind, she stepped onto a faded Oriental rug on the scuffed wood floor of a shadowed entry. A tarnished brass lantern hung overhead. "Dak?" Her voice echoed up a narrow stairway to the right, but nobody answered.

She moved toward a rectangle of light at the rear, glancing into the rooms she passed. It was a shotgun house, long and thin. Dark hall down the center, a parlor to the right dominated by a big maple TV cabinet, its rabbit ears perked over piles of magazines and catalogs; a dining room to the left with a chandelier of dulled crystal. A bunch of stuff was piled to one side, and the table had been pushed up to the windows. Unlike every other dust-covered thing, its top gleamed from a recent polish. A laptop sat in the middle with a few spiral notebooks stacked neatly nearby. The walls throughout sported faded floral wallpaper, dingy corners, and fingerprints. The furniture, circa 1940-something, was worn. Everything smelled musty, despite open windows where yellowing lace curtains fluttered.

She paused in the kitchen. It was gray. Gray counters, gray linoleum rubbed white, white appliances that had grayed. Not even a pair of curtains to enliven the room. The whole house lacked warmth, lacked *life*. No wonder Dak hadn't returned.

About to call again, she started as the back door creaked open. Before Dak stepped in, she started talking. "Nobody answered so I—" She sucked in a breath. It was Florida, not Dak.

Florida froze. "Alcea Addams, as I live and breathe . . . I see y'all have added breaking and entering to your many accomplishments." Her mouth crooked. "Love the 'do, by the way."

It took an effort to keep her hand from flying to her hair. "I *wasn't* breaking in. Dak is expecting me, but nobody answered. And if anyone has issues with morality, it's—"

Florida held up a hand. She looked tired. In fact, she looked green. "I don't have time for this. I'm already late for work." She motioned toward the back. "He's out there." She pushed past Alcea and moved down the hall.

Alcea stared until she'd stepped out the door, but Florida didn't look back. Was she sick? Time was they could have traded insults for at least ten minutes before someone really lost her temper.

The door creaked again, and this time it *was* Dak. To her satisfaction, his eyes lit up. "Ah, you're here."

She looked him over. He wore work boots and a black T-shirt the same shade as his hair. Normally she preferred button-downs and sleek suits, but the way that shirt stretched across his chest suddenly made her reevaluate her T-shirt position. He was eying her in the same up-and-down manner.

She blushed. "I— Florida let me in." She let the lie sneak out.

"C'mon out." He held open the door.

When she brushed by him, she smelled male and soap. The scent set an alarm off in her head, the hair on her arms stood up, and her brain shouted, *Escape*! But her feet kept moving. Stepping down to the patio, she almost tripped on the crumbling concrete. Righting herself, she looked around. A newer-looking glass-topped table with a striped umbrella and four matching chairs looked out of place on the network of cracks. In the middle of the table, a sponge sat in a pool of water.

"I like the hair," Dak said, letting the screen door bang shut.

She jumped and glanced back, certain he was joking. "Easy if you have an eggbeater."

He smiled. "It's natural. It suits you."

Natural suited her?

He moved past her, swiped up the water, and dropped the sponge in a bucket. "Picked these up at the Swap 'n' Shop yesterday. I like spending time out here, and aluminum lawn chairs wouldn't do it. Maybe the new owner will buy them with the house."

Considering what it looked like inside, she'd spend most of her time out here, too. She started to murmur something polite, but the words died on her lips. Spellbound, she stared across the ragtag property at the monstrosity hunkering at the rear.

Dak followed her gaze. "Don't mind the torn skirting and the overgrowth. I'll take care of that." He started toward the trailer on a path of erratically spaced concrete blocks sunk in the dirt. When she stood rooted, he paused and looked back. "Coming?"

She detected challenge. Making an unintelligible sound, she followed.

"New paint, though. Julius painted it," he continued.

Painted? It looked like someone had doused the thing with Pepto-Bismol. "Rusty's Hardware had a special?"

"Maybe." Now she scented amusement. "It has a new water heater, and Julius says the window AC still works, although he recommends you bang it every once in a while. Nothing is rotted, although you might keep an eye on the corner of the main bedroom. Looks like some chipmunks might have tried to get in out of the cold this winter. If you stuff the hole with mothballs and steel wool, it should keep them out." She couldn't see his smile, but it was there. She knew it. "I sprayed it for spiders. Snakes, though"—he motioned at piles of scrap lumber littering the yard—"snakes might be a problem."

The walkway stopped at a gravel drive that led from the alley running alongside the property to a none-too-sturdy carport. They crossed the drive and stepped onto a patio formed by more concrete blocks. Weeds snaked up between the cracks. From there it was up a few steps to the entrance, an ill-fitting door on the front of a small one-room addition.

Dak stuck in a key and the door squealed open. "I'll oil that." He pointed toward the alley. "Dumpster's over there. Don't keep trash cans outside. Raccoons will just tip them over."

He *was* enjoying himself. She straightened her shoulders. She wasn't a complete wimp. "Any instructions for marauding tigers?"

He looked back and his smile flashed. He motioned her inside. "Welcome to the Pink Palace. There's really nothing in here a little elbow grease can't fix. That is, if you're up to it." His tone told her that, just like Peg, he thought she was afraid of work.

Alcea's spine hardened. As she stepped inside, it wilted again. Yellowing linoleum lined the floor of the tacked-on room. A washer and dryer leaned against one cheaply paneled wall. A table, early-fifties Formica complete with cigarette burns, stood in the middle. The best thing about the room was a ring of grimy windows. Open on nice days, the place would become a screened-in porch. She eyed the rusted hardware. If they opened.

"Washer and dryer work. Place does need airing out."

Dak opened a second door to the trailer. A ripe smell pinched her nose.

"I take it Julius had a cat."

"A tom named Whiskers."

"Lovely." She pivoted, intending to leave. Enough was enough.

"I showed it earlier this morning to Tansy's grandson, Andy," Dak said mildly. "He said he'd rip out the carpet. Of course, that's a lot of work."

Alcea hesitated. He gave her a smile. She glared, held her breath, and stepped into the living room. It was divided from the kitchen by a finger of counter. Dak stepped around it, into the kitchen, and tugged a cord. A fluorescent bulb hissed and blinked to life. Alcea blinked back.

Pink stove. Pink refrigerator. Pink chipped sink. Pink counters. Pink and white—or at least it used to be white—tile tripped out of sight down a brief hall. She told herself to breathe.

Dak leaned an elbow on the counter. His eyes were a caress. "I'd rather rent to you, though. Florida tells me Andy has had some troubles with the law."

"Andy likes to drink." She cleared her throat. "This place is certainly . . . pink."

"I like pink." There was that hint of challenge again.

"I do, too." She hated pink.

Dak raised his eyebrows but didn't comment. He stayed behind while she explored both ends of the trailer in a trip that took less than a minute. Bedrooms flanked both ends, each with a bed so ancient she wouldn't be surprised if the mattresses were stuffed with hay. She reminded herself she had mattresses. She slid open a closet door, thought of her double-wide walk-ins, felt faint, and snapped the door shut. She returned to the kitchen.

Dak still lounged against the counter. "What do you think?"

Frankly, she thought a burly man with a bulldozer might do it some justice. She couldn't live here. She just couldn't. "Um, I have a few other places to look at before I make a decision."

His gaze softened. Maybe he'd had his fill of fun. "I'd help take out this carpet."

"Thank you. I'll, uh, let you know. Monday?" Mentally, she prepared Monday's To-Do List. *Tell Peg no. Tell Dak no. Collect money from Lil.* Her stomach churned. Being beholden to Lil would be painful, but it was better than this. Wasn't it? Her options depressed her.

"Monday's fine."

She picked her way across the walkway. After he'd locked up, he caught up and swung along at her side, his stride easy and unhurried. The backs of their hands brushed and her skin burned. He didn't seem to notice.

"How about a cup of coffee?"

"I really should—" She halted. The only thing waiting at home was a bunch of rooms to pack so she could move—where? Until she knew how much Lil would float her . . . Suddenly, the idea of keeping company with only her own thoughts was unbearable. "Okay."

When they reached the patio, Dak motioned her to a chair, then went inside. Through the open window, she could hear the clatter of crockery. She tilted her head up to catch the sun's rays. They felt . . . hopeful. She wished she felt the same.

Dak returned and set a mug near her elbow, then settled himself beside her, locking his ankles on top of a bucket. The sun was now well up over the horizon. For a moment, they stared at the verdant Ozark hills in the distance and the wisps of clouds scuttling across a sky as blue as the cornflowers that grew in her mother's garden. She slid a sideways look at Dak. He seemed totally relaxed, head tipped back, eyes half closed, hair lifting off his forehead in the breeze.

She shifted, picked up her coffee. "So what have you been up to for the last twenty years?"

"Traveling. Writing. And you?"

"Marriage, motherhood."

"But no pastry chef's hat?"

"Only for my family. And lately some cakes and cookies for Peg's."

"Hmm." His eyes followed a barn swallow taking flight across the fields. "You sounded so passionate about it in high school."

"Well, back then, in my family, it was the easiest way to get attention. I'm afraid a little praise from them on my baking made me a maniac on the subject." She chuckled as though she found the memory of her young self amusing, but she didn't. She'd harbored that dream for a good two years after Dak had left town, even writing to some culinary institutes for brochures. She hadn't shown them to her parents. She'd known they couldn't afford it. "I must have been a bore."

"I didn't find you boring." The look he sent her said he still didn't. It also said he didn't believe her.

She took a sip of coffee, unable to ignore the sudden tension in her body but equally determined not to show it. Years at the country club had given her an ease with social niceties, although—what a surprise—they'd never come naturally. "So, tell me, what do you write?"

"Stories, articles." His shoulder rose and fell.

"Do you—" She'd been about to ask if he made much money, but stopped to rephrase. "Do you sell many?"

A smile played on his mouth. "Enough. And I enjoy it, so what more could I ask?"

A lot more than this. Her gaze swept the confines of his "inheritance"; the scraggly yard, the pink trailer, the narrow house. "Did you ever marry?" The words slipped out.

"Once. A long time ago. We were both still in college." He spoke easily. No artifice, no evasion. "It only lasted a few years. Nobody's fault."

She watched him for a moment, wondering if she'd

ever be that blasé about her divorce. "And no children?"

"We never got around to thinking about it before the marriage was over." His smile darted in and out. "And since then I've been careful. What about you? Only the one daughter?"

"Stan only wanted one." Actually, he hadn't wanted *any*. "He said he was happy as an only child." Although his mother would have liked more children. Ellen had once confided she would have had more if her doctor hadn't advised against it. Stan had been a difficult birth—big surprise. "But the real reason was because Kathleen was too much competition for Stan." Alcea realized she sounded bitter—which she was—and matched Dak's shrug. *"C'est la vie."*

"The reason for your divorce?"

She squirmed at his directness. *Oh, what the hell.* "Stan's a shit."

That bright smile winked again. "That says it all."

She shrugged. "He was a serial adulterer. After Kathleen was born, he had an affair because I didn't pay enough attention to him. At least that was his excuse, and I forgave him that one. But not the twenty gazillion other ones that came after. He was discreet about it at first." She halted, surprised at herself. She wasn't one for the current rage of baring her soul. But just like when she was sixteen, she was telling him things she usually kept to herself.

"At least he showed you that small courtesy." Dak's voice was dry.

She snorted and decided to forget discretion. "Oh, it wasn't because of me. His mother, Ellen, would have killed him—or worse, changed her will—if she'd gotten wind of anything. She had a real thing about infidelity. But when she died, he got worse than a cat in heat."

"But you stayed with him until, what, four years ago?"

That was right. He'd know when they'd divorced, because of Florida. For a moment, she'd forgotten it was his half sister who was the final straw for a pretty rickety camel. Somehow, instead of ruffling her feathers, his knowledge made her feel more at ease. "Call me a chump. Or call me a wimp. It seemed easier to stay. Fact is, I didn't leave because I didn't know how I'd support Kathleen." She looked at the trailer. She still didn't.

"I wouldn't call you either of those things," he said quietly.

She eyed him. He didn't look judgmental. She relaxed further. "I guess one day I'd just had enough. When Lil got married and I saw how happy she was . . . Well. My pride had taken all it could take. I knew if I didn't get out, I'd . . . lose myself." She took another sip, then thunked the mug on the table. "I don't even know what I mean." Nor did she understand why his presence caused an alien to take over her mouth.

"I felt the same way about my marriage. And about my career. There's no shame in making changes, you know. The shame only lies in continuing in the same rut if you're not happy."

"Yes. Well." She looked at the trailer again. "I guess I've dug a whole new rut."

"You never know what lies around the corner. Maybe you'll like this rut better."

"Maybe. Kathleen won't." She stopped, startled again at her frankness. Obviously, she'd been way too long without a friend. She'd had them, of course, but when she'd married Stan, she'd taken a step up in the world and her old friends didn't belong to the country club. She'd never gotten close to the women who did. They fit so easily into a moneyed world, while she'd felt like the proverbial square peg.

"So Kathleen learned at school about the foreclosure."

On the verge of telling herself Dak wasn't exactly

a friend so she should shut up, instead she said, "And she's not exactly thrilled by the change in our circumstances."

"Gave you a hard time, huh?"

"*Hard time* doesn't begin to cover it. Screaming, throwing things, refusing to come out of her room. *That* begins to cover it. I can't blame only her, though. I spoiled her." Good *God*. With or without that imp on her shoulder, she was clear-eyed enough to know she'd always lavished Kathleen with too much attention, too much money, too much everything. Kathleen had provided a distraction from her marital mess, but she didn't normally blab about her failings as a mother.

"I can't say I know a thing about raising kids, but from what I hear, they're adaptable."

"You don't know Kathleen."

"She'll adjust."

"She won't."

They fell silent.

Alcea picked up her mug and studied her coffee. "Do you remember that night?" The question felt normal, natural. And she wanted to know. For a short while, he'd had a profound effect on her, and she'd always wondered if it had all been as lopsided as his later behavior had implied.

He locked gazes with her. "Sure, I remember." He didn't pretend not to know what she was talking about.

She looked away. "Why wouldn't you take me to the senior dance? I practically put the invitation right in your mouth." And had embarrassed herself in front of the entire school.

At school following their encounter on the water tower, she'd been starry-eyed. After more than a week of waiting and hoping Dakota Jones would ask her out, she'd finally screwed up her courage. She'd bypassed her usual cafeteria table and joined him at his, where he sat alone. Whispering behind their hands, her classmates had followed her with their gazes. Alcea O'Malley always sat with the popular crowd. What was she doing paying attention to the kid who'd kept to himself for the last four years? Dak was strange. Everyone knew that.

But for the very first time in her life, maybe for the only time, she didn't care what anyone thought. Something deep inside her had shifted during that nighttime encounter. She felt empowered by the possibilities Dak had uncovered—dreams she'd hardly dared to admit even to herself. And his kisses. Oh, his kisses. She'd experienced her first taste of passion. She wanted to experience it again.

She slid into a seat beside him and he looked up from a book, surprise lighting his chameleon eyes. Surprise that turned to wariness that turned to disinterest. But she ignored all the signals. Determined, she plunged in, attempting to engage his attention like she had that night. He answered in monosyllables. She countered by tossing her hair and laughing too loud. Her classmates' whispers turned to snickers.

Then, in a voice made loud by desperation, she trilled, "So, tell me . . ." Flutter of eyelashes. "Who are y'all taking to the senior dance?"

And while she'd sat there with a bright smile growing brittle and a face flaming red, he'd looked at her for a long moment. Around them all the usual clatter had ceased.

"Nobody," he'd answered. "Excuse me."

His voice had resonated in the silence. He'd left her sitting alone in the middle of her classmates' muffled laughter, her eyes now starry from barely held tears.

Although she didn't look at him now, she could feel his gaze resting on her. "We were young, Alcea." His voice was gentle. "And I didn't handle things with much sensitivity. But you were barely sixteen, and I was about to leave for college. And . . . there were differences in what we wanted. I thought about you all the rest of that night, if that makes any difference, but there didn't seem to be a point."

"I guess not." She looked at him again. "But did you ever wonder what if?"

"No." This time he averted his gaze. And for the first time she wondered if he was being honest. "What if isn't very useful." He smiled. *"Do, or do not. There is no try."*

Ha. One she knew. "Yoda. *The Empire Strikes Back*." She reached for her mug. "So you live by doing. No holding back. Damn the torpedoes and full speed ahead?"

"I suppose. I guess I'd say I'm a little more self-assured than I was back then." His eyes hooked hers, and she sucked in a breath. "I know what I want. And I pretty much go after it." His gaze dropped to her sandals. "You have very pretty feet."

The air suddenly radiated sex.

In the process of taking a drink, she almost choked. "Um, thank you." For a moment, she was grateful that she'd used the coral polish on her toenails, and in the next moment, she wished she'd stuffed her feet into snow boots. Fumbling, she set the mug back on the table, stood up, and reeled in her heartbeat. She needed stability, not some wandering storyteller who would only be here for the length of an affair. "And thanks for the coffee, too, but I'd better get going."

He smiled slightly but ushered her into the house. The walk down the hall seemed interminable. She wasn't embarrassed she'd brought up that night, but her thoughts were confused, and it didn't help that she could feel his eyes pinned on her backside.

When they reached the porch, she paused. He leaned his haunches against the railing—a risky business—and hooked his thumbs in his pockets. Such a casual pose shouldn't be so sexy but it was. "So, I'll see you tomorrow," his mouth said, while his eyes said, *Want to complete what we started all those years ago*?

Her mouth went dry. "Tomorrow?"

"The birthday celebration?"

"Uh, sure. Tomorrow." As she rattled off her parents' address, she didn't meet his eyes lest she be tempted to follow him back into the house. She didn't want an affair, but his obvious admiration was a shot in the arm. More than a shot. A high-powered dose of amphetamine.

She walked carefully down the steps, down the walk, and didn't look back. She felt his gaze on her the whole time. As soon as she was out of sight, she stopped and pressed a hand to her chest. Whoa, what had just happened? She'd spilled her guts as though she'd known him her entire life. And then she'd come *this close* to throwing caution aside and following through on his unspoken invitation. Wow. She should feel alarmed, but what she felt was . . . thrilled.

She smiled. She didn't know she still had it in her.

She threw back her head and took a deep breath. The sky was achingly blue, the tulips bowing in the window boxes on the shops along the square a vivid red. The world looked clean, fresh—and, for once, conquerable.

Fingers of breeze lifted her hair as she crossed Maple Woods Drive and walked up Main toward her car. Her pace picked up until she positively bounced. She called out a greeting to Paddy, sweeping outside his Emporium. He gaped. She waved at Patsy Lee, dusting the window at Merry-Go-Read, for once not thinking anything scathing about the peasant dresses her sister-in-law usually wore to hide a plump figure. Patsy Lee blinked round robin eyes and waved back. Spotting Serena Simpson mounting the steps to Stan's bank, her dark curls sweeping the back of her pink silk blouse, she didn't even feel her usual urge to spit. Serena could have Stan. With Alcea's blessing.

When she reached home, she actually sang as she placed Post-it notes on the furniture she intended to keep. The rest would go in an estate sale to add to whatever Lil loaned her. There was a limit to what she could take from her sister. She even reconsidered her decision to tell Lil about Michael and the Indian, although she reserved her final verdict for the morrow.

After school, a friend dropped off Kathleen. Alcea's pleasure stumbled in the face of her daughter's continued belligerence, but even the silent treatment she received all evening didn't bother her as much as it had the night before. She reasserted her unaccustomed optimism and decided to believe Dak. With time, Kathleen would adapt to their less-than-palatial circumstances.

And as she dropped into a dreamless sleep, she realized she was actually looking forward to the O'Malley Spring Birthday Party. She didn't pause to examine why. She already knew.

Chapter 6

Just past one on Saturday, Dak swung up Maple Woods Drive, checking addresses. The O'Malley home lay a few blocks south of Main and Cowboy's Tow. Overhead, the trees were green lace against a blue-and-white backdrop. He glanced up in appreciation, but not for too long. The sidewalk buckled over determined roots. He passed a row of bungalows, big and small, all looking like the torsos of stolid matrons with hands on their hips and lapfuls of front porch. He picked up his pace when he spotted Alcea's Taurus parked a few houses down.

Then slowed while he reined in his libido. Had she crooked even her little finger while they'd stood on the front porch yesterday, he would have given full vent to the attraction between them, but, upon reflection, cooler thought had prevailed. He felt drawn to Alcea, much as he'd briefly been mesmerized by that girl on the water tower, but she was a woman in crisis. She had a relationship of some sort with that fellow Kemp. She also still seemed to want exactly what he wouldn't offer—a long-term relationship with roots.

It wasn't his habit to play with people's emotions. In the towns he visited, there was usually some woman of his ilk who would take a liking to him, and he to her. They would enjoy each other while it was convenient, and he'd left no broken hearts behind. He didn't plan to start now.

Plus, he liked Alcea. Just like he remembered, she was still an unlikely mix of insecurity and arrogance, now tempered by a self-deprecation he didn't recall, and an added softness likely created by experience. And she was smart. Given her current situation, it would be interesting to see which direction she'd choose. He'd offer her friendship, but nothing more.

At the walkway, he brushed past a discreet O'MALLEY BED & BREAKFAST sign posted in the dappled shade of maples. The rambling two-story house was white alleviated by brick red shutters. He mounted broad steps, glossy with gray paint, to an expanse of wraparound porch. Swings and buckets of pansies faced each other from either end. He could hear the squeals of children at play out back. In case Alcea answered his knock, he schooled his features into friendliness untouched by any shadow of seduction. It would be a good thing if she turned up her nose at the Pink Palace. Having her that near would definitely test his sense of ethics.

Instead of Alcea, though, the door was opened by a man somewhere in his sixties who looked vaguely familiar. "Mr. O'Malley? Dakota Jones."

The man smiled around an unlit pipe, his face crinkling into well-used lines, especially at the corners of a pair of brown eyes topped by a shock of white eyebrows. He swung open the door. "Come in, come in. And call me Tom."

The men shook hands. Dak felt his six-foot length fade into insignificance, not only because the man was broad shouldered and at least five inches taller, but because Tom's orange-and-purple plaid shirt packed a punch. Obviously, the O'Malley daughters had gotten their height from their father. He wondered if any of them had also inherited his outlandish taste.

Dak followed Tom through the house. They passed through a parlor dimmed by vines crawling up the windows. Doilies rode on the backs of overstuffed furniture, a beaded lamp cast light over a faded Oriental rug, and lace anointed a table in the dining room. Then they stepped into the kitchen. Dak's eyes widened.

This room popped. Wallpaper burst with cabbage roses over a lavender chair rail. Baskets and copper urns stuffed with plants, magazines, and skeins of yarn elbowed for space in every nook. Children's drawings and ceramic handprints crowded the walls, dominated by a large landscape of the Ozark hills rendered in broad strokes and bold colors. He paused to admire it.

"That's Mari's work. She used to do lots of painting but says work doesn't leave her much time for it anymore." Beaming, Zinnia came toward him, wiping her hands down an apron embroidered with violets before grasping his hands. "I'm glad you made it. Let me get you something to drink." She turned to her husband. "Tom, get him something to drink from the icebox. I'm sure the lemonade out on the table has gotten warm." The oven timer dinged. "There are my brownies. You go on back and we'll introduce you to everyone. Tom, you get on out there with him so he doesn't feel like a stranger."

Dak thought he saw why Alcea and her mother might butt heads.

"Yes, dear." Tom handed Dak a glass of lemonade, eyes twinkling. "I've learned it's better to obey than raise an objection."

"Oh, pish," Zinnia said with a frown. As she turned toward the oven, Tom gave her behind a pinch. Zinnia whipped around but she was smiling. "What's this boy going to think of us? Go on with you, now." She waved them to the door.

What Dak thought was he'd just seen a real marriage in action. For a moment he wondered what life was like being raised by two parents like this, in a house like this. Just an idle thought, really. He'd loved his own mother, and he was happy with his life.

Tom led the way out through a screened porch. In the deep back yard, blossoms nodded and waved from every spot that wasn't doused in shade. Lil, a man he recognized as Lil's husband, and another woman with unnaturally black hair streaked with equally unnatural red were gathered in lawn chairs off to one side, intent on their conversation. Opposite them, near a detached garage, a short woman with long brown hair poked at the coals in a barbeque pit with a long-handled fork. A little girl, three or four, held the folds of the woman's peasant-style dress away from the fire.

"Pop? Can you come help?" The woman was barely audible over the kids playing volleyball in an area worn clean of grass.

"Coming, Patsy Lee." Tom looked back at Dak. "My daughter-in-law is one of the birthday girls. Sweet as a peach, and shoulders of iron. She's carried on well since Henry passed." He pointed to the five kids ranging around the makeshift volleyball court. "Along with the one hanging on Patsy Lee's skirt—that's little Lily—three of those are hers. Rose." Tom indicated a thin-limbed blond mop top Dak would judge as being midway through grade school. Tom's finger moved. "Daisy." Daisy was a taller version of the mop top, maybe fourteen or fifteen. Her pale hair was curlier than her sister's. As she brushed it away from her face, Dak grinned. Outlandish taste *was* an inherited trait. A layer of purple eye shadow ringed her eyes, ill matched with the red-and-white T-shirt she wore.

"Hank! Pay attention!" Daisy leaped for a serve and sent the ball spinning toward her teammate, a lanky boy with equally lanky honey hair. He looked to be a couple of years younger. He stood staring up at the trees, and the ball simply landed with a thud at his feet.

"Aw, Hank!" Daisy stomped around in a circle, shaking her head in disgust, while Hank looked at the ball, surprised.

"That daydreamer is Patsy Lee's son." Tom shook his head. "And history repeats itself. Three girls and a boy, like with Zinnia and me. Patsy Lee has her hands full."

On the other side of the net, another boy of about Rose's age whooped, while a girl near Daisy's size pumped her arms in a victory signal. "That's another point for the Van Castle team!" Both of these kids had straight brown hair, long bangs, and straight, thin bodies. The girl's eyes were serious; the boy's full of mischief.

Tom smiled. "Those two are my daughter Lil's stepchildren—Jon's kids. Melanie, another birthday girl. She's turning fifteen. Michael is, let's see, ten now. He and Rose are in the same grade. And the last birthday girl is Alcea's daughter, Kathleen." He motioned to a bench, angled to face the volleyball court. Back facing him, Alcea sat next to but not touching a girl whose shape was a miniature of her own. "Kathleen will be fifteen, too, in early May."

Dak scrambled to keep up. Light, curly hair—Patsy Lee's bouquet of four children. Dark, straight hair—Lil and Jon's pair. Kathleen, a candlestick between them. He couldn't imagine having a family this size, let alone remembering all their names and ages.

"Pop?" Patsy Lee called out again. "I'm afraid these hot dogs are almost goners."

"Don't worry, we've got plenty!" Tom called back. He started toward her with a wink over his shoulder. "Don't tell Zinnia I left you alone to get acquainted."

Forgoing the party in the lawn chairs for now, Dak sauntered across the lawn toward Alcea. When she caught sight of him, she flushed and touched her hair. "I didn't think you'd come."

But she'd hoped he would. The unbound hairstyle said it, as well as what she wore. She looked lovely in—he gave an inward grin—pink. From the starchy, overpressed look of her blouse and shorts, he'd guess the outfit was new. Her bare legs, tinged with the beginning of a summer tan, were as long as her sisters. A tiny gold chain was looped around an ankle as graceful as her feet. Her toenails were pink today. As were her ears. She was completely aware of him and couldn't hide it. He felt a stirring in his loins, and hoped what he was feeling didn't show in his face. "Wouldn't miss it. And this is—"

"My daughter, Kathleen. Move over, sweetheart, so Mr. Jones can sit down."

The girl gave him a disinterested glance and scooted farther down the bench. Dak sat, sandwiching Alcea between them. Even without touching, the warmth from Alcea's legs radiated to his own. "Happy birthday, Kathleen." He leaned forward to see her. "Not a volleyball player?"

When his question went unanswered, Alcea rolled her eyes. "She's a good volleyball player, but I can't convince her to join her cousins."

"It's a dumb game. I mean, like, look at Hank."

"Kathleen!" Alcea glanced at him with some embarrassment. "Mr. Jones—"

"Dak," he inserted. "If you call me Mr. Jones, I'll be looking around for my grandfather."

"Dak," Alcea repeated, giving him a smile tinged with mortification at his meager effort to ease the situation. The smile about blew him off the bench. Sincerity became her. "Dak is a writer, Kathleen. A published one."

Inwardly, Dak sighed. Generally, when people discovered what he did, things got awkward, as though writing held some vaunted place on the hierarchy of talents. It didn't. Everyone had talents. But this time when Kathleen looked at him, he didn't see what he thought of as ill-placed admiration, but real interest. "Do you write?" he guessed, and was rewarded by another smile from Alcea.

Kathleen twirled a piece of hair around her finger. "Some."

"What do you write?"

She darted another look, like making sure he really wanted to know. "Short stories. Poems. And I work on the paper at school." She dropped her hair and slid her hands under her thighs, palms down, probably to stop their fidgeting. "I guess you think that's pretty lame."

"Youth doesn't have a lot to do with talent. I started writing in high school, too. I was published in *Ploughshares*—it's a magazine—when I was sixteen. Have you submitted yet?"

Now he had her full attention. "I didn't know there was any place that took kids' stories."

"There are lots of places. No guarantees, though. Every writer has to handle rejection."

She frowned. "I'm probably not good enough. Although Mr. Eagleton likes my stuff."

"Eagleton? Good God—I thought he'd retired. He must have age spots on his age spots by now." He made a mental note to call Eagleton. If he'd followed the success of his former student, Dak didn't want him blowing the news around town.

That got a smile. "He does. But he's, like, a good teacher."

"One of the best," Dak agreed. "And he says you're good?"

She nodded.

"Then you are. He's the one who showed me the publishing ropes. If he thinks you're good, I'm surprised he hasn't done the same for you."

"He did mention something yesterday about maybe I'm ready. But I thought he just said it to make me feel good because—" Kathleen's eyes grew stormy.

"Because they're growing morons at Cordelia High. I could just kill—" Alcea bit her lip.

"Dad," Kathleen completed her sentence. "It's not *his* fault. It's yours."

Alcea's color heightened, and Dak intervened. "Eagleton wouldn't mention anything to you if he wasn't serious. Tell you what. Let me look over what you've got, and I'll give you another opinion." As soon as the words left his mouth, he wanted to call them back. Getting mixed up with Alcea's daughter wasn't on his play card.

Kathleen's remaining truculence fled. She was as pretty as her mother when she allowed it. "You'd do that? And you'd be honest, not, like, just say nice things because you know my mother or something?"

He nodded. "Keep in mind, though, that I'm just one opinion. It's subjective, you know. Even if I love it, the next person may not. And if I don't, it doesn't mean someone else won't."

Kathleen watched Pop deliver a tray of hot dogs to a picnic table set up on the patio. "Okay. Maybe I could bring some of it to you Monday?" She glanced at her mother. "If you'll take me after school?" The question was stiff.

Alcea glanced uncertainly between them. "Sure, if Mr.— if Dak is sure."

"I am," Dak said, even though he wasn't. He leaned forward with elbows on his knees, watching the volleyball game. He simultaneously saw the ball thunk at Hank's feet again and felt Alcea's smile once more brush his face. He liked the feel of it.

Daisy gave a snort, scooped up the ball, and ran over. "Kath? C'mon and get your butt out here. Mel and Michael are making me look like I suck."

Kathleen looked up. "You do. And you've got too much gunk on your eyes."

"So what? You've got too much starch in your pants, so we're even." Daisy set the ball on her hip. "Come on. You play better than Hank. Of course, anyone plays better than Hank."

The thin brown-haired girl—Melanie—waved from the net. "Puh-*lease*, Kathleen."

A smile tickled Kathleen's lips and some of the tension faded from her body. "Okay."

Daisy tossed her the ball. "You serve." The two ran off.

Alcea watched them. "They're inseparable. There used to be a lot of differences between them, but they found a common link a couple years ago."

"Writing?"

"With Melanie, maybe, but with Daisy . . ." Alcea snorted. "Boys. They're constantly scheming, but I don't think they've caught any—yet."

"I wouldn't think Kathleen had much trouble in that department." He glanced at Alcea. "Any more than her mother did."

Her face went as pink as her toenails. "Actually, Kathleen is known as a bit of a brain. And she's tall. Not a match made in heaven for most boys. And Melanie is shy around boys. As for Daisy . . ." The curly-topped blonde ran past, whooping and sweating. Her eye shadow formed two purple rivulets down the side of her face. "Need I say more?" Alcea turned to face him, her color returned to normal. "Thank you for offering to help Kathleen. I hope it won't be too much of a bother. That's the happiest I've seen her since she found out about the house. I should get her counseling or something, but . . ."

"But you can't afford it," he said matter-of-factly. "Don't worry about me. Us writers have to stick together." But he knew it wasn't Kathleen he really wanted to get stuck with.

"Hey, Hock!" A voice rang out from the trio near the house. The black-haired woman. "You going to keep a queenly distance all day?"

Alcea's mouth puckered. "It looks like Mari has finally shut up long enough to notice you're here. It's not me she's interested in."

"Hock?"

"My clever sister learned a long time ago that *Alcea* was the formal name for hollyhocks. The flower thing—remember?"

"And Rose, Daisy, Lily . . ." He watched her daughter, lithe and graceful when she wasn't self-conscious. "But Kathleen?"

"It didn't make my mother very happy, but I wasn't about to saddle my baby with a name kids would turn into a joke."

He smiled wryly. "I understand. I'm always explaining Dakota."

Her smile held mischief. "Then explain it again."

"Born in South Dakota."

"You and Stan share a link, then. Lucky you. His father was from there."

"Hock!" Mari called out again. "Soup's on."

Alcea got to her feet. "C'mon. She won't shut up until we've paid homage."

After they'd filled their plates, Dak and Alcea joined her sisters in the lawn chairs. Despite urging, the kids refused to be pulled away from their game. Tom still busied himself at the barbeque, helped by Patsy Lee.

Eyes as blue as the hyacinths blooming behind her, Lil greeted him. She motioned to the woman whose hair—except for the bright red streaks—soaked up light like a black hole. The sprinkle of freckles across her nose indicated she might naturally be a redhead, just not that color red. "Have you met Mari?"

Settling next to Alcea and balancing his plate on his lap, Dak reached across to briefly grasp the hand Mari held out, amazed she could lift her slim arm; her wrist held forty pounds of chunky bracelets. Mari's eyes, twins of Lil's, were lit with curiosity. He prepared to enjoy himself. This kind of family gathering was the stuff from which characters grew.

Mari crossed long legs that ended in three-inch platform heels, and gave Alcea a once-over. "Mom should be glad you finally unearthed that outfit from your closet. She only gave it to you umpteen years ago, and you've never worn it. Did you finally get over your allergy to pink?"

"Don't be silly." Alcea glanced at him, face flushing. "I've always liked pink."

"Hmph. That must be why you practically strangled her with the belt when you saw it." Unlike the others, who drank lemonade, Mari twirled a wineglass between two fingers.

"Mari," Lil admonished, tone gentle. "Leave Alcea alone."

Alcea's brow lowered at Lil. "I don't need you to defend me." She looked at Mari. "I'm at least wearing more suitable attire than that sackcloth you have on." Belted with macrame, Mari wore an olive tunic over black tights.

Mari's eyes narrowed. She carefully set her wineglass on a table near her elbow. "What's wrong with what I have on?"

Dak tried to deflect the squabble. "Where's Zinnia?" His voice barely penetrated the rising babble of female voices as Lil also tried to play mediator. Tom and Patsy Lee approached, took a gander, and retreated into the house.

"Zinnia's always so busy at these things, she forgets her own stomach. Which is fine because, believe me, this is enough to handle." Lil's husband, Jonathan Van Castle, emerged from the screened-in porch, dragging some lawn chairs. Dak had never met the man, but he certainly recognized the singing sensation that had ruled the country charts for numerous years.

Jon set down the chairs and looked at the three sisters. "Never a dull moment," he murmured. He turned to Dak and held out a hand. "Jon Van Castle."

Dak shook his hand, struck by the vibrancy of Jon's catlike eyes.

Jon opened a chair between Dak and Lil. "Don't bother to try to get in a word," he advised Dak with a crooked smile. "Lost cause."

At his words, there was a chorus of objections as all three sisters hit on a point of agreement concerning men who spoke up where they weren't wanted.

Jon rolled his eyes. "See what I mean?"

The kids abandoned their game and attacked the picnic table like a swarm of locusts. They settled around the bench under the oak, and for a short while there was silence while everyone ate. Mari finished first and tossed her empty plate at a garbage can. She missed.

"Hell. I never used to miss." She picked up her wineglass and stared at Dak over the rim. "So, what do you do, Dakota Jones? I hardly remember you at all, but then you're closer to Alcea's age, so that isn't surprising." She made *Alcea's age* sound like her sister was teetering on the edge of her grave. She looked between the two of them with ill-concealed interest. "Did you guys date in high school or something?"

"No, we didn't—"

"He's a writer—"

They spoke simultaneously, and stopped.

"Mari has a habit of speaking without thinking." Lil's look at her sister held a warning. "Don't you, Mari?"

"If you mean I'm up-front and honest, then it's not a habit I want to break. Unlike some people, I don't try to pretend to be something I'm not." She arched her eyebrows at Alcea.

Squeezing her hot dog so hard Dak wouldn't have been surprised to see it pop out of the bun, Alcea opened her mouth. Lil cast a wild look at Jon seated close beside her, but before anyone else could speak, Dak responded. "Alcea and I only knew each other in high school. I'm afraid I always had my nose in a book, and most Saturday nights would find me studying, not dating. I was a pretty boring kid, if you want the truth. And, of course, Alcea was popular—and gorgeous enough to make a boy like me incapable of doing more than stammer in her presence."

Alcea's color heightened again, but at least his compliment had the result of loosening her grip on her hot dog. Mischief spoiled, Mari settled for *hmph*ing again.

"Not hard to imagine, looking at Alcea now." Jon smiled at his sister-in-law and gave Dak a look of approval. "And you write?"

"Jon reads a lot. Would we know anything you've written?" Lil asked. She'd relaxed against Jon's shoulder, apparently no longer worried her sisters would yank each other's hair. Jon's hand rested on her back.

"He writes stories and articles," Alcea said, repeating what he'd told her.

"For some rather obscure magazines," Dak added. That was true. He didn't write articles very often, but when he did, they were published in periodicals usually known only in literary circles. And he wrote those under a pen name, just like he did with his books. If Jon was well-read, though, he might recognize Dak's nom de plume. Probably would where his books were concerned. The *Road* series had never hit the heights of his first novel, but then he wasn't interested in that kind of high again. Dak didn't like to shave the truth; it was just more comfortable to omit details. "Florida tells me you're retired?" he asked Jon, changing the subject.

A pall fell over Lil and Alcea, and Mari squirmed. Damn, he'd forgotten his half-sister's name was mud in this group.

Jon smoothed over the moment. "From singing and performing. Not from songwriting, but I'm able to do that anywhere." He smiled at his wife and slid his hand up to rub the back of her neck. "One hotshot entrepreneur in the family is enough. Somebody's got to do the cooking for our crew. Michael eats enough for eight people."

Lil smiled, her gaze wandering over to the children. "How is Kathleen, Alcea? Melanie told me she was pretty upset."

"She's fine." Alcea's voice was clipped.

"Patsy Lee told me Daisy said things were a little rough on her at school." Lil sighed. "Children can be so mean."

"Maybe I should have told her how things were, but I didn't want to worry her." Alcea still sounded defensive. "I'd hoped—"

"You'd hoped Kemp Runyon would have come up to the mark by now."

"Mari!" Lil frowned at her. Alcea turned red.

"Well, she did," Mari said. "You can't tell me she didn't. Mom keeps me up to date on everything that goes on around here, whether I want to know it or not, and she told me Hock had cast her crown at the new CEO of PicNic. It's disgusting."

"It is not." Alcea's jaw was tight. "He's a very nice man—not disgusting at all."

"He's not disgusting. You are. You've never seemed to realize you could do something more with your life besides marry well. Not that you even did that. It about makes me want to puke. Look at you! You're beautiful and smart and yet you act like some throwback to the fifties. You give women a bad name."

Alcea's mouth dropped open.

"Shut up, Mari." Jon's voice was mild but the look he cast her wasn't. "Not here. Not now."

Mari looked contrite. "Me and my big mouth. I'm sorry if I got everyone's panties twisted, but it just makes me so . . . *mad*." She stood up abruptly. "Maybe I'd better go see if Mom needs help in the kitchen."

"Please do," Lil said, tone firm.

Usually, he was interested in the underpinnings of family relationships since he had nothing to compare it to, but this was more than he'd wanted to see. He realized it bothered him to see Alcea embarrassed. And that bothered him even more. As Mari teetered toward the house on her two-story shoes, Dak took a pretend look at his watch and stood. "I've got an appointment at three. Fellow coming over to give me an estimate on roof repair." The appointment was actually at four.

From the looks on Jon and Lil's faces, he hadn't

fooled them. But they didn't object, likely as uncomfortable as he was. They made their farewells, Lil's mixed in with an apology for her little sister. He turned to Alcea. Since Mari had left, she'd sat staring straight ahead, face stony, nose suspiciously pink. His heart went soft around the edges, and he touched her shoulder. "Walk me out?"

She stood up, unnaturally stiff. Without a word she led him along a brick path that rounded the house. When they reached the walkway, she would have let him go with only a murmured *Thanks for coming.* He almost followed her lead, wanting to leave behind the odd feeling of even momentary involvement in the O'Malleys' life. He didn't know why he'd abandoned his usual dispassionate observation, first butting into Kathleen's business, then acting the rescuer with Alcea. But he hesitated, then caught up her hand as she turned away.

"Will I see you Monday after school with Kathleen?" He shouldn't encourage her, but he couldn't help it.

Her hand was limp but she raised her eyes. He sucked in a breath. They were so dark. Confused. She stood at a crossroads, past life crumbling, new one uncertain, and she knew it.

"It was kind of you to offer to help Kathleen, but you don't have to." She was offering him an out in case he'd had enough of her and her problems.

"I want to." He suddenly realized he did. And he wanted a lot more. Holding her gaze, he raised her hand and pressed his lips to the back. A pulse leaped under his lips. Reluctantly, he let her hand go, but couldn't resist touching her again. With the side of his finger he tilted her chin up. "You look better that way. Just that way. Don't let anyone defeat you."

A light glimmered at the back of her eyes as she searched his.

"Play the music you hear," he murmured, his finger still gentle on her skin.

A trace of a smile crossed her lips. "Yoda?"

"No. Me." He gave her a slight grin and caressed the contour of her chin with his thumb. "But I'll admit to pillaging from Thoreau. Follow your own heart, even if it means running contrary to popular opinion."

"And if you don't know your own heart?"

Electricity shimmered between them. He didn't know how his heart was feeling, but his body was leaving little room for doubt. He dropped his hand. "Then go with your gut."

Her chin had stayed tilted. She considered him for a long moment, then drew in a breath. "I'll try."

Hugging herself, Alcea watched Dakota Jones saunter down the sidewalk, then turned toward the house, still feeling warm from his touch. Dak didn't have much, yet he sat comfortably in his own skin and didn't seem to want for more. In a lot of ways, he confused her. She shivered. Although the way her body flushed when he was near wasn't confusing at all. It was the result of way more than four years of nunhood and a marriage bed that had never warmed past tepid. But no matter how tempting Dakota Jones was, she had to remember he couldn't give her what she needed. Well, in most ways. In one way, she was pretty certain he could give her far more than she could handle.

Still, there was no risk in listening to his advice. *Play the music you hear. . . .*

Thinking of Mari's comments, her cheeks heated, even though a grudging part of her acknowledged it was possible Mari was right. Both of her sisters had achieved far more than a knack with baked goods and a busted-up marriage. Even her timid sister-in-law had a career of sorts. Not that being right gave Mari an excuse for humiliating her in front of Dak. In front of anyone, for that matter.

She entered the front door, and by the time she hit the dining room, her footsteps sounded like the drumbeat in "The Battle Hymn of the Republic." Planning to storm straight outside and confront Mari, she pulled up short at the scene in the kitchen. Through the open windows, she could hear the children still at play, but everyone else was seated around her mother's oak table, except her mother. Zinnia was pouring a fresh pitcher of lemonade. She'd already put out cookies. Even though nobody would touch either one. These meetings had a way of taking the edge off the old appetite.

Nobody noticed her arrival. Pop sat at the head of the table as usual, although everyone knew who really ran the show. Hands linked over his chest and chewing on his unlit pipe, he listened quietly to Patsy Lee, who leaned toward him. Across from Patsy Lee, Mari slouched, feet stuck straight out in those ridiculous shoes. Her bright eyes followed the conversation between Pop and Patsy Lee. Foreheads touching, Lil and Jon murmured together. Some paper and a pen lay on the table, as though someone might want to record the event for posterity. Between Lil and Mari a chair sat empty. That was her mother's. The seat across from her, the one next to Patsy Lee, was the hot seat. The place where her mother's latest victim was forced to meet the eyes of the Inquisition.

Play your own music. Ignoring the hot seat, Alcea grabbed a chair from the foot of the table and scraped it back. Everyone looked up. Keeping her expression neutral, she sat down, back straight. Her sisters' eyes grew round. Pop glanced at Zinnia, who still had her back to them.

Holding the pitcher, Zinnia turned around. "Here we go." Her footsteps hitched when she spotted the change to the traditional seating, but she continued forward without a word. Alcea felt a silly sense of victory.

Silent, everyone watched as Zinnia put down the pitcher. Looking like he'd rather be anyplace else, Jon leaned back, one hand drumming on his thigh. Eyes downcast, Lil sat upright, hands folded on the table in front of her.

Alcea studied Lil, marveling at her sister's constant composure. Lil hadn't always been so contained. When they were little, they'd romped together, squabbled together, and fallen into scrapes more times than she could count. Then they'd end up crowded next to each other in the hot seat, pinned by Zinnia's gaze as she'd doled out punishments that ranged from weeding her garden to a week's worth of laundry. Alcea's gaze shifted to Mari. When Mari had come along, a "late, little mistake" as her mother fondly put it, the two older sisters had united against the toddler's uncanny ability to find them wherever they hid. Then, almost overnight it seemed, Alcea had turned around to find Mari and Lil joined at the hip.

When had she and Lil drifted apart? Maybe when Lil had become inseparable from her first husband? Maybe when Stan started holding center stage in her life? She couldn't name a specific moment, but their relationship had grown stilted somewhere between Barbie dolls and prom. Lil raised her head and their eyes met. Alcea dropped her gaze first and it landed on the rock glinting on Lil's finger. Pawn Lil's wedding ring and it could support a small country. She thought of her plan to ask Lil for a loan. It hadn't seemed like a big deal before, but now she broke out in a sweat.

Her mother angled her chair so she could look at Alcea directly. Pop winked, just like he always had at every person who had ever landed in the hot seat. "So." Zinnia's glasses glinted as she looked around the table. "What are we going to do about Alcea?"

Alcea shifted. "Maybe Alcea could figure that out for herself."

"Now, honeybunch, we only want to help. When do you have to be out of your house?"

"Three weeks."

"Will you get anything at all from the sale?"

"No."

"Do you have any money left?"

"Some." She figured if she kept her answers short, there wouldn't be much to argue about. She'd ask Lil about the loan when she could catch her alone. She wiped her brow.

"I just can't believe Stan would do this to you." Zinnia shook her head. "Lord love a duck, Alcea Caroline, I wish you'd never married the man in the first place. Of course, you did get Kathleen out of it. That's a blessing." That wasn't exactly the term Alcea would use right now, but she was glad her mother recognized at least that much.

Mari snorted. "Marrying for money is perfectly stupid."

"At the time, I loved him." She glared at her sister.

"Sure you did. You loved the house he bought, the country club he belonged to, the—"

"What do you know? You were a child."

Mari glared back. "I've grown up. And I know women like you."

Women like her? Alcea turned her shoulder on Mari and looked at her mother. "I think you made your thoughts on my marriage perfectly clear a long time ago."

"He was a selfish scoundrel then, and I told you he wouldn't change his colors. But you wouldn't listen. You were as stubborn as an old mule. Always have been, always will be."

"Rather like your mother." Pop smiled and squeezed Zinnia's arm, taking the sting from his words. "What's done is done, Zinnia."

"You're right—no need to rehash the past." Zinnia's head bobbed. "Well, we'll help where we can, Alcea. We've got no room, what with our guests, but we got some extra put by, so—"

"I don't need anyone's help. I'll get a job." The words popped right out, taking her by surprise. And everyone else. Their eyes held the same disbelief she'd seen in Peg's and Rosemary's. It hurt more coming from her family. She tilted her chin up. "You know, a job? Something you do when you need money?"

Her mother wet her lips. "That's all well and good, honeybunch, and I'm proud you want to earn your way, but, uh, what do you plan to do?"

"I can do lots of things!" Nobody had ever thought she was anything more than pretty. And pretty in the O'Malley household didn't count for a whole lot. Tears burned under her eyelids. "I've run charity committees and organized events at the country club and worked for the PTA. Those ought to count for something."

"Mmm," was Zinnia's only comment. Mari made a rude noise.

Lil had watched the exchange with level eyes. Now she spoke up. "She can work for me. That wouldn't be a problem, would it, Patsy Lee?" Patsy Lee managed Lil's Cordelia store while Lil divided her time between it, her family, and overseeing the other two stores in her chain, one an hour away in Sedalia, the other three hours distant in Kansas City. Even for trips to Sedalia, Lil always booked a hotel—a daily commute in the winter could be dicey at best. In the summer, the tourist traffic was murder. She was lucky she had Jon to carry the childcare load at home.

Patsy Lee cleared her throat. "Um, we'd love to have you at Merry-Go-Read, Alcea." Patsy Lee spoke with her usual gentle voice, but didn't meet Alcea's gaze.

Sure, Patsy Lee would be thrilled. They'd never been close. In fact, Alcea had always scorned the back-to-Mother-Earth lifestyle her brother and sister-in-law had adopted. After Henry had died, she'd even felt Patsy Lee and her brood shouldn't have expected much more than the penury that was Henry's legacy. She wasn't proud of her thoughts. She should have done more to help, but, of course, she hadn't needed to. Lil had ridden to Patsy Lee's rescue.

"Didn't you tell me you were overstaffed?" Why

was she giving Lil an out? She should leap at the offer. "That you wish you'd told Patsy Lee to let go of last year's holiday help?"

"That doesn't matter. You're my sister." Lil reached across the table and covered Alcea's hand. Her big gem wobbled sideways. Alcea bit her lip. It wasn't as if one more person at Merry-Go-Read would hurt Lil's financial picture. "What would I do?"

"Clerk and help with inventory."

Alcea started to nod, but her head stuck midbob. "I've never used a cash register."

"That's easy to learn." Lil pulled the paper toward her and uncapped a pen. She sketched out a chart, started lettering in the days of the week. "You and Patsy Lee will have fun."

Alcea glanced at Patsy Lee, who had a sickly smile on her face. They'd have a riot. "Won't I cut into someone else's hours?"

"Oh, no." Lil looked up with a bright smile, then bent her head again to the chart.

Oh, no? Oh, yes. Lil was never a good liar. Alcea could imagine how popular she'd be, waltzing into Merry-Go-Read under Lil's benign eye and Patsy Lee's tolerance, having just taken money from her co-workers' pockets. With the act she'd put on for the past four years, they might not know she was desperate. *Then follow your gut.* "Maybe this isn't the best—"

"There." Lil put down the pen. "That schedule would give you thirty-five hours a week, and allow you to be home when Kathleen gets back from school and on weekends."

Like most of the shops on the square, Merry-Go-Read was closed Sundays. But Saturdays, too?

Mari slouched back, looking disgusted.

"I'm not sure—" Patsy Lee looked worried. "I mean, Lil, everyone takes turns working Saturdays."

Lil gave her a look. "They'll understand."

Uh-huh. "And how much would you pay me?"

Lil named a figure that was minimum wage times three—Patsy Lee's mouth dropped open—and obviously as much as she paid Patsy Lee.

Zinnia gave a vigorous nod. "There. That's settled."

"I can't take the job." This following your gut stuff was pure insanity.

Patsy Lee sagged with relief. Lil's glow went out. Mari un-slouched and looked interested. And Jon glanced at his wife and frowned. "Why not?" he asked Alcea.

"I just can't."

The table fell silent.

How could she explain? Her reasons weren't clear even to herself, but they were all wrapped up in her past. She hadn't stepped forward to help out Lil when her first husband had died, leaving her sister with a piddly amount of life insurance. She hadn't helped a pregnant Patsy Lee when Henry had died. Nor her parents when they'd taken out a second mortgage to put Mari through college. Not that she hadn't itched to play Lady Bountiful, but Stan had scotched her ideas. *And you didn't push him very hard, because you felt it was tit for tat after your family's everlasting lack of faith in you. You liked feeling superior.* God, self-revelation was a bitch.

Looking at the faces around the table, the scene of a similar family meeting flashed into her head. A time when Lil was in similar circumstances, before Jon came along and gave her his kingdom. Lil had listened to every one of her mother's arguments about what she should do, and then she'd gone and done exactly as she damn well pleased. Passive resistance par excellence.

She set her shoulders. If Lil could do it, so could she.

"Have you found a place to live?" Zinnia's face had colored. "You have a daughter to think of, you know."

"I realize that."

"How do you plan to take care of her when you're turning down a perfectly decent job?"

"I'll find something else."

"I admire your pluck, but pride has its place. And it goeth before the fall. Lord love you, now's not the time to look gift horses in the mouth."

Alcea's face heated. "And I suppose that's the only way you think I'll find a job—if someone hands it to me all wrapped up with ribbon?"

Pop harrumphed. Jon's fingers beat faster. Mari smiled with a look of grudging approval. And Patsy Lee was suddenly fascinated with a spot on the table.

"That's not what I'm saying, honeybunch. I'm just saying you don't have much time, and no telling how long your job search will take."

Lil looked between the two red faces. "At least move into the store's upstairs apartment. At least let me do that for you."

"No!" Lil's face registered hurt, and Jon's frown deepened. Alcea didn't mean to hurt Lil, but the idea of hours cooped up with Kathleen in two rooms and Lil and Patsy Lee literally underfoot didn't bear thinking about. "I mean, I've already looked at something else."

Zinnia's eyes narrowed. "What?"

"Well, I—"

"Doesn't that just take the cake?" Zinnia shook her head. "First, turn down a job, then turn down a free bed. There's just no reasoning with you. You aren't lady of the manor anymore, and if someone is willing to offer you a hand up, you've got to take it."

Alcea shot to her feet and her chair fell back, landing with a crash. "That's the whole point! I want—need—to do this my way. I just can't crawl back home. I can't take anyone's handouts. Even before I married Stan, even before things got to this point, you never thought I'd make anything of myself. It was always, 'Lil's so sweet, you should take a lesson from her,' or 'Why can't you get good grades like Lil?' or 'Lil plays piano like an angel.' " So much for *passive* resistance. Alcea felt foolish, spouting off her version of Mom-likes-you-best, but, dammit, it was the way she'd always felt. "When she got valedictorian in high school, you gave her a four-pot-roast dinner and invited all your friends. When I won the Miss Cordelia pageant, you gave me a pat on the head and said, 'Remember, beauty's only skin deep.' Nothing I ever did was good enough for you."

"Oh, no, Alcea." Lil's eyes were wide. "You couldn't have thought . . . Mother never thought I was better than you."

"And you!" Alcea rounded on Lil. "For all the years I was married to Stan, you treated me like I was some object of pity. I know you and Mari have laughed about how stuck-up Alcea got her just desserts when Stan started playing around. Did you ever stop to think how much he hurt me? How much you hurt me? Did you think Mari would keep her remarks—and yours—to herself?" She almost mentioned Michael and Rose's escapade with the Indian, but decided not to sacrifice their little souls on the altar of her own resentments. Good for them if they got away with anything against this group.

Mari squirmed, and Lil looked at her hands. "We joked a little, but we didn't mean anything by it, Alcea. I always admired how you held your head up and just went on. I didn't mean to pity you, but I was always sad your marriage wasn't what you'd wanted it to be."

Zinnia's face had folded in on itself. "I was proud when you won that crown, honeybunch. I was just afraid you'd try to skate by on your good looks. But I didn't play favorites. I always loved each of you just the same."

"Well, it sure didn't seem that way from where I was sitting." Alcea's chin quivered. "You had Henry to dote on, Lil to be proud of, and Mari was always the cute one. I never had a special place."

For a moment, the two men shifted uncomfortably, and three females dabbed their eyes.

But Mari rolled hers. "Puh-lease, spare me. You're talking to the 'late, little mistake' here. Don't blame everyone else for your choices. Stan was a stupid move and you know it. Divorcing him was the smartest thing you ever did, and what you've done for the last four years is one of the dumbest. That was a great life plan—trying to keep up with the Joneses while slowly going broke—and now you're flat busted. So what? It's not the end of the world. Everyone else sitting at this table has been in the same exact spot at least once in their lives, and we all dug our way out one way or another." She addressed the rest of the table. "Either she'll get a job on her own, or she'll crawl back to Lil on her knees, or she'll marry Kemp Runyon or someone else like him and let him support her. Huge waste if she chooses old Kemp, if you ask me, but either way she'll survive. I don't see what the big deal is."

"Mari!" Lil started to jump to her defense.

"No," Alcea said slowly, staring at Mari. "She's right." Mari *was* right. But that still didn't mean Alcea didn't want to slap her silly. She took a deep breath and looked at her mother. Behind her glasses, Zinnia's eyes still reflected hurt, and her father was frowning. "I'm sorry if I hurt you, Mother." Her words sounded stiff even to her own ears. "Or you, Lil." She glanced at her sister. Lil still looked ready to cry. "But I'd appreciate it if you'd let me figure things out for myself." She pinned Mari with her gaze. "And if I ever decide to remarry, I'd thank you to keep your opinion about it to yourself."

Mari shrugged. "Fine by me. I hate these stupid meetings."

Zinnia squawked a protest, Mari grew belligerent, and Lil jumped in as mediator. Pop's harrumphs got louder, Jon still beat a nervous staccato on his thigh, and Patsy Lee still had her eyes down.

Alcea stood up. "Excuse me while I use the powder room." To her relief, nobody even glanced her direction. She skirted the stairway that led up to the bathrooms, slipped out the front door, and walked toward the back to gather Kathleen, pausing for a moment at the side of the house to clear her head. *Now what?* drummed through her brain, picking up Jon's beat. *Now what?*

Chapter 7

The noise in her head hadn't subsided by the next day. Fine thing to declare your independence; another thing to actually do something about it.

Early light slanted through the folds of linen draped across Alcea's bedroom windows. She plucked at the sheets, listening to Stan's and Serena's voices at the front door. The bell had rung at nine, and Kathleen had answered. The promise of a full day's shopping in Kansas City, two hours from here, had blasted Kathleen out of bed an hour ago (the only thing that would do it on a Sunday). But Alcea hadn't bothered to get up, unwilling to face the same silent treatment from her daughter that she'd gotten last night.

After they'd reached home, Kathleen had headed directly for her room and slammed the door. She grudgingly emerged for supper—a paltry affair of left-over hot dogs and potato salad snagged from the picnic table—but refused to mumble more than a sullen yes or no to Alcea's attempts at normal conversation. Then when Alcea broached the subject of moving, Kathleen stood up abruptly, dropped her half-finished plate into the sink, and without even glancing at her mother, marched straight back upstairs.

Pushing her potato salad around, Alcea had stayed at the table wishing she had the funds for Kathleen to talk to a therapist or psychologist or something.

Still fingering the sheets, she heard the front door

close, cutting Serena off midtrill. She didn't feel equipped to help Kathleen through this transition—hell, she didn't feel equipped to help *herself*. Well, at least today would be free of sullens and snide asides. They wouldn't bring Kathleen back until late. Alcea swung her legs out of bed, deciding the absence of her glowering daughter was a good time to start packing.

She pulled on jeans and a tank top. Like she had for months, she'd skip services at St. Andrew's. It was too late for the last one, anyway, and she had no desire to take her usual seat in the O'Malley pew. Not only did she not want to face her family, knowing things had been said that couldn't be unsaid, but she'd had it up to the eyeballs with tradition. She really did love them, but she wanted—needed—some distance. As she snapped her hair into a rubber band, her mouth twisted wryly. After yesterday, she'd probably get plenty.

In the kitchen she pushed open the windows, spooned coffee into a basket, then waited for it to perk. Leaning her elbows on the counter, she stared outside. It was a glorious spring day. The daffodils along the drive swayed complacently, birds chirped a song. The earth stirred after winter, and she felt an echoing reply in her body. She held still, trying to identify the source of her unexpected euphoria. It was more than spring. She realized it was hope. And anticipation. Maybe there was something to be said for a blank slate.

She took a long look across the acres of green, then turned so her backside leaned against the counter's edge. Her gaze wandered over the Corian counters and sharp-edged mahogany cabinets of a kitchen worthy of a spread in *House Beautiful*, past the stainless steel of the appliances and the wide glass-fronted refrigerator, and up to the plate rack where she'd once displayed her Flow Blue platter collection. She realized she didn't miss them. She'd only collected the china because it had been something to do when the country club women had invited her antiquing. It had looked pretty against the beige walls. The same beige walls that complimented the beige Berber carpet in every other room of the house.

Her mind journeyed through those rooms, cataloguing the belongings she hadn't yet sold, from the Rauschenberg prints in the foyer to the leather-bound volumes of Shakespeare on the library shelves. (Her current copy of the *National Tattler* always remained out of sight in a drawer.) It was one big pile of stuff. Artwork that she didn't understand and books she'd never read and old plates she'd picked up while she was bored out of her mind. All in an attempt to add color to a lifeless house. And every single item, every last thing, had been created out of her marriage to Stan. She'd held on to Stan way too long. And she'd held on to the garbage of their lives far longer. For what?

She hugged herself against a sudden chill as euphoria dipped and sharp regret rose.

Sunlight slanted across the tiled floor; the warm breeze was sweet on her back. She'd wasted so much time. On Stan. On this house. On designer labels and Ethan Allen furniture and coq au vin. Determined to outachieve Lil, out-Martha Martha Stewart, out-mother other mothers. Desperately trying to prove Alcea O'Malley counted for something. The lifestyle had never fit. But even long after she'd known her marriage was over, long after the divorce was finally final, she'd stubbornly persisted along the path she'd cleared for herself, stopping only now when there was a wall too big to climb over.

And through it all, she'd never given her *self* a chance.

Never.

The revelation walloped her right in the gut. Suddenly, she couldn't breathe. She sucked in air, and a keening rose in her throat. Her knees buckled and she sank to the floor. Still hugging herself, she wept and rocked. Her tears purged self-pity and regret and resentment until finally she slumped back against cabinet doors. For a while she simply sat limp, stretched out, arms loose, and eyes closed, letting the chirrup of the birds, the wind chimes on the porch, the soft hum of the refrigerator lull her. Like Mari had said, she'd dig her way out. Like Dak had said, this time she'd play the music she heard. She just had to learn the notes. *She had to.*

Feeling drained but more clearheaded than she had in four years, she gathered herself up and went to the phone before her brain got muddled again. First, she called Peg and accepted the job. Maybe it wasn't her dream career, but it would serve to put food—ha ha—on the table. They agreed she'd start Wednesday. Then she called Kemp and left a message reconfirming their supper date for tomorrow. She'd leave all options open. He *was* a nice guy, and some of the better marriages she'd seen had grown out of friendship, not passion.

And then she phoned Dak. When he answered, the soft tenor of his voice sent her skin quivering where it shouldn't quiver, but she told him she'd take the Pink Palace, trying not to think what living only yards away from him would do to her equilibrium.

"I'm . . . pleased." His tone conveyed a mix of approval, surprise, and wariness. The wariness upped her pulse. Seemed he might be concerned about his own equilibrium. "Give me a couple of days. I'll get that rug ripped out and the skirting fixed."

Thinking of the cat-perfumed carpet, she decided to take her mother's advice and not look this gift horse in the mouth. They decided she'd pick up the key on Tuesday so she could clean and measure for furniture, and she'd move in next weekend. The sooner, the better. She was suddenly impatient to get started on . . . whatever she'd started.

Business concluded, he seemed reluctant to let her go. "I take it you survived yesterday's onslaught."

"It wasn't pretty, and I marched all over everyone's feelings, but nobody ended up dead, so I consider it a success."

His chuckle vibrated somewhere in her lower regions. She squeezed her knees together.

"And a job?" he asked.

"I start Wednesday at Peg's. How could I not? Kathleen will be thrilled to have an entree into the world of the greasy spoon, and I look great in orange." Kathleen would be embarrassed and outraged, and Alcea looked hideous in orange.

"Better than you do in pink?" His tone was teasing.

She blushed. Damn Mari and her wagging tongue. "Much better," she said firmly.

"Maybe Peg will give you a chance to do more baking."

She hadn't thought that far, but she considered his words. "Maybe she will." She heard a buzz in the background.

"Florida is here so I have to go." Of course. Brother and sister would spend Sundays together. She'd have to get used to seeing Florida more frequently. What fun. Waitressing, the Pink Palace, *and* Florida. "See you tomorrow?" She didn't know how he did it, but he managed to make the question sound seductive.

She sighed with regret. She'd already decided less was more where he was concerned. That equilibrium thing. "I have an engagement early tomorrow evening. So I just thought I'd drop Kathleen off after school. She can walk over to my parents' afterward. So I can, uh, keep my engagement and you can, well, do whatever it is you do. I'll just pick her up there. At my parents, I mean. In case I'm late." Oh, good God, why didn't she just say she had a date? "And there's something else. Since I can't be there . . . well, will Julius be around?" She instinctively trusted Dak, but still her daughter was young and she hardly knew him. So until she knew him better . . . She stopped her thoughts. She wasn't planning on knowing him *better*.

He caught her drift without further explanation. "Julius is always around." He sounded irritated. "This will be just peachy."

Peachy? Was he irritated at her request? Or because he'd guessed she had a date? A thrill tingled through her, but she only mumbled a thanks before she hung up. She was pathetic.

For the rest of the day, she boxed some things and set aside others to be sold or given away. Feeling expansive, she even earmarked the Shakespeare volumes for Julius, and, after a moment's hesitation, the Rauschenberg prints for Mari. The activity helped keep her mind off her worries and off Dak. But every once in a while, she'd think *Peachy,* and smile.

Late afternoon, she finally stopped. She didn't want to be packing when Kathleen got home—it would be like waving a red flag at a bull. After a shower and a quick meal, she hauled out butter and eggs, bittersweet chocolate and other supplies. Maybe arriving home to the scent of peanut butter–fudge brownies would sweeten Kathleen's mood. Besides, Alcea could use the therapy. She knew it was crazy, but to her, the transformation of simple ingredients into something wonderful bordered on mystical. It was an art, and she always lost herself in its rhythms. She blushed at her lofty thoughts as she chopped some pecans. That was the same drivel she'd spouted to Dak on the water tower. She was just baking brownies.

Still . . . Maybe as Dak had suggested, she would get the opportunity to show off her skills at Peg's. Not just brownies, but cakes and pies and fancy breads. As she measured flour and baking soda, she daydreamed. And for the first time found herself looking forward to her job. Lost in a glow of optimism, she'd just slid the brownies into the oven when she heard a car in the drive, the slam of a door, the car pulling off.

Kathleen pushed through the kitchen door, arms laden with sacks. She greeted her mother with a frown. "You look like the Pillsbury Doughboy."

Alcea's glow faded. Thinking of the vision Serena must have presented, Alcea self-consciously brushed flour off her shirt and reknotted her ponytail. "Did you have a fun day?"

"It was awesome." Kathleen pushed aside a bag of peanut butter chips and dropped the bags on the table. "I not only got the dress *and* shoes *and* a purse for the spring dance, Serena made Dad buy me, like, a whole new summer wardrobe. She is way cool. Just wait till you see."

She should be happy Kathleen wouldn't pester her for clothes she couldn't afford, but jealousy bit her. Serena and Stan had put a sparkle on Kathleen's face, when all she'd put there lately was a scowl. She sighed. And the scowl would be nothing once Kathleen found out where she'd be working—and where they'd be living. "Serena *made* Stan buy you all this?"

"You know how they flirt around. He didn't really care—he just likes to have her hanging all over him."

Lovely image. "Well, I'm glad you're happy." That much was true. She was glad Kathleen had at least momentarily forgotten her misery. And her anger at her mother.

Arms folded, she *ooh*ed and *aah*ed at each item Kathleen pulled out. After Kathleen had emptied the last bag, she thunked in a chair and stared happily at the dresses, jeans, shoes, bags, and jewelry mounded on the table. Alcea eyed the pile with trepidation. It would fill one whole closet—make that *two* closets—in the Pink Palace. She'd better come clean.

Alcea took a seat across the table and caught her daughter's eyes over the pile of clothing. "Um, we need to talk." Kathleen frowned, and Alcea dropped her gaze. "I think you know I have to work." Alcea fingered a Saks price tag that dangled from a skimpy pair of shorts. The cost could have covered at least fourteen yards of material. "Right away. And since I don't have the luxury of taking a long time to look, I've, uh, accepted a job with Peg."

"To bake for her? You're already doing that."

"I probably still will, but . . . uh, that isn't all I'll do." Alcea took a deep breath and glanced up. "I'll work as a waitress."

"A waitress? At Peg's?" Kathleen's eyes popped. "You can't! Things are bad enough at school. This will make things *worse*."

"Your classmates' mothers work—and most of them don't have high-paying professional jobs." Not in Cordelia.

"But they were *always* like that." Kathleen struggled against tears. "None of them ever belonged to the country club, and they didn't ever have a big house or a Lexus or . . . *Why* can't you understand? They're all *laughing* at me!"

"Whoever 'they' are, they're not your friends if they think your change in circumstances is funny. Besides, none of this is your fault." Alcea dropped the price tag and reached around the pile for Kathleen's hand. "I do understand, sweetheart, but I don't have any choice." At least none she could live with.

"You're right." Kathleen snatched her hand away, tears gone, anger surfacing. "None of this is my fault—it's yours! You're the one who divorced Dad. *He* never said he wanted one."

"Do you really think I should have stayed with him?" Alcea clamped her mouth shut as soon as the words were out. She hadn't discussed with Kathleen all the reasons she'd left Stan—she'd simply used the tired "We don't love each other anymore, but we both still love you" lecture and left it at that. Bad-mouthing Stan would only make her daughter feel conflicted. That's how the psychology books put it.

"Yes! You never said anything about his affairs for

years, so why couldn't you at least like, *wait* until I was grown up?"

Alcea's mouth dropped open.

Kathleen gave her a look that said she was the queen of morons. "Like nobody knew? Duh. Did you think my friends didn't *tell* me?"

"Quite a nice group of friends you have." It stung that Kathleen blamed her for the divorce, but Alcea reined in her temper. "And knowing what you know, you still think I should have stayed in the marriage?"

"Lots of people do it. 'For the sake of the children.' " She parroted in a falsetto voice. "So why couldn't you?"

The oven dinged. Alcea got up to take out the brownies, conscious of Kathleen's glare. She reminded herself her daughter was young. Kathleen thought hopes and dreams stopped somewhere around the ancient age of thirty. She thought the only reason Alcea had been placed on the planet was to be her mother. And this was a difficult situation for her—it would be difficult for any child, doubly difficult for a child raised like a princess. She could think of no way to defend herself—well, at least for her defensible acts—that Kathleen would understand. She set the brownies on a cooling rack and returned to her seat. "I couldn't stay with your dad, Kathleen. Not any longer than I already had. I was . . . losing myself." She repeated the words she'd used with Dak, yet this time she had a better understanding of what she meant. "Does that make any sense to you at all?"

"Well, I sure hope you *found* yourself. Since we've lost, like, everything else."

Alcea felt a wave of guilt at how she'd mismanaged their lives since the divorce. When she didn't respond, Kathleen heaved a long-suffering sigh. "So now what? Where will we go? To Grandma's?"

"No! I mean, Grandma doesn't have room for us, not with her paying guests."

"Aunt Lil's?" Kathleen suddenly looked hopeful.

Alcea managed to refrain from spouting a big fat no again. She smoothed one of Kathleen's new shirts. "That wouldn't be . . . fair . . . to Aunt Lil. She has her own family to take care of. You wouldn't want to feel underfoot all the time, would you? And, uh, have to share everything with Melanie?"

"I guess not." Kathleen's face fell as she had to give up the idea of Lil and Jon's private pool and stables. "So we won't be going to Aunt Patsy Lee's either, thank God. Daisy's fun, but I don't, like, want to *live* with her. And I especially don't want to live with Hank and Rose and Lily. So where?"

Alcea twisted the shirt hem. "I, uh, decided we needed some place private, just for the two of us. Mr. Jones—Dakota—had an idea."

"Is he selling you Cowboy's house? It's kind of small, but like that wouldn't be too bad. I'd practically be able to walk to everyone's house except Mel's, and I can hang out at the ice cream parlor. Everybody's always there. And you'll keep looking for a different job, right?"

"It's not exactly Cowboy's, although it's still near the square." Hell. Just *tell* her. "It will just be temporary until I can find something else."

"Do I have to guess or something? Is it—" Kathleen stopped and her eyes widened. "Not that old pink trailer behind Cowboy's? *Please* tell me that's not it!"

Alcea couldn't meet her gaze. "Um, would you like a brownie?"

"A trailer? You expect me to live in that piece of shit?"

"Kathleen!"

"Don't 'Kathleen!' me!" Kathleen shot to her feet, arms rigid at her sides. "I'm not going there, and you can't make me. I-I'll go live with Dad! Serena won't care. She likes me. She—she—" Her face twisted. "You've *ruined* my life!"

"I know it might seem like it now. But this will all pass, and then we'll laugh about it." Alcea rose and rounded the table. "It won't be so bad, sweetheart. We can make it fun. Like camping or something." They'd never camped in their lives. She touched Kathleen's shoulder, but her daughter jerked away and fled. Alcea stared after her until she heard footsteps pound through the hall and a door slam.

Heart thunking, she sank onto Kathleen's chair, every bit of the optimism gone. Oh, God. Surely Dak was right. Surely Kathleen would come around. Because if Kathleen thought Stan would rescue her, she'd have her heart broken. She plucked at a pair of shorts. Stan would throw as much money as Serena wanted at Kathleen, but bring her to live with him . . . Alcea snorted. Fat chance. Stan had been a rotten father, and that wasn't going to change. Somehow *she'd* have to make them a better life.

Kemp Runyon's image surfaced. Then she thought of Dak. Making a disgusted sound, she wadded the shorts and tossed them aside.

Chapter 8

On Monday, in a continued blur of packing, Alcea managed to forget both men until it was time to fetch Kathleen and deliver her to Dak. Then she couldn't shake his image. At least not until she stopped at Peg's to pick up her uniforms. They were even more orange than she remembered. For a moment she questioned her mental stability, something that seemed to be consuming more and more of her time. Then she threw the things in the trunk where Kathleen wouldn't see them, and went on to Cordelia High. As she waited for school to get out, she slouched in the seat, the brief euphoria she'd felt yesterday gone. Orange—and pink—had a way of doing that to her.

She looked around at the other cars, manned by other mothers like her who didn't work and could afford the luxury of taking their children to school. She sighed. She supposed it hadn't occurred to Kathleen that in short order—like tomorrow—she'd ride the bus. But when Kathleen hopped in the car and Alcea broke that news, it didn't get a reaction beyond "Duh." Kathleen carried a folder stuffed with papers and a happier look than Alcea had seen in a long time.

"Mr. Eagleton helped me pick out what he thought was my best work." Kathleen bubbled, as though she didn't have a surly bone in her body. "I can't wait for Mr. Jones—I mean, Dak—to see it." Her forehead puckered. "Do you think he'll like it?"

Alcea patted her hand and, wonder of wonders, Kathleen didn't yank it away. "I'm sure he will. You're quite talented."

Kathleen thought a moment. "Maybe he will. He's not immature like Joey Beadlesworth. Joey thinks I'm a dork because I love to write."

Privately, Alcea thought Kathleen's classmate was a dork. She put the car into gear. "Maybe he's just jealous."

"Maybe . . . But he's *so* hot, and he hardly even knows I'm *there*." She turned her face to the window. "And now he's making fun of me, along with the other kids."

Guilt wormed under her skin. "I know this is tough on you, but—"

"I don't want to talk about it."

From the jut of her jaw, Alcea knew she meant it. Unwilling to spark another argument, she kept quiet. They drove the rest of the way in silence.

When they arrived at Cowboy's, Kathleen's mood lightened again. She traipsed up the steps of the glum-looking house parked next to the service garage, equally gray but with the added cachet of a few old tires stacked next to a rusting FIRESTONE sign. Julius was lounging on the front porch, and he gave Alcea a thumbs-up. She sighed with relief, glad she didn't have to bring up the chaperone thing again. In her present mood, she'd decided that Dak's *peachy* had been mere annoyance at her request, nothing else.

Wearing tight-fitting jeans and a loose-fitting shirt, Dak wandered out the door. His dark hair looked combed by the wind, his feet were bare, and suddenly the whole place looked brighter. Watching him greet Kathleen, she realized it was *herself* she didn't trust, not him. *Kemp*, she told herself firmly, putting the car in gear before she could give into the urge to hop out of the car. *Kemp*. The mantra worked, and she managed to drive off with an airy wave before she drooled over the smile Dak flashed her direction. She *was* a sorry case; no more mature than the schoolgirl that had once had a crush on him.

Kemp, Kemp. She kept him firmly in her head while she barreled home and prepared for her date. She wanted to look her best, and after two days' packing, her fingernails were ragged. She'd have to hurry to fit in a manicure, but she could do it.

By the time Kemp Runyon handed her into his Lincoln Town Car, her nails gleamed with bronze polish that complimented a few strands of antique beads that draped over the cowl neck of a simple but expensive taupe sheath. This was their fourth time out, and the second Monday Night Discount Dinner they'd shared at the country club. Their first date had been a St. Andrew's potluck; the second, brunch at Peg's. She supposed this meant she was moving up in his eyes. She glanced at him. His eyes had definitely lit up when he'd seen her. That was a good sign, although the getup wasn't just for him. She needed every bit of self-confidence she could muster to face the country club, now that her empty coffers were a full-fledged topic of gossip.

As they neared the club, Kemp's face was in profile against the green carpet of the golf course. His nose had a little hook. She averted her gaze. So what if it did? He was a sweet man, stable, well-groomed, *well-heeled.* What more did she want? An image of blue jeans and bare feet surfaced. She gave herself a mental shake. Dak was nothing—nothing—like the picture Kemp presented in a midnight blue suit and platinum cuff links. Kemp even smelled expensive.

She dismissed her comparisons and smiled at him. "Did you have a good trip?" Kemp had left Thursday for PicNic's home office in Texas.

"The boys are satisfied with last quarter's earnings, and Glory's doing fine. Looking forward to graduation in another month." Glory was Kemp's daughter. She'd graduate from the University of Texas in May. Rare for Kemp, he took his eyes off the road and gave her a brief look, half hope, half consternation. "We were talking and . . . Maybe you'd like to go to commencement? Glory said to invite you."

Huh? It was quite a leap from Monday Night Discount Dinner to a weekender in Austin. She gripped her clutch bag. She'd misread him entirely, hadn't realized that in his mind things had moved along at quite a pace. "You . . . uh, *she* won't think it's too soon?" *I do*. The thought of a trip alone with Kemp—in bed with Kemp—filled her with panic.

"Glory accepts I'm dating again, and feels enough time has passed since Marjorie left us." That was Kemp's euphemism for his wife's death after an illness last year.

"Um, well, I'll have to see. There's Kathleen, and . . . I'm starting a new job. . . ." What was it with her and turning down opportunities? "I—I'll have to check my calendar."

He glanced at her again and his face went red. Despite his business acumen, it hadn't taken her long to realize that Kemp found dating awkward after more than twenty-five years of marriage. "I didn't mean—" he stammered. "What I mean is, I'll stay at Glory's apartment, and we'll book you a hotel room nearby."

Still flushing, Kemp looked away to devote his attention to the turn into a curving driveway. Set back from the road so it wouldn't get dust on its white stucco, the club was a long building, bent in the middle by a portico. One end was devoted to a pro shop and bar; the other, to dining.

Of course they'd have separate sleeping arrangements. With Kemp, how could she have thought anything different? With the removal of the threat, though, she felt perversely disgruntled. She'd bet Dak would never book her in a separate—she halted, aghast at the direction her thoughts kept taking. "Yes." She blurted. "Yes. I'll see if I can get off then. I'd really like to meet Glory."

Kemp pulled to a stop, and a uniformed valet opened

her door. Kemp dropped the keys into his hand, and offered his arm to her. She took it, feeling nothing at the contact. "What job?" he asked, escorting her into a marble-floored lobby.

Oh, balls. She'd planned to approach the subject of her new employment with more flair. "It's just so amusing. I'm going to be a waitress at Peg's. Can you believe it?"

He stumbled. "At Peg's?"

"She's had that HELP WANTED sign up forever, and the other day—that day when I saw you—she asked me if I'd be willing to help out. Just for a while."

Kemp halted, pulling her up short. "Alcea," he said, frowning into her eyes. "Are things that bad?" He hadn't become a CEO because he was stupid.

"Oh, no. I just thought it would be fun. You know me—always ready to try something different. Always ready—" With his gaze on her, she couldn't continue. He didn't deserve her lies. "Yes," she said quietly. "Things are that bad."

"Mr. Runyon—and Ms. Addams!" The hostess, a formidable woman with sharp features and black-winged hair, approached, holding out her hands. "How lovely to see you this evening. We have your table all ready. If you'll just follow me."

Still frowning, Kemp motioned her ahead. She followed the hostess, who glanced back at her with a speculative look. When they entered the dining room, the tinkle of ice cubes and silverware paused. Faces turned toward her, brows raised. Hell. She might as well get used to it. At least these people were too well-bred to be outright nasty. Either that or they were afraid she might one day become Mrs. Runyon and be able to buy and sell the whole lot of them. The idea made the trip to Austin sound more appealing.

Shoulders back, Alcea let her gaze sweep the room. It landed on a strawberry blonde seated at a table in their path. She stopped, and Kemp crowded against her. Oh, good God. What was Florida doing here? It was the one place she'd always been sure she wouldn't run into the woman. Stan had always held at least a few places—if not their own bedroom—sacrosanct. Her gaze moved to Florida's dining companion, a crane of a man with craggy features and a mop of white hair. Mr. Eagleton? Had Florida set her sights on the old English teacher?

"Excuse me." A low voice sounded in her ear, and she started. Dak smiled. "Evening, Alcea. Kemp, isn't it?"

As the two men shook hands, Alcea attempted to recover her wits. Dak looked . . . stunning . . . in black slacks, gleaming dark hair curling over the collar of a black shirt, and a casual jacket. He'd eschewed a tie in favor of a bolo with a turquoise clasp. Kemp's cuff links suddenly looked way too flashy. The two men were moving toward Florida and Eagleton. Somehow Kemp had gotten ahead of her, and Alcea realized she looked like a loon standing frozen in the middle of the room. A number of eyes had sharpened.

Pinning on a gracious smile, she swept toward the table. "Why, Mr. Eagleton. So nice to see you." She nodded toward Florida without looking at her. "Florida."

Florida murmured, "Alcea," her voice cold enough to chill glass.

Creaking like an old hinge, Mr. Eagleton rose. "Glad you suggested we get together, Dakota." He shook Dak's hand, then Kemp's, while Dak seated himself. He squinted at her through half-glasses. "Ah, Alcea O'Malley. I thought that was you. Your daughter is the spitting image. Except for the nose. Straighter, I think, like Dak's here. Fortunately, she also inherited her brains from someone else. Wonderful student, Kathleen."

Florida tittered and Alcea's smile grew rigid. There was a reason why she'd never liked English lit. For her daughter's sake, she swallowed the retort that sprang to her lips. She glanced at Dak, who quickly wiped his face free of expression.

"I just saw Kathleen's work for the first time. I was impressed." Dak briefly explained their meeting, then looked at Alcea. "She's safe at your parents' house."

"I, um, hope I didn't inconvenience Julius."

The look he gave her was amused. "Not at all." Their eyes held a moment until Alcea realized Florida had raised an eyebrow. Alcea looked away.

"She's quite, quite talented, that girl." Eagleton sat down and drew a linen napkin across his lap. "Reminds me some of you at that age, Dakota. Different voice, of course, but an amazingly mature writer for her age. So, tell me, when can we expect your next book? Quite enjoyed the last one. Set someplace in Maine, wasn't it?"

"Book?" Alcea could have sworn Dak had mentioned only magazine articles.

"That's right—you don't read." Eagleton shook his head. "Our Dakota Jones is quite a well-known writer in some circles. Under a pen name, though. *One for the Road* is the name of his series. In fact, for a few years there, he was a real sensa—"

"She may not be a student of literature, but have you tasted those cakes she sells at Peg's? She's an artist in her own right." Dak inserted smoothly. Looking surprised, Florida flicked a glance between her brother and Alcea. "Besides, my books are obscure. Part fiction, part travelogue. They've had modest success, but it's not surprising Alcea hasn't read them." He made it sound as if she'd read everything else.

Gratitude sparked at his defense, but she was still puzzled. "But you told Jon—"

"He doesn't like to talk about it." Florida said. "I think your hostess is waiting."

Alcea flushed and looked over her shoulder. Welcoming smile frozen, the hostess stood tapping her toe at a table that overlooked the golf course. Alcea's flush deepened. Focused on Dak, she'd forgotten the hostess and ignored Kemp.

"Come along, m'dear." Kemp nodded at the trio. She felt Dak's eyes on her back as Kemp led her to their table.

After the waiter had taken their drink order and left them with menus, Kemp picked up their private conversation where they'd left off. "Just how bad are things?"

"Pretty far from dandy." Alcea sat back. Just a glance to his left and Dakota Jones was pinned in her sights. She fixed her gaze on Kemp, and only Kemp. She might as well tell him everything—it wasn't as if she could hide the Pink Palace. He'd see it the next time he picked her up. If there was a next time. She gave him a brief summary of what she'd decided to do and concluded, "I'm selling almost everything—I contacted the Soroptomists and they'll be over this week to catalog the lot for an estate sale weekend after next." She'd leave it in their hands. Once she moved, she wouldn't return.

"If I can—"

Afraid he was about to offer a loan, and, worse, afraid she'd take it, she hurried on. "With child support, my income, and a bit of a nest egg, we'll be fine." Barely. She'd also spent part of the day drumming up a budget for the first time in her life. Math wasn't her strong suit, but she thought she could make ends meet if she could wean Kathleen away from designer labels. "I've rented a place for us to live. It—It's a trailer."

The concern on his face didn't change into disgust. Instead his hand reached for hers. She went still, hoping, wanting, to feel even a remote thrill, but gratitude was all the emotion she got. "You're a very brave woman." His face was so grave—like she'd just volunteered to lead a death squad into the jungle—she wanted to giggle, then felt ashamed. He *was* a nice man, a very nice man. "If I can do anything at all to help, you let me know. I mean that." He hesitated. "I know it's way too soon for this conversation, but I think you know that since I've met you, I've felt more content than I have since Marjorie left. Knowing you are here has made me glad I decided to move to Cordelia."

Content. Nice. The wild stuff dreams were made of. Suddenly restless, Alcea edged her hand from under his and reached for her menu. "Thank you. I'm starving—aren't you? Let's see what the special is."

"I didn't mean to make you uncomfortable, m'dear. I just wanted you to know you can count on me now." Kemp's smile was all understanding. "And—" His tone dropped in a meaningful way. "In the future."

"Uh-huh." Fortunately, at that point the waiter arrived with their drinks, and she didn't have to think of any other reply.

Nearing eight, Kemp led her from the dining room, luckily choosing a route that didn't go by Dak's table. She was no longer up to repartee with Florida, jabs from Eagleton, or the kind of shivers Dak sent down her spine. They moved through the doorway into the lobby and she stifled a yawn, telling herself she was tired, not bored stiff from almost two hours of conversation that had centered around Kemp. But without his chatter to distract her, her mind immediately leaped to her problems. Maybe by the time she got home, Kathleen would have thawed. They could have the kind of heart-to-heart they used to have. Maybe if she could convince Kathleen that now wasn't forever, Kathleen would see her life wasn't over, that her mother hadn't destroyed her, that—

"Oof." Lost in her thoughts, Alcea hadn't noticed a couple had entered the lobby from the bar, drink glasses in hand. She plowed right into them. Kemp grabbed her arm to keep her steady. When she looked up, she looked straight into Serena Simpson's wide green eyes. The twenty-something looked fresh as peppermint in a pink-and-white striped dress. Or had until Alcea had sloshed Serena's screwdriver all over her. And Stan.

"Uh, so sorry." Alcea clumsily patted at Stan's gray vest that went so well with his black hair and its sprinkle of silver. Her hand slowed. There wasn't as much of Stan to pat. He'd lost weight. She frowned at his silk tie. And the thick chains he'd once worn were gone. She glanced at Serena. It must be love.

Clucking like a mother hen, Serena pushed her hands away and blotted with a tissue she'd pulled out of the smart little purse hanging over her shoulder. A tiny frown edged between her arched brows. "Orange juice shouldn't stain. The dry cleaners will get it out." Her brow cleared and she smiled up at Stan. He just stood there, looking down like a lovestruck puppy. She tore her eyes from his for a second to glance at Alcea. "Don't worry about it, Alcea."

She hadn't. "No vodka?" Stan used to drink like a fish.

Stan started as though just realizing she was there. Glancing between first wife and current mistress, he rubbed a hand over his neck below the razor-sharp edge of his haircut. His hair waved like Dak's, and he'd once worn it the same way—over his collar—thinking it made him look younger. On Dak, the style held charm. On Stan, it had just seemed pathetic. "I quit drinking." The hair. No booze. It *was* love.

Serena patted Stan's arm. "I'm so proud of him."

Stan colored, apparently registering Kemp's bemused gaze. His chest puffed out like a rooster, probably so Kemp wouldn't think he was henpecked. "How's it hanging, Runyon?" Oh, brother. Serena still had her work cut out. The men launched into business-speak. Stan's was the only bank in town, although Kemp said PicNic used a bigger bank in Warsaw for most of its business.

"It's so nice to run into you," Serena said to Alcea, then giggled. "Well, I didn't really mean *run* into you. But I was just telling Stan how much I enjoyed the outing with Kathleen. Did she show you her clothes? Weren't they adorable? And she's so *sweet*."

Sweet? Alcea eyed Serena, but she looked perfectly sincere. Jealousy stabbed her. *Sweet* wasn't a side of Kathleen she saw much of anymore. She hadn't intended to drag out her dirty linen in front of Kemp, but her green-eyed monster had other intentions. "Yes, I saw. Too bad Stan didn't feel it necessary to tell her that while he was giving with one hand, he was taking away with the other." She looked at her ex-husband, and he broke off eye contact midsentence.

"Oh, Stan told me about your house." Serena actually looked regretful. "He said you'd gotten behind in the payments, and there wasn't anything else he could do."

Kemp murmured, obviously ill at ease. Alcea didn't care, nor did she care if there was any truth in what Serena said. *What Serena said . . .* Alcea eyed her again, suddenly thoughtful. Stan would do—or at least try to do—anything Serena told him. Maybe she didn't understand what had happened. And maybe—if she was that fond of Kathleen—she would help if she did. "You do realize what Stan's doing to Kathleen, don't you? She's a mess, being thrown out of her home, knowing we'll live in a trailer." She winced. She hadn't meant to reveal that much.

"A trailer?" Serena's eyes went wide.

"Yes, a trailer," Alcea said through gritted teeth.

"I didn't have a choice, Alcea. The bank's board . . ." Stan blustered. "I thought you would go to your parents'. Or Lil's. Surely your family will help out."

"They—they . . ." Stan knew her family well. She couldn't very well tell him they wouldn't, nor did she want to get tangled up in explanations of why she'd refused.

Kemp cleared his throat. "Uh, Alcea. Our car is here."

"In a minute." She barely gave him a glance. "Kathleen needs a therapist, Stan. Somebody neutral she can talk to. She's upset with m— *both* of us, and she won't open up with me. I can't afford it, so you have to—"

Serena laid a hand on her arm, face overly eager. "If you're worried about Kathleen, maybe she could live with us. We'll get her a therapist. I know a good one."

Live with them? "I would never—"

"Don't you think that would be an ideal solution, babycakes?" Serena turned an adoring gaze to Stan.

Babycakes? Alcea wanted to retch, even as fingers of fear crept up her back. *This* was the reason Serena hadn't leaned on Stan to stop the foreclosure. She wasn't that dumb. And she wanted Kathleen.

Shifting as though his pants had just grown too tight, Stan ran a finger under his collar. "Is Kathleen driving yet?" he asked Alcea.

She almost went limp with relief. He hadn't changed *that* much. "No." She was happy to tell him. "And she's involved in *everything.* She needs rides *everywhere.* Lots and lots of rides. Afternoons. Evenings. There's lots of *waiting.*"

He turned to Serena. "Honey, I know you enjoy having Kathleen around, but full-time I'm afraid she'll wear you out."

But Serena was having none of it. She pouted. "I can take her anywhere she needs to go, and be back before you're even home. You're gone all day, and you work late nights, and I get so lonely. She won't be a bother. She'll be fun. Like having a sister." She clutched his arm. "Please. You won't even know she's around."

The fear was back. "Kathleen requires *a lot* of attention," Alcea said.

Both of them ignored her. "And," Serena added, squeezing out a tear, "it will be just like having the daughter I lost."

Alcea frowned. "What daughter?"

Neither answered her. They were lost somewhere in each other's eyes.

Kemp spoke close to her ear. "I think I heard Serena miscarried some years ago."

Oh, great.

"Are you sure this is what you really want?" Stan asked Serena.

She nodded happily. Stan looked back at Alcea. If he'd still been wearing his chains, she'd have him in a choke hold. "That is," he stammered, making an accurate interpretation of her expression, "maybe it could be a temporary arrangement."

Serena frowned, opened her mouth, but then also looked at Alcea and blanched.

"Stan"—Alcea kept her voice even, although fear was rapidly changing to panic—"think what your parents would have said." This line hadn't worked when she'd begged him not to foreclose, but she was desperate. "Your mother would have said a daughter belongs with her mother. Ellen never would have *countenanced* this suggestion." At her use of one of his mother's favorite words, Stan winced and looked over his shoulder as though he might see her ghost. Alcea felt she was halfway home. She'd never known his father, but she might as well yank him out of the grave, too. "And your father—"

Stan's face suddenly lost its haunted look. "My father would have thought Kathleen would be fine with me. Maybe more so than with you."

He would have? "But—"

Serena tugged Stan's arm. "We need to think about what's best for Kathleen." She gave Alcea a triumphant look. "And right now, that's us. I mean . . . a trailer?"

Ignoring Serena's triumphant look, Alcea protested. "Wait a damn minute—"

Stan held up a hand. "I think Serena's right. We do share custody, and it's time she stayed with me." He paled at the murder she felt in her eyes, and backtracked. "At least temporarily. We'll call and invite her tomorrow."

"But—"

"So nice to see you, both of you." Serena took Stan's arm again and hustled him toward the dining room.

Feeling more defeated than she had since Eddie-Freddie had slipped the foreclosure notice into her hands, Alcea stared after them helplessly. "Temporarily! Whatever Kathleen decides"—like there was a question—"don't forget, it's *temporary*."

As she yelled the last word, Dak and his party exited the dining room. Seeing Stan, Florida cringed. Eagleton merely glared at Alcea like he had when she'd talked during reading time. But Stan's reaction was more dramatic. He did a double take, face paling, eyes wide on Dak. Good. She didn't understand his reaction, but hoped he was having a heart attack.

Dak didn't seem to notice Stan's stare. He just frowned at the couple, then looked back at her. Their eyes connected. His were filled with concern, and that was all it took for tears to prickle in hers.

Murmuring something that was supposed to be comforting, Kemp took Alcea's arm and pulled her toward the exit. She jerked out of his grip, poked out her chin, and walked out the door. Until she was home and locked in her bedroom, she didn't let a single tear spill down her cheeks.

Chapter 9

Dak was watching from the door when Alcea pulled up to the curb in front of Cowboy's the next morning. Dawn had opened its eyes under a heavy mauve brow, and now the weight of the atmosphere foreshadowed rain. He felt an inner tumult that matched the clouds boiling in the west. Seeing Alcea last night at the country club had left him wanting . . . more.

He'd enjoyed Florida and Mr. Eagleton, the arrogant old cuss, but Alcea's presence had interested him far more. Despite the enthralled tilt of her head while Runyon had talked, he'd seen her squirm one time, yawn behind her hand another, and had caught her wandering gaze more than once. He thought of bare feet and raspberries, a flash from dark eyes and the scent of cinnamon. Amused, he'd smiled to himself. Despite the upswept hair and elegant apparel, Alcea didn't fit in the confines of the country club—or with as staid an escort as Runyon. He wondered if she knew it.

But his amusement had faded when he'd entered the lobby. Alcea's eyes, shadowed with fear, had tugged at his compassion, even though he had no desire to understand the emotions that had suddenly spiked all around him. Stan Addams had jumped like he'd spotted a ghost, and the encounter had left Florida nauseated. He frowned. Later, he'd asked Florida if she was well. After she'd poured out her woes, he'd been sorry he had.

And he didn't plan to butt his way in anyplace else. Alcea still sat, her hands clenched on top of the wheel. He pushed open the door at the same moment her forehead dropped on her fists. Stifling the urge he always had to run to her rescue, he halted and let the door drift closed—she was far from a woman who needed saving, nor was he the guy for the job. After a moment, she raised her head, tilted the rearview mirror, and swiped under her eyes. When she got out of the car, her shoulders were straight, eyes veiled. He walked out on the porch, relieved she'd composed herself. "Good morning," he called.

"Morning." She started up the walk. The snap was gone from her step, and her expression matched the bedraggled denims and overlong T-shirt she'd worn to do her intended cleaning. As she reached the porch, thunder sounded.

He glanced up. "Looks like we might be in for it. Come on in. I'll grab the keys, and we'll make a dash for the Pink Palace."

She trailed him to the kitchen. A light spatter of rain sounded on the roof. He scooped up the keys and held open the back door. When she didn't follow him, he turned around with raised eyebrows.

"I'm coming." She was biting her lip. "I—I'm sorry. I'm a bit of a mess this morning."

She looked vulnerable without the mask of makeup and pride. Unwillingly, his heart stumbled. "Do you want to do this another time?" He wouldn't ask. If she wanted him to know, she'd tell him. But he hoped she wouldn't. Thunder rattled the windows.

Her lips firmed. "No, let's do it now."

With him in the lead, they sprinted through the yard. They were halfway across when the skies opened up. Rain slashed, puddling on the already soggy ground. He heard a squawk behind him and turned to see Alcea sprawled bottom down in the mud.

"You all right?" he called, starting toward her.

"I'm fine."

Her voice was shaky, and he picked up his pace, thinking she was hurt, then slowing when he neared and realized laughter had caused the tremor. A smile tugged on his mouth. She was a mud-covered mess.

Pushing aside a hunk of wet hair, she looked up at him. "I thought I couldn't sink any lower. Guess I was wrong."

He laughed and offered his hand. "Neither mud nor raspberry sauce gets you down, does it?" He pulled her up, and, still laughing, she stumbled against him. Their gazes locked, and over the rain, he heard the quick intake of her breath. Her laughter faded, replaced by a slight frown as she searched his face, her eyes as dark as the drenched earth. Uneasily, he dropped her hand, and she turned away. Without another word, they ran the rest of the way to the trailer.

Inside the one-room addition, the rain drummed on the corrugated tin roof and a pool of water was spreading fast around Alcea's feet. Covering the lingering awkwardness between them, Dak grabbed some rags he'd left in here earlier and bent down to swipe up the mess while she slipped off her sneakers. Only inches away from his face, the sight of those high arches and pink toenails made his breath hitch. He mopped faster, willing himself to keep his mind on his task, and wishing she'd worn socks.

Finally feeling he'd regained his self-control, he straightened. She was looking unconcerned, squeezing the water out of her hair with another rag. "We can't go in there like this." He had to raise his voice to be heard.

"Why not?" She frowned. "You said you'd tear out the old carpet."

"I did tear out the carpet." He smiled. "I also had new carpet put in. It was supposed to be a surprise."

"I— You— You didn't need to do that." She flushed, then looked down at herself. "Maybe I *should* come back another day."

"That's one option," he agreed, the continued view of those feet suddenly making him feel reckless again.

She looked up at him, eyes wary. "And what's the other one?"

He motioned at the washing machine and saw objection bloom on her face. "We'll be covered," he pointed out, his gaze indicating her long T-shirt. His shirttail would be enough. She stared at him thoughtfully for a moment. Her color had heightened even more, but he couldn't read her expression.

"Well, then." She continued to blot at her hair, then suddenly she threw down the rag and faced him with a look that was half excitement and half confusion. He didn't know what to make of it. "Okay. You first." She pointed at his jeans.

Without hesitation, he kicked off his shoes and stripped off his jeans.

She stared at the hems of his boxers. "No fair."

He made a gimme signal with his fingers. "C'mon."

"Turn your back."

He did, and was rewarded by a thwack when her wet jeans hit the back of his head. "Now, *that's* no fair."

When he turned around, she was laughing again. She looked young and carefree, very much like the girl he remembered in high school. He sighed. And just as he'd thought it would, the length of her top kept her modest. Still, he couldn't resist sweeping a gaze over her legs. When his eyes returned to her face, that odd expression was back. Her eyes looked too big for her face.

"Well, into the wash." He scooped up her jeans and stuffed them with his into the washer. By the time he switched it on and turned around, her face was composed. He felt strangely deflated. "Shall we?" He opened the trailer door and they stepped inside.

"Ooo, nice." He watched her toes wiggle into the deep pile of the carpet he'd had installed. "Turn on a light so I can see it better." When he did, she looked around wide-eyed. "It really makes a difference."

He looked around, too. It did. He hadn't created a silk purse, exactly, but the carpet was a definite improvement. He'd also stripped away the old curtains, leaving only some slatted blinds. "The bedrooms got the carpet treatment, too. And I threw out the old mattresses. You said you had some?"

"Plenty of mattresses." She'd wandered on the other side of the high counter that separated the kitchen from the living room and stared down at the linoleum. "And you took bleach to this floor." She looked at him. "I said I'd clean. That's why I'm here."

He shrugged, inordinately pleased that she was pleased. "You start your new job tomorrow. Your last day of freedom shouldn't be spent scrubbing floors."

"Well, thank you." She'd started pulling open drawers and cabinets. He'd already taken most of the old stuff to the rummage basement at St. Andrew's, thinking she'd want to use her own.

"What's this?" She'd opened a cabinet that was stocked with a few things he'd picked up. All unessential . . . a few cans of a pricey clam chowder, gourmet cookies, deli crackers, and a package of Andre's Mints.

"Consider it a housewarming gift. Kind of like a fruit basket."

"Who wants fruit?" Looking delighted, she rummaged around. He leaned against the counter, watching her. When she raised her arms her shirt slipped up, revealing the smooth sweep of her thighs. She unwrapped a mint, popped it in her mouth, and opened the refrigerator. "And all this, too?"

All this consisted of a round of baby Swiss cheese, a six-pack of diet soda, some condiments, and one dozen brown eggs that he'd bought off a farmer who sat out in front of the garage with Julius most mornings. She'd bent over to peer inside. He shut his eyes against the sight. When he heard her move, he opened them.

Frowning, she held out a can of diet cola. "Maybe a jolt of caffeine would help."

He was far from needing any more jolts, but he took the soda. They popped lids, and she brushed past him into the living room, taking a seat on one of two stools that sat at the high counter. He took the other. For a moment, she just swung her feet and looked around. He could tell from the way she studied the room, she was planning just where to put what, and what curtains to sew for the windows—did she sew? Undoubtedly. That nesting instinct was nothing he'd ever developed. Then she swung around and placed her can on the counter, wrapped her hands around it, and stared at the kitchen. He did likewise. There was something comfortable about lounging here with the rain and Alcea as companions. Her gaze flipped to the oven and she suddenly looked dispirited.

"Not exactly Jenn-Air, is it?" He knew she was thinking about baking.

"A campfire might work better." One of her shoulders rose and fell, making interesting things move under her T-shirt. "Oh, well. Beggars can't be choosers."

He was quiet a moment. "You need to think bigger."

"Like that's all it will take? I don't even think a bigger oven would fit."

"That's not what I meant. Think Peg's."

She tilted her head and eyed him curiously. "You mentioned that before. No question she'll have me bake cakes, but—"

"But a few a week, even a day, won't be enough, will it?" He knew her. He didn't know how, but he knew her.

"I already thought I'd ask her about putting scones or breakfast breads on the menu instead of that god-awful cardboard that Tansy passes off as pastry. She must use *margarine.* But what with my waitressing duties . . ." She grimaced.

"Why not ask her about turning that space she's renovating into a bakery? She can still use some of it for overflow. She can always look for another waitress if she set you up as a baker and it was a success."

"She'd think I was nuts."

"You don't know that." He contemplated her. "You have a talent to share."

"A piece of cake?" She rolled her eyes. "The world is waiting with bated breath."

"*Salivating* is the better word. I tried that chocolate thing."

"I use a special cocoa with a higher percentage of butterfat. It melts in your mouth, doesn't it? . . . Gads. I sound like *Gourmet* magazine, sorry."

"You have a passion for it." He smiled at her. "Being a baker can be a calling, too. Just like any art. Any work, for that matter."

"A baker . . ." She said the word as if she could taste it. She turned her head and stared out into space. "Maybe . . ."

"No maybe. '*There is no try* . . . ' Remember?"

She laughed. "You make it sound so easy." She turned to look at him again, and her eyes softened. "Thank you. For everything."

Their linked gazes lasted too long for either of them. They both looked away at the same time, and he took a swig of soda to wet a suddenly dry throat.

Alcea cleared hers. "I wouldn't have pegged you for diet soda. Somehow it doesn't fit with the grabbing-life-by-the-horns image."

"It does when you feel like you ate the whole steer. That steak was pretty good, I'll say that for the Cordelia Country Club." He rubbed his stomach.

Her gaze followed the movement. Then she looked

at him again. Their faces were only inches apart. He was suddenly aware of how very alone they were, cocooned in the Pink Palace, the rain providing a curtain between them and the outside world.

"So where's the rental contract?" Her tone was suddenly brisk.

"No contract. We'll play it by the month." He shrugged. "You don't know how long you want it, and I don't know how long I'm staying. It's easier that way."

"And you'd said no deposit, right?"

"On this old heap?" He smiled. "What's the point?"

"Guess there isn't much I could do to hurt it, is there?"

"Although teenagers have been known to be rather inventive."

"Teenagers? Oh, you mean . . . Kathleen." She suddenly looked bleak.

Had she fought with Kathleen? He probably should steer clear of the topic if it would upset her. And if he didn't want to get involved. But resolve failed him. He wanted to know about her. And not just because he was angling to understand some family dynamic for a book. "Eagleton's right. She's very talented."

"Yes, she is," Alcea said simply. She paused. "Why didn't you say you wrote books?"

"No nefarious reason. It's just easier that way." He traced a line in the dew on his soda can. "The towns I visit . . . become as much a character as anyone in the book. And the characters are often based on real people, even though they're fictionalized. I get a deeper portrait if folks don't know the fellow who likes to sit around their diners and talk away the afternoons is planning to write a book about them."

"Why haven't I heard of you? I *do* read, you know." She sounded defensive.

"Eagleton is an old goat. Don't worry about him." He thought of the literary circles he'd once frequented in the East and was again glad he'd left that self-absorbed world. "I use a pen name. People tend to want to make a writer a celebrity." The images of a time in California drifted through his mind. He shrugged. "I don't like celebrity."

"Will you write about Cordelia?"

"Probably. It depends on how long I stay."

"And how long will that be?" She pinked as she asked.

"I don't know." He said the words slowly. It was important she understand this. "As long as it takes to sell this place. That could be only a few weeks. But more likely a few months, considering the state it's in."

"I hope—if you're here for a while, that would make *Kathleen* happy." Her face had turned even rosier.

"Alcea . . ." Their hands, still wrapped around their soda cans, were only an inch or so apart. He let a finger touch hers. She didn't move. "There's an . . . attraction between us. We both feel it. But just like before, there's no future for us. I *will* move on."

She leaned into him until there was only a small gap between their mouths. Her lips were parted. Her eyes were darker, deeper . . . dangerous, and that expression was back. "I—I don't think I care."

It took only a slight movement for his lips to settle on hers. They were soft, pliant, and the kiss was sweet as her scent, cinnamon and vanilla, the same flavor as that very first kiss they'd shared on the water tower. But back then, he'd only had a vague yearning for what he'd never experienced. This time, he was damn certain of what he wanted.

He nipped her top lip, kissed a corner of her mouth, then loosened his grasp on his pop can to bury his hands in her hair. She sat still with a steel grip on her soda. He covered her mouth with his and let the kiss deepen. She made a noise in her throat and her body sagged against him. Her mouth opened. He explored it thoroughly, his breath growing more rapid as her tongue met his.

"Sorry." He pulled away, the movement so abrupt she barely kept herself upright. "I can't make promises. You want things I've never wanted." He dragged a hand through his hair, staring at her, unable to keep the hunger from his eyes. "It wouldn't be fair."

Her face changed, suddenly darkening with anger. "And what *is* fair? Nothing, as far as I can see."

Abruptly, she stood up and yanked her shirt over her head.

The movement was so unexpected, his jaw dropped even while his eyes devoured her body, now clad only in lacy underwear and a half-cup bra. She was pure ivory, a little soft around the belly, long limbs still firm. His gaze moved from her lovely feet up her thighs, pausing a moment at the shadow between her legs, then skimmed over her abdomen to the full mounds of her breasts, nipples taut against her bra. She was much better in reality than the boyhood flights of imagination that had fueled some pretty wild dreams. Some very recently. His breathing grew hoarse. He was hard as a rock.

"Do you have condom?" she demanded.

He swallowed. He did, but . . . "Alcea, we shouldn't—"

She stuck her hands on her hips. "I want you. Go get it." She was blushing furiously, but she tilted her head back defiantly.

"Shit."

He made it to Cowboy's in record time, hoping to God nobody saw him running around in his boxers. The rain hadn't wilted his erection a bit by the time he returned. She still stood where he'd left her, only now biting on her lower lip.

"Are you sure?" he asked, thinking if she wasn't, he might have to kill himself.

"I am damned sure."

He started toward her. She met him halfway. Again

he took possession of her mouth, devouring, demanding. She answered with a need more fierce than his own. Her hands skimmed up under his shirt, over his back, then around to his chest. His nipples were so tight they hurt, and his groin screamed for more.

One of her legs wrapped around him, her inner thigh sweetly smooth on his skin. His hands moved down the silk of her back. He cupped her buttocks and pulled her tight. She moaned. She dropped her head back, offering the sweep of her neck, the temptation of her breasts. Without hesitation, he took hold of one tip through the film of her bra, nipping gently, then sucking hard. She shuddered. It wasn't enough. He wanted to taste her. Realized he'd always wanted to taste her. The fantasies of his youth melded with adult passion until he hardly knew if the present was separate from the past.

With one hand he fumbled behind her back until her bra fell loose, then he nudged the material aside, intentionally stimulating her with the coarse stubble on his chin. As he tugged on a nipple again, she whimpered and pulled back, as though the sensation was beyond what she could stand.

But he held her firmly in place, the arch of her back across his arm, the invitation in front of him unbearably exciting. Her breathing grew rapid. He played his mouth and fingers over both breasts, then dipped a hand between her legs, under the band of her panties, puzzled at her sudden mew of protest. He murmured her name and withdrew his hand, but it was too late. "Oh!" She made a sound of surprise and shook as she came. He held her tight to keep her upright, and slowly moved his tongue back up her neck to recapture her mouth.

When he could hardly stand any more, he felt her fingers grasp the elastic of his shorts and he tugged on her panties, until both pooled on the floor. She kicked them aside and pulled him tight, legs entwining with his as if she wanted to climb him.

They sank to the floor, his hands filled with the rounds of her bottom. Both of them still on their knees, he tried to explore more, but she pushed his hands away. Instead she lay back, golden hair fanning around her head, and parted her legs. When he would have dipped his mouth to meet the dark triangle, she gripped his buttocks, guiding him surely until he was on her, in her.

God! Had anything ever felt so good? It was his last coherent thought before he gave way to the fiery sensation he'd been imagining since the age of eighteen.

Underneath them, the trailer floor shook as the washer hit the spin cycle.

A little more than three hours later, they still lay entwined. The dryer rumbled. He'd gotten up an hour ago to move the clothes. Alcea's head nestled on his shoulder, and her breathing was soft. He wondered if she'd fallen asleep. The rain was no longer ferocious, but still fell in a steady tattoo. Dak looked up at the ceiling, feeling no inclination to move. God, she'd worn him out. Three bouts of lovemaking . . . He hadn't even known he'd had it in him.

Just as she'd taken the lead the first time, she'd guided their actions the second. Only that time, she had explored him like she was rehearsing for the Discovery Channel, her mouth and hands unskilled, but all the more exciting for it. She'd continued to resist his more intimate forays, allowing him only brief encounters with her most secret places. It was only when he'd mounted her that she let him guide the way, that time in a slow waltz that had crescendoed into an explosion of feeling. At least where he was concerned. But her? He'd finally cradled her in his arms and asked, "Did you come?"

She stilled, and he knew the answer. "I haven't— I mean, it's been a long time. It hurts . . . a little. And with Stan . . ." She blew out a breath and it stroked his cheek.

He raised up on an elbow and studied her. "You never have, have you? During intercourse, I mean."

She'd blinked up at him, flushing. "No."

So the third time, he'd gently made sure of it. Starting with his mouth running along the slender lovely arches of her feet, he'd worked his way up, finally pinning her wrists in one hand while he stroked and nuzzled until he'd driven her into a frenzy of need. Then he'd taken it long and slow until he'd felt her contract against him. He'd given to her gladly, gratified and relieved that he could.

She stirred, stretched languorously against him, then sat up. He lazily traced a finger down her back and she shivered, looking over her shoulder at him with a smile. He was surprised and glad that in the aftermath of their passion, he saw no more embarrassment. In fact, she looked more relaxed than he'd seen her before.

"Don't start something we can't finish," she said.

"Why can't we finish?" Four times in one—what was it? Afternoon? Morning—would be some kind of world record. For him, anyway.

Her face grew serious. "Dak, I think . . ."

He tensed, dropping his hand and locking it with his other behind his head. He'd encountered this before when he hadn't been careful. Women always had a need to explore the parameters of their relationship, to talk about the future. Or to talk about how they had none, and how all this had been a mistake. He felt a pang and hoped it wasn't the latter. He really might be here for some time, and having her only a backyard away but out of his reach would be a mighty test of his fortitude. But might as well get it over with. He put what he hoped was an interested look on his face. "What do you think?"

She studied him a moment. "I think," she said

lightly, "that was better than I ever imagined it could be." Then she turned her face away and shook out her hair. "And I think we need to put our clothes on. I still need to measure some things."

The release of his breath was almost audible. "And then I'll take you to dinner. Or lunch. Or whatever. I'm hungry."

"I can't. I have to pick up—" Her body went stiff.

He raised up on an elbow. "What is it?" Had she heard someone coming?

"Oh, God. I'd forgotten. For a while I'd forgotten."

He was totally confused. "Forgotten what?"

"Kathleen." There was a hiccup that might have been a sob.

Still puzzled, he pulled her down beside him, and she buried her head on his neck. He felt the warm moisture of tears. He tightened his hold, murmuring platitudes, wondering what was causing all this. Finally, she rolled onto her back.

"Did something happen to Kathleen? Is she all right?"

Alcea dashed her tears while anger swept her face. "She's all right. Right where she wants to be. Right where Serena wants her to be." Her voice broke but remained harsh. "Last night, Kathleen decided to move in with her dad and Serena. They couldn't even wait until today to ask her. We agreed it would only be for the summer. But then Kathleen said she wouldn't move back if I still lived here. I knew Stan and Serena wouldn't support me if I insisted she *promise* to come back, and she was getting ready for a real tantrum, plus she's so *unhappy*." Alcea rubbed her hand across her eyes.

"So you said she could decide at the end of August. Sounds reasonable to me."

"But it's just *not right*. I should never have promised her it could be her decision."

"Kids are pretty smart. She'll make the right one."

"You don't know Kathleen. I taught her . . . I taught her to think things were more important than people."

She curled back against his side, and he held her some more and murmured some more, and tried to understand her pain. The rain pattered on the rooftop, giving him no answers. Eventually, he drifted off, feeling the dampness of Alcea's tears on his chest. His final thought before sleep overcame him was, try as he might, he couldn't really grasp how she felt.

Chapter 10

Not until ten days later, on the first of May, did Alcea realize that the rainy Tuesday with Dak had been the proverbial edge of the cliff. With the strip of a T-shirt, she'd leaped right off and into a life that had ceased to be at all familiar. Like in the Carroll classic she'd picked out from a pile at Cowboy's to read when she and Dak curled up on his sofa, she was Alice down the rabbit hole.

And she liked it there. She had plenty of new concerns, but freedom from the house, from family interference, and even, she admitted, from Kathleen, was an intoxicating experience. And where Dak was concerned . . . well, she was flat out punch-drunk. In her head, she called him her Fling. She hadn't stopped long enough to examine the stirrings of her heart that murmured he might be something more.

It was nearing four, an hour past closing time at Peg's. Bearing an armful of plates, Alcea pushed through the swinging door into the kitchen. She piled them next to the three-bin sink where Rosemary was holding forth.

"You're looking downright peaked, Peg, and you know Doc said you gotta watch your blood pressure. Doesn't she look peaked, Alcea?" Up to her elbows in soapy water, Rosemary talked over her shoulder to Peg, who was standing, fists on hips, in the doorway to a cubby she euphemistically called an office. She didn't wait for Alcea to answer. "You just go on now and call Doc up, and I'm sure he'll fit you in even though it's late. Mama Butz always said no time like the present."

"Grill's clean." Tansy pushed through the door, an unlit cigarette clamped between her thin lips. She shouldered past Alcea to dump some more dishes, giving her a glance through narrow eyes. "Good catch today. You're not bad, girl."

Alcea glowed. Until now, Tansy had only muttered in Alcea's presence, smirking every time she'd send Alcea's order skidding down the countertop where, despite Alcea's gymnastics, they'd smashed to the floor. (Alcea considered them practice.) But today when the old bird had sent Erik Olausson's "eggs up" flying, Alcea had leaped Freddie Steeplemier's workboots (she'd learned to tell him apart from Eddie) and snatched it up like a pro, earning her first round of diner applause.

"If I have to leave early to see Doc, then who in tarnation is going to clean this joint?" Peg was Mrs. Clean. Along with the usual daily mop-up, she insisted the diner be thoroughly scoured on Fridays. She took turns with Rosemary and Tansy and was on the schedule for today. Alcea would be added into the rotation when she'd "learned the ropes a bit better, sweetness."

Rosemary looked stricken. "I'd do it for you, except Betty Bruell invited me over to Up-in-the-Hair to show me the latest in perma-waves, can you imagine? I'll be a step ahead of those gals when I start at Sedalia Beauty School. Ooo, I can't wait till I start taking those classes." She patted Alcea on the shoulder, leaving a wet handprint. "You're such a peach, Alcea-doll."

Alcea's glow flamed brighter. When she'd started at Peg's ten days ago, she'd quickly learned Rosemary yammered more about her dreams of beauty school than anything else except possibly Mama Butz, her deceased (witch of a) mother. At first she'd wanted to stick a dishrag in Rosemary's mouth, but then she'd noticed Rosemary was rushing to claim the customers Alcea was ready to strangle.

That first week of work had seen a steady stream of country club ladies, drawn not by Peg's Meatloaf Special but by the sight of Alcea in her bright orange waitress uniform. But if they'd hoped to regale her with catty remarks while she served them their coffee with skim milk, they'd been disappointed, because Rosemary beat her to the punch every time. So when Alcea had finally bluntly asked Rosemary why she just didn't enroll at the beauty school, and she'd learned it was because Rosemary couldn't get away from work, she hadn't known who was more surprised—her or Rosemary—when she'd volunteered to shoulder both their burdens one afternoon a week.

Rosemary looked at Tansy. "If I don't stay, maybe Tansy—"

Tansy, who had stood straight backed at the grill all day, suddenly slumped, her shoulder blades sticking out like a bird's wings, and muttered something about "these tired old bones."

"I'll do it."

All three women looked at Alcea in surprise.

"What? I think I can figure out how to use soap." Good God, she'd been cleaning up after Stan and Kathleen for years.

Peg studied her a moment, then gave a brisk nod. "You'll do, Alcea. You'll do."

Alcea warmed again, knowing Peg was talking about far more than her skill with a mop.

A half hour later, the dishes were done and Rosemary and Tansy had left. Alcea carried a bucket into the kitchen, dumped the dirty water, then turned on the faucet for fresh. She was pouring in disinfectant when Peg emerged from her office. "Doc'll see me in an hour. How you getting along?"

"I'm about to do the last row of booths." Alcea

cast a look at her. Peg's footsteps were heavier than usual and the enamel butterfly pinned among her orange coils drooped. Rosemary was right to insist Peg see her doctor.

Peg followed her back into the diner, took a seat, and watched as Alcea started on the back row. Under Peg's gaze, she took her time instead of swiping things in a hurry like she had been doing. She'd go home to Dak tonight, just like she had every night since Jon and Pop had helped them move her into the Pink Palace last Sunday. She'd spent precisely one night in the trailer. With Dak. And the rest of the nights she'd been at Cowboy's. With Dak. Yep, punch-drunk.

"That's the way, sweetness." Peg sighed and kicked off her shoes. "Got any more info for me on that bakery idea of yours?"

Two days into her job, thinking of Dak's "think bigger" speech, she'd asked Peg to consider a bakery. Workmen had already gutted the interior of the building Peg had purchased, but no finishing work had started. To her delight, Peg had leaped at the idea. But it was Alcea's job to do the planning and present a budget.

"Just that it's not going to be cheap." She'd started her research bubbling over with ideas, but just a few evenings at Dak's laptop in Cowboy's dining room pricing commercial equipment had left her feeling hopeless. If it weren't for Dak's continual cheerleading, she'd have dropped the whole idea. "It really *is* expensive, Peg. Even a ten-quart planetary mixer is close to a thousand, and it would be easier with bigger. A convection oven will run twice that, and a display case another two. And that's not refrigerated. We'd need refrigerated. Add mixing bowls, paddles, beaters, bakery scales, pans . . ." A dough sheeter was out of the question. She'd have to make do with arm muscles and a rolling pin. "I *am* looking into used equipment. Maybe somebody nearby will go out of business. And Old Ben said we could have his stainless steel prep table for next to nothing since he's getting a new one." And since she went and groveled to the owner of Sin-Sational, apologizing for her fleas-in-the-ice-cream remark.

Peg didn't look concerned. "You just bring me what you find. I got a mite set aside." Her jowls drooped. "And nobody much to give it to now that Cowboy's gone. Oh, Florida, of course, but she seems pretty well set."

Alcea swallowed a snort. Florida's jewelry, expensive suits, and her little Miata were all gifts from Stan. She knew because she'd seen the credit card records during her divorce. But she said nothing. Florida slipped into the diner's kitchen almost daily, looking for Peg and avoiding Alcea. Rosemary, of course, had filled her in on the closeness between the two women.

"Say, I noticed your family came in today. I hardly had time to say hello. How are they doing?" Her parents, Patsy Lee, and Lil had arrived at the noon hour.

"They're fine." She dipped her rag into the bucket, wrung it, and started on the tabletops. "Mother and Pop are busy with guests arriving this evening. Lil's crew is off to Lake Kesibwi for a week." She'd hardly had time to exchange more than a few words, but she'd kept a smile on her face, hoping it would help them forget her tirade at the family meeting. And even though she suspected her mother was on a mission. She darted a glance at Peg. "Did Mother ask you how I was working out?"

"Why? Did you think she'd check up on you?"

Alcea snorted. "*My* mother?"

Peg paused in rubbing her bunions. "You know, Zinnia's not spying on you—she's just concerned. About you *and* Kathleen."

So Mother *had* checked up. "Kathleen's doing okay." Through the open door, squeals sounded from the after-school crowd at Sin-Sational. Kathleen was likely among them. "She's spending tonight and tomorrow night with me. Stan and Serena are spending the weekend in Branson." Which was a fortunate excuse. Kathleen didn't know Alcea had insisted to Serena that her daughter spend at least Saturday nights with her. "It seems she's adjusted. Actually, when I caught up with her at the ice cream parlor this week, she seemed happy as a clam." Especially because Joey Beadlesworth had stopped making fun of her since she'd moved into Serena's condo. Her chances of getting Kathleen into the Pink Palace seemed to be growing dimmer and dimmer.

"Then why the long face?"

"Because she doesn't miss me as much as I miss her." *If* Kathleen missed her at all. Except for one weepy hug with her mother last Saturday when Stan had loaded her things into his Humvee for her move to the condo, her mother's absence from her daily life hadn't seemed to faze her a bit. "I'm fixing up her bedroom. When I get home I'll finish the curtains I'm sewing." That is, if she could keep her fingers on thread and needle instead of on Dak. "But it will take more than that to top where she's living now. The condo has a swimming pool and tennis courts. I have a bucket under a leaky roof and an old badminton net I found shoved under the trailer."

Peg waved a hand. "From what I've seen, mothers and daughters have a way of gettin' the best of each other, but they usually find their ways back. Leastways, most of them. Florida, now . . . Well, that's a different story."

Alcea's wiping slowed. "What *is* the story?" She couldn't care less about Florida, but unlike most men she'd known, Dak rarely talked about himself and she wanted to know *everything*. "Did you know Dak when he was little?"

"Didn't even know he existed until Tamara dropped them on Cowboy's doorstep."

"You didn't?" Alcea abandoned the bucket and slid into a chair across from Peg.

"Nope. Tamara was a wild 'un, like her mama before her. That gal ran off with some sweet-talkin' salesman and left Tamara with her daddy. Then when Tamara got outta high school, she ran off, too. Cowboy didn't see hide nor hair of her for another fifteen, sixteen years, though he knew about Dak because—" The look Peg threw at Alcea puzzled her. "Well, that's all water under the bridge. Enough said that Cowboy hadn't known about Florida. When Tamara left them here, it caused quite a ruckus, but then Tamara was always good at ruckuses."

"She just dumped them and took off again?"

Peg nodded, staring off through the windows. "I stepped in and did what I could for them, but Dak . . . he was hurt bad. Not so's you'd notice unless you looked careful, though. Kept his feelings to himself." Peg sighed. "And Florida got most of my attention. She was only six, poor mite. She ranted and cried and generally got it all out of her system, but she ended up hating Tamara. Always felt bad about that. Girl shouldn't hate her mama, not that I blamed her much. And maybe that's better than what Dak done."

"What did he do?"

"Forgave Tamara. Made up excuses for her. Poor Dak. Cowboy . . . well, he handled things as best he knew, but I always thought—" Again the odd glance. "Well, doesn't matter what I thought."

Alcea wondered what else lay behind the story, but from the looks of Peg's clamped lips, she wouldn't get many more details even though her rendition didn't jive with Dak's. He was far from thinking of himself as *poor Dak*. "I think his childhood sounds pretty warped, but it doesn't seem to bother him."

Last night as they'd held each other, Alcea had asked about the years before he'd arrived in Cordelia. He'd talked about the things his mother had given him—a love of freedom, "a willingness to explore new horizons." And he hadn't seemed at all perturbed by the fact she'd left him here. He seemed to accept it as just part of her nature.

"Dak said Tamara used to write long letters to him in loopy handwriting, full of Shakespeare sonnets and poems and whatnot. And that he wrote her back, but Cowboy had to wait until he heard from her to mail his letters on."

"Dak said, did he?" Peg gave her an appraising look.

"We, uh, well, we see each other a lot now that he's my landlord."

"Mm-hmm." There was a raised eyebrow in there somewhere.

Alcea knew she should drop the subject before she dug herself in deeper, but she was intensely curious. "What about his father? Dak said Tamara didn't tell him who it was. That she had men in and out of her life."

And when she'd frowned, he'd laughed and said, "Don't look like such a prig. It was the sixties. Free love and all that. No ties, no regrets. She was a product of her time." Alcea hadn't laughed back, because Dak was so obviously a product of Tamara. *No ties, no regrets.* And when she'd protested she wasn't a prig, he'd asked her to prove it, and that had been the end of their discussion about his childhood.

But Peg was no longer giving her that raised-eyebrow look. She'd busied herself retying her shoes and didn't look at her at all. "There wasn't a father's name on Dakota's birth certificate." Her lips pressed together, she yanked the strings tight and finally looked up. "There wasn't one on Florida's either. Poor mites. Dakota pushed me away when I tried to take his mama's place, but Florida . . . Well, I know it wasn't the same. Still, she's the closest I've come to having a child of my own." Her face drooped. "I sure would have liked to have had a couple of those."

Alcea frowned at the sad expression she rarely saw on Peg's face. She hesitated, then asked, "Why didn't you, Peg? You would have been a good mother."

"Simple." Peg fixed her with her blue-shadowed

eyes. "I fell in love with the wrong man. Oh, Cowboy was a *good* man, and he had a quiet way with him that'd just charm you right out of your head. But it 'bout broke his heart when his wife left him, and no matter how hard I tried, he never did want to take another chance on marriage."

"But the two of you were a couple for years."

Peg's butterfly bobbed. "Almost forty, and that's a fact."

"Forty years?" Alcea sat back, astounded. "Why did you stay with him?"

"Because I loved him," Peg said, her eyes welling. "And right up until the end, I thought maybe *this* year might be the year he'd put a ring on my finger. Well, we was happy, but I sure do wish I could have had a baby or two of my own."

Silence fell. Alcea tried to swallow past the lump in her throat, unsure if it was caused by melancholy at Peg's story—or a sudden feeling of panic. *Forty years?*

Peg glanced at the clock. "Lands alive, look at the time! Doc said he'd stay late, and here I am jabbering on." She stood up and bustled about, swiping at her eyes, leaving final instructions for Alcea. Handbag over her arm, she paused by the door. "You know, they say the apple don't fall far from the tree. The Jones family don't seem much in the habit of marryin'. You remember that, sweetness."

When she'd left, Alcea put her hands up to cool her cheeks. Even though with every blink she saw Dak in her mind's eye . . . how the shadows of his angular face subtly shifted with his emotions, how he'd fire a smile at her smallest quip . . . how he flung his bare feet up on the coffee table and chewed on his lower lip when he was reading, how his eyes were tranquil as the sea at dawn as he gazed at a sunrise and turbulent as the surf when they made love. Even though he was never out of her head, she'd avoided thinking of him too hard because he was just . . .

A Fling.

Well, they'd flung all right. They'd flung on the new carpet, in his bed at Cowboy's, on every mattress in the Pink Palace, and even one memorable time across the kitchen table. She'd lost all of her initial modesty. Until Dak, she'd never been touched the way he touched her, had never felt the shuddering passion he evoked, had never felt a man's mouth on her . . .

Never mind.

She got up, dumped the bucket, and fetched a bottle of cleaner and a rag to polish the mirror that ran along the back wall. She clambered up on a booth to reach it and her image stared back. Eyes too big and dark, mouth too full. And her expression? Pure hopelessness.

In little more than a week, she'd undoubtedly made love more times than she had in the entire fourteen years of her marriage. She'd certainly experienced things she'd never experienced with Stan. And felt things. Thought things. And in the space of the seventeen measly days since Dakota Jones had returned to Cordelia . . .

Just face it, Alcea. You've fallen in love. Goddammit. She bit down on her quivering lower lip. Some *fling*.

As they'd watched the sun rise this morning, she'd drummed up the courage to ask more details about his first marriage. "We were young, still in college," he'd said. "She was an Eastern blue blood. Boston. Girls' prep schools, DAR, the whole nine yards."

It didn't sound like the type of woman he'd choose. Look at who he was with *now*. "What was the attraction?"

"Trite, maybe, but opposites do attract. For me, I suppose all that money was heady stuff. I don't know if it was *her* or the old brownstone her parents set her up in while she went to college. I wanted to write. She wanted to support me. Not that I'm proud now that I could be bought, although I did think I loved her. And it was through her I met some people who would be important to my career."

"Was that when you first published a book? While you were in college?"

He was silent. She shifted to look at him, loving the way his hair waved back from his face, the crease between his eyes when he thought hard. Right now he wasn't even with her. He was lost in the past. "Yes," he finally said without elaboration.

"Were you married by then?" she prodded.

"All these questions . . ." He reached over and tucked her hair behind her ear, touched a fingertip to her nose. "We got married the year before I graduated. When her parents got wind of me, they disowned her." There was no acrimony in his voice.

"That must have hurt."

"Not me." Yeah, right. "But it hurt her. At first she thought it was a lark, clipping coupons, living on a shoestring. But that gets old pretty fast." He leaned back, latching his hands behind his head.

She could relate. Although with Dak's example in front of her—with Dak himself *beside* her—she thought she could adjust to pretty much anything. "So that's why you had problems."

He went still. Just as he had after they'd tumbled around on the floor in the Pink Palace on that rainy Tuesday when she'd sat up and shook out her hair and turned to look at him over her shoulder, wanting so badly to say that it had all *meant* something to her. But then she'd seen his expression. He hadn't wanted to hear it. She hadn't spent almost half her life looking for signs of betrayal in Stan's face without learning how to read resistance.

His hands stayed latched, but he finally spoke. "Money was a problem, and . . . Well, the trouble really started after my book was published." He smiled at her. "This is all ancient history. We simply discovered we had different ideas about success."

"She couldn't stand living on a writer's paltry income?" she'd asked.

"Something like that. And so we divorced."

And so they'd divorced. He'd said the words as though getting a divorce was not much different from dumping the garbage. *Something like that.* Alcea stared at herself in the mirror for a long moment. Something like *Peg.* My God, *forty years*!

She scrubbed furiously at the glass. She'd allowed herself her insanity. She'd stripped off her T-shirt and invited his advances out of some wild need to grab something for herself. He was an addiction, or maybe a twenty-year thirst she'd finally gotten to slake. She *had* to look at it that way. Because no matter how many sunrises they shared, no matter how often she felt his eyes on her or how close he held her at night, there was a space between them she couldn't cross. He'd never be hers. He'd never be anyone's. And if she let their . . . *flinging* . . . continue, the hurt would only be more intense than going cold turkey now.

She'd break things off tonight. Her hand slowed. Would his eyes glaze with hurt? Would he give her a soulful look and promise to stay by her side?

Dream on, Alcea.

She rubbed harder. Most likely he'd just shrug, smile, and continue on as though they'd never even met. The glass under her cloth creaked, and she lessened the pressure before it cracked. Just like her heart.

Outside the diner windows, the sun slanted through the trees on its way toward sunset. Inside, the linoleum gleamed. Feeling more wiped out than the work warranted, Alcea was putting away the mop and bucket in the back room when she heard the bells over the door jangle. *Now what?*

Stomping toward the front, wondering why people couldn't read a damned CLOSED sign, she stopped short at the sight of Kemp standing uncertainly just inside the door. Shame and guilt replaced aggravation. Pleading exhaustion from moving, and finally leaving her answering machine unplugged, she'd avoided him since that Monday Night Discount Dinner, feeling guilty about her betrayal even though they had no promises between them.

But now, or at least, *after* she talked with Dak tonight, she might be looking at her future. Although when she confessed—of course, she'd have to confess—Kemp might just walk away and never look back. And it would be no less than she deserved. She tugged a weary hand through her hair. How much had she screwed up while she'd danced through a dreamy fog with Dak? Dak . . . Her heart twisted.

"Alcea!" Kemp took a step toward her. "I'm sorry if I scared you. . . ."

"No . . . uh, no. I'm glad you're here."

"You are?" He darted an almost incredulous look at her. "I mean, you haven't gotten in touch, and I was worried. So I stopped by your new place—"

She stilled, hoping he hadn't encountered Dak. Dak had never broached the subject of Kemp. Like with most things, he seemed content just to listen to whatever she wanted to tell him and never pushed for more. But with that laissez-faire attitude of his, he could very well have said—

"—and Julius told me you were still here."

She let out her breath. "I'm sorry, I've been busy and . . . well, you know." He didn't know; she had to tell him. She motioned to a table. "Um, maybe we should talk."

Kemp took a seat, his concerned eyes on her. "So why haven't you . . . I'm sorry, it's really none of my business. I'm sure you would have called if you had a free moment, and I shouldn't be asking—"

She felt like pond scum. She sat down and clasped her hands on the table. "Kemp, it's not just that I've been busy. I . . . well, I met someone and I thought I . . ." Would roll around on the floor with him? She didn't know how to say this.

He looked away and said it for her. "I thought it was something like that. Is it Dakota Jones?"

Now for the hard part. The begging-for-forgiveness part. "Yes, but I realized this afternoon that—"

"Alcea, I like you and admire you." She wondered if there was anything lower than pond scum. He reached for her hands and rubbed her waterlogged knuckles. "But I'm not going to stand in the way of your happiness."

"Well, but I decided—"

"And if Dakota Jones makes you happy, m'dear, then I'll bow out. I know how it is when you meet that special someone. When I met Marjorie . . ."

While he talked about his wife, she studied their hands. He had strong hands, not aristocratic like Dak's, but capable-looking, with short blocky fingers and carefully buffed nails. When he'd grasped her hands, she'd felt nothing. She still felt nothing. Nothing beyond a glimmer of warmth for the generosity of the man. Her heart didn't speed up, the hairs on the back of her neck didn't stand up, there was no delicious tingle running up her spine. Nor was there the warmth, the connection, she felt between her and Dak. And she suddenly realized she couldn't let him go.

Shit, shit, shit. *Forty years?*

"You're a sweet, kind man, Kemp Runyon." She broke into his reminiscences, giving his hands a squeeze and wishing she could love *him,* not Dak. "Thank you for being so understanding. I—I really am grateful."

He squeezed back and stood up. "I guess that's it, then. Good luck, Alcea," he said softly. "If you ever need anything, I'll be here. I mean that. Anything at all."

After he'd left, she continued to sit. Kemp was right. Dak did make her happy. As happy as she could ever remember. And she thought, in some small ways, she made him happy, too. Maybe that was enough for her now. And later . . . Well, even though he'd told her one day he'd leave, maybe . . .

Maybe he wouldn't.

Chapter 11

As May's fine weather slid by, Alcea let her concerns about Dak slide with it, helped by her preoccupation with supervising the workmen as they put the finishing touches on the space that was to become what she thought of as *her* bakery.

Buoyed by Dak's belief she could do it, she persisted and finally found a bakery going out of business in Columbia that put her equipment within a budget Peg could afford. A bargain-basement refrigerated and lighted display case, four-burner stove, giant refrigerator, and double convection oven had joined a *thirty*-quart planetary mixer and Old Ben's prep table, placed center stage, where people could watch her work (if they had nothing better to do at dawn). All were in pristine condition after a thorough scrubbing, and fine working order after Julius had fiddled with some parts. Only the automatic shutoff on the oven was iffy, but she'd get that fixed at a later date.

Pink streaks edged the eastern sky on the Saturday before Memorial Day. The square was still quiet, but inside Peg's, Alcea had hustled for most of the night, preparing for opening day. She wasn't tired, though. Her body hummed with excitement and an overdose of caffeine. Hands on hips, she stood in the middle of the bakery and looked around with pride. Not a vanity kind of pride, but an I-baked-it-myself kind of pride.

The place was a glow of stainless steel, pastel yellow, and light oak.

To save money, Dak and Jon had wielded paintbrushes for her. About a week ago, her mother had bustled in with advice and a number of baskets from her kitchen that were now filled with Tropical Blend Banana Muffins and Blueberry Bright Scones. Cakes and brownies held sway in the case, next to the display cards Mari had whipped out on one of her graphics programs. Catching her excitement, even Kathleen had helped, bringing her a bolt of gingham she'd bought at a foray to the Swap 'n' Shop with Daisy. Lil and Patsy Lee had hemmed it into shapes that lined baskets, frilled the windows, and draped the chalkboard where she would post daily selections. Yesterday the health department had made their final inspection and the fire marshal had signed off on the sprinkler system. She was now good to go. Looking at her dream, her heart swelled. She flung her arms out and twirled around.

"Uh, Mom?"

She'd thought she was alone. Alcea staggered sideways and caught her balance against the display case. She looked over her shoulder to see Kathleen hovering in the doorway that adjoined the bakery with the diner.

"Can I help run the register or something today?"

Alcea stared. Not only was her daughter here at dawn, but she was also outfitted in one of Alcea's orange uniforms *and* offering to help. Surprise didn't begin to cover it. She wanted to fall to her knees in thanksgiving, but afraid she'd spook Kathleen, she settled for "Of course you can. I'd love it."

Kathleen's face broke into a smile. "You'll have to, like, show me how."

"C'mon over here. Nothing to it." She kept her voice nonchalant but her heart hammered as Kathleen joined her behind the counter. She'd finally, *finally* done something that didn't merit a "So what?" or worse. Arms brushing, Alcea took Kathleen through the cash register's paces, then stood back while she ran some test receipts on her own. From the diner, she heard Peg and the others arrive and start setting up for the morning. She studied her daughter's face. Orange looked as hideous on Kathleen as it did on her, Kathleen's hair was flat on one side—obviously she hadn't risen early enough to style it—and she was chewing on her lower lip. When she quit gnawing, her teeth left red dents above her chin. She'd never looked lovelier.

"I think I've got it." Kathleen looked up and encountered her mother's gaze. Her face went quiet. "This is way cool, Mom."

Alcea's heart squeezed. She touched Kathleen's shoulder and found herself wrapped in a tight hug that went on for long moments.

Kathleen finally squirmed away, looking embarrassed. "Hey, there's Dak."

Out on the sidewalk, arms crossed, Dak was lounging against a light pole. When he saw he had her attention, he saluted, his mouth quirked in a told-you-so smile. And no wonder. A small throng had gathered outside the doors.

Peg poked her head in. "My, my, it smells as heavenly as it looks in here." The enamel butterfly nodded with approval. "And Kathleen, you're a good girl to help your mama. You gals ready?"

"More than," Alcea said. "And Peg? Thank you."

Peg's gaze rested on her. "You done all the work, sweetness. It's you I got to thank." And with that, she flung open the doors. Alcea took a deep breath and greeted her first customer, Paddy O'Neill.

For the next eight hours, the cash register chugged under Kathleen's fingers while Alcea scurried to serve customers, both locals and tourists who'd stopped in town on their way to the lakes, lured in by the aromas drifting out of the open door. She noted the locals went for the muffins, while the tourists snapped up the scones. She'd need to plan her wares by season. Leaving the bakery in Kathleen's hands while she helped Rosemary and Peg clean up after noon in the diner, she returned to find Kathleen handing off the last Dark Cocoa Buttermilk Cake. Everything else was gone.

When the customer had left, Kathleen gave Alcea a smug look. "She only wanted to buy a slice, but I talked her into the whole thing."

Alcea laughed. "A saleswoman is born."

"And now that I've sold *everything*"—Kathleen looked around in satisfaction at the empty case and baskets—"I think I'll go to Mel's. Aunt Lil said she'd pick me up when I was through."

Their family had all stopped by, although Alcea hadn't had time to chat. She'd see Lil again this evening, though. In the last month, potluck with her sister and her husband had become an every-other-Saturday-night affair, sustained by the friendship growing between Jon and Dak.

"What time will you get there?" Kathleen asked. "Is Dak coming?"

"Six, and yes . . . You like him, don't you?"

Kathleen shot her a grin. "Not more than you do."

Alcea blushed. Even though she and Dak moved to separate sleeping quarters when Kathleen was around, they hadn't fooled her much.

"It's okay, Mom." Still grinning, Kathleen patted her arm, then took off her apron and looked around. "This was fun. Do you think I could help out like, you know, on a regular basis?"

Alcea wanted nothing more but, "School needs to come first."

Kathleen frowned, then her face brightened. "But, like, when I don't have a lot of homework?"

Alcea nodded, optimism rising. "That'd be great." Maybe the next step would be the Pink Palace.

"And maybe you could pay me?"

Optimism drooped. Alcea kept the disappointment out of her voice. "I'm not the boss around here, sweetheart. Peg is. And I don't think she can afford anyone else now."

"Whatever. It was just an idea." Kathleen shrugged and untied her apron.

Some of the day's excitement drained away. Money was still powering Kathleen.

Kathleen paused in the doorway and fiddled with her hair. "You know, Dak says I'll be a better writer if I fill as much of my time as I can with new experiences and people I like to be with." She paused. "Even if Peg can't pay me, I'll try to come for a few hours on Saturdays."

Before Alcea could recover her power of speech, Kathleen had left. Tears sprang to her eyes. They'd made strides today. Some bridge had just been crossed, and Kathleen's casual promise was sweet icing on her success.

When Dak came in a short time after she'd turned the CLOSED sign to the window, he found her weeping into her apron. He frowned. "I thought everything went great."

She flung her arms around him. "It did!" she wailed. "I'm just *so happy*."

And until Lil's birthday, she was. Those three weeks between Memorial Day and a hot sapphire Monday in mid-June, filled with early risings, long hours, busy evenings, and nights held in Dak's arms, sped by in a blur of delight with her work *and* Dak. Lulled by Kathleen's appearance at the bakery each Saturday, she'd even allowed herself to think they might be a Big Happy Family by the time September cooled the air. And even if niggling doubts kept her awake some nights, she was far too busy to consider them under the daylight.

"Ready to go?" As he'd done every day since the

bakery had opened, Dak sauntered into the diner shortly after closing. As always, her heart bounced at the sight of him, hair tousled after spending the day running his hands through it while he wrote. He'd said this book wasn't moving along with quite the same ease as his last one.

Alcea had been waiting. On the way home, they sometimes detoured into Sin-Sational to share a malt, or O'Neill's Emporium to poke around, or even Stan's bank so she could drop off the nightly deposit. Once a week, Dak brought the Jeep and they'd run the errands they now combined. Today they were meeting Lil at Merry-Go-Read. She snatched up a cake box tied with a string and called out good-byes.

One hip plumped on her stool, Peg looked up with a drawn face from counting the cash drawer. The bakery had brought in more money but had also made more work for all of them. So maybe it was only tiredness that made her look at Alcea hanging happily on Dak's arm and snap, "You be careful about what yer doin', sweetness."

Alcea flushed. "I *am*." It was the same kind of advice her mother had hissed at her when she and Dak had gone to her parents' for dinner last Sunday. And the reason why she'd drummed up an excuse so they wouldn't have to return *this* Sunday.

Dak looked at her as they walked out of the diner. "What was that all about?"

"She—she's just concerned I'm overextending myself." A flat-out lie. Both women were concerned at how she'd latched on to Dak like there was no tomorrow. Well, she didn't want to *think* about tomorrow. Her family—both her real one and Peg—would have to like it or lump it. Speaking of family . . . "Have you heard from your sister?"

Despite her apprehensions, she'd rarely seen Florida around Cowboy's since she'd moved to the Pink Palace. She supposed Dak did, but someone was taking care it wasn't under her nose. *Probably Florida,* she thought with grudging gratitude, because Dak wasn't prone to shape events or think too far ahead.

He'd paused to browse the Emporium window and only spared her a look of mild surprise. "Not lately. Why?"

"I heard some gossip today. She and Stan had a rousing fight at the bank."

"Oh?" He bent down to study a ghastly pair of pink pig salt and pepper shakers. "These would fit right in at the trailer." He arrowed a grin her direction.

"Aren't you even curious why?"

"Not particularly." He looked back at the pigs. "Maybe I'll buy them."

She narrowed her eyes. His casual disinterest was too studied, even for him. "Well, nobody knows. They were shouting behind closed doors, and I guess Florida walked out in a huff and didn't go back after lunch. Everyone thinks she quit."

"Huh."

Giving a mental shrug, she gave up on the subject of Florida. "C'mon." She tugged on his hand. "I told Lil I'd be there by four thirty."

She'd made a special cake just for her sister. Unlike the cakes she sold at Peg's, where she didn't have time to do more than feather the icing with a spoon and maybe add a dollop of caramelized nuts to the center, for Lil's she'd put in some effort. Starting the process five days ago, she'd created crystallized flowers to decorate the concoction, fudging by using African violets instead of more appropriate lilacs that were no longer in season. The gum arabic and fine sugar had dried completely by last night, and Lil's cake now had a pretty posy of sparkling flowers right in the middle.

Because the O'Malleys usually celebrated en masse, Lil would be surprised at Alcea's thoughtfulness. Hell, *she* was surprised at her thoughtfulness. And not just where Lil's birthday was concerned. It seemed these days she viewed the entire world through fine-sugar glasses. She gave a little skip.

Dak laughed. "You bubble much more and you're going to disappear in a cloud of effervescence. Where did all this energy come from?"

You, she wanted to say but didn't. At any hint of the depth of her feelings, she knew he'd withdraw. "I don't know. But it's bound to benefit you later." She winked.

"Oh-ho." He stopped and pulled her into his arms, talking against her mouth. "But you said you planned to finish *A Midsummer Night's Dream* tonight."

"Hmm." She murmured as he kissed her. "Maybe I just want to create my own."

Many nights, she curled up beside him, usually on Cowboy's old horsehair sofa (that she'd covered with a pinstriped throw that matched the curtains she'd sewn for the windows), and they read. Dak shunned television, but she'd found enough books to keep her busy—if not always entertained—among Dak's cache and Cowboy's mess. She'd first made her way through some of Dak's *Road* series. They transported her to the towns he'd described, but she couldn't quite connect with his characters' emotions. Sometimes she couldn't even *find* the emotions. Not that she'd mentioned it. She didn't want him to think she was dense. And speaking of dense . . . She was plowing through Julius's Shakespeare volumes so she could join some of Kathleen and Dak's discussions. But they made her eyes cross. Another thing she'd neglected to mention.

Shakespeare and the *Road* series aside, she actually enjoyed reading. Take *that,* Eagleton. Especially the Jane Austen novels she'd found in the cellar. One rainy Sunday while Dak was writing, she'd rummaged through a trunk, unearthing all kinds of junk. Books. Old love letters from Peg (she'd read one, then felt like a voyeur and had returned the rest to her boss), newspaper clippings announcing the opening of Cowboy's Tow and Service (which she'd passed on to Julius), and one weird note: *Thanks for the money, you fool. You'll never see the damn kid again.* It was signed *T.*

Curious, she'd shown the note to Dak, but the only *T* he knew was his mother, and the sharp, slanted handwriting didn't match hers. He'd handed it back with a grin. "Cowboy was a pack rat. Keep searching and maybe you'll find the answer to your mystery writer."

For a while, she'd treated the mystery like her mission in life (preferring it over Shakespeare), foraging around in spare moments and neatening things up as she went, but she'd never found another clue. The note now marked her spot in *A Midsummer Night's Dream.* As soon as she was done, she'd show it to Peg. If she was ever done.

Releasing each other with a last kiss, they swung into Lil's bookstore. Tiny chimes sang out. Inside the primary-colored space, Lil and Zinnia looked over from the counter at the rear. Alcea stopped short near a display of sing-along books, pulling Dak to a halt. Despite the potlucks, she hadn't caught Lil alone long enough to smooth over any lingering bitterness her sister might still feel over the family meeting. She'd hoped that the cake would be an olive branch. But she hadn't expected to offer it in front of her mother.

Lil paused in rearranging a massive bouquet of garden flowers. "Look what Mother brought me. Aren't they gorgeous?"

"Beautiful." She walked over. They were. More so than her stupid sugar flowers.

Dak moved off to study the books, undoubtedly helped along by the chill he must feel blowing off Zinnia.

"Put him in any bookstore and he's lost in a fog," Alcea said lightly.

"Yes. Well." Her mother's gaze followed Dak, and Alcea prickled. With only two words her mother had registered her disapproval. She turned to Alcea. "And what have you got there, honeybunch?"

"Just one of my cakes." Alcea set the box on the counter with a snap.

Lil lifted the cover. "Oh, how pretty!" She smiled at Alcea. "This will be perfect. The children and Jon are preparing a birthday feast, but I'll bet they forgot a cake."

She'd bet they hadn't. Jon didn't forget anything where Lil was concerned. He'd likely flown in a cake decorated by some pastry chef in New York. "Well, I just wanted to give that to you, so I guess we'll be—"

Looking distracted, Patsy Lee hurried in from the back room. She clutched a backpack. "Lil, thanks so much for filling in for me the last hour. And on your birthday, too." Seeing Alcea, she added a breathless hello before turning to Zinnia. "I told Daisy to heat up some of last night's spaghetti for the children's dinner, so they should be fed. Except, knowing Daisy, she might have forgotten."

"Don't give it another thought. We'll pick 'em up in a little while, and if they haven't eaten, we'll feed them. You just learn lots tonight."

"Learn lots?" Alcea said.

Her sister-in-law blushed. "I decided . . . well, after CMSU opened that satellite campus last year . . . I probably won't get very far, but—"

"Pish!" Zinnia interrupted. "We'll be watching your graduation in no time at all." She turned to Alcea. "Our Patsy Lee has decided to get her degree in business from Central Missouri State. How about that?"

Patsy Lee blushed. "Lil's done all this." She waved a hand vaguely at the store. "And I've watched Rosemary go off to school. Now with you and the bakery . . . I don't want to get left behind, I guess."

Her sister-in-law *admired* her? She stared at Patsy Lee.

Zinnia patted Patsy Lee's arm. "Get on with you, and don't you worry. We'll get something figured out for next week."

"What's next week?" Alcea asked.

"Patsy Lee has classes on Tuesday evenings," Lil explained. "There's a bit of a snag next week. Mother has guests coming, and we'll be at Kesibwi."

Dak returned to her side, and she felt the same warmth she always did when he was near.

"Oh, please don't worry about it," Patsy Lee said. "I should have organized things better, but I'll find someone to watch the children."

What was she? Chopped meat? "I'll do it. Kathleen and Daisy will help."

Dak looked taken aback, and Alcea almost retracted her offer. But when a shy smile spread across Patsy Lee's face, she felt a surge of pleasure and kept her mouth shut.

Silence fell after Patsy Lee left. Lil's eyes rested on her, surprised but warm. Dak looked resigned. And Zinnia was studying her like she'd grown wings. "Seems like our Alcea Caroline is knee-deep in good deeds these days. What's going on?"

"Can't I offer to do something for a member of our family without you thinking the world's flipped upside down?"

"And not just a member of our family." Zinnia set her purse down on the counter and leaned an elbow on it, still staring at Alcea. "I've heard tell you've upped and offered your help to any number of people recently."

"Like who?"

"Like, haven't you shouldered Rosemary's shift as well as your own so she can attend that beauty school she was always so hot about? I even heard you're the one who talked her out of her dead mama's constant objections." Zinnia shook her head. "Never did like that Butz woman, God rest her."

Dak smiled.

Alcea shrugged. "We always do favors for each other at the diner."

"And," Lil piped up. "Whose idea was that coffee

can on the counter to collect funds to send Tansy to Nebraska?"

"She needs the money for bus fare," Alcea said, feeling defensive, although both women were now smiling. "No-Account Andy got drunk and disorderly when he was there visiting relatives, and she needs to bail him out."

"And," Dak added, "she spends Sunday evenings baking cookies to raise money for the high school."

"And"—Zinnia actually winked at Dak—"cakes for my Ladies' Auxiliary benefits."

Alcea knew her face was bright red. "It's not that big a deal."

Zinnia's face sobered. "But that's the thing, honeybunch. It *is* a big deal to the folks you're helping." She reached out and squeezed Alcea's arm. "I'm proud of you. Only wondering where the change came from." Zinnia considered Dak for a moment, only this time without looking like she'd smelled sour milk.

"It's—it's nothing. Really." Alcea's eyes watered and she studied the ceiling.

Zinnia gave a nod, as if she'd just decided something. She picked up her purse. "I'd best go get supper on. We have guests tonight." She gave each daughter a brief hug, then took hold of Dak's hand. "I hope you're here for a very long time."

Her voice was so warm with meaning, Dak actually blushed for the first time since Alcea had met him. She blushed again herself.

When Zinnia had left, Dak glanced at her, his color still high. "I'm going to pop into the Emporium, see what Paddy is up to. Collect me when you're done, okay?"

The words were nonchalant, but she could sense his withdrawal. Damn. Why hadn't her mother kept her mouth shut? Feeling confused but also afraid, Alcea started to follow him. But then Jon burst in, almost colliding with Dak.

"Sorry, old man. Hey, birthday girl." Jon caught up Lil and twirled her around.

Lil smiled into his face, and Alcea felt a stab of envy. She glanced at Dak. His face held an expression she couldn't read.

"You ready? The kids are waiting at home." Jon set Lil back on her feet.

"Almost. Give me a few minutes, okay? I want to talk with Alcea."

"Sure." He turned to Dak. "Why don't we grab a cup of joe and leave them to their hen talk."

"Go on with you, then." After Lil had shooed them out the door, she turned to Alcea. "Share a piece of cake?" When Alcea hesitated, she added, "It's my birthday, so you have to."

Olive branch, Alcea reminded herself. While Lil dished out cake onto paper plates she'd grabbed from the back room, Alcea took a chair at the children's table in front of the display window. Lil settled across from her. Even with their knees up in their chins, it reminded Alcea of all the pretend tea parties they'd once shared.

For a while they chatted, covering familiar ground. Lil shared stories about Melanie and Michael, confessing that as her mischievous stepson grew older, he was giving them fits (and Alcea was glad she'd never added to the burden by telling Lil about the Indian). Alcea concentrated on Kathleen's summer activities, which, along with her writing sessions with Dak and her help at the bakery, included swim team, weekly trips to a therapist, and a lot of shopping, all courtesy of Stan and Serena. Lil asked about the bakery, and Alcea waxed poetic.

Lil forked a piece of cake into her mouth. "I don't see how you can do this and not eat it all yourself. It's so good."

"Fear of looking like Peg, maybe." Alcea laughed, then sobered. "I can't keep her out of my cake batter, although the doctor told her she needs to lose weight. She's not looking good."

"You really care about her, don't you? And all the people at the diner. All those things you've done . . ."

"Just a regular Girl Scout, aren't I?" Alcea laughed again, trying to head off more I'm-proud-of-you moments. She was glad her family didn't view her as a total washout, but it also hurt to realize how little they must have thought of her before if a few good deeds had them doing handstands. "If you think I'm a do-gooder, you should have seen Dak this week. Eric Olausson sprained his wrist trying to out-arm-wrestle Paddy, and Dak did Eric's mowing." She smiled, feeling mischievous. "And he looks downright cute dressed in overalls, sitting on that John Deere."

She'd laughed and told him all he needed was a piece of straw between his teeth to look like a real native. He'd returned a rude gesture with his hand. She smiled, remembering. He'd been a good sport, though. She'd badgered him into it, her "it will be a new experience" argument finally winning a reluctant grin and agreement.

"Dakota is the reason why you're, well, different, isn't he?"

Alcea started to bristle but stopped at the deep look of concern in Lil's eyes. Lil meant well. She always meant well. It was what Alcea couldn't stand about her—and what she loved about her. "Dak has taught me a lot, I guess." She spoke slowly. "Like to 'play the music I hear.' Carpe diem. And maybe that money isn't everything."

"Play the music?"

"You should know what that means better than most." Alcea held Lil's eyes. "I'm only doing what you did. I'm following my gut even it seems crazy sometimes."

Lil was quiet a moment, undoubtedly remembering she'd once thought her own marriage would never work out. "It's not always easy," she finally said. Then, "Are things serious between you and Dakota?"

"We haven't booked a church, if that's what you're asking."

"From everything I've heard, it sounds like he doesn't make future plans." Before Alcea could spring to Dak's defense—and her own—Lil put down her fork. "Mother doesn't disapprove, and she likes Dak. I hope you realize that. She's just worried—like I am. You're so happy now, Alcea. I can hear your laughter clear in here sometimes, and I see you swinging down the sidewalk with Dak after work every day. We just don't want you to be hurt."

Trust Lil to bring up the fly in the ointment. Alcea stiffened. "He hasn't made any plans to leave. He used to talk about selling Cowboy's, but he hasn't taken a single step yet to get repairs made to the place." Lil couldn't know how hard Alcea had held on to the fact that the painters and repairmen he'd discussed had never materialized.

"So you think maybe he's ready to settle down? With you?"

Lil's face was so tender, Alcea couldn't utter the retort that immediately sprang to her lips, something ruder than "Mind your own business."

Still, the joy she'd felt during the day evaporated. She didn't know anything more about Dak's intentions where she was concerned than she had when she'd first stripped off her T-shirt and offered him her body. He didn't talk about leaving much anymore—but he also didn't talk about staying.

The frustrations she'd buried under the busyness of their lives surfaced in a feeling of aggravation at Lil for pointing out what she didn't want to look at. So before she could say anything that would break the olive branch, she stood up. "Look at the time. Kathleen is coming over and I have to—"

"Are you gals done yet?" Jon sauntered in. "Dak's waiting for you at the Emporium, Alcea. Something about buying a pair of pigs?"

Lil laughed. "I saw those. Why don't you come on

in and help me close, Mr. Impatience?" To Alcea, she added. "He's worse than his son."

"I'll help only if you'll let me put the CLOSED sign up." He wiggled his eyebrows. "And I'll show you I'm no comparison to any little boy."

Lil's face flamed, but she was still laughing. Alcea thought it high time to make an exit. She let herself out, making sure the door was closed—and locked. She smiled. When she got home she'd thank Dak properly for her new salt and pepper shakers. She turned toward the Emporium but halted when she saw the small crowd gathered outside Peg's. Faces looked worried; voices were raised. Rosemary separated herself from the group and hurried toward her. "Oh, thank God. Alcea!"

"What in the world—?"

Rosemary grabbed her arm. Her curls were a disheveled mess. "It's Peg. She collapsed right smack in the middle of the diner a few minutes ago. I rounded up Paddy and Dakota and they've hauled her off to the hospital. Stupid paramedics! We called them, but they take forever and a day to get anywhere. Mama Butz always said—"

Alcea grabbed her arm. "How is she?"

"I don't *know,*" Rosemary wailed. "I don't know what I'll do if—"

Before Rosemary could utter the words, Alcea took off at a run toward home and her car. Rosemary puffed along behind.

Peg had to—just had to—be okay.

Chapter 12

But Peg wasn't okay.

When Alcea arrived with Rosemary at the hospital, a throng had gathered in the waiting room. Most of the regulars were there, sitting on an assortment of sofas and chairs, elbows to thighs, hands drooping between their knees and fingering their hats. It was quiet, unnaturally quiet. A few hopeful eyes glanced up at their arrival, but then returned to study the floor. Alcea's stomach clenched like a fist.

From a chair near the door, Julius looked at them from red-rimmed eyes. "They've done what they could." He spread his hands helplessly. "But they say she won't last the night."

Alcea's head whirled. Rosemary broke into tears. Paddy got up, wrapped an arm around Rosemary, and led her to a corner. Looking like a frail bunch of bones on the sofa, Tansy sniffed and turned her head away.

Numb, Alcea looked around. Tears burned behind her eyelids but refused to fall. She approached Tansy feeling near desperation. "Is she—? Can I—?" She didn't know what to do, where to go.

More people crowded into the room behind her. News about Peg was spreading.

"She's awake," Tansy muttered, wiping at her nose. "In and out, the doctor said. She asked for you."

"For me?" A wave of gratitude swept over her. She at least had a chance to tell Peg how much she meant to her, before . . . before she had to let her go. She whirled toward the door. "Then I have to—"

"Wait." Tansy touched her arm. "Florida's in there now."

Florida. Anger flushed her, but then she thought of Peg. "Of course. Of course she is." She swallowed hard. *Hold on, Peg. Hold on so I can say . . . goodbye.* The tears started then. Watching her from the corner, Julius's features knotted and he covered his face with his hands. Cheeks wet, Rosemary awkwardly patted his back. Alcea stood alone in the increasingly crowded room, feeling grief suffocate her.

A hand fell on her shoulder and she turned. Dak. Lil and Jon hovered behind him. Dak's eyes were bright with his own unshed tears, but they stared steadily into hers, loaning her a measure of strength, like he always did. Still, a sob escaped her lips. He gathered her close. "Cry, Alcea," he whispered. "You'll want it all out before you see her." So she cried. She felt Lil's soft touch on her back as she poured her anguish onto Dak's shoulder.

Jon spoke softly. "Florida is here."

Alcea turned from Dak's embrace. Florida hesitated in the doorway, looking like someone had punched her in the stomach. Knotting her hands in the folds of a bulky CMSU sweatshirt, her gaze swept the room erratically and briefly landed on Alcea. For that instant, there was a communion of mutual grief. Then Florida's knees buckled and she sagged against the door frame. Dak rushed forward and caught her before she slumped to the floor. Behind them, a nurse appeared. Spotting Alcea, she beckoned her forward. Alcea used the tissues Lil handed her, then straightened her shoulders. For Peg, she had to be brave.

Florida leaned heavily against Dak, her face turned into his chest. As she passed them, Dak reached out and squeezed her shoulder. "I'll take Florida home," he said. "And then I'll be back."

Alcea only nodded, not trusting her voice. Then she

followed the nurse's starched white uniform up a hallway toward Peg's room.

But Dak hadn't come back. He hadn't been there after Peg had murmured, "You'll do, sweetness, you'll do" to Alcea one last time before Alcea left her room to sob against a wall in the corridor. Nor when Rosemary and Tansy had each taken their turns, and Peg had then asked for Julius. And he hadn't been there when Peg had finally slipped away from them a couple of hours ago.

It was nearing midnight when Alcea pulled up to the curb in front of Cowboy's. Lights still glowed in the parlor windows, and she felt relieved Dak had at least waited up. Her heart too full of sorrow to allow anger, she'd already forgiven him his lapse, unwilling to believe he was so fearful of ties he wouldn't even allow himself to face the one he'd had to Peg. Undoubtedly, Florida had required his support, just like Rosemary had Alcea's. She'd taken Rosemary home, then had phoned Tansy and waited for her to arrive before she left. Rosemary had been too hysterical to be alone.

Rubbing a hand over her face, thinking of all the arrangements that would need to be made for the funeral and at the diner—wondering who even owned the diner now—she started up the walk, head down. A deep weariness weighted her steps. She wanted nothing except a hot bath, a bed, and Dak's arms around her.

"Alcea?" She started as a figure rose from the front steps. "It's only me," Julius said, coming toward her. In the cast of the streetlamp, his face was ravaged by grief. "I—I didn't want to go home." He waved a limp hand at his apartment over the garage.

"Oh, Julius."

They clasped each other, and Alcea's tears rose again. Julius had been the last person with Peg. He'd stayed with her until she'd died.

Alcea finally pulled away. "Do you want to come in? It looks like Dak's still up."

"Nah." Julius wiped his sleeve across his eyes. "Think I just want to set out here awhile is all."

They seated themselves at the bottom of the porch steps, silent for a moment. Julius squinted up at the Milky Way sparkling over them. "Think Peg's up there?"

"I know she is." Alcea smiled slightly. "Making the angels polish their halos."

An answering smile flickered across his grizzled face. "While she kicks up her feet and has a piece of the best chocolate cake ever made."

They fell quiet again, then Julius whispered. "I loved her, you know."

"We all did."

"No, I mean I loved her like she loved Cowboy and like you love Dak."

Alcea looked at him, not knowing if she was more surprised by his revelation about Peg or his knowledge about her.

He glanced at her face. "I got eyes, you know. It's pretty clear how you feel about him—at least to me. Maybe that comes from being in your shoes for most of my life."

"What do you mean, my shoes?"

"One that loved not wisely, but too well," he murmured. *"Othello."*

She moved impatiently. "Speak my language."

"Ah, Alcea. I fell in love with Peg when there was only the half of her to love, red hair trailing down her slim back, and blue eyes that sparkled with laughter, and enough sass in her to give a man plenty of sleepless nights." His gaze explored the stars. "But I never told her."

"Why ever not?"

He turned his head to look at her. "Why haven't you told Dak how you feel?"

She paused. "Because he'd probably leave."

"And if I'd told Peg how I felt, knowing how she felt about Cowboy, and me and him being such good friends and all . . ."

"You would have lost both of them."

"Yep." He sighed. "I fell in love with the wrong woman." Julius's words echoed Peg's. *I fell in love with the wrong man.* "I thought maybe after Cowboy died and some time passed . . . But there wasn't enough time left." Julius turned his head away, and she was certain from the quiver in his shoulders that he was crying again.

She placed a hand on his knee and they sat with only his snuffles breaking the silence. She didn't voice what she was thinking. She remembered the wistful look on Peg's face when she'd talked about wanting babies. It would be cruel now to tell Julius that if Peg had known how he felt, she might have given up Cowboy and given them a chance.

But even as the thought passed through her head, she knew it wasn't that easy. You couldn't dismiss your feelings as easily as you changed your clothes. Was that her own destiny? To gather just crumbs of happiness instead of a full loaf? Would I FELL IN LOVE WITH THE WRONG MAN be her own epitaph?

She squeezed her eyes shut. *Oh, Peg.* She couldn't bear a life like her friend's.

She felt Julius stand up, and she opened her eyes.

"Think I'll go on home."

"You sure you don't want to come in?" she asked.

He shook his head. "Thanks—you're a sweet'un, but I want to be alone now."

After he'd left, Alcea sat for a long moment thinking of Julius's tale and letting the starlight bathe her hurt. Then she pushed to her feet. In case Dak had gone to bed, she was careful to let herself in quietly. But he wasn't asleep. Upstairs a light glowed down the hallway from a bedroom, and voices murmured from the parlor.

"But I just think Joey's so *hot*." Kathleen's voice. God, she'd forgotten Kathleen.

"Maybe your Mr. Beadlesworth is the hottest thing since, uh, Leonardo DiCaprio, but . . ." Dak's voice. About to announce her presence, Alcea stopped just short of the doorway, wondering what he'd say next. ". . . Maybe it's me, but I think the guy's a jerk if the only way he'd ask you out is if you'd give up something you love. The writing is a part of you, Kathleen. If you have to jump through hoops to change yourself, is the guy really worth it?"

Why hadn't she thought of giving Kathleen that advice? She grimaced. Probably because she didn't know how to live it herself. She sagged against the wall. And wasn't that exactly what she was wanting from Dak? For him to change? Kathleen murmured something, but busy with her own thoughts, Alcea missed it.

Dak responded, "I'm not saying people can't—or shouldn't—change. I'm just saying that real change is driven from within—because of your own wants and needs. If you do it solely for someone else's, you won't be happy. Not with that person, and not with yourself."

Well, that boded well for any future together, didn't it? Too drained to consider his words any further, Alcea pushed off the wall and paused in the doorway. Feet up, Dak sat on one end of the sofa. Kathleen curled on the other with her legs tucked under. Kathleen was continuing the conversation. "Did you change a lot when you went to college?"

Dak's chuckled. "Well, Harvard overwhelmed me when I first got there—" He broke off as he spotted Alcea and got to his feet.

Harvard? She faltered a moment before continuing toward him. Just another item from his life that he'd neglected to tell her. But she couldn't summon up any real anger, not even over his failure to reappear at the hospital. He looked as weary as she felt. Peg's death had obviously dealt him a blow, and he must have had a time of it with Florida. His eyes were red, filled with clouds, and . . . she hesitated again . . . an odd glint of dread.

Before she'd reached him, Kathleen scrambled to her feet and rushed to hug her. "I'm so sorry about Peg, Mom. I know she was your friend."

Alcea held her close, relishing the contact. "We're all sorry, sweetheart." Dak approached, hovering uncertainly until she held out her hand and pulled him into their embrace. His cheek was rough against hers. She pulled back a little to lay a kiss on Kathleen's forehead. "And I'm sorry I forgot all about you."

"That's okay." Kathleen broke the circle, but Alcea didn't move. She gathered Dak closer, pressing her cheek against his shoulder, her head turned to see Kathleen. "Dak and Fl—" Kathleen's gaze traveled from Dak to the doorway, and she stopped.

Alcea lifted her head and looked between the two of them. "What?"

"I need to tell you something." Dak cleared his throat and pushed the hair away from her face, his gaze holding hers with what she could only interpret as an apology. "I didn't come back because I was helping Florida. She's—"

She smoothed his lips. "Not doing so well. I know you couldn't leave her alone." His gaze shied away, and she frowned. "Florida *is* doing okay now, isn't she?"

"As well as I can, I guess." A familiar drawl sounded from the doorway.

Alcea wrenched around. Florida drooped against the frame, arms folded. Alcea's gaze took in her tear-swollen face, the green tint under her pale complexion. . . .

. . . and then the mound of luggage piled against the wall just inside the entrance.

"Dak said y'all had room for me here. I'm moving in."

* * *

Alcea paced between the kitchen, living room, and tacked-on entry of the Pink Palace. Late afternoon sun slanted across the floor, doing nothing to lighten her mood. After catching only a few hours' sleep last night, she'd spent the day divided between the funeral home and the diner, where a never-ending stream of townsfolk had made Peg O' My Heart their pilgrimage. Peg's high-backed stool had become a memorial, covered in so many wreaths and offerings, it was next to impossible to get to the cash register.

It seemed everyone else—including Florida, who should at least be taking a hand in the funeral arrangements—was too grief stricken to do what had to be done. Alcea was exhausted. But the idea of Florida lurking somewhere behind the narrow walls of Cowboy's house prevented her from falling straight into bed. Anger had added its bite to her grief. She wanted to know how long Florida would live there and, more important, why Dak hadn't even bothered to consult her before making this decision.

She glanced between the candy-striped curtains she'd hung at the entry's windows, looking across the scrabbly backyard for Dak. He hadn't shown his face at the diner today, the coward, yet she knew he was home. His Jeep sat in the driveway, parked behind Florida's Miata. And he knew she was home because her Taurus was perfectly visible from his kitchen window. He was hiding out. Banking on the fact she wouldn't storm in to confront him with Florida present.

How could he have done this? She strode around the small space. He would know this would change their entire lifestyle. There would be no more cozy evenings, no leisurely late-afternoon lovemaking, no sublime mornings watching the sun rise. Not with that she-devil around. And if that hadn't been enough to stop him from making Florida some kind of houseguest, you'd think he would have considered *her* feelings at being asked to welcome the woman into their home, because . . .

As quick as her anger had risen, it fell. She slumped in a chair. He hadn't asked. He hadn't asked because it wasn't *their* home; it was *his* home. She was a tenant. A transient tenant. In a transient relationship. For a moment, she let despair swamp her, then she gave herself a shake and stood up.

If she wanted him to stay . . . If she wanted him to even *consider* staying, launching a tirade the moment he appeared would be completely boneheaded. Much as it galled her, she'd have to shrug off Florida's visit as no concern of hers. She headed for the kitchen, needing to lose herself in a mixing bowl of *something*.

An hour later, a pan of pastry was crisping in the oven while she slopped dishes around in the sink, thinking this was certainly a time when baking had failed to calm her. Dak appeared in the doorway. And even though she had an overwhelming urge to screech like a shrew, her unruly heart stuttered at his sheepish grin. Her unspoken words died on her lips. Instead she pasted on a welcoming smile.

Dak ran fingers through his hair. "Smells great. I see you're performing your magic."

"Apricot tarts," she said brightly. She'd thought tarts were appropriate.

"Oh, boy," he said with glee, and she knew they were both overacting.

For a while they tiptoed around the subject uppermost in both of their minds. He asked about her day and Peg's funeral arrangements, and told her she looked tired. She asked about his day and his novel, and studiously avoided telling him he looked guilty. Finally, apparently having decided she wouldn't bite him, he sidled up and slid his hands around her waist from behind. He nuzzled her neck. His stubble tickled, and she scrunched a shoulder.

"I was afraid you'd be upset about Florida," he murmured.

Honey, you don't know the half of it. "Is that why you went underground for most of the day?" She worked hard to keep her tone light, and twisted to see his face. She caught the flash from his smile and it nearly broke her heart. God, how could she love this man so much and not have her feelings returned? She turned back to the dishes before he saw her anguish.

"Maybe a little," he admitted, letting his hands slide off. "I know it must have been a shock, coming on top of Peg. I'm sorry I didn't tell you before."

Didn't tell her *before*? "You knew about her plans before last night?" She managed to keep her voice even.

Dak moseyed around to the other side of the counter and took one of the stools. She kept her eyes on the sink.

"That night at the country club, she told me she was pregnant—"

Her gaze flew to his. "Pregnant!" Her mind cast over Florida's recent appearance. Bulky sweatshirt, green face . . . "Pregnant." Her voice was flat.

"—And that she might need my help. I told her she could count on me." He shrugged. "What else could I do?"

She lowered her eyes again. "Nothing. She's your sister." A sister who could count on Dak more than his lover could. "But why did she move in with you?"

"She quit her job. She can't pay rent."

"That makes sense." The words were sarcastic. Quitting made no sense at all.

"Look, Alcea, she's not having an easy time of it. She just said everything became too much for her to handle."

The pregnancy? Or seeing Stan every day with Serena? She'd wondered how Florida had coped with that situation. Okay, to be truthful, she'd relished Florida in that situation. The quitting didn't surprise her, really. The timing did. "But why would she quit now? She'll need money more than ever."

"I don't know. I don't understand it myself." In other words, he hadn't asked. "What's done is done. Now she just needs somewhere to stay until the baby is born. Then she'll look for a different job."

"And how long will that be?"

"She's four and a half months along."

Florida would be at Cowboy's for four to five months? Alcea plunked a plate in the drainer with enough force it almost broke. Dak looked at her in surprise. She smiled at him. "Oops." Then a thought hit and her smile faded. Dak might not even be here that long. Panic swept her. Maybe this pregnancy was a good thing. Maybe he'd stick around to see his niece or nephew born, and then . . . Well, anything could happen then. She'd have to grit her teeth and bear this.

She turned away to take the tarts from the oven, and kept her voice conversational. "Did she happen to mention who the father is? Couldn't he help her?"

She'd already done the math. The obvious choice—Stan—didn't fit. Serena and Stan had moved in together shortly after Serena had arrived in Cordelia more than six months ago. If she was halfway through her pregnancy, Florida hadn't become pregnant until a couple of months after that.

"She didn't say, and I didn't ask."

Of course he hadn't. She wanted to brain him with the tray, but instead she set it on the stove. If *she* knew who the father was, she'd beg him to take Florida off Dak's hands. That is, unless . . . "He's probably married."

"Now, Alcea . . ."

"Well, it fits, doesn't it? She doesn't say. Her history and all."

"What she does with her life isn't any of my—or your—business."

He was wrong. "It was very much my business once upon a time."

"But not this time." Dak's clear gaze found hers. "Give her a chance, Alcea. Come over to the house for supper later. She's got a casserole in the oven. You could bring your"—he motioned at the stove—"tart things."

She stared at him in disbelief. This was taking *live and let live* a mite too far. "I'm tired. I want to go to bed."

"I know. But you still have to eat."

His insistence was incredible. "As you have often implied, what you decide to do with your life is your business. You have made the choice to invite Florida into"—she bit back *our*—"*your* home. I am doing my best to accept that. But if you think we're going to become friends, you must be losing it." She yanked the hot pads off her hands and threw them down. "Dakota Jones, sometimes you are as dense as a doorknob. Your sister helped destroy my marriage. Okay, maybe it deserved to be annihilated. Maybe it would have ended without her. But to ask me to forget—"

"I'm not asking you to forget. I'm asking you to forgive. There's a difference."

"Maybe in your woo-woo world, but not in mine. You made a choice here. I can understand it, but I don't have to like it."

"So . . ." Dak stood up and put his hands in his pockets. "That's it?"

His casual question pulled her up short. Was *what* it? Did he mean, was that her final word on Florida? Or did he mean that unless she accepted his sister, their relationship was over? She was so afraid it was the latter, her knees started to tremble. She gazed into that beloved face, those shuttered eyes, and knew she'd do anything to keep him. What a *wimp*. "I'll try to be civil," she finally said. "That's the best I can do."

He nodded as though she'd said something profound, and her fear almost vanished in the desire to throw the whole tray of tarts in his face.

"That's all anyone can do," he said. "And all that I ask."

It would probably be all he'd ever *ask.* And she wanted him to ask so much more.

Chapter 13

Balancing a casserole dish on each palm, Dak shouldered into the crowded kitchen at Cowboy's three afternoons later. He still felt guilty about manipulating Alcea. He'd known his simple question the other day would throw her into turmoil, but for the life of him, he hadn't known what else to do.

He looked at the table overflowing with food, just like the one in the dining room, and hoped adopting a helpless expression would bring aid from one of the women that had commandeered this part of the house. Behind him, voices murmured from the parlor.

That morning, following a short graveside service, they'd buried Peg. Julius's eulogy had been touching, but what had really yanked at Dak's heartstrings were the images of all the faces that had come to pay their last respects. And now every last one of them was here. Since he and Florida—particularly Florida—had been the closest thing to family that Peg had left, they'd assumed the burden of the funeral arrangements. His gaze fell on Alcea. Or rather, Alcea had.

She was busy at the sink, standing shoulder to shoulder with her mother and Mari, who had driven in from Kansas City for the service. Somewhere behind him, Lil and Tom O'Malley unobtrusively replaced empty platters, picked up dirtied plates, and kept things tidy. Jon was presiding over a table of iced tea and lemonade. Patsy Lee and Dak were rotating positions at the front door, greeting people and taking their offerings. The O'Malley family might have their differences, but in a crunch, they pulled together. For a moment, he wondered what that would be like. Always having someone at your back.

Alcea turned and spotted him. Guessing his dilemma, she approached with a wan smile. Despite the crescents under her eyes, she looked lovely with her gold hair pulled back and set off by the black dress she wore. She'd worked so hard these last few days, accepting the money he gave her for the funeral but shrugging off his thanks. With less finesse, she'd also shrugged off Florida's stilted offers to help. Looking at the weariness in her face, he thought both he and Florida should have insisted on doing more. Not only had she handled the bulk of the arrangements, she'd also struggled to keep the diner open for at least a few hours each day. She hadn't wanted to disappoint the stream of patrons who came in memory of Peg.

Peg. A sense of loss swept him, its intensity taking him by surprise. He hadn't been close to his grandfather's longtime paramour, at least not since he was in high school, and perhaps not even then. Unlike Florida, he'd shunned Peg's efforts at mothering. But now, with both Cowboy and Peg gone, he felt oddly orphaned. He shrugged off the sensation. It was the occasion making him glum.

Alcea took a casserole dish from his hand. "Heard anything?"

He shook his head. The contents of Peg's will—most important for Alcea, the disposition of the diner—hadn't been made public. Peg's lawyer had been out of town and had only returned last night. But this morning before the services, the lawyer had arrived to meet with Florida. From the expression on Florida's face after the meeting, Dak thought he knew what had transpired. So far, Florida had stayed mum, and he hadn't asked any questions. It was her concern, not his. But looking into Alcea's hopeful face, he suddenly wished he'd made it his business.

She pushed a wisp of hair off her forehead. "The waiting to know—it's hard."

He knew she hoped Peg had willed the diner to some distant relative who would leave its management in her hands. He doubted that was the case. He took a deep breath. "The lawyer—"

"Let me take that." Florida took the last casserole from him and glared at Alcea.

Zinnia turned around, took in the standoff, and started in their direction. But Alcea only glared back at Florida, and then both women turned and walked away in opposite directions. He sighed.

Beside him, Zinnia said, "Got yourself into a pretty pickle, haven't you?"

"I don't know. Detente has lasted for three days, so I'm hopeful."

"Don't be. I know my daughter." She gave him a sharp look. "And I hope *you* know what you're doing."

He shifted, uneasy. It was the closest an O'Malley had come to asking his intentions. Jon had circled around the subject but backed off when Dak grew silent. But he didn't think Zinnia knew the meaning of restraint.

He decided to purposely misunderstand. "I'm doing what I can."

Zinnia wasn't buying it. "And what's that? You're stringing her along, far as I can see."

He'd been right. *Reticence* wasn't a word in her vocabulary. "Alcea and I have an understanding. I've never lied to her." He spoke the words in a quiet voice, but he wanted to squirm. He wasn't an idiot, and he knew Alcea's feelings ran deep. He also knew he shouldn't have allowed things to go this far.

Every morning when he woke, he told himself to end it all now. But then Alcea would smile at him, or slide her arms around him, or cuddle against him, and he couldn't summon the willpower. Not that there had been much cuddling since Florida had arrived. When Florida had declared her intentions of moving to Cowboy's, he'd felt she'd had more right to be here than he did. But he hadn't looked very far ahead. If he had, he might have thought up some other arrangement.

"Hmph," was Zinnia's reply. "That girl is in lo—"

"Mother." Alcea materialized and put a firm hand on her mother's shoulder. "Why don't you help me carry some food to the patio? Maybe we can get people to move outside. It's getting stuffy in here, and at least there's a breeze out there."

Zinnia threw him a pointed look, then picked up a dish and followed Alcea. Before they reached the door, Florida intercepted them with a hand on Alcea's arm. Florida's face was too pale, her hair dull. Partly due to grief, partly due to the pregnancy she could no longer keep hidden under loose shirts.

"We should set up a table on the front porch instead. The backyard is a mess."

Zinnia's gaze riveted on Florida. Or, actually, on the swell of her abdomen.

Alcea shrugged off her hand. "There's already a table set up in back."

"This is *not* your house," Florida hissed.

"And last time I checked, it wasn't yours, either. Not that those kind of details ever bothered you."

Zinnia pulled her gaze off Florida's stomach. "Alcea Caroline," she whispered. "This is not the time or the place—"

"What is *that* supposed to mean?" Florida narrowed her eyes.

"I'm glad you asked. You have a habit of staking a claim on territory that isn't yours." Alcea pointedly looked at Florida's increasing figure.

Florida flushed. "This is not—"

"Do you remember that time I came home—to *my*

home—and found a trail of *your* clothing leading up to *my* guest room?"

Florida swept a look around the room. While all the women except Zinnia remained studiously busy, the chatter had stopped. Red faced, she put up her chin. "You never understood Stan the way I did."

Beside the sink, Mari frowned and opened her mouth, but Alcea spoke first. "A trail of clothing. And you in bed. With *my* husband, by the way."

"That still didn't give you any right to lock us in"—Florida lowered her voice—"and without our clothes!"

"But it was so amusing when the fire department answered Stan's call."

"I will never forgive you for that, Alcea. Never."

"Forgive *me*? Excuse me, but I think it's you who should be begging forgiveness. You have some nerve—"

Dak recovered his wits and grabbed Alcea's elbow. *"Out here."* He steered her toward the back door.

"Florida, *in here*." Zinnia found her voice at the same time. She herded her into the dining room.

As soon as they stepped out the door, Alcea deflated, and he let go.

"I'm sorry," she murmured. She took a seat at the patio table and dropped her forehead on to her hand. "Mother was right. It wasn't the time or the place."

Dak leaned a thigh against the table and studied her. "You'll have to learn to get along with her if—"

Alcea raised her head. "If what, Dak? If we're going to keep doing whatever it is we're doing?"

He'd been about to say, *If you want to keep your job,* but now he stilled.

She watched him a moment. "Cutting too close to the bone, aren't I?"

He wasn't sure what she meant, but the way she looked, he thought she might call the whole thing quits right now. Dread tickled him, and he frowned. Of course it had to end. But some other day, not today. Not on the same day they'd buried Peg.

She looked away. For a long moment, she stared off at the Ozark hills wavering under a mid-June haze. Then she stirred. "Have you ever realized that no matter how many times we see things happen in our own lives, or other people's, we seem to always make the same mistakes?" She'd gone from belligerent to pensive.

He took the chair beside her. "What do you mean?"

"I'm not sure. Peg and Cowboy. Me and Stan . . . Peg and Julius."

"Peg and Julius?"

"Julius was in love with Peg." She tilted her head. "You didn't know that?"

He shook his head. He'd never even suspected.

"I guess I'm not surprised. He never told her. He was waiting until she was ready, and now it's too late." Her voice quavered. "And maybe . . . maybe he could have been the one to give her what she wished she'd had with Cowboy."

He still didn't quite understand, but her sadness sounded an echoing chord in him. He edged his chair closer and smoothed her hair. "Peg and Cowboy were happy," he murmured, hoping the words would bring her some comfort.

She pulled away from his touch. "You mean *Cowboy* was happy." When she looked up, he was surprised to see her eyes blaze. "Peg wasn't, Dak. Peg. Was. *Not.*"

Something inside him withdrew and folded in on itself.

Alcea's eyes veiled. "I'm sorry Mother badgered you."

"Zinnia just loves you." As he uttered the words, he again felt a sense of loss, one that went deeper than today's occasion. "And she doesn't understand what we have."

"That makes two of us."

Dak shot her a look, but her face remained inscrutable. She got to her feet. "I'd better go back inside. Make some amends. Maybe some changes."

He felt relief, not the least because she didn't seem inclined to explain that last remark. "Florida will meet you halfway." He hoped there was some truth to the words.

Alcea looked at him like he was beyond hope. "I wasn't just talking about Florida. For somebody who is supposed to be so perceptive, you can be amazingly slow-witted."

She turned her back and walked inside.

Turning Alcea's words over in his head, Dak stayed put. Alcea was wrong. He wasn't slow-witted. He understood she'd drawn parallels between their . . . situation . . . and Cowboy and Peg's. It saddened him that Julius had lived with the throes of unrequited love—he winced—exactly like the situation he'd forced on Alcea. Hell. He scraped back his chair and threw his feet up on the table.

The back door squeaked open. He steeled himself for another encounter with Someone O'Malley, but when he turned around, he saw it was Jon and relaxed.

Jon dropped into the chair Alcea had vacated. "Tough day, eh?"

"That's for sure."

For a while, they only shared the silence and the view, punctuated by a few inane remarks about the services. From the way Jon's fingers drummed his thigh, though, he was working around to something. He finally spoke up. "Alcea really is a great gal."

Dak sighed. "I'm aware of that."

"A lot like Lil in some ways."

Now, that statement surprised him. "How?"

"Both women figure out what they want and they go after it, no holds barred." Jon smiled. "So the only question a man's got to ask himself is, Am I going to make things easy or hard?"

Maybe he *was* slow-witted. Did Jon think he didn't have a choice? "I don't know what you, or any of the rest of Alcea's family, thinks, but I've never deceived Alcea for a moment. She knows one day I'll leave."

"Uh-huh. That's what you think."

His tone was teasing, but Dak bristled. "Look, Jon, I don't know when, but I *will* leave—believe it. And while I'll miss Alcea—" To his embarrassment, his voice roughened. He cleared his throat. "While I'll miss her, in some ways having it over would be a relief."

"Believe me, I understand." Jon looked out at the hills. "There was a time when I tried like hell to get Lil out of my life. But she wouldn't have it. She fought tooth and nail until I came to my senses." His eyes softened. "And I thank God every day that she did."

"I'm not you. Alcea's not Lil. I'm not what Alcea needs or wants."

Jon barked a laugh. "Do you know how many times I thought that—said that—to Lil? You gotta give it a chance, man. It's the right thing to do for both of you."

Dak thought back to the scene in the high school cafeteria. The right thing to do would have been to leave things right there.

"Don't believe me, do you?" Jon eyed him, jocularity gone. "You should."

"Dak!" Zinnia poked her head out the door. "I think you'd better get in here."

Simultaneously relieved and irritated, Dak heaved to his feet. "Hell. What now?"

When he got inside, Zinnia motioned him to the dining room. Florida stood at one end of the table, Alcea at the other, broken crockery at her feet. She looked stunned.

And Florida looked smug. "That's right, Alcea. You'd better watch your step, as y'all are looking at your new boss."

Dak groaned and wanted to hide. Dammit. This was

what he got for messing around with domestic life. If he'd thought things had been tense around the household for the last few days, he knew he hadn't seen anything yet.

He wasn't wrong.

The remnants of his peace unraveled completely over the next week. There was no place to hide from the slammed doors, barbed remarks, and quarrels that came like bursts from a shotgun over everything from a dish in the sink to a towel on the floor. He'd thought each woman would retreat into her own corner—Florida upstairs in her old bedroom, Alcea to the Pink Palace. But Alcea had apparently decided to stake a claim at Cowboy's, too. She wandered in and out like she had before Florida had arrived, purposely taunting her, banking on her relationship with Dak to keep Florida from throwing her out. And if the atmosphere at home was bad, Peg O' My Heart was a war zone. Gone was the lively banter. Anyone courageous enough to brave the place kept his head in his coffee cup and out of the line of fire.

He was sick of it.

Early Friday morning, he sat at his laptop in the dining room, trying to take advantage of the few hours he had when the house was empty. Trying to write. But no matter how long he stared at the screen, the words refused to come. Some weeks ago, he'd finished reading the galleys on his last book and had started a new novel for *Road*. Set in Cordelia, he'd made the diner the focal point, planning to weave his impressions of the town around a story based loosely on the lives of his grandfather and Peg.

He reread what he'd written yesterday and gave a snort of disgust. The dialogue was stilted. As Eagleton had once pointed out, emotion was his weak point. But this time, it wasn't just weak. It was crap. He backed up the cursor, highlighting four paragraphs of text, and hit DELETE. This should be easy. He knew these people well. But maybe that was the problem. Maybe he knew them too well.

Or not at all.

He propped his chin on his hand and stared through the gauze on the windows. From here he could see the breezeway and the front of the service garage, where more old-timers than usual had congregated in the folding chairs Julius kept out front. Their hands were wrapped around StarMart cups instead of the Styrofoam ones Peg had always kept on hand. No surprise.

That old itch to move on had risen with increasing urgency over the past week, but he'd tamped it down, concerned about Florida. Concerned about Alcea. But now restlessness seized him by the throat. His gaze roamed the room, falling on a vase of wildflowers he'd picked with Alcea on the day of the funeral. They'd wilted. Irritation surged. And undoubtedly, Florida would notice, make some biting comment to Alcea, and they'd go at it again.

He kicked back his chair, picked up the vase, and dumped the flowers in the trash. With each movement, his aggravation increased. What was he doing here, worrying about posies? He banged down the vase, strode through the hallway, and took the stairs two at a time. In his bedroom, he threw some clothes into his duffel, hauled it downstairs, and parked it next to the front door. He headed for the kitchen, grabbed a set of keys, and was headed back when the door flew open.

Alcea stepped in—stomped in, more like it—and he halted. Her hair was disheveled, her face red as fire. He didn't have to be Einstein to guess Florida was the cause. Knowing it was cowardly, he briefly hoped she was mad enough that she'd stride right by him, jaw locked, and go somewhere to cool off. She'd done it before in a futile attempt to shield him from their arguments.

But she stopped at the sight of him. "She fired me!"

He leaned against the newel post. Only a few short steps away, freedom beckoned. He was sick of playing mediator. "And this is a surprise?"

Wound up with outrage, she didn't seem to notice the sarcasm. She dropped her purse where she stood. "As a matter of fact, it is. Since she took over the diner, I've done my best to teach her what she needs to know—"

"By using those twin tools of effective mentoring—ridicule and shouting."

Her eyes narrowed. "Are you defending her? Since the very first day, she waltzed in there like—" She stumbled to a halt.

"Like she owns the place? It's a reality. Get over it."

Her color heightened even more. "I thought for once you might—just might—side with me. Maybe even help me. Talk to her—"

"Oh, no. I'm as neutral as Switzerland. You're special to me, Alcea, but Florida is my sister. You can't ask me to choose sides."

"If that's the way you want to look at it, then go right ahead!" She stooped to pick up her purse, and her gaze locked on his duffel. She straightened, the anger in her eyes replaced by near panic. "Where—? Are you going someplace?"

"Maybe to Kesibwi." Then he thought of Jon and Lil, who were there almost every weekend. His luck, he'd run into them. "Or maybe the Lake of the Ozarks."

"For—for how long?" She'd tilted her chin up as though steeling herself for a blow.

Dammit. He wanted to be able to stalk right past her and go where he wanted without caring what she thought. But watching that beautiful face struggle between pride and tears, he relented. "Just for a few days."

Biting her lip, she eyed him. "And you weren't going to tell me?"

He sighed, took a seat on the steps, and patted the space beside him. She sat down, and he tried to choose his words carefully, not wanting to hurt her any more than he already had. "Look, Alcea. Sometimes I need time away, sometimes I need a breather. And I'm not used to having to explain myself." He realized his irritation was growing again at the need to do so.

"I understand that, but . . ." Her eyes wandered to his bag again. "Do you have to go today? I need . . ." She hesitated. "I don't know what to do now."

He gathered his patience. "What do you *want* to do?"

"I want to work in the bakery. I want things to be like before. I want Peg back." Her voice shook, and suddenly he wanted to hold her and reassure her and tell her everything would be all right. Simultaneously, he wanted to run.

But for her, he tried. "I miss Peg, too." He paused. "I know you loved her, but can you imagine what Florida is feeling? It's like losing Tamara all over again. Peg took her place for Florida."

Alcea played with the hem of her apron, then finally spoke. "You're right. I should be more understanding. Even though my mother is a pain, I can't imagine what life would have been like without her." Her hand quieted, and she gave him a curious look. "Who took your mother's place for you?"

The question came out of left field, and an unexpected stab of pain shot up from deep down. Without examining it, he shoved it back and shrugged. "Cowboy, Peg. But we can't change what's done." Before she could pursue the topic, he changed direction. "What do you think you'll do now?"

She studied him, her gaze thoughtful, then looked away. "I don't know. Lil would help, but I don't want to ask. Peg paid me a good wage—at least for this town. And I loved my work. To do something similar, I'd have to leave Cordelia." She looked at him again.

"But I don't want to do that because I don't want to leave—"

"Kathleen." He filled the blank before she could say *you*.

Her lips tightened. "Yes, Kathleen." She stood up. "Since you won't be here, I'll get my belongings so I'm not around when Florida comes back. Considering how things stand, I doubt I'll stay here anymore."

He should feel relief, but he didn't. Without her . . . His urge to flee grew stronger.

She hesitated halfway up the stairs. "You'll let me know when you get back?"

He nodded, then added gently, "Alcea, if—when—I leave for good, I won't sneak off in the middle of the night."

Some of her spirit flashed in her eyes before she turned her back. She mumbled a "Gee, thanks" under her breath, and a corner of his mouth crooked. She'd be okay. No matter what happened, she'd be okay.

He thought of something and called up as she reached the landing. "Say, I phoned the painters you told me about a few days ago. If they show up and you're here, will you show them around?" When she stumbled, he wished he could retract the question. She was hurting, and all he could do was give her a chore?

But her expression when she looked at him was neutral. "Sure thing. Why don't you just leave me a list of everything you want done while you're gone? God knows I have time." She moved into his bedroom. He stared after her, perversely upset at her composure. Then she poked her head out. "And while you're at it, make a list for yourself. The number one item should be sensitivity training."

Despite the pall in the atmosphere, he chuckled, feeling a wisp of the same magic they'd conjured before Florida had arrived. Still smiling, he rose and started upstairs, intending to catch her around the waist and make her pay in oh-so-sweet ways for that remark. Plus, it had just crossed his mind that without her job, maybe she'd come with him. He'd like to show her a taste of a life unbound by convention.

He was halfway to the landing when he stopped. If he wanted to distance himself, this was no way to do it. Reluctantly, he reversed course, picked up his bag, and stepped outside, shutting the door behind him. Digging into his pocket, he pulled out the keys and cursed. They were hers. Hell. Even something as simple as this was tangled up in her life.

Not wanting to risk another scene, he quietly let himself back in. The unmistakable sounds of Alcea's weeping floated down the stairs. His heart clenched. He hesitated at the newel post, then moved on to the kitchen and pocketed the right keys. To remove the temptation of doing anything else, he exited through the back door. He had to leave. He had to leave right now. Because if he didn't . . .

If he didn't, he might be tempted to stay.

Chapter 14

Alcea lay listlessly in her bed at the Pink Palace the day after Dak left. It was nearing noon and she'd lain awake for hours, but she had nothing to do and nobody to get up for. The phone had rung a few times but she'd ignored it. There wasn't anybody she wanted to talk to. She could look at the want ads, but she already knew she'd find only a big fat zero. Like her love life. Damn Dak. How *could* he have left her alone on the day her dream had blown up? She'd wanted to throw his bag in his face but—damn her stupid heart, too—she couldn't stand it if he didn't come back.

On the other hand, she couldn't stand much more of this relationship without a future, either. Not that it wasn't fitting, considering she didn't *have* a future anymore. No daughter. No job. No lover. She plucked at the sheets. Of her empty bed. When he got back, she'd tell Dak to get lost. No, she'd tell him to go to hell. She'd tell *both* the Jones children . . .

A pounding sounded on the outer door. Dak! Scrambling up, she didn't even bother to grab a robe. She finger-combed her hair as she flew down the hallway, threw open the trailer door, and stopped short. Not Dak. Through the window she saw the light-defying black spiked hair of her sister Mari. Dragging her feet, she opened the door to the addition. "I thought you'd left."

"Well, hello to you, too. I thought I'd stop by on my way out and say good-bye. Plus, I never did thank you for those Rauschenberg prints." Mari pushed past Alcea and into the trailer, giving her a scornful glance over her shoulder. "New fashion statement?"

"Some thanks. Look, Mari . . ." Alcea trailed after her, still pulling her fingers through the tangles on her head. "This is a bad day. A very bad day. I won't be responsible if you don't get out of here alive."

"What, your job? There are other jobs. You're good at what you do. You'll find someplace else."

"I'm good at—" Alcea stopped in the doorway. "Would you repeat that? If I'm not mistaken, that was a compliment. And how did you know I lost my job, anyway?"

"Who doesn't know?" Mari snorted. "Paddy was in the diner when Florida chased you out with a spatula."

"So Mother knows?"

"She tried to call you." Mari prowled through the room, picking things up and setting them back down, looking like a caped crusader in a black skirt and wide silver bracelets. "She wanted to call a Family Meeting. You can pay me later for stopping her."

Alcea slumped onto a stool. "Thanks."

"And don't give me any false modesty. You know you're a good at what you do. You always have been. It's a mystery to me why you love spending time in the kitchen, but I'll admit your cakes and cookies and stuff are better than anyone else's. There are jobs out there for bakers." Mari stopped and put her hands on her hips. "Of course, you might have to move."

"I can't, Mari. There's Kathleen."

"And she's handcuffed to something here? C'mon. She can move, too."

"Stan's decided to be a father all of a sudden. She has friends here. Family. School. She's happy. I can't just yank her away."

"All right. Then you'll figure something else out. In fact, I wouldn't be surprised if Florida begged you to come back. The bakery was closed this morning, you know."

Now this was interesting. "It was?"

"Like someone is going to buy Tansy's pastries?"

"She'll find someone else." Alcea plowed her hair back. "Women like her have all the luck."

"Oh, yeah. She's pretty damn lucky. Pregnant, saddled with a business she knows nothing about. No friends. Dumped by the guy she loved who now has a new girlfriend."

Alcea frowned. "Do you feel *sorry* for her?"

Mari looked away. "You know, Hock, this place isn't too bad. I like it a lot better than that sterile layout you used to live in."

Two compliments in one day from Mari? She must be sick. "Do you want a cup of coffee?"

"Yuck, no, but I'll take some OJ if you have some." Alcea got up, poured her a glass, and Mari chugged it down. She set the glass on the counter. "Better. I went over to the Rooster last night to catch up with a few old friends. And I had a few too many. Drinks, that is, not friends."

Alcea poured herself some juice and settled back on the stool. "How are the friends?"

"Same. Boring. Most of them have some drone of a job and two-point-five kids. Like No-Account Andy, they're losers." Mari sat on the other stool and swung her legs. "I never will understand why anyone wants to stay stuck in this backwater. You really should move."

Alcea bristled. "I like Cordelia. Is Kansas City really all that much better?"

"I guess you take your problems wherever you go." Despite Mari's nonchalant shrug, Alcea caught a shadow passing across her face.

She frowned. It was the first time Mari had ever hinted that her life was anything but roses. Mari had never confided in her, not like she did with Lil. Maybe it was the age difference, or maybe it was because she always got defensive around her. Mari always seemed so certain about everything. She spoke carefully, afraid Mari might bolt. "Is something wrong?"

Mari's legs stopped swinging. "You and Stan and Florida . . . I was off at college when all that was going down. I heard stuff, but nobody really talked about it much, at least to me." She paused. "When you found out, why didn't you toss Stan out on his ear right away? Was it money, or were you afraid, or did you still love him, or what?"

Puzzled at her questions, Alcea set down her mug and studied her sister for signs she was about to launch into yet another commentary on Alcea's pathetic life. But Mari looked honestly perplexed. "That's all history. Why do you want to know?"

Mari tilted her juice glass and studied the pulp on its sides. "I dunno," she said, although Alcea thought she did. "It's just that, well, Florida isn't all that much older than me, and I remember I was jealous of her when we were growing up. All that strawberry blond hair, and she was so smart. But I felt sorry for her, too, because her life was lonely. No family, really. And I wonder why she didn't get out of here and why she latched on to Stan after college, and—" Mari slanted a look at her. "You're not going to like this, but, yes, I feel sorry for her."

Alcea was incredulous. "After what she did to me?"

"I said you wouldn't like it." Mari hunched forward, still holding her glass. "Think about it, though. How alone she is. All she has for family is a brother who can't stand still long enough to take a piss." She darted a look at Alcea. "Uh, sorry. I know you like the guy."

Alcea ignored the last comment. "Mari, Florida Jones carried on an affair with my husband. Pardon me if I don't get out my hanky."

"But don't you think he fooled her as much as he fooled you? And wasn't your marriage already pretty well shot?"

Alcea ignored that, too, and stood up. Charity toward Florida wasn't in her genetic makeup. "What is this all about, Mari? Do you really think I can forgive—" She broke off as a thought hit her. "Are you . . . Are you seeing a married man? Is that why all this sympathy for Florida?"

Mari didn't meet her eyes. "I have a guy in my life, yeah. And he's . . . he's still living with her, but they're getting a divorce." She didn't sound convinced.

"Oh, Mari. Don't you know a guy will say anything? I'm sure Stan did. He probably told Florida—" She stopped, aghast she was about to make excuses for Stan's ex-mistress.

"That's what I'm afraid of." Mari's nose had pinked. "Is it all just talk?"

Alcea took Mari's hands. "Dump him. Now. You can do better than that."

Mari sniffed. "Like you have?" She dropped her gaze. "Sorry, that was cheap."

A retort in Dak's defense sprang to Alcea's lips, but she swallowed it. Mari had a point. She was embroiled in her first relationship since Stan—if you didn't count Kemp. And just like Mari—my God, just like Florida—she'd chosen someone who was married. Not to a woman, but to a way of life she couldn't share. She dropped Mari's hands. "Balls. We're both morons."

That earned her one of Mari's quick grins. "You said it." She glanced at her watch. "I've got to hit the road. And, really, thanks for the prints."

They walked to the door together and impulsively Alcea reached out and pulled her little sister into a fierce hug. Despite the clothes, the hair, the bravado, Mari was only twenty-six. Hardly grown up at all. She suddenly wanted to tell her so many things, but all she whispered was, "You take care of *yourself,* you hear me?"

Mari hugged back, then broke away. She looked

down to straighten her clothing, but not before Alcea saw tears in her sister's eyes. "You take care of yourself, too," Mari whispered.

After she'd left, Alcea sat thinking about their conversation. She felt a glow over the first real connection she'd ever felt with Mari, but a gnawing sadness over what linked them. For a moment, she tried to imagine Mari in Florida's shoes. Her sister, the Other Woman. But just like always whenever she thought of Florida, the image of the tramp in Stan's arms rose like a specter and turned her vision red. When she'd discovered them that day, she'd never before felt as humiliated, as embarrassed, as . . .

Suddenly, she realized that out of all the emotions she'd experienced when she'd walked in on Stan and Florida, a sense of loss wasn't one of them. Her heart hadn't been damaged. Only her pride.

She looked down at her rumpled nightgown. Did she have any pride left? Maybe a little. She heaved to her feet. She'd take a shower, eat something, straighten up the trailer, and—she sighed—look at the damn want ads.

A day after Mari's visit, having found the expected zero in the want ads, she'd begged a part-time job out of Old Ben at Sin-Sational. Three days post-Mari, Paddy had told her he'd like her help mornings at the Emporium. And five days later (not *a few*), Dak had returned, and she'd stuffed her resentments under her relief at having him back, although it was short-lived. Because since he'd returned, they'd failed to recapture the easy rhythms of their life before Florida moved in. She avoided Cowboy's, her schedule was chaotic, and there was a distance between them that couldn't be measured by the Jeep's odometer.

Now, almost three weeks after she'd talked to Mari, Alcea swiped a forearm across her forehead, thinking her situation was about as stagnant as the air outside. The afternoon temperature was a bull's-eye on a hundred, but what could you expect in the middle of Missouri in the middle of July? The air-conditioning in Sin-Sational ran in fits and starts, despite Old Ben's promises he'd get it fixed. The pizza oven didn't make it any cooler. She dropped her ladle into a bucket of butter crunch ice cream and reached for an oven mitt, noting her forearms looked like Iron Mike's. If something else didn't turn up, she could always take up prizefighting. As she slid another pepperoni from the oven, the door to the ice cream parlor swung open, admitting her mother and Lil.

"Just some coffee, Alcea," her mother called. They seated themselves at one of the tiny ironwork tables scattered across the green-and-white checkerboard floor.

Old Ben tilted back his paper cap. "Won't be much of a crowd until evening. Go ahead and rest a spell." Alcea smiled a thanks. They rubbed together well, but she still longed for Peg. And for her bakery. She fetched coffee and joined her mother and sister.

Zinnia was eying the room. "Lord love a duck, change decor and this is Peg's."

Alcea followed her gaze. All the old-timers that used to crowd the diner had gravitated to Sin-Sational. At first Old Ben had grumped about tables filled by dollar-a-bottomless-cup coffee orders, but Alcea had convinced him to see it as potential profit. He'd given her a jaundiced look until she'd added deli sandwiches and cookies to the ice cream and pizza. Now folks stuck around for lunch, and Sin-Sational was as full at noon as Peg's once was. Old Ben was happy, and the old boys were out of the heat, and that gave her some pleasure, too. She squirmed, though, admitting to herself that her satisfaction wasn't just because her friends had a haven. She liked knowing that whatever business was here wasn't at Peg O' My Heart.

"We haven't seen you in a month of Sundays, so we figured the only way we'd catch up was to come on over." Her mother looked at her from over the rim of her cup. "I wanted to thank you for keeping up the baking for the Ladies' Auxiliary. Those cakes sell like wildfire, and the money's helping some needy souls. I still think you should peddle them yourself."

"You know the Pink Palace isn't big enough for me to bake in quantity." She'd already tried to live on that income and it hadn't worked. She waved a hand. "And no thanks necessary." Because it wasn't charitable feelings that had her baking for her mother's church group and the summer PTA fund-raisers. Mixing, measuring, and experimenting with her recipes brought her the only real peace of mind she'd found since Florida had kicked her out of Peg's. She and Dak certainly couldn't consume all that she baked. She frowned at her cup. Not that he'd been around that much to consume anything.

"It must keep you a mite busy. And with two jobs . . . Lord love you, child, can't you drop one of them?"

She glanced around the room. "And let down my fan club? Besides, Paddy needs me." He claimed. She suspected Paddy had offered her a job out of pity and a bum knee more than anything else, although she'd returned the favor by arriving early many mornings to whip his junk pile of a store into shape. "And I need the money."

Actually, her expenses were so minor without a full-time Kathleen, she might slide by with only one job, but she was squirreling away part of her income, adding it to the small nest egg that had remained after Stan had foreclosed. Someday she'd own her own bakery. Maybe when she was ninety.

Her mother's eyes sharpened. "You got enough?"

"I do. Dak offered to let me have the Pink Palace rent-free—"

"Well, that's good."

"—but I refused." It had felt too much like the way she'd lived off Stan. "I'm sure he needs the money as much as I do." She knew he was having trouble with his current book, and his publisher had already pushed back his deadline. He wouldn't receive another check until he delivered.

Lil laid a hand on her arm. "I wish you'd let me—"

Alcea smiled. "We've been over this before. I can't take your money."

"But at least I could hire you. I'd pay better than this."

"And interfere with everything Patsy Lee is doing for you?" Alcea shook her head. "She'd be crushed. Didn't you tell me she'd proposed some new inventory system she learned in those business classes? I don't think she wants to share her job, and you know me—I like to order people around."

Zinnia looked at her with approval. "You just do what you need to do, but keep in mind, your family is here."

"How could I forget?" She smiled to soften the words, but averted her gaze to the windows to indicate subject closed. Outside, Florida passed by on her way home from the diner. She was just shy of six months pregnant, but already her footsteps were slow and her face weary. Alcea frowned, remembering the excitement and pampering that had surrounded Kathleen's impending arrival. She couldn't imagine going through it alone. Of course, Florida wasn't *really* alone. She had Dak. Her frown deepened. At least as much as anyone did.

With that scary ability of hers, her mother picked up on her thoughts. "Haven't seen that young man of yours lately."

"Jon was saying just this morning that he hasn't seen Dak since we went to watch fireworks on the Fourth," Lil added. "Every time Jon calls, he's on his way somewhere."

"He . . . he's taken some trips lately." Alcea sat back. "You know, for his book." Liar. The book was about Cordelia, and all the information he needed was under his nose. She didn't tell them that, nor how his trips had grown more frequent since that first one. Sometimes he was gone a night; sometimes three. And each time he shouldered the damn duffel, she told herself she'd never watch him walk away again. And each time the vow lasted only as long as it took him to return. She was a weak-kneed idiot. "And he's not my 'young man.' He won't ever be anyone's young man." Maybe if she voiced it often enough, she'd eventually believe it. And act on it.

Zinnia eyed her. "And that's enough for you?"

"Yes, it is." *No, it wasn't.* "So don't badger him like you did at Peg's funeral."

"I didn't badger him." Zinnia plopped her cup on the table and hooked Alcea's eyes. "But maybe someone should. Don't forget, I used to know his mother."

"What does that have to do with anything?"

"Because if he's as irresponsible as she was . . . well, let's just say Tamara didn't walk the straight and narrow. Very free with the milk, so it wasn't any big surprise when nobody bought the cow."

"Mother!"

Lil tried to shush her, but Alcea waved her hand, morbidly fascinated. "Go on."

"Well, it's true." Zinnia threw a defensive look at Lil. "Tamara lay down for pretty much anything that moved. Rumor has it, half the men in town . . . why, even S.R. Addams, if you can believe it."

"Stan's father? Impossible. Ellen would have strung him up by his ba—"—Alcea glanced at her mother's frown—"big toes if he'd wandered. Besides, from everything I've heard, Stan's parents adored each other."

"They did." Zinnia nodded emphatically. "But this would have been pre-Ellen, if I remember right, and S.R. sowed a passel of wild oats before she came along. Stan didn't fall far from *that* tree, you've got to admit. So if Dak's anything like Tamara, then you just watch you don't find yourself in a family way. He'd probably just skip away like nothing happened."

Now it was her turn. "Mother!" Alcea didn't quite

follow the logic, but she flushed. "He's not like Tamara." He was very much like Tamara. "And I resent—"

Lil intervened. "I heard Dak hired the Jackson boys to paint his house."

"Yes, he did." Alcea felt a stirring of guilt.

"Did you warn him those no-goods take forever?" Zinnia shook her head. "They wait for pay day, and then don't come back to finish the job until they've drank it all up."

That was the point. "I, uh, forgot to mention it. They should be done in another week, though."

"And then is he selling?"

Alcea met her mother's eyes squarely. "I don't know."

They stared at each other a moment while her mother's eyes grew sad. "Guess this *is* your business. But do be careful, honeybunch. I just *worry* about you is all."

"I know," Alcea answered, afraid if her mother teared up, she would, too. She shifted topics. "Did I tell you Dak has helped Kathleen submit a few stories to some magazines? She's excited because he thinks she's good enough to get one accepted."

"Just how close are the two of them?"

Alcea clenched her teeth. *Good God, Mother. Drop it.* But all she said was, "They get along." Although she, too, worried what Dak's departure would do to Kathleen. "I'm not worried about her," she lied. "Even though I still want her with me, I have to give Serena some credit. That therapist seems to have helped."

And Dak had helped, too. Her daughter positively glowed under his attention. And Dak was much less guarded with his emotions when Kathleen was around. She wondered if he'd realized Kathleen was the same age he'd been when his mother had left him at Cowboy's. She also wondered if leaving Kathleen would hurt him more than it would her daughter.

The door opened. Rosemary stepped inside, peered around, and Zinnia frowned. "More hot air."

"Now, Mother," Alcea said. "She's got a good heart."

"I was talking about the draft." Zinnia rounded her eyes.

"Alcea! I just couldn't wait to tell you— Hi, Ben. I don't mean to bother Alcea while she's working but I just had to come right over." She fanned herself. "Oo, what a scorcher. Mama Butz is probably turning right on over in her grave about now."

"Because it's hot?" Alcea got up to hug Rosemary.

"No, because . . . well, I'll just never be able to thank you enough for helping me out so I could take those classes." She beamed around the table. "Betty Bruell has given me the shampoo assistant job over at Up-in-the-Hair. And she's going to teach me how to do those perma-waves and everything, like an apprentice, kind of. Right now I'm only working one afternoon a week and every other Saturday when I'm not at Peg's, but it's a start, isn't it? Mama Butz always said, 'Make hay while the sun—' "

"Take a load off." Looking resigned, Zinnia motioned to an empty chair. "Seems all you gals are working two jobs."

Rosemary adjusted her hips onto the tiny seat. "Betty says she'll put me on full-time soon's I pass my tests, and it won't be any too soon for me. I hate it at Peg's. Florida's destroyed the place. Even Tansy's threatening to quit. That Florida barks orders all over the place like a body has four hands and we don't know what we're doing. Maybe that worked for her at the bank, but it ain't working there." She lowered her voice and leaned forward. "And, my, my, don't dare ask her about the father of her baby because she's like to take your head right off your shoulders. Everybody wants to know who it is, but she's not telling, that's for sure."

Hearing of Florida's woes, Alcea waited for the

same wave of satisfaction that had swept over her before. It didn't come. She just couldn't relish Florida's current ranking at the top of the gossip column, having headlined so recently herself. And she knew Peg wouldn't be happy about the state of the diner . . . or Florida's state. Alcea tuned Rosemary out and watched Zinnia. Her mother was exchanging gardening talk with Erik Olausson, head bobbing for emphasis as she made her usual I-know-best declarations. But instead of feeling annoyance, love warmed her. No matter how much they butted heads, she'd never have made it this far if she hadn't inherited Zinnia's backbone or had her mother's support, whether she acknowledged it or not.

Alcea thought of Florida, raised slapdash by her grandfather and Peg. And she felt something for Florida Jones that she'd never, ever expected to feel. Compassion.

She was still in that frame of mind four days later when Florida knocked on the door to the Pink Palace.

Alcea admitted her with raised eyebrows, noting Florida's tailored jumper, the neatly brushed-back mane of hair, and the carefully applied makeup that was beginning to melt in the heat. Good grooming. No spatula. Her hopes rose.

"I'm sorry to bother you." Florida's speech was formal. "I have something I want to discuss."

"Sit down." Alcea motioned to the sofa, glad she'd used her first free afternoon in a while to clean the trailer until it shined. Dak had actually called last night to say he'd return later this evening, and she'd wanted everything perfect. "Let me check on my cake." She had a cake in the oven and a roast in the Crock-Pot, hoping Dak would arrive hungry. "Can I get you something to drink?"

Florida looked startled at the courtesy. "Uh, sure. If you have anything decaf."

Alcea ducked into the kitchen out of Florida's view

and smoothed down her sundress with trembling hands. As she poured two glasses of 7UP, the thoughts that had raced through her mind ever since she'd seen Rosemary on Friday tumbled through her head. When she breezed back into the living room, Florida was shifting from haunch to haunch on the sofa. She stilled when she saw Alcea.

Alcea handed her the 7UP, then seated herself on a chair opposite. "Preparation H," she murmured, sipping at her own glass.

"Huh?"

"When I was pregnant with Kathleen, I had them, too. It helps."

"Oh." Florida reddened. "Uh, thanks."

Inwardly, Alcea smiled, watching as Florida struggled to regain her businesslike demeanor. "So," Florida started. "I'm aware that the way we parted was not under the best of circumstances. However, I am hoping we can let bygones be bygones and—"

Unable to resist, Alcea interrupted. "Brandishing a spatula at me at least left me no doubt about my job status."

"I, uh, tend to get a bit overwrought when I'm angry." Florida swallowed and choked out the next words. "I'm sorry."

Alcea merely nodded. "Go on."

Florida cleared her throat. "I may soon have a work shortage at the diner. Because of this circumstance, I have decided—"

"Do you mean everyone's quitting?" Alcea tucked her legs up under her and adopted a look of mild interest.

Florida again looked disconcerted. "Well. I don't know. I mean, Tansy said if I didn't . . . and Rosemary may not be there much longer. . . . Then, with the baby coming . . ." Her voice trailed off and she straightened. "However, I am hoping we can let—"

"Bygones be bygones. I know." Alcea studied a

point over Florida's head. "Seems to me you might be able to get along without hiring anyone else."

"How is that?"

Her gaze returned to Florida's face. "Because you've driven away most of the customers."

Florida flushed. "Maybe taking meat loaf off the menu was a bad idea."

"And?"

"And buying baked goods from the Ladies' Auxiliary." Florida grimaced. "They charge more than you did for exactly the same thing."

Alcea hid a grin. So that's where the L.A. had been selling her cakes. Score one for Mother. "As was telling Rosemary she needed to put her hair in a net."

"That's a health regulation!"

"Strictly applied. But Rosemary? And wearing hose? And telling her to shut up about Mama Butz already? C'mon, Florida. Even I couldn't believe you were boneheaded enough to do that."

"Okay, okay! I've made some mistakes." Florida squirmed. "Maybe a lot of mistakes. I want you back. Will you do it?"

"No."

Florida went white. "I was sure you . . . look, Alcea, if you want me to beg, I'll beg. You have *got* to help me. This is all I have left. Not just for myself, but from Peg. And—and . . ." Her eyes filled. "I'm positively *ruining* everything!"

Alcea was silent a moment. She wanted to be a big person, but having Florida's brilliant blue eyes beseeching her for a favor was a moment to treasure. She finally relented. "I'll come back. But I have a condition."

"Just name it!"

"I'll return. But only as your partner."

Florida went bug-eyed. "You and me? Partners?"

Chapter 15

For the next hour, stopping only once to get up and take her cake out of the oven and twice so Florida could use the bathroom (she remembered that part of pregnancy, too), Alcea spoke concisely and convincingly (or at least she hoped so) about the plans she'd formulated over the last few days.

She envisioned bolstering their sales to the tourist trade with ads in the Kansas City and St. Louis papers. Or maybe a direct mail campaign.

"Mari would design the ads. Nobody wants to go on vacation and cook, but everyone wants to eat well. All these people pass through to the lakes from spring through fall—people with money. We could prepackage casseroles and meat loaf and homemade soup. Instead of just cakes and cookies, I want to add more scones and dessert breads . . ."

She went on in this vein for a while, her ideas tumbling faster the longer she talked. After Florida recovered from her initial shock, she listened thoughtfully, inserting pertinent questions. Alcea felt a grudging respect for the woman's business acumen. And was glad she'd anticipated Florida's possible concerns and objections.

When she finally stopped to draw breath, she pinned hopeful eyes on Florida. "What do you think?"

"It all sounds great," Florida said slowly. "But it'll take money."

"I have money." Alcea named what amounted to

her entire nest egg, what she had left in her savings account, what she'd salvaged from the estate sale, plus the portion of her salary she'd been setting aside. She wanted to invest her money and her knowledge in the business in return for a percentage. It was a flying leap of faith, but she felt ready.

Florida's brows raised. "Y'all are just full of surprises."

Another two hours passed while they discussed terms and conditions, and argued—albeit moderately, for them—about division of work. All the while, Alcea kept an eye on the clock, wondering if Dak would appear before the roast was way overdone.

Finally, both women sat back, eying each other warily.

"You know," Florida finally said. "This just might work. We have different strengths. You in operations, I guess you'd call it. Me with finances. And we're both Idea Women."

Alcea liked being an Idea Woman. She felt her hopes rise so high she thought they'd burst out the top of her head.

"So," Florida continued, "If we can just stay out of each other's way . . . tell you what. I'll call a lawyer I know and we'll see what he can draw up. That okay with you?"

"Yes." Alcea could hardly breathe the word she was so excited. If everything worked out, she'd own a bakery. Or at least part of a bakery. And part of a diner.

The outer door rattled. Both women looked at the inner door, and Dak appeared, his duffel slung over his shoulder. As usual, Alcea's heart flew into her throat. He looked relaxed, the lines of strain in his face gone—at least for a time.

He stopped short at the sight of his sister and Alcea, obviously unnerved that they weren't tearing at each other's hair. "What's going on?" The amazement on his face was so great, Alcea laughed.

Florida grinned, too. "Let me introduce y'all to my new partner."

"Partner?" He dropped the duffel and looked at both smiling faces. When his eyes latched on Alcea's, his grew warm, promising, and she blushed. "Well, I'll be damned. Did hell freeze over while I was gone?"

"Might have," Florida said.

Dak perched on the arm of Alcea's chair as Florida briefly outlined the terms they'd agreed to. Wanting so badly to welcome him properly—or maybe not so properly—Alcea had a hard time concentrating on Florida's words.

"So you see," Florida concluded, "the cash infusion from Alcea will help me pay off the loan for the bakery equipment."

That got Alcea's attention. "Peg took out a loan? She told me she had money saved."

"She believed in you." Florida's gaze was level. "And if she hadn't, I wouldn't have entertained your ideas for a minute."

Omigod. Oh, Peg.

"Anyway," Florida continued. "We also need extra insurance. Peg never contacted the insurance company to reappraise the business after she expanded. She was probably waiting until the bakery started turning a profit. And we also need to get a licensed electrician in. The guys who did the renovation were fine, and a sprinkler system is well and good, but it's only viable on the first floor. The second story of the building still has old wiring. And then there's . . ."

Alcea was listening with only half an ear, wishing there was some way she could repay Peg's goodness. She straightened. She could. By doing the best job she knew how.

Florida was still talking. "Alcea's money will help me—us—get the place back on its feet, since I practically ran it into the ground."

Dak frowned. "I'd be willing to give you whatever you need."

Startled, Alcea glanced up. What was he trying to do—steal her thunder? Besides, while the amount she'd invest wasn't a fortune, she was certain it was more than Dak had. He could hardly afford a spare toothbrush.

"And you'd be throwing good money on a bad proposition without Alcea. I need her skills as much as—no, more than—I need the money. And the percentage I'll give her buys me her talent." Florida pushed herself up from the sofa. "So save your gold, Midas. Invest in more Microsoft stocks or whatever you do with your riches. I've got to get going."

His gold? His riches? Alcea smiled up at Dak, but there was no answering grin. Her smile faded, and her jaw went slack.

Florida wasn't joking?

Chapter 16

As the outer door closed behind Florida, Alcea continued to stare at Dak. There was still no laughing protest. No joking denial. In fact, while he looked vaguely disgruntled, mostly he looked just as he always did—totally unperturbed.

She opened her mouth, but before she'd uttered a word, his head dipped to tease her lips with his.

"Just when I thought I might be able to tear you away from this place every once in a while . . ."

Was that the reason for the shadow she'd seen on his face? She pulled back, startled again. He'd never before indicated any desire to take her on one of his jaunts. And from the shutters that descended over his eyes at her surprise, it appeared he already regretted it. She moved impatiently. She was tired of veiled eyes and omissions. "You're rich." It came out like an accusation.

"Not in a Trump way." He bent his head again, nuzzled her neck. "Not in a Jonathan Van Castle way, but well enough off."

She closed her eyes, feeling her body respond. When she opened them again, his had gone cloudy with awakening desire. She struggled to hold on to her thoughts. "But how? I mean, you didn't inherit a fortune from Cowboy. And you said your books don't bring in all that much . . ."

He withdrew his mouth and stood up. She suddenly felt cold.

"What difference does it make?" He took a turn around the room, then flopped on the sofa.

"It—it doesn't make any difference." But now, without the distraction of his kisses, she knew it did. Her whole concept of him had just flipped upside down. "I'm—I guess I'm just curious."

"It's not that big of a deal." Despite the casual words, she could tell from the jerk of a muscle in his jaw that this wasn't a topic he wanted to discuss. "Back when I was in college, I wrote this novel. Sprang out of nowhere, really. It's nothing like I wrote before. Or since, for that matter. My agent showed it around, and it got the attention of some movie mogul before the publishing world ever took notice." One shoulder shrugged. "The movie was a hit, so the print rights went for big money. It was a fluke."

"Would I know it?"

He hesitated. "Maybe. Probably." He grimaced. "*Torn from My Arms*. Piece of schlock."

"Omigod." It *had* been schlock—melodramatic schlock that had sold millions of tickets, then gone on to win a few Academy Awards. Later she remembered seeing the book on every book stand in every drugstore and grocery store, and in the hands of many people she knew. She hadn't read it, but she'd seen the movie. "I don't remember seeing your name. I'd remember your name."

"I wasn't interested in fame," he said shortly. "Besides, they turned it into a soap opera. I refused to lend my John Henry to the project." His voice turned dry. "Who really wrote it is still a matter of speculation in certain literary circles. At least according to my agent and editor, who would like nothing more than for me to turn out another piece of dreck like that so they can ride piggyback on that first book's success. Ain't gonna happen. Once was enough."

She frowned. "But your pen name for *Road* is different than the name on *Torn from My Arms*."

"Correct. I don't want anything to do with that book." His gaze was so intense, she winced. He lightened his tone. "This is old stuff. I'm a starving man."

She picked at the chair fabric. He wasn't going to tell her anything else. "The roast should be ready."

His smile blinked like a shutter. "Not that kind of starving."

She rose but hesitated, feeling an odd uncertainty about him. Then he raised his eyebrows, and that was all it took for her to go to him. Still, while he thoroughly kissed her, a part of her mind was dredging up what she remembered about that movie. It had been a tearjerker, the story of a child ripped from his mother's arms. And as Dak bent her over his arm and slowly undid each button on the front of her dress, she remembered something else. When that child had grown into a man, he'd destroyed his own life because of his inability to make a commitment to anyone else. Dak's mouth found a breast, but her mind wouldn't shut up. *Torn* must have been wrenched out of the soul of a young man who had not yet learned to hide himself from the hurts of his past. Dak's hands moved down and under the elastic of her panties. But the man was still hiding from the words he'd written.

She squirmed, and he mistook her movements for passion, sliding his jeans down, lowering himself on top of her. She closed her eyes and tried to concentrate on what he was doing, but confusion distracted her. He not only hid from himself, he hid from everyone around him, lying by omission, hoarding his secrets, afraid of attachment.

She opened her eyes. His face hovered above her, eyes closed, beautiful brows arched, the tendons in his neck stretched as he strained forward, rocking her back and forth, back and forth, and taking her nowhere. Who was this man? Suddenly needing distance, she forced her body into shudders and let out a moan, faking an orgasm for the first time since Stan. And after he'd relaxed, she gave him only a second to collect his wits before she struggled out from under him. "I need to go turn off the Crock-Pot before the roast is history."

"I didn't come."

The morning sun had just lightened the sky in the east. Padding barefoot outside to join her on the patio Dak handed off a mug of coffee and looked confused. "Didn't come where?"

She set the mug aside. She'd already downed three after waking at four this morning, finally able to call last night's confusion—which she'd covered from the time she'd left the sofa, served the damned roast, and then pleaded tiredness when he wanted to make love again—what it really was. Livid anger. "Last night. I faked it."

His brow lightened. "Oh. Well, I didn't." He shot her a grin. "Want to go two out of three?"

"Don't joke. I thought I should tell you—in the interest of honesty. You know honesty? It's that thing where people don't try to fool other people."

His grin faded. He ran a hand through his hair. "Alcea, what are you getting at?"

"Why didn't you tell me you were rich? Why didn't you tell me about *Torn*?"

Jaw tightening, he lowered himself onto another chair. "Like I said last night, what difference does it make?"

"It's more things you never told me about. Like writing books. Or going to Harvard. Only this is bigger."

"No, it's not." His tone hovered on the edge of patience. "I've told you before, I don't tell people about any of it—including the money—because when they know, they treat me differently."

"And that's all I am? One of the unwashed masses?"

"Of course not. Look, this isn't a conspiracy. I'm not used to talking about these things with anyone. Why should I? They don't matter. Or they shouldn't." His eyes narrowed at her.

And Alcea's went wide. "Are you implying I would have done things differently if I'd known you had money?"

"Apparently, you've forgotten Kemp Runyon. I haven't."

Alcea fell silent. She *had* forgotten Kemp, even though he'd continued to visit Peg's, and then Sin-Sational. She'd told herself Kemp's patronage had nothing to do with her, although she'd been conscious of his gaze following her as she worked.

"That was then." She knew the defense was feeble. "This is now. I'm not after your money. I'm upset you didn't tell me because . . ." She struggled to find the words to explain something she only vaguely understood herself. "Because it hurts to find out I don't really know the person I lo— care about."

His glance was impatient. "Money—or the lack of it—doesn't make me a different person."

Alcea felt equally impatient. "Not a different person, maybe, but it sure as hell influences your choices. Since you've had money for more than a decade, maybe you've forgotten that."

He didn't respond. Not liking the set of his shoulders or the way he kept his head turned away, she tempered her tone. "Don't you see? All this time I've thought of you as a struggling-artist type. You were my . . . example. Whenever I thought I'd have to throw in the towel, I'd think about how you lived, what you said, what you'd done. And I'd think, If he can do it, so can I. I'd ask myself what you would do, what you would risk. And now . . . now I find out my perceptions were all wrong."

"That doesn't mean your choices were any less right."

"Maybe not. But then why do I feel like an idiot?"

Dak didn't answer. The silence, broken only by some quarreling sparrows and a delivery truck trundling down the alley, surrounded them until Alcea couldn't stand it anymore. "Dak, try to understand. I'm upset because—"

Dressed in painter's whites, a couple of fellows emerged from around the corner of Cowboy's house. "The Jackson brothers have finally deigned to appear." Dak stood up. "I think I'll go see how much longer this paint job will take." He picked up his mug and strolled toward the house.

Like he'd flipped a light switch, her anger changed to alarm. Dak hailed the Jacksons with a raise of his mug, and her heart nearly broke. Sometime in the future, perhaps the very near future, he'd walk away from her just like that, his stride nonchalant, the sunlight glinting off his dark hair. And with no look back. When that moment came, she'd never forget it. And she'd never forget him. But she was horribly afraid she'd just pushed him well on the way to forgetting about her.

Chapter 17

On the last day of July, on a Friday evening washed free of the usual humidity by thunderstorms that afternoon, Alcea lounged in a lawn chair on the Pink Palace's patio, a book in her lap. Near a washtub of petunias, a squirrel scrabbled for acorns and chattered with frustration. She knew how he felt.

For the last nine days she'd felt Dak slowly slipping away, just like the way his hair slid through her fingers. He made love as if it was an apology, their conversations were inane, and she'd catch him watching her when he thought she wasn't looking. She hated that last most of all. For God's sake, he didn't have to commit her to memory. She'd give him a damn picture.

She watched the squirrel, wondering if he'd share his supper with a companion. She sure wouldn't. When she'd arrived home from work, jazzed after her first full week back at Peg's as an *owner,* she'd found a note from Dak. Nothing new. It was similar to the one he'd left four days before *this* and three days before *that,* telling her he'd be away at least overnight. With typical understanding, she'd crumpled it and thrown it at the wall. That was their pattern. When he was gone, she moped and threw things. When he was home, they played games. Or at least she did. He didn't seem to notice.

Her gaze wandered from the squirrel, across the back of Cowboy's freshly painted house and up to a stack of shingles on the roof. The Jacksons had finally finished, and Dak had hired an electrician to fix some wiring, and someone else to patch the roof. And as the stream of repairmen had plodded through the door, she'd become June F'ing Cleaver. No pearls, but she'd measured out the welcoming smiles, clean house, and fresh-baked cookies, along with a soupçon of sex, until the concoction nauseated her. She felt stretched thin—transparent—in the same way she had with Stan. For Dak, she desperately wanted to be a woman who lived for the moment. But, dammit, she really wanted forever.

She looked down at the edition of *Torn* in her lap, wondering if plowing through was worth it. She read it when he wasn't around. And hid it in the clothes dryer when he was. Through the words he'd penned, she was struggling to understand him, hoping to find some chink in the barriers he'd erected between himself and the world. Between himself and *her*.

She shrugged and opened the book. What else did she have to do? As the squirrel abandoned his efforts and scurried up the oak overhead, she set aside her bookmark, that odd note she'd found stuffed away in a trunk in Cowboy's cellar. Remembering spring, when she was newly in love and stupidly hopeful, tears welled in her eyes. Impatiently, she dashed them away and bent her head to the book.

An hour later, as streaks of violet painted the western sky, she shut the book on the last chapter. Hands resting on the cover, she watched the fireflies welcome the dusk. Lights flickered on inside Cowboy's as Florida settled in for the evening. Her mind rambled back through the pages she'd read. Good God, couldn't Dak see himself in what he'd written? Unlike his other books, *Torn* was a storm of emotion, a heartfelt cry. She shook her head. Maybe he thought he'd only spoken for the character, but his anguish was clear in every line. And he thought *she* had difficulty grasping metaphor?

As the cicadas stirred into song, she tried to imagine him at the time he'd written *Torn* . . . not much older than the boy she'd met on the water tower . . . a recent refugee from the only home he'd ever known . . . married into a family where he could never hope to measure up. She had to hand it to his wife, though. The love he'd felt for her must have weakened his defenses, or he'd never have poured out his soul on these pages. Or maybe the boy just hadn't shored up his walls the way the man could now.

Rubbing the spine with her thumb, she fast-forwarded his life. Once the movie had started production, or maybe when the book had soared in popularity, Dak must have sensed the torment he'd put on the page lurked within *him,* but he just couldn't face it. So he'd hidden behind outrage over the screenplay, a pen name, and a go-with-the-flow attitude. And he'd not only buried the emotions, he'd buried the marriage that had helped him unearth them. So what in the hell could she do now to convince him love—her love—could heal those wounds?

"Just call me Freud," she grumped. Restless, she got up and carried the book back to the dryer. Slamming the door on it, she leaned her palms on the machine and stared across the darkening yard. She was assuming all her psychobabble was right. And she was assuming there was something she *could* do. She might be dead wrong on every level. But maybe she wasn't. Pushing herself off, she went to find Florida.

Florida called, "Come in" when Alcea yoo-hooed through the back door. Alcea found her in the dining room, pencil pushed into the bundle of hair tossed up on her head, a laptop open, and a spreadsheet glowing on the screen. She motioned Alcea to a chair. "I just finished up last quarter's income statement, which I should have done before y'all signed those papers yesterday. But Baby's not cooperating. I'm just always so danged tired. Or scatterbrained and hysterical. Hormones, I guess."

Alcea settled herself at the table near a fan of papers, wondering how to broach the subject she wanted to discuss. Over the last week, hostility had given way to a kind of guarded friendliness, although Florida might still be a far cry from welcoming the personal questions Alcea wanted to ask. "I remember how it was." Alcea took the paper Florida pushed in her direction. After perusing the numbers, she sighed. "You'll have to interpret."

"Basically, it says Peg O' My Heart is a healthy business." Stretching, Florida leaned back. "But Peg spread herself pretty thin when she purchased that old building, and then took out a loan for equipment. I'm not worried, though. We'll have to operate on a shoestring for a while, but with the way the profits are heading—*were* heading until I started balling things up—we'll be back in the black after another quarter." Frowning, she dropped her arms and settled her hands over her abdomen. "But I don't think we should purchase extra insurance right now—or anything else. It's not the smartest thing to wait, but it will only be another few months."

"Okay." Alcea pushed the paper back. She'd have to trust Florida until she could bone up on business accounting. Hell, on business, period. Sounded boring, but she'd bet it would beat Shakespeare. "I'll put my ideas on hold until you tell me we have the money. If nothing else, I've learned something about frugal living."

Florida smiled and reached across the table to gather up the papers. "How's life at the Pink Palace?" When Alcea didn't answer, she gave her a sharp look. "Dak gone again?"

"Yes." The word was a sigh.

"Dang it." Florida snapped the laptop closed. "I sure am sorry."

"*You're* sorry?"

"It's probably my doing. He and I had a boot-stompin' fight this morning. At least, I stomped. He just sat there with one of those expressions he has that makes you feel like a bug under glass."

She knew it well. "Wielding the spatula again?"

"Uh, no. A mixing spoon." Florida looked shame-faced. "But, dammit, the man did deserve a clunk on the head."

"You actually hit him?" Alcea wished she could summon the guts.

"No, but it sure did tempt me. When he came in this morning, he caught me weeping in my Rice Krispies over nothing. But instead of letting things be, he made the mistake of trying to empathize." Florida sighed, pulled out a chair, and put her feet up. She motioned to them, looking mournful. "Just look at those ankles. Big as footballs, and they used to be so pretty." She looked up at Alcea. "What in the hell does a man know about carrying a baby?"

"So he said something wrong."

"I'll say. There I am, sitting with this baby bulging between us, and he has the nerve to ask me why I hadn't considered abortion."

"Abortion?" Did the man have *no* sensitivity?

Florida took a look at Alcea's face, and the irritation faded from her own. "I'm making it sound worse than it really was. He didn't say that was what I should have done. He was . . . oh, curious, I guess. You know how he is, always trying to figure out what makes us mere mortals tick. And motherly love would be a foreign concept to him. I know it is for me." Her voice softened. "Or at least until this little dickens came along, it was."

It was the opening Alcea had wanted, but she broached the subject gingerly. "It—it must have been hard growing up without a mother."

"Far as I was concerned, it was hell." Florida waved a hand around. "This dim house. Constant quiet. When Tamara left us here, I cried myself silly for a month straight. Grandpa had conniptions over me, so Peg stepped in to help. She was a comfort, but it wasn't ever enough. I felt so different without parents. And no friends. I envied every kid I ever tried to be friends with." She shrugged. "So I ended up without any."

"I can't even imagine how tough that would be." And she couldn't. No squabbling over the last piece of apple pie, no riotous Christmas mornings, no dunking for apples on Halloween. God, the very idea even made her thankful for the O'Malley Family Meetings. She thought of Kathleen. Instead of viewing Serena and Stan as rivals, maybe she should be glad Kathleen had so many people who cared about her. Maybe she should be glad so many people cared about *her*. *Should* was the operative word. "Dak, though . . . Dak says he didn't mind being left. That he understood Tamara."

Florida threw her a shrewd look. "Trying to figure him out, huh? Well, good luck. I never have understood him. Back then, he didn't shed a tear. Least not that I saw. And since he's been back, any time I bring up Tamara, he only yammers about how great she was. Well, she wasn't. She was a lousy mother and a stinkin' human being. I've tried to tell him because if he only knew—" She broke off, maybe feeling she was saying too much. "Let's just say I've quit discussing our mother with him. Good riddance to her. You're not the only one trying to make life easy on him so he'll stick around. He's the only family I've got."

Chagrined that Florida had seen right through her June Cleaver act, Alcea's face heated. The Jones siblings weren't the only ones that could benefit from a stint on a therapist's couch. Still, she wanted to know more. "What about your father?"

"Mine was some drifter like Tamara. Cowboy told Dak his was, too."

Alcea caught the discrepancy and her antenna went up. "You mean, Cowboy knew who Dak's father was?"

"Um, no." Florida pushed some stray strands of hair into the knot on her head, her arms shading her face. "I just meant Cowboy told Dak his father was a drifter, too."

Alcea didn't think that was what she'd meant at all.

Florida lowered her arms, pushed herself up, and started stacking papers. "Let me get this stuff out of the way and get us something to drink." Her hands stilled. Catching her bottom lip between her teeth, she looked up at Alcea. "If you don't mind, could we talk babies for a while? I, um, could use a friend, and I know I've got some nerve to ask *you,* but . . ."

What the hell. Alcea returned Florida's gaze with a level one of her own. "I can't say I'll ever forget what happened, Florida, but I'm willing to try to put it behind us."

Florida's smile was shy. "That's more than I should probably expect. Thank you, Alcea."

Alcea watched Florida head for the kitchen, but she only spared a moment to think how strange life was before her thoughts reverted to Dak. Florida hadn't told her much more than she'd already known, but Dak's sister had confirmed her backseat psychoanalysis. Dak had not only painted over his hurt, he'd cemented his so-called understanding of Tamara with a life modeled on hers. Exposing his buried emotions would take Rambo with dynamite, not June Cleaver, and she was fresh out of ammunition. That might be a good thing. There was a risk that a blast of that kind would destroy not only his illusions, but the man himself.

"Where's Alcea?" Back from an overnight journey to Kansas City where he'd spent most of his time sitting on the banks of Brush Creek while the swirl of Friday night revelers on The Plaza went on around him, Dak stepped into the diner. He always felt a mixture of guilt and relief when he slipped away, but he hoped his sporadic absences would eventually make it easier on Alcea when he finally left for good. And not just easier on her.

"She's in back with Florida doing inventory." It was after closing time, and Rosemary was buffing a booth. Her sponge tore on a piece of duct tape, and she flung the pieces aside. "Dang it. Alcea says we'll replace these some day. It'll be none too soon for me. But—can you imagine—she says they'll be in this same red color. Pooh. To heck with tradition—they never went with orange uniforms. And even though Mama Butz always said variety is the spice . . ."

Rosemary's voice faded as Dak pushed through the swinging door to the rear. A murmur of voices came from the storeroom and he moved toward them.

Florida's laughter trilled. "You really hit Stan while you were in labor?"

"So hard his nose bled." Alcea sounded prosaic. "No man should ever tell a woman he knows what she's going through at that particular moment."

While the chatter continued, Dak hesitated outside the entrance. As much as he'd missed Alcea, he'd like to turn right back around. It seemed all he heard anymore was talk about this baby. Of course, since he'd pretty much banned his finances, his book, his past, and their future from their conversations, he hadn't left Alcea with a whole heck of a lot to discuss. He turned his back to the wall and leaned against it. In fact, he hadn't left her with much room to maneuver at all. He hated that she was trying to shape herself to fit his needs.

Because he was quite happy with her just the way she was.

The thought took him unawares and he frowned. He *was* happy with Alcea. Happier, at least, than he'd been with any other woman, including his wife. She demanded nothing of him. She never complained that his writing ate up too much time, never objected when he hied out of town, didn't criticize that his clothing was rumpled or his hair unkempt.

She . . . fit him.

But he didn't fit her. He didn't fit anyone. Face it: He'd immersed himself in the life of a roaming scribe and, right or wrong, he liked his personal space—and plenty of it.

"Florida, are you nuts?" Alcea penetrated his thoughts, her voice a scold. "Give me that crate, sit down over there, and don't you dare try to lift anything that heavy again or I'll ship you straight back to the bank come Monday." There were shuffling noises. "And from what I hear, they'd take you back in a second. Roberta Franks isn't working out as the new supervisor."

There was a moment of silence, then Alcea spoke again, this time with an apologetic tone. "Just call me Mari. I'm sorry. I shouldn't have brought up the bank."

"It's okay." He heard Florida sniff. "I'm just a bundle of emotions, that's all. And when I think about what Stan paid me . . . Sometimes I just wonder how me and this baby'll survive."

Dak frowned. He'd help if his sister needed him.

Alcea seconded his thoughts. "Dak would help you, wouldn't he?"

"But I want to support us myself."

"I guess I can't quibble with that, can I?" There was a pause. "Why *did* you quit with the baby on the way?"

On the verge of entering the storage room, Dak pulled back again, curious about Florida's answer. He'd never understood himself. One of the boneheaded reasons he'd brought up abortion yesterday morning. He needed to apologize for that.

"I— There were reasons. And watching them together was eating up my soul." Florida's sigh was audible clear out here. "What goes around comes around, doesn't it? I guess you felt the same way when you found out about Stan and me." Her voice trembled. "I'm truly sorry, Alcea. I didn't think about how it would hurt you. I only thought about myself. And Stan. I thought your marriage was awful—at least from what he said."

Another pause, then, "Our marriage *was* awful. You— Um, you weren't the first."

"I wasn't? But in this town . . . Why wouldn't I know?"

"Stan was discreet. At least up until the day his mother died."

"And"—Florida's voice was dry—"with me, up until he met Serena. And if I hadn't guessed then, I surely should have known after he—" She stopped abruptly.

"After he what?"

"Nothing. I just wish—"

Alcea snorted. "I've found out wishing doesn't do much good. Neither does praying."

Dak's lips tightened. He hated hearing the pain behind her flippancy.

"You really loved him, didn't you?" Alcea continued.

"Hell of it is, I still do."

"Then it seems we have something in common besides the diner. You've lost your man, and I'm about to lose mine."

A long silence followed, and Dak wished he were somewhere else. Then Alcea sighed. "God . . . aren't men pricks?"

Florida laughed. At the same moment, Dak looked up to see Rosemary pushing rear first through the swinging door, her arms full of dishes. Time to make his presence known or get caught for the lurker he was. He cleared his throat and stepped into the storage room. Alcea and Florida were sitting side by side on a stack of boxes. Alcea looked up and a veil fell over her eyes. Damn, sometimes he wished she'd just let him have it.

"Back so soon?" she said lightly, getting up to give him a peck, her cheek soft against his stubble.

"Couldn't stay away," he said, equally jovial and feeling like a jerk.

Over her shoulder, he saw Florida frown. The frown turned to a grimace. "Ooo." Florida gasped and cradled her abdomen.

Alcea turned around, brows raised. "You didn't start labor with all that lifting, did you?"

"Relax," Florida smiled. "Here, feel."

Alcea dragged him over toward Florida and before he knew what was happening, she'd trapped his hand under hers over Florida's bulge. He felt flutters, butterflies dancing under his fingertips.

Florida smiled up at him. "I swear I'm growing a field kicker."

Alcea smiled, too, but her eyes were on him. An ache had started somewhere in the pit of his stomach—probably the result of the burrito he'd had for lunch. He wanted to pull away, but with both women staring at him, he felt he had to say something. "Great. That's great." His voice sounded hollow.

Florida's glow went out. Alcea turned away, but not before he saw her face. He gave an inward sigh. It shouldn't surprise her at this point to know he wasn't a family man.

She stooped and picked up a clipboard. "You stay put," she said when Florida started to push herself up. "Here." She thrust it in his hands. "You can help me."

Following her to some shelves, he looked at the list while she clambered up on a stool.

"I'll count. You mark the tally," Alcea instructed, then in a low voice added, "You asked her why she didn't have an *abortion*?" Her eyes were dark with accusation, although sorrow lay at their depths. A defense sprang to his lips, but she didn't wait to hear it.

She looked over her shoulder at Florida. "I always wondered what Kathleen would turn out to be. She leaped around inside me so much I had high hopes for the first female champ of *WWE SmackDown*!" To him, she said, "Ketchup, four gallons. Creamer, two cases. Napkins . . ." She poked around. "Florida, we need napkins."

He dutifully noted the numbers. When he looked back up, she was climbing down, her shoulders slumped. "I get so afraid I'll lose her. That at the end of the summer, she'll refuse to come back. I should *never* have promised to let her decide for herself."

It was the same litany he'd heard before, but at the drawn look on her face, his heart gave a little lurch. He opened his mouth, but Florida beat him to it. "If Kathleen should insist on staying with them . . . I don't know if it will make you feel any better, but from what I saw of Serena at the bank, she's not all *that* bad. She was never nasty to me, even though I might have given her a few reasons to be." To him, she added, "Write a note on the bottom about napkins."

That was probably better than the "destiny will take its course" speech he'd been about to offer as comfort. Feeling clueless, he bent his head back to the clipboard. When he looked up, Alcea was looking at Florida with raised eyebrows. "What reasons?"

"Oh, you know . . ." Florida flushed and waved a hand. Looking disappointed at the lack of information, Alcea stooped and pushed some boxes around on a bottom shelf. Florida continued. "But I just hope my child is as talented and pretty as Kathleen. She looks just like you, you know, so sometimes I wonder—" She broke off and her color deepened.

"Wonder what?" To him, she added, "Make a note about needing sugar packets, too."

"I just wonder what mine will look like. What this baby will grow up to be."

"It's hard to tell." Alcea peered farther into the depths of the shelf. "Cake flour, twelve pounds. Alkalized cocoa, five containers." She looked back at Florida. "Kathleen didn't get her writing talent from me, that's for sure. Or Stan. Stan's dad S.R., though, he had some talent. Pop told me he used to write editorials and short stories for the *Daily Sun*." Alcea pushed to her feet. "We've got enough Styrofoam cups to last a lifetime."

"Well, wouldn't it be something if I was carrying another Shakespeare?"

"Oh, God. I hope n—" Alcea glanced at him and colored before turning back to Florida. "I mean, maybe you are. Dak's talent had to come from somewhere, didn't it? So—"

"That's not what I—" Florida broke off again, and looked flustered. "Oh. Of course."

"Of course." Something was dawning across Alcea's face as she watched Florida's confusion. Florida looked like she wanted to hide.

He frowned, trying to tout up the disjointed conversation, wondering at the wheels he could see spinning behind Alcea's eyes.

Before he had a sum, Alcea had knelt in front of Florida and laid a hand on her knee. "I suspected it before, but since Stan and Serena were together before this happened . . ."

Florida's face screwed up. "You must think I'm some kind of s-slut. But I loved him Alcea, I *loved* him."

Alcea gathered her close. "Shhh."

"What in the hell is going on?" He tossed the clipboard down.

Alcea gave him an impatient look. "Florida's baby is Stan's." Her grasp on Florida grew tighter. "Stan played around on me. Then he played around on Florida. And then he played around on Serena."

"It was all my fault!" Florida cried into Alcea's shoulder.

"No, it wasn't. Okay, part of it was. But the man just can't keep his zipper up, and he doesn't care who gets hurt." She pulled back to look at Florida. "And that's why you quit, isn't it? You told him that day at the bank, he said he wouldn't acknowledge the child, and you fought."

Florida gulped and nodded.

"Well, this time he doesn't get away with it. He *owes* that baby some support. He owes *you* some support." Alcea stood up, with that martial look in her eye that he knew meant business.

Florida grabbed at her wrist. "You don't understand!"

"I understand enough."

"No! You can't say anything about it." Florida took a deep breath. "I planned it, Alcea. I seduced him one night when we were working late, and I knew I'd probably get pregnant. I *wanted* to. I thought . . . I thought maybe he'd come back to me if I was."

Alcea hesitated, then her jaw tensed. "That doesn't matter. Maybe what you did wasn't at all right, but what he's done is worse. Love drove you. It doesn't drive him. It takes two to dance the horizontal mambo, and he needs to pay the piper whether he wants to or not. Think of your *baby,* Florida. You grew up not knowing your parents. Does your child deserve to know only one?"

"But that's not all. He told me—" Florida stopped, casting a wild look at Dak.

He interpreted it as a plea for help. "Alcea, if Florida doesn't want anyone to know, I think you should—"

Alcea whirled on him, her frustration clear. "What do you know about it? Maybe you're content without any parents, but most people don't cope quite so well."

"Promise me you won't tell, Alcea," Florida pleaded.

Alcea looked between the two of them, then whipped off her apron. "I have never seen a family so screwed up before." She stomped out of the room, leaving Dak and Florida staring at each other. A moment later, they heard the clank of bells as the outer door slammed.

"She didn't promise," Florida whispered.

"Does it really matter?" He sat down beside her and stroked her arm. "Nobody thinks it was an immaculate conception, and probably more people than Alcea suspect Stan's the father."

She didn't answer. She only looked at him, fear lurking at the back of her eyes.

He patted some more. "She'll go someplace and cool down. And when she's collected herself, I'm sure she'll keep quiet." He wasn't sure at all. When Alcea was on a mission . . .

Florida's expression didn't change. She placed a hand on the side his face. "Whatever happens, please don't leave."

Confused, he frowned. Because from the way she studied him, the fear shimmering in her gaze wasn't for herself. It was for him.

Chapter 18

Last night, Alcea hadn't said another word about Florida or Stan or Dak's damnable lack of understanding. She'd let the banging of pots and pans do her talking for her, unable to summon June Cleaver up from her depths.

Dak had taken her tantrum with his usual aplomb: no comment, no reaction. But for the first time in their history together they'd gone to bed without touching, each rolling a back to the other.

She'd lain awake long after she heard his steady breathing, her ire at everything in general finally zeroing in on Stan. Florida's state of affairs had resurrected every last bit of hurt her ex-husband had dealt her.

So this morning, after lying to Dak about needing to check on something at the diner, Alcea headed to the country club golf course. Stan had always had a tee time at ten on Sundays. If she got there fast enough, she'd catch him in the parking lot. While he might have slimmed down, stopped drinking, and started exhibiting some interest in his daughter, she didn't think he'd changed all his habits. Especially in light of Florida's condition.

Her foot pressed harder on the accelerator until the trees were a green blur out her window, and dust plumed in her wake. Her ex-husband was about to own up. His shenanigans, past and present, stopped right here. Her wheels hit the asphalt of the parking lot. Spotting Stan's Humvee, she whipped into an adjacent place just as he was pulling out his clubs. She slid out of the car and slammed the door.

He looked up and blanched. "What are you doing here?"

"We need to talk." She leaned against her car and crossed her arms.

He dragged his clubs over. "About Kathleen? Call the condo. Serena can—"

"Believe me, this isn't something you want Serena involved in. It's about Florida."

His eyes widened, then he dipped his head and fumbled with a buckle on his golf bag that looked perfectly in order to her. "What about Florida?" he mumbled.

"You know exactly *what* about Florida. She's pregnant with your child. And you've washed your hands of the matter."

He looked up and his dark eyes narrowed. "She told you?"

"I guessed. It didn't take a wild leap. You can't just act like this didn't happen, Stan. You may be a rotten father, but you're the only one that baby has. That child deserves your help—and your attention."

He straightened. "It wasn't my fault! She threw herself at me."

"Spare me. I've heard it all before. And this time I'm not going to hide my head in the sand and pretend it never happened."

"We're not married anymore. This isn't any of your business."

"I'm making it my business. Would you rather be having this discussion with Serena?"

"You can't tell her! Promise you won't tell her." He pulled a cloth from the bag and mopped the back of his neck. "You don't know the whole story."

She wasn't going to promise anything. "Then tell me."

"She did it on purpose. Florida got pregnant on purpose." Stan peered at her like he expected this news to stun her. When it didn't, he added, "She's just like her mother."

"Tamara Jones? What does she have to do with anything?"

"Ah, so you *don't* know everything." Stan leaned back against the Humvee and crossed his ankles. He smiled. "Florida does. And she doesn't want anyone else to know, so you came here for nothing."

She'd heard enough double-talk from Stan to last a lifetime. "What's there to know?" she asked impatiently.

"Just that Florida's mother did the exact same thing. She got pregnant on purpose, thinking she'd trap my dad."

She remembered her mother telling her S.R. had likely hit the sack with Tamara, but there had been no whisper of a baby. "Wait a minute. Back up. You're saying Tamara Jones and your father had a child together?" Alcea examined him for signs he was lying, but she didn't see any eye twitching. "How would you know that? You were only thirteen when your father died."

"Mom told me." He examined his nails. "Before *she* died. Tamara Jones and my father had a fling before he met Mom. Then when he fell in love with Mom, the slut threw herself at him and got pregnant, thinking he'd go back to her. Just like Florida did to me." When he looked up at her, his face was triumphant. "And in case you don't know, the last thing Florida Jones wants is any comparison with *her* mother."

Oh, for God's sake. Bad enough that Florida saw her pregnancy as an embarrassment, but the parallel must have rocked her to her toes. It explained her pleas that nobody find out. "You creep—you told her all that?" Stan's smile was answer enough. "And you think you're so smart because you're blackmailing her with the information. That way you don't have any obligation, Serena doesn't have to know, the town won't know—" She stopped. "Wait. Why doesn't the town know about S.R. and Tamara? God knows they ferret out everything else."

"Nobody knew. S.R. paid her to go off to some relative before the baby was born. He wanted to spare Mom the embarrassment of the gossip."

There were holes in this story. "Then how did Ellen know?"

Stan shrugged. "He told her, I guess. And Mom told me when she found out her illness was terminal. She was afraid the love child might come back someday and claim part of my inheritance, so she wanted me to be forewarned. And sure enough, he did." Stan frowned. "Although if he wants my money, he hasn't said anything. Maybe he doesn't know."

"He?" Omigod. Stan had to be kidding. "Did . . . did Ellen say where the baby was born?"

"Yeah. South Dakota. Dad still had relatives there." Stan looked happy at the expression on her face.

"Dak is S.R.'s son?" Alcea was stunned. "You're half brothers? And Kathleen is his niece?" Good God, how would this news affect Dak? And why hadn't Florida told him if she knew?

"Amazing, isn't it?" Stan was still smiling. "And tell him that if he has any intention of making a claim, my mom's will—"

"He doesn't need your money." She wanted to rake the smug expression off his face. "And none of this matters where Florida's child is concerned. Maybe you'd better measure up to your father. S.R. had the guts to tell Ellen, and I think it's time for you to have a heart-to-heart with Serena."

His smile faded without her having to resort to fingernails. He blanched. "You can't tell her, Alcea. . . . I love Serena. I mean, I really love her."

You know, she actually thought he did. "You have a strange way of showing it."

His face hardened. "Well, before I say anything to Serena—*if* I decide to say anything at all—maybe *you* should have a little talk with the Jones siblings first. Maybe they don't want their mother's *peccadilloes* made public."

Stalemate. She knew Florida wouldn't. As for Dak . . . Who knew what Dak wanted? But it was only right that he know. She watched as Stan picked up his golf bag and walked off. Her only satisfaction was when he stumbled over the curb as if he hadn't seen it.

Leafing through the Sunday paper, Dak looked up from the glider Alcea had unearthed in the backyard two months ago, repainted, and then had him drag to the front porch. Her Taurus turned into the alley. Alcea waved and disappeared around back.

"The prodigal returns," he said to Florida, who was watering some impatiens that Alcea had hung in planters along the rafters.

"It's about time," she said, tugging the hose and moving to the next pot. "She wanted to make a three-layer cake before Kathleen gets here this afternoon. Makes me sorry I said I'd go to Rosemary's for Sunday dinner, but I have a few fences to mend there, so I guess I'd better." She pinched off a dead tendril. "I still don't know why Alcea went to the diner."

He didn't answer, only folded his paper, certain Alcea hadn't gone to the diner and suspecting her actual destination. He flipped a look up at Florida, wondering if the friendship growing between the two women would withstand Alcea's meddling. The banging pots and pans last night had almost been a relief after all the cheeriness Alcea had forced on him the last weeks, but when she'd rolled her back to him at bedtime, he'd felt disgruntled. Before he'd fallen asleep, he'd pondered how to ease the situation but couldn't see a way unless he bought into her feelings. And he didn't. Despite that odd sensation he'd felt as

Florida's baby had moved under his hand, her pregnancy wasn't his concern—or Alcea's.

"I didn't go to the diner." Alcea walked around the edge of the house. The corners of her mouth were tight and the look she tossed him was full of disquiet, not too unlike the way Florida had looked at him yesterday. He shifted against a sudden uneasiness.

Florida glanced over her shoulder. "Where did you go, then?"

"To talk to Stan." Alcea stopped midway up the steps, holding Florida's eyes.

"Oh, God." Florida snapped the sprinkler wand shut. "Don't tell me you—"

"I did."

"So you know about Tamara and S.R.?" Florida dropped the hose and lowered herself next to Dak. The glider squealed and fell silent. "Oh, God," she repeated. "Everything?

"I don't know. *You'll* have to tell *me*."

"What in the hell are you two talking about?" At the mention of Tamara, the sense of uneasiness verged on the edge of apprehension.

Florida ignored him. Her eyes flashed. "You promised. You said—"

"I didn't promise anything. Stan has some obligation here, Florida. He owes it—*you* owe it—to the *baby*." Alcea seated herself on the top step and leaned back against the newel post. "And Dak needs to know."

Florida's face switched from anger to alarm. "No, he doesn't."

"Yes, he does. Tell him."

"Tell me *what*?" Despite his words, he suddenly didn't want to know. The expressions on the two women's faces spooked him. "Look, you got pregnant to get him back. People have done dumber things, and I doubt you raped him, right? Looks like the only person you hurt was yourself, and that's not going to change, no matter how many people know whatever there is to know." He frowned at Alcea. "So give it a rest."

Florida laid a hand on his knee. The gesture smacked of comfort. Why did he need comfort? "Don't forget, I hurt Serena, too. She never did anything to me." Florida flicked a glance at Alcea. "Until recently, I didn't much think about anyone but myself. And Stan." She turned her head to Dak. "And you."

"And me?" He didn't have anything to do with this.

"Yes, you."

Florida exchanged an undecipherable look with Alcea, who nodded while her eyes found his, holding them level as though her gaze could keep him steady. What was going on?

Florida took a deep breath and met his eyes. "You see, when I told Stan I was pregnant, I found out . . ." She faltered and dropped her gaze.

"Found out *what*?"

Alcea waited a beat, then spoke softly. "She found out that Stanley Randall Addams—Stan's father—was your father, too."

Bewilderment shoved him back in the glider as Florida's hand tightened on his knee. "S.R. Addams was my father?" he whispered. The idea that his father had a name rocked him even without the added knowledge it had been someone from this very town. "I— How—" His gaze darted between the two women, then settled on Florida. "Why didn't you tell me?"

"I didn't know how you'd take it, and I didn't want you to get hurt." Her voice lowered to a murmur. "I didn't want you to leave."

"Why would knowing hurt me?" He aimed for nonchalance, but it *did* hurt. In the maelstrom of emotions that were swirling through him, one thing stood out. Tamara had lied. She'd lied by omission. There wasn't just a father he could have put a face to a long time ago, but, my God, he was related to Stan. And to Kathleen. He looked at Alcea.

Alcea sighed. "It might hurt, because there's more."

"No, Alcea, don't tell—" If Florida could have popped out of her seat, she would have. As it was, she struggled to lean forward.

"No more secrets, Florida." Alcea pleaded with her. "This doesn't just affect you and Dak and your child. It affects Kathleen, too." She looked back at him, took a breath, then spoke in clipped sentences, as though brevity would make it easier to swallow. "According to what Stan learned from his mother, Ellen, Tamara had the same plan Florida did. Tamara loved S.R. He loved Ellen. Tamara thought if she got pregnant, S.R. would leave Ellen. So she got pregnant. But he didn't leave Ellen. Instead he shipped Tamara off to South Dakota to have the baby. To have *you*." She slumped back against the post. "End of story."

"Yes, end of story." For unknown reasons, Florida looked relieved. He remained silent, trying to let the information soak in. Florida sat back. "So can you understand why I don't want anyone to know? It's bad enough Tamara was my mother. The fact that I behaved just like her is something I'd rather keep quiet."

"Hold on," Dak said, thinking his mother must have had her reasons for not telling him about his father. Good ones. He *knew* her. "Maybe it should give you a better understanding of Tamara. She only did just what—"

Alcea rode over his words. "But, Florida, you can't keep this quiet! It's not fair to your child. And it's not fair to Kathleen." She motioned at Dak. "He's her uncle, and she deserves to know that. And your baby—that's Kathleen's half sister or brother. In fact your baby has a whole damn family in the O'Malleys because of the connection. Don't you want your child to know it? To know us?"

Florida looked stricken. "There is that. . . ."

Dak sat forward. Things were playing out way too fast. His mind couldn't quite wrap itself around what it was learning. But he did know one thing. "I have a say here."

"What?" Both women spoke in unison.

"Right now only the three of us and Stan know about my—my paternity, right?" He couldn't force out the word *father*. "So what *wouldn't* be fair is telling Kathleen and asking her to keep it a secret. Or realistically, even expecting her to, no matter what she might promise."

"Why does it have to be a secret at all?" Alcea's face tightened. "True, there's Serena to consider, but wouldn't it be better—in the long run, anyway—for her to know, too? And if Stan blabs about S.R. and Tamara—and I'm not sure he will; it's his father they'd be gossiping about after all—that all happened almost forty years ago. These kids—Kathleen and Florida's baby—deserve clean slates, no secrets."

"Are you done?" Dak glared at Alcea, and she winced. He'd never spoken to her like that before, but she was pushing too hard. "Before *you* decide anything, could you remember this is my life, too, that we're talking about? I need time to *think*."

Alcea's lips pressed together. "Then go on. Go *think*."

Without another word, Dak got up and went inside, slamming the door behind him.

Several hours later, he'd joined Alcea in the kitchen. Kathleen would be here soon. Florida had left for Rosemary's with only a brief admonition to him not to decide *anything* until she returned. From his bedroom, where he'd lain on his bed with his hands knotted behind his head, he'd heard Alcea slam things around. But now she was quiet, her frustration at him apparently spent.

Or so he thought before she thrust some plates in his hand, her eyes hard as mahogany. "Would you set the table?" She spoke pleasantly, but with an edge.

He found he welcomed it. It would make what he needed to do easier if she was still upset with him.

He'd reasoned everything out. His father had to be somebody. Did it really matter if he was a scion from Cordelia or a South Dakota drifter? Not in the grand scheme of things. S.R. Addams was long dead, and considering his lack of interest in his son's life—in Tamara's life—Dak hadn't missed much. But still, the knowledge of his paternity sat uneasily on his shoulders. As did the knowledge he had a half brother (that he didn't like) and a niece (that he did). He'd never wanted a family, and now relatives were popping out of the woodwork.

Laying the plates on the table, his gaze moved up Alcea's straight back, over the fall of hair across her shoulders, the proud chin with the soft skin underneath that he'd kissed so often. It would be tough, but it wasn't fair to her to continue this way. It wasn't good for him, either. Whether this place was ready for sale or not, it was time to call a halt. Tonight. He wanted out before things got more tangled up than they already were. He needed to sort out his head, and he couldn't do it with Alcea sucking him deeper into her family.

"So what did you *think* about?" Alcea spoke without looking at him. "And when will you tell Kathleen she has an uncle?"

"I'm not telling her. I'd appreciate it if you didn't, either."

Alcea turned around, her eyes flat. "You're just going to ignore the connection? With Stan, too?"

"What's the point?" On the other side of the table, he put down the last plate and looked at her. "Alcea, you know I won't be here forever. What difference will it make to Kathleen or Stan if I'm related to them?"

Alcea turned her back, and when she spoke again her voice was soft. "I couldn't care less what impact it has on Stan. But Kathleen adores you, and she'd be thrilled if she knew."

"She won't be thrilled when she understands it may be another twenty years before I come back." He gripped the back of a chair and gentled his voice. "Or it may be never.

"I still think Kathleen should know." He could tell she was crying, although she was making an effort to keep it out of her voice. "Are you afraid I'll insist you have some obligation to her?"

"No. All I'm saying is Kathleen and I already have a friendship. Whether I'm her uncle or not, that won't change anything."

"Right." She banged a broiler pan on the counter.

"Alcea . . ." Today's events had almost overwhelmed him. They'd overwhelmed her. He'd like to take her in his arms and lead her upstairs and hold her. But he couldn't. He couldn't even think of anything to say to ease her distress. "So you won't tell her?"

"No, I won't tell her." Alcea turned around. Despite the glisten of tears, her chin went up. "I wouldn't hurt Kathleen by telling her she has an uncle who doesn't want her."

"Don't twist things around."

"If anything's twisted here, it's you."

They stared at each other. The door buzzer sounded.

"Must be Kathleen," he said, looking away first. "I'll let her in."

Glimpsing Kathleen through the door, his heart lightened, warmed after the chill in the kitchen. He supposed part of it was fueled by the new knowledge they were related, but the fact was, he'd always liked Alcea's daughter. He could admit her admiration stroked his ego, but he really did enjoy the time they spent together. She took him for what he was and didn't try to figure him out.

"So did you have a fun time at Daisy's last night?" he asked as they walked toward the kitchen. There'd been a slumber party, if he recalled right.

She shifted the package she held in her arms and shot him a look. He realized his voice had been overly hearty. "It was way cool. But wait until I tell you what happened. Way *more* cool." Her voice was high and excited. She pushed past him into the kitchen.

Alcea turned around, her fake cheerfulness fully back in place. "What's up?"

Kathleen twirled around. "I got a letter yesterday from *Carousel* magazine. They publish kid stories and stuff, and they really liked the one I sent them, and they're going to publish it and pay me a whole sixty-five dollars!"

"That's terrific!" Alcea swiped her hands on her jeans, then pulled Kathleen into a hug.

Kathleen leaned back, smiling at her mother. "I wanted you to be first to know. I haven't told anyone else yet."

"Not—not even Serena? Oh, sweetheart." Kathleen stirred uncomfortably as Alcea teared up. Alcea must have noticed. She sniffed once, and then her voice turned brisk. "So, how are you going to spend the money?"

Kathleen pushed away. "Is that what you think I'm excited about?"

"Why, no." Alcea stammered. "Not just that. I know you're excited about getting your story published. I just—"

"No duh. And they could even publish it for *free*."

Alcea threw him a desperate look, and he stepped in. "I guess my editorial skills have finally been confirmed. My opinion of your writing validated." He knew by Alcea's expression he was overplaying the jocularity. He settled for hugging Kathleen's shoulders. He *was* proud of her. "Way to go, kiddo."

She pushed the package at him. "I got this for you. As thanks for helping me."

Alcea beamed, and Kathleen rolled her eyes. "What? It's not like I never do anything nice. It's just that you never notice."

Dak waited for Alcea to retort, but she didn't answer. She just studied Kathleen with a thoughtful expression.

"So what's this?" Wanting to sweep the tension under the rug, Dak turned the package over in his hands. "Can I open it before we eat the feast your mother's prepared?"

Kathleen looked at the steaks marinating on the counter, the twice-baked potatoes ready for the oven, and the three-layer cake cooling on the counter. "Oh, Mom, you didn't have to make such a big deal out of a Sunday afternoon visit." But Kathleen looked happy that she had.

"I must have known there'd be a reason for a celebration. Besides, I need to make sure you remember your poor old mom when you're rich and famous."

Kathleen's grin widened. "Do you think one day I really will be?"

Alcea nodded. "I'm sure of it. You have everything it takes. Talent, determination, smarts . . ." Her voice softened. "Plus, you're a *very* nice person. I promise to keep that in mind."

Dak watched as a look passed between them, and suddenly felt a boy's aching for his own mother. For a father. He gave himself a mental shake. It was just the day, that was all.

"Well," Alcea said. "Why don't you two skedaddle outside to the patio and let Dak open his present. I'll finish getting things ready."

Glad for the dismissal, Dak followed Kathleen outside and took a seat at the table. He watched while she followed suit, carefully tucking under the miniskirt she wore, fluffing out her hair. Maybe there was something of the bloodline they shared in the slant of their eyebrows or their noses or . . . He halted his thoughts. This was ridiculous.

"So are you going to open your present?" Kathleen gestured at the package.

He'd forgotten he was holding it. He turned it over

in his hands, trying to remember the last time anyone had given him a gift. Unexpected emotion stuck in his throat, but he managed to flash her a smile before he ripped off the paper. It was a journal. Leather-bound, and much fancier than the spiral notebooks he usually used.

"Do you like it?"

"It's something. Really something."

He ran a hand over the leather, and his mind suddenly flashed back to a time when he was seven, maybe eight. Occasionally, Tamara would pick up workbooks and give homeschooling a try. She usually lost interest before they'd gotten very far. But various people they'd encountered had taken pity on him, picked up the slack, and he'd learned to read and write. He couldn't get enough of it. Often he begged Tamara for scraps of paper, pencils, books. . . . And then one day, she'd tossed a Big Chief tablet at him. He remembered catching it before it hit the floor. With wonder, he'd rubbed his hand over the smooth surface, just like this. "Here," she'd said. "Maybe this will keep you out from underfoot." His hand stilled. That couldn't be right. He hadn't been the one always underfoot; that had been Florida. Except . . . Florida wasn't born then. And pity? Why would anyone feel sorry for him? He'd lived the kind of Tom Sawyer existence anyone would envy.

"Is something wrong?" Kathleen was frowning at him.

"Nothing's wrong." He rubbed his thumb along the spine. "It's the nicest journal I've ever owned."

"I thought so. I've seen that stack of junky spirals."

"Much nicer. Thank you, Kathleen. I'll treasure it." Like he had the Big Chief notebook. He shook his head and laid the journal aside, along with his thoughts of the past. "So, what have you been up to?"

"A new story. Do you want to hear about it?" He nodded, and she filled in the details, then frowned.

"But I can't seem to make it come out right. Do you ever have that problem?"

"I'm having it now. The Cordelia manuscript isn't coming easy."

"Writer's block." Kathleen gave him a smug look. He hid a smile. "Sometimes I get that when I try to make the words work the way *I* want to, rather than just let them come out the way *they* want to. That's sounds lame, doesn't it?"

His smile died. It didn't sound lame. "You're further along than you know. And it's not just the writing itself. Sometimes I have problems progressing with a current manuscript if ideas for something different won't leave me alone." He hesitated, not really wanting to discuss the new idea that had dogged him mercilessly. But Kathleen looked so eager, he relented. "I have some thoughts for another book that are tripping up my efforts on the one I owe my publisher."

"I know what you mean." Kathleen nodded sagely. "What's the idea?"

"I, uh, don't like to tell. It interrupts the process." True, but that wasn't the real reason.

"Oh, c'mon. Can't you even give me a hint?" She wheedled. "Please?"

"Okay, okay." He gave a dramatic sigh, and she grinned. "It's a love story." A love story. Jesus. "Nothing like anything I've ever written before." Also not completely true. It was very much of the same ilk that had produced *Torn,* and he never wanted to go there again. Briefly, he outlined the story he couldn't shake—without revealing the person who had inspired it—watching the expressions flitting across Kathleen's face, so like Alcea's when he'd first met her. Suddenly, he was struck by the realization that this could be the last time he'd enjoy Kathleen's companionship. Once he'd severed his relationship with her mother, Kathleen might not have the opportunity—or the desire—to continue their friendship.

Yet . . . she was his niece.

He abruptly stopped and stood up. "I'm hungry, aren't you? I'll go snag some peanuts."

Kathleen touched his arm. "Um, before you go, could I ask you something?"

He looked down at her. A tiny line marred her smooth forehead. "About a new story?"

"No . . . It's personal." She looked down and picked at the wrapping paper on the table. "And I don't have anyone else I can talk to."

Uneasily, he sat again. "Not your mom? Or Serena or your dad?" *My half brother.*

"Especially not them. You see . . . Serena and my dad are planning to get married soon. I don't think my mom knows yet."

"I don't think that's a problem." Especially since, if Alcea revealed the paternity of Florida's baby—hopefully after he was gone—there likely wouldn't be a marriage. "I know your mother and Serena have had their differences, but I don't think she'll be upset."

But Kathleen was shaking her head. "That's not it. They're going to build a house. And they want me to help plan it because . . . because they want me to live with them. Permanently."

"Well, that's nothing new, is it? They want you, your mom wants you. Kind of a nice position to be in." Although he himself had never experienced it. A bitter taste flooded his mouth, and he swallowed.

"But . . . I just kinda thought I'd go back and forth, you know? Like maybe I'd stay with them for a while, and then maybe with my mom. I didn't think this would be, like, a *forever* kind of decision." She sighed. "But Serena says she wants to adopt me. She says I have to decide one way or the other."

Oh, Christ. If this marriage came off and Serena made a push for adoption, Alcea would go nuts. He tried to focus on Kathleen, not her mother. "And what do *you* want?"

"I—I'm not sure. I like it with them, and they'd

have a pool, and I'd have a suite of rooms—that's what Serena calls it. But I know it would hurt Mom if I did it." She sighed again. "How do I decide?"

"Maybe look at other things. Like who can teach you the most about life. My mother . . ." He faltered a moment, then plunged on. "My mother taught me a lot."

"I thought you didn't have a mother. I mean, I know you *had* one, everyone has one, but Mom said your mother left you." He frowned, and she hurried on. "I'm sorry. Maybe I shouldn't bring that up. It must have, like, hurt a lot."

God, had it hurt. The strength of the thought startled him. Well, of course it had hurt. At least until he'd thought it through.

Kathleen was frowning. "Are you okay?"

"I'm fine." He'd always been fine. *Always*. "It's true my mother wasn't around later, but she did teach me a lot about life. I think you're better off with your mother. In fact, I know it." The last words were uttered with such force, Kathleen looked surprised. He was surprised himself. "I mean, you're only fifteen."

"Isn't that the same age you were when your mother left? And you turned out fine."

She was right; he had. "But a, uh, girl needs her mother."

A *child* needs his mother. And his father. His head churned with barely remembered feelings, with the memory of the last time he'd seen Tamara. Gold sun glinted off gold hair as she'd walked away. Leaving him with the understanding he didn't even have a father. His fists knotted. "Why did you move in with your dad in the first place? Why didn't you stay with your mom? Was it all about money?"

She blinked at the harshness in his voice, but she did exactly what Alcea would do. She pushed out her chin. "It's not like I haven't thought about it. That therapist and I have talked about it. And . . . and, like, I can admit it was partly the money. I mean, would you want to live *there*?" She motioned at the Pink Palace.

"I would have lived anywhere if—" He stopped, aghast at himself. He tempered his tone. "So it wasn't just the money. What else, then?"

She looked away. "Mom and I weren't getting along. Sometimes we still don't. I . . . Well, she was just so stupid about the divorce and about the house. I mean, I know my dad cheated on her. But, like, he'd done that for years, so why did she stay with him all that time? And why leave him when she did—why not stay until I was older?"

"Maybe she tried all those years, maybe for you—but then she reached a point where she just couldn't take anymore. Aren't there times when you feel that way? Like you've just flat run out of patience?" That's what had happened with Tamara. She'd loved him. She had just reached a breaking point.

"Maybe you're right." She plucked at the paper. "I would *so* not stay with a boyfriend that cheated on me. But what about the house? I hear Dad and Serena talk. Mom couldn't afford to keep it even right after they got divorced. But she didn't do anything about it. She didn't get a job. She didn't move us someplace else that would have at least been better than that." A nod toward the Pink Palace. "She didn't even *think* about what people, my friends, would say. She couldn't *face reality*." He heard an echo of her therapist behind the words. Her eyes darted to his, then away. "Maybe she still can't."

He knew she was thinking about his relationship with her mother. Just like with Alcea, he'd never let Kathleen think his stay would be forever. "Kathleen, look at me. Whatever is going on between your mother and me doesn't matter. Your mother has met more challenges in the last four months—hell, last few years—than many people face in a lifetime. She's going to make mistakes—she's human. Look at what she *has* done. And think about *her*. As a person, not just as your mother." He was back on safe ground again. That's what he'd always done with Tamara. "Everyone does the best they can. Whether it's as good as what someone else could do is a different matter. But nobody sets out to do a bad job. And she's never intentionally tried to hurt you. In fact, she saw keeping that house as a way to protect you."

Just like Tamara had protected him. *Of course.* That was it. She'd known it would be harder on him to know he had a father who couldn't be bothered with him, rather than believing his father was some fellow who had briefly passed in and out of Tamara's life. His felt his brow clear. But Kathleen looked more perplexed.

"Give it some thought, and maybe you'll figure out what I'm trying to tell you. Don't just write her off. Every kid needs a mom." And Alcea certainly needed Kathleen. If Kathleen decided to stay with Stan and Serena, Alcea would be . . .

Alcea would be free.

"Or . . . or maybe you'll decide you're happier with your dad." He felt like a jerk, even minimally encouraging Kathleen in that direction, but the idea that had just risen in his head was too tempting to resist. Suddenly, he decided to postpone his talk with Alcea.

Kathleen frowned at him, but before she could say anything else, the back door banged open. "Come and get it," Alcea called.

As he stood up to follow Kathleen, his words echoed back at him. *Every kid needs a mom.* He'd lied. Not every kid. After he'd turned fifteen, he hadn't. Maybe Kathleen didn't either.

Through dinner, Alcea wrapped her mouth around a smile and encouraged a stream of chatter from Kathleen, afraid if there was a lapse she'd slap Dak silly. Or collapse into a sodden heap. Dak's none-to-subtle reminder he'd be leaving—and probably soon—had been a blow coming on top of everything else that had happened today. And now she had caught some undercurrent between Kathleen and Dak that she didn't understand and was too tired to figure out.

In fact, she was glad when the doorbell rang before she'd served dessert, indicating Kathleen's ride home had arrived. After her earlier encounter with Stan, she wasn't surprised when she opened the door to Serena. It only took a glance at the woman to know Stan hadn't told Serena a thing. In pink shorts and top, Serena glowed from her glossy dark hair to her shiny green eyes. "Stan had a meeting, so he asked me to fetch Kathleen."

Right. A meeting on Sunday. Alcea swung the door open without comment and led the way to the kitchen. While Serena and Dak exchanged small talk, and Kathleen bagged some books she was borrowing from Dak, Alcea wrapped a wedge of Kathleen's cake on a paper plate, grudgingly adding enough for Stan and Serena.

Smoothing the wrap, she turned around. "Here you—" She stopped dead at the naked hunger on Serena's face as she watched Kathleen. Serena turned to her with a smile, the look gone so fast, Alcea thought she'd imagined it. Given her present frame of mind, she probably had. She handed the plate to Serena. "Dessert."

"That's so sweet of you." Serena smiled.

She returned a tight smile and trailed Serena and Kathleen to the door. Kathleen hugged her and slipped out, but Serena hesitated in the doorway. "I have something I want to talk to you about. Are you free tomorrow?"

"I'm at the diner all day, and I have an obligation tomorrow night." At least she hoped Dak would still be here. She smiled sweetly. "If you'd like to see me, though, I'll be at the bakery at four thirty tomorrow morning."

Serena didn't even blanch, dang her. "Four thirty it

is." She pushed open the door and waved over her shoulder. "Toodles."

Alcea stepped out onto the porch and crossed her arms, watching until Serena's brake lights flashed around the corner. Behind her, she heard Dak rattling dishes as he cleared the table. She hadn't a clue what Serena wanted to discuss. It could be anything from Kathleen's therapist to Kathleen's schedule. But somehow she didn't think it was anything that mundane. Dread wrapped an arm around her shoulders.

Chapter 19

The next morning, Serena showed up promptly at four thirty. By five thirty, she'd scurried out the door in the face of Alcea's anger. And Alcea was left to manage the rest of the day with her dread realized.

Trying to put the conversation out of her head, she set herself on autopilot and attended to all the demands of her business, for the first time enjoying none of it. She snapped at customers, snapped at Rosemary and Tansy, and bit off Florida's head for lifting another crate. The clock ticked with all the speed of a tortoise on Valium. Finally, closing time arrived, and to her great relief Dak appeared to walk her home. She hadn't been sure he would, even though last night after Kathleen had left, they'd cleaned up the kitchen in an uneasy state of truce. She'd been too weary to do more than mention Serena's request for a meeting, and Dak had looked beaten over the day's revelations. But when they'd gone to bed, they'd surged together, holding each other with a sense of desperation, not making love and not talking, both alone with their thoughts. Hers had been unbearable. But didn't hold a candle to how she felt now.

Insisting she'd close up alone, she shooed everyone out, including Florida, clapped the placard to CLOSED and leaned her back against it. Dak watched her, his expression bemused.

"How *dare* she waltz in here and tell me what's best for my daughter?"

"I take it Serena kept her appointment."

Alcea pushed off the door, rounded the counter, and picked up a spatula. "She most certainly did. She informed me she and Stan were getting married, they plan to build a house, and she wants to adopt Kathleen. And, get this, she was quite certain I'd just say *yes*! Like Kathleen didn't already have a mother. She wants us to make the decision for Kathleen. Said decision, of course, in favor of Stan and Serena."

He nodded.

She waved the spatula. "The nerve of the woman!"

"The nerve," he agreed.

Furiously, she scraped at the grill. " 'I know you'll agree, Alcea,' " she parroted Serena, " 'that she'll have more advantages if she's living with us.' " She threw down the spatula. "To hell with her and her advantages! Kathleen is *my* daughter. I'm the one that raised her. I'm the one who wiped her nose, and read her bedtime stories, and went to five thousand PTA meetings, and four hundred teacher conferences, and three goddamned Girl Scout camping trips where I got poison ivy . . . every . . . single . . . time." She realized she was crying, and it made her more angry.

"So what did you tell her?" Dak studied her with a thoughtful expression she couldn't fathom. Damn his composure. This wasn't the time for *calm*.

"I told her to get out. I told her I'd never agree. That Kathleen would never agree. But, Dak, I don't know what Kathleen wants. And I'm so afraid she'll want *them* and their goddamned house." She dashed at her tears, bent her head back to the grill. "I should have just told Serena about Stan and Florida and been done with it," she muttered.

"Why didn't you?"

She turned around. "Because of you. Because of

you and Florida. And not wanting Kathleen to be hurt because you . . . God, I'm so confused!"

Dak moved around the counter. Gently prying her fingers off the spatula, he pulled her against him. "It sounded to me like Kathleen was uncertain about what she wanted."

Lost in the comfort she'd looked for all day, his words took time to penetrate. She pulled back. "*Sounded?* You knew? You knew about the marriage, the house, the *adoption,* and you didn't tell me?"

His silence was answer enough. She flung herself away. "That really blows, you know it? It's one thing to keep everything about yourself secret, but this is about *me*. My life!"

"I would have thought," he said quietly, "that this was about Kathleen's life, too."

"Quit splitting hairs, dammit. You know what I mean."

"Look, Kathleen talked to me confidentially. I couldn't betray her trust."

"To hell with trust!"

"And I know it's a surprise."

"More like a fist in the gut."

He pulled out a chair and sat. "If you don't calm down, we can't discuss this."

"For God's sake." She followed him. "What's to discuss? Serena wants Kathleen. I want Kathleen. And she's better off with me. End of discussion."

"But does Kathleen agree?"

"She's fifteen. I don't care what she wants," she mumbled. But she did. Although sometimes she wondered if she shouldn't just forget her promise and stamp her foot and insist on her way. But how could she drag Kathleen off to the Pink Palace and expect they'd both live happily ever after? She flopped down in a chair next to him. "Okay. Maybe she's too big to order around. So what do I do?"

"Maybe you shouldn't do anything. Maybe you should let things fall where they will."

She stared at him. She'd waited all day for his advice, and this was all he could offer?

"Don't look at me like that." A line furrowed his brow. At least it was a hint of emotion, even if the irritation was directed at her, not at Serena. "All I'm saying is maybe you should consider what Serena has suggested."

"I should—? You *are* nuts. You think I should give up my daughter?"

"Not give her up. Let her choose, like you promised."

"Well, we all know what choice she'll make, don't we?" Alcea tasted bile. "Serena's right. She would have more advantages with Stan—monetary ones. Not the things that are important." She narrowed her eyes. "Is this your way of telling me Kathleen has already decided to stay with them?"

"She doesn't know what she wants to do."

"I need to talk to her." Alcea made to stand up.

Dak put a hand on her arm. "Cool down first or you'll get nowhere."

She jerked her arm away, but sat back down. "You're right. I'm a mess." She rubbed a hand over her face. "What did you mean, I should consider Serena's suggestion? What exactly has she offered besides a bigger house, a swimming pool, a *suite* of rooms, for God's sake?"

Dak hesitated, then held her eyes. "You could look at this from a different perspective. From your perspective."

"I believe that's exactly where I'm looking at it from." Exasperation colored her voice.

"If you knew Kathleen was safe—and happy—like she has been for the past four months with Serena and Stan, wouldn't that be . . . liberating?"

"Liberating?" She frowned. "Speak plain English."

"You'd be able to do whatever you want."

Her frown deepened. She glanced around the diner. "I *am* doing what I want."

"You could go with me."

The words fell between them. For a moment she couldn't speak. He wanted her with him.

But only on his terms.

Her outrage broke through. "I can't believe you'd ask me that."

He frowned. "This is the first time I've wanted anyone with me. I thought you would—"

"Be happy? Delighted to leave everything I've built? To leave my family? Kathleen?"

"If you don't want to go, just say so, but you don't have to yell." The flicker of hurt that flashed across his features only maddened her further. His selfishness was astounding.

"Don't have to— Do you realize what you're asking?" Unable to sit still, she jerked to her feet. "Of course you don't. You're flawed, Dak. You're incapable of understanding maternal love because your mother—"

"Leave my mother out of this."

"Face reality! Your mother abandoned you and—"

A muscle leaped in Dak's jaw. "She didn't abandon me. She had to be true to herself. I understood that. I still do."

"Play the music you hear, huh? Well, she was completely tone-deaf. A mother doesn't just abandon—"

"Quit using that word."

"—her children and traipse off because she just feels like it. She damaged you, both you and Florida, like it or not, and you can't face—"

Dak's chair clattered back. He stood, fists on the table, and leaned toward her. "I've faced that what I want out of life is different than normal. I have Tamara to thank for that, not blame. She gave me an understanding that—"

Alcea leaned right back. "An understanding that doesn't include the knowledge that when you love someone, you don't ask them to choose between you and someone else. I already chose once between you and Kathleen today. I could have told Serena what I knew. It might have guaranteed Kathleen would end up with me, but instead I thought about you."

He interrupted. "I never said I loved you."

"Why would you think—" She stopped and sucked in her breath. "What?"

"You heard me."

"Then why . . . why would you ask me to go with you?"

"It was . . ." His gaze fell off hers. "It was just an idea." He shrugged back into his composure. "If it's not going to work, then okay, it's not going to work."

"You . . . you . . ." Alcea couldn't find the words to express the fury that rose in her throat. "You're unbelievable. You can't even admit . . . Dakota Jones, look me in the eyes. Look me straight in the eyes and tell me you don't love me."

His head rose and he gazed steadily into her eyes. That same muscle quivered once more in his jaw, then fell still. "I don't love you."

There was a moment of silence. Alcea felt like someone had just ripped out her insides. Tears threatened behind her eyelids but she refused to release them.

She poked her chin up. "Then get out. Get out of here. And get out of my life."

He flushed but turned toward the door. It was only after he'd slammed it behind him and she'd rushed forward to lock it that she let the tears fall.

The afternoon sun had reached its zenith when Alcea raised her head. It was over. The day she'd dreaded hadn't crept up in bittersweet moments but had fallen on her like a cast iron skillet. She shoved back her chair and scrambled to her feet. To hell with him, then. He could return to his wandering waste of a life, but she had responsibilities, commitments, and her own life to lead. She grabbed a mop and a bucket.

As the sun splashed into sunset, she scoured the diner. As dusk muted the square and the streetlamps flickered on, she attacked the back room. By the time night pressed full against the windows, her fury was spent, the diner gleamed, and she moved to the bakery, where she lost herself in the familiar rhythms of measuring and mixing. Occasionally, the ring of the phone broke the silence, but she ignored it.

Near midnight, she stepped back from a row of apple coffee cakes cooling on the counter and wiped a forearm over her brow. While she'd scrubbed and straightened and baked, she'd thought and remembered and finally her mind had gone blank. But now the events of the day crowded back in. Serena. Kathleen. Dak . . .

She didn't want to think about him. He was selfish beyond words, and she'd already wasted four months on him. Still, she felt a flicker of regret at the words she'd hurled. She shouldn't have brought up his mother. Wearily, she gathered her belongings, let herself out, and turned toward home. Home, where nobody awaited her. The night air was cool but heavy.

Expecting to see Cowboy's shrouded in darkness, she was surprised to find lights glazing the windows and a figure moving on the front porch. Thinking it was Dak, her heart caught in her throat. She would have faded into the alley that led to the Pink Palace, but before she could, the shadow came toward her.

"Alcea, thank God!" Florida, not Dak. Alcea floundered between disappointment and relief. In the wash of lamplight, Florida's face was unnaturally pale. "Where's Dak?"

"I don't know." *Nor do I care.* "What on earth are you still doing up? Something wrong?"

"Wrong?" Florida's laugh held a tinge of hysteria. "Nothing's wrong. Everything's just hunky-dory. Dak only tore in here looking like death hours ago, jumped in his Jeep, and took off. And you didn't come home at all. Did something happen? Did you tell—"

"No, I didn't tell Serena." Alcea sighed, took Florida's arm, and steered her toward the house. "And I'm sure Dak's fine. He takes off all the time."

"Not like that, he doesn't. He didn't take anything. Not his duffel, not his laptop."

Alcea felt a trickle of unwanted concern.

Florida shrugged off Alcea's hand. "And where were you? I called the diner. I've called everywhere!"

"I just . . . had some things to do."

"Did y'all fight? Is that it?"

"Florida, calm down. You've worked yourself up. I'm fine. I'm sure Dak is fine, too." But despite herself, she frowned.

"You're *not* sure." Florida's voice held a note of triumph. "Alcea, you need to find him. I've never seen him like that."

"Don't be ridiculous. Even if I thought he needed to be found, I wouldn't have the slightest clue . . ." But her voice trailed off and she wondered.

Florida pounced on her hesitation. "You think you know!"

Again she tried to guide Florida up the porch steps, and again Florida pushed her hand off. "If you won't go, at least tell me where to look."

Oh, she'd like to. She'd like to hand the whole thing right off to Florida and go to bed and forget Dak ever existed. But if Dak was where she thought he was, Florida would never make it. She looked at the mulish set of Florida's chin and realized she'd either have to go look or spend the rest of the night arguing with her. "All right. I'll check out the one place I've thought of, but if he's not there, we both go to bed. Deal?"

Florida smiled. "Deal."

From where he sat on the railed ledge of the water tower, Dak felt he could see halfway across the continent. Only the knowledge he'd be dumping a pile of problems in Florida's pregnant lap had kept him from heading there seven hours before. The feeling of responsibility irritated him. His gaze swept over the stars pinpricking the black sky. Somewhere nearby, an owl hooted. A half-moon night. Bathed in its soft blue haze, Cordelia slept under the sentinel of the church steeple. Just a few lights glowed from windows, and only a few cars sped along the highway. As he watched, one vehicle separated itself, making a turn onto the dirt road that led to the tower.

He knew who it was.

Alcea's decision stung. He'd known his idea was only half-baked, but he'd screwed up his courage. . . . His thoughts stopped. Courage? He'd simply thought traveling with her would be fun. No big deal that she couldn't go. And maybe for the best, if she thought his offer had implied a lifetime commitment . . . or that Tamara had a bearing on their relationship.

He shifted and looked at his feet. Clad in sandals, they were only shadows against the earth. Twenty years ago from this same spot, he'd wiggled his tennis shoes and they'd looked like moths fluttering in the darkness. That night she'd arrived unannounced by headlights. He'd heard her before he'd seen her, and had scrambled to his feet, his heart pounding in his chest. When he'd finally glimpsed the intruder to his nighttime aerie, her hair gleaming near-white in the moonlight, he'd almost fainted with relief. It was just a girl from his high school. Alcea O'Malley.

Spotting him, she had inhaled sharply, then stumbled. He'd grabbed her wrist, surprised at the fragile feel beneath his fingers. Which was at odds with the haughty look, dark eyes flashing in the moonlight. "What are you doing here?"

"I was here first." He dropped her wrist and sat back down, hoping she'd leave.

"But I've been coming here longer."

He hunched his shoulders. It was a childish exchange, and he couldn't argue with her last statement, anyway. She knew he was a transplant. Everyone did. He'd never fit in. Nor had he tried. She settled herself within six feet of him, and he frowned. At least she could have moved to the other side of the tower. For a while, they both stared at the view, resolutely ignoring each other until silence grew more uncomfortable than conversation.

He spoke first. "What do you think about up here?"

Without hesitation, she pointed to a hilltop where a white house stood tall, solitary, and whitewashed by the moon. "I want to live there someday."

"That's all?" That figured.

"Of course not." She tossed her hair back. "I think about who I'll marry. And how many children I'll have. I want to raise a family. In that house."

A family. A home. He heard Tamara's breathy laugh and shifted uneasily. "But what about *you*?"

"What do you mean, what about me? That *is* about me. I'd be a wife, a mother, and I'd put a garden right there . . . and a swing set over there. I'd have a kitchen bigger than my mother's, and when my kids came home from school, there would be fresh-baked cookies. Or maybe a cake three layers tall. And when my husband got home from work . . ." She continued in this vein, and he watched the light play over her features. He couldn't relate to her fantasy, yet his stomach churned with yearning, familiar for years, yet unnamed until she'd put words on it. It made him feel disloyal. To his mother . . . to himself.

A wind sprang up. Its rush rode over her speech and he moved closer, until only inches lay between them. He wanted to hear. At the same time, he wanted to clap his hands over his ears. She didn't pause, and he finally interrupted. "Seems to me that's all limiting yourself to doing what other people expect."

All around him, his fellow seniors were preparing for college or marriage or work. Like her, they were so certain. Did they realize they had choices? They were stifled by convention. But sometimes he envied them, and despised himself for doing so.

These weren't the normal musings of a boy his age. He knew it. But he wasn't normal, and he took pride in that. His life—or at least the one he'd lived with Tamara—had prepared him for something exciting. Something different. Something beyond the confines of his grandfather's narrow house and his clingy little sister. But sometimes, when he watched parents applaud their children's efforts at the St. Andrew's Christmas Eve Pageant, or walk with linked hands along the town square, or, like now, listening to Alcea O'Malley chatter on about the family she envisioned . . .

He realized Alcea had stopped and was staring at him. "What do you mean, I'm limiting myself?"

He shrugged. "It takes a husband to be a wife. And children to be a mother." He glanced at her. Usually, he didn't care what other people thought, but he was suddenly afraid she'd think he was weird. But her brows were knit, not raised in amusement. "I mean, is that enough? Don't you want something that's just for yourself? That you can be without anyone else?"

He expected her to roll her eyes, but instead she pondered his question. "I've never thought about it that way." She sounded shy, no longer full of self-assurance. And suddenly he knew the self-assurance was only skin deep.

It made him feel closer to her, so he tried to explain. "Is what you want all tied up in what you think other people want you to do?"

"Part of it, I guess." She tilted her head. "Do people want you to do certain things . . . I mean, after you graduate?"

He frowned. His grandfather had never said anything. His sister was too young to care. And his mother . . . Well, Tamara wanted him to follow his heart, of course, just like she had. A sense of isolation hit him. He shifted and his arm brushed hers. It was warm, smooth. And it suddenly struck him that he was a boy, she was a girl, and they were alone. "I don't think I want anyone to expect anything from me. Because . . . Well, listen. If there wasn't anything stopping you, if nobody cared what you did, and time or money weren't a problem, what would you do?"

Without losing a beat, she blurted, "I'd be a baker." Her voice was too loud. She looked startled. He was, too. He'd expected her to say *movie star* or *model.* "I just like it, is all," she muttered. "But it's stupid, isn't it? Even my littlest sister thinks I'm dumb to spend so much time in the kitchen."

"It doesn't sound stupid if that's what you like."

"Then that's what I'd be." She gave him the same look he'd just given her. Like she was afraid he'd think she was strange. When he just waited, she finally said, "It's just . . . well, you take all these things—sugar, flour, spices—that aren't much by themselves, and maybe you follow a recipe, or maybe you don't. It's better if you don't. Like"—she hugged her knees—"I tried lemon juice instead of all milk in the sponge cake last week. Everyone thought it was great. It's like being an inventor. Or a magician. Even my mom can't bake as well as I can. But she says I won't get rich that way."

"And that's important to her?"

"Not really." She hesitated. "I guess she thinks it's important to me."

"And is it?"

"Well, everyone wants money."

"My grandfather always says to use the brains God gave me and everything will turn out okay. Maybe it's the same kind of thing . . . using the talents you're given." She looked skeptical, and he tried again. "I mean, if you're happy, does money really matter?"

He expected her to say "Of course it does," but she scrunched her nose in thought. She had a cute nose. "My mom says money doesn't buy happiness. And you're saying if you're happy . . ." She shook her head and giggled. "I'm getting all mixed up."

She had a nice laugh, too.

"Then why don't we talk about . . ." He culled his

mind for what she'd be studying in her English class. ". . . Steinbeck?" He grinned.

She shot him a look to make sure he wasn't serious, then smiled back. "How about home ec?"

But they didn't talk about that, either. For the next two hours, while the constellations shifted over their heads, they talked about lots of things, although he shied from questions about his childhood. Nobody ever understood that. Finally, she leaned back on her hands, dropping her head back to study the stars. He did likewise.

She turned her head to look at him. "You're different, Dakota Jones."

He met her gaze and their eyes held. "Different how?"

"Different nice."

She leaned toward him. He leaned, too, until their shoulders touched and their faces were so close together her two dark eyes had merged into one deep pool. Her hair brushed his cheek.

And he kissed her.

He'd shared a few kisses before, but never had lips felt this soft. His hand moved up to her neck to hold her head steady when he kissed her again, and again after that, but other than his fingers brushing the smooth skin at the nape of her neck, he didn't touch her. He wanted to, but . . . but soon he'd graduate and leave Cordelia.

They shared warm kisses until dawn glowed beneath the blanket of the night sky, acting like an alarm. Laughing, they'd scrambled down the ladder, then had headed off in separate directions, without any promises. Her, he'd suspected, because she'd thought the course of their immediate future was implied. Him, because he'd already known they didn't have one.

Back at school, they hadn't seen much of each other. Over the next week—in the cafeteria, an assembly, in the schoolyard, he'd glimpsed her. Holding a question, her eyes would meet his above the heads of the popular crowd she was always a part of. But he had made no attempt to approach her. It was too late. He'd shrugged. Such was life. Then had come that time in the cafeteria. She'd shunned her crowd. He'd shunned her. And just like that, it was over.

Dak shifted his gaze from his sandals to the car that pulled up underneath him. The headlights blinked off. Alcea got out, looked up, and headed for the steps.

Just like this, it was over.

He sat silent while she ducked under the railing and settled herself near him. Not too close, not too far away, just like that first time.

"Florida's upset, worried about you. You need to go home."

He tamped down the unexpected disappointment she hadn't said something else. "I'll leave in a minute."

"And then you need to leave for good." There was no question in her voice.

"Yes." He shifted. "I never meant to hurt you, Alcea, I just—"

"Don't. You don't need to explain. It's just . . . the way you are. I shouldn't ask you to be what you're not." She took a deep breath. "And I shouldn't have said some of the things I said. About your mother. I had no right . . ." Her voice grew bitter. "You gave me no right."

He ignored her comment. His earlier feelings had exploded out of nowhere and he'd examine them later, not now. "I still want you to come with me." He looked at her.

"I . . ." Emotions played across her face, anger not the least of them. But it was resignation that won out. "You know I can't. Maybe that's why you asked." She looked at him straight on. "You know what? I don't like Shakespeare."

He didn't feel like smiling, but his lips quirked, anyway. "I know."

She gave a satisfied nod, and some of the tension between them relaxed.

He swept his gaze across the horizon. "I'd forgotten how much I love this view."

Alcea was silent, then she blurted, "Of course you love this view." Like that time long ago, she leaned back on her hands, face turned toward the sky. Angry tears glittered in her eyes. "It's how you like everything."

"What do you mean?"

"From up here, everything is at a safe distance. Reality never intrudes."

"I've made my peace with reality, Alcea," he said gently. "It's just not a reality most people understand."

She shook her head. "You aren't at peace. You should read *Torn*. It's all there."

"You read that?" He was startled. When she didn't reply, he just shrugged. "That book was a piece of postadolescent garbage. Fiction, not reality."

Her smile was grim. "You've never seen reality, Dak. You spend only enough time in one place to fall in love with it, with the people, maybe even with a woman. Then you leave before your fantasies are tarnished. You leave before leaving is hard."

She was wrong. "Leaving you will be hard."

"I know." She sighed and got to her feet. She stood there a moment, looking down at him. "But that's only because you stayed too long."

He watched her go, watched her shadow climb into her car, watched until her taillights merged with the distant lights of Cordelia.

Then he looked out at the spot in the distance where the highway escaped into the hills. And waited for the siren song of the road to thrum once more through his veins.

But all he heard was the hoot of the owl.

Chapter 20

By mid-August, summer's hand lay heavy on Cordelia. The atmosphere was saturated. Birdsong had given way to the hum of air conditioners and the constant drone of locusts. As he stepped out the back door of Cowboy's house near four in the afternoon, Dak's skin went damp. The Realtor he was escorting grimaced. Monica Pratt had swept her unnaturally blond hair on top of her head, but with extra pounds and a red power suit bundled on her frame, the heat must be overpowering. Still, she didn't pause in the sales-patter voice she'd used on him for the entire time they'd toured Cowboy's house and garage.

"Like I said, the buildings seem sound—we'll know more at inspection—but there are some repairs you still need to take care of before we put it up on the market."

She ticked off things on her lacquered fingernails, and he sighed. Finding help more reliable than the Jackson brothers around here wasn't easy. When he and Alcea had parted two weeks ago, he'd hoped that by now he'd be further on his way to leaving Cordelia than this. He'd tried to dispel his images of Alcea, but reminders of her were all over the place. Hell, *she* was all over the place. He'd never had a woman stick in his head like this. Probably because he'd always said good-bye on one day, then left the next. But this time . . .

He felt mired, unable to move forward, unwilling to go back.

Still looking back at him, Monica continued. "The cosmetic updates you've done so far are nice, but you'll need to do more if you want to sell fast, even though we'll price it slightly below market, just like you want." She didn't look happy at his insistence on that point.

He shrugged off the memory of Alcea humming in the next room, painting the parlor while he worked on his book, and just nodded. With the way his manuscript on Cordelia was going—or not going—his time would be better spent with a toolbox anyway.

Monica turned around and hauled in a breath. "What is *that*?"

Dak followed her gaze. Kemp Runyon's Lincoln Town Car sat in front of the Pink Palace. His mouth tightened. "It belongs to a friend of my tenant."

"I don't mean the car, I mean that *thing*."

"Oh." He flushed at his mistake. "The trailer. There's one tenant. No lease. The new owner can keep it there, or I'll help move it, get rid of it, whatever." He tried not to feel a pang for the time he'd spent under that corrugated aluminum roof.

Monica pulled out a pad from the briefcase draped over her shoulder and jotted a note. She capped her pen, looked once more at the trailer. "If it stays, it has to be painted."

"I like it pink."

She looked at him like he was nuts. "Then at least an allowance for paint to the new owner."

He nodded. Once he was quit of here, what did it matter?

Her gaze raked the acreage. "Nice-sized property. We'll need to have it surveyed, and you'll have to clean out all the scrap. And take down that badminton net."

Alcea had unearthed that old net from under the

trailer. Kathleen and her friends sometimes used it. "Fine."

His voice was shorter than he'd intended, and she gave him a sharp look. "Sorry. Sometimes I get too caught up in the 'talk' and forget sellers have feelings." She gave his arm a maternal pat. "Making these changes is hard. It helps if you just concentrate on where you'll be going." Her eyes sharpened further. "Have you bought anything yet? If not, I've got . . ." She started rattling off her listings.

"I'm not staying in Cordelia." Nor had he formulated any idea of where he'd go next. Instead of beckoning him, his future seemed to yawn emptily. He gave a mental shrug. Whenever a book was a struggle, everything was a struggle.

Monica wore an oh-well-I-tried expression. "I think I've seen enough. I'll contact a surveyor. Let's get these papers signed. You can get back to me when you're ready for market."

He followed Monica into the kitchen. She plopped her briefcase on the table and began pulling out forms. He turned to close the door and saw Kemp and Alcea emerge from the trailer, Kathleen trailing behind them. They paused to talk next to the Lincoln. Kathleen leaned against a pole on the carport, gaze idling across the yard. His niece.

When she spotted him, she straightened and waved. "Dak! Hey, Dak!"

Both Kemp and Alcea turned his direction. Embarrassed for the second time that day, he waved back to Kathleen, then firmly shut the door.

Monica was bundling the now-signed forms back into her case when Florida came in the front door. "Whew! It *is* a hot one." She entered the kitchen, tugging on the front of her uniform. As she'd increased, she'd borrowed one of Rosemary's, but even that one wasn't going to wrap around her for much longer. "Whose car is in the—" She stopped short when she saw Monica.

He introduced them before escorting Monica out. When he returned, Florida had poured two glasses of iced tea and had taken a chair. She'd scooted it back, but her abdomen still brushed the table. She pushed a glass at him. "So y'all are really going to do it."

Groaning inside, he sat. "It will still be a while." He didn't want to talk, but he knew a discussion was overdue. Florida hadn't said anything about Alcea in the last two weeks, although she had to know. Even if Alcea hadn't told her, there was the fact he now went to bed alone every night. "Lots of repairs to do yet. And, Florida, I've told Monica we need to leave the close date open-ended for now. We'll make sure you have a place first."

"I suppose I should be grateful for small favors, hmm? Maybe I should get with this Monica and see what kind of shack I can afford."

"I've wanted to talk to you about that."

"Then why didn't you? I've been around." Her tone was waspish.

He held on to his patience. As her pregnancy had advanced, Florida's tolerance had vanished. He couldn't blame her. New business. Single motherhood . . . No home.

"I want you to take the money from the sale. I don't need it. You do."

"Thanks bunches." But she didn't sound grateful.

He frowned. "You said you didn't want this place."

"I don't. Big old money pit. And my memories here aren't the best."

"Cowboy did—"

"The best he could. If you tell me that one more time, I'm gonna punch you."

"It's true."

"Right." She set her iced tea down hard. "He did the best he could. Peg did the best she could. But none of it mattered, Dak. I wanted a mother."

"Tamara did—" He broke off when she glared at him.

"No, she did not." She looked down at the mound in her lap. "I haven't even birthed this child, and already it has me wrapped around its little finger. There's no way in hell I'd ever drop it off with some relative and go my merry way. Let alone do what she did to—" She bit her lip.

"To us?"

"No. Yes. I just meant . . . She was selfish. Purely selfish. We were a bother, and she didn't want to be bothered."

"She only—"

"Oh, shut up." Florida leaned back, eying him. "You've defended her ad nauseum. Which is a laugh, coming from you. And I've never bought it."

What did she mean, *coming from you*? "But she didn't abandon us, not in the usual sense."

"She ran away. Just like her mother ran away from her. Some legacy, huh? Because you're just like her. Do you want to know what she did? She—"

Temper flashing, he stood up. Florida winced. "I'm not like her. I'm not—" He halted, aghast. He *was* like Tamara. And it had always made him *glad*.

"Okay, okay," Florida soothed, although her face was tight with frustration. She ran a finger along the condensation on her glass. "But you've changed, haven't you, since you came to Cordelia?" She looked up at him. "And none of this Monica stuff is making you happy. Maybe you should examine how and why."

"Just leave it alone, Florida."

She hesitated. "Then promise me something, Dak. Promise me you'll come back. At least to visit."

He didn't want to make promises he didn't know that he'd keep. "Florida, I've made a lifestyle choice. That's all it is. It has nothing to do with anyone else."

She blinked back tears. "My mother abandoned me, my grandfather died, Peg just died, I'm about to have a baby . . . and now you're running off." When he didn't respond, she slammed down her glass. "Shit. Why don't you just leave now?"

He started.

"I'm serious. I'll handle all this. Just pack up and go."

"Don't be ridiculous. You need—"

"I don't need *you.* And whatever else I need, Julius or Alcea will help me." She stood up. "I'm beat. I'm going to lay down." She paused in the doorway. "You know, you're hurting a lot of folks. Like it or not, people around here care about you, even though you don't know how to return the favor."

He watched until she'd rounded the newel post, feeling unutterably weary. What was it with everyone? Just yesterday, he'd run into Jon and Lil on the square as she was closing up her bookstore. Lil had been courteous for a few heartbeats, then she'd turned her back and busied herself with checking the door, although he suspected she knew it was already locked.

Jon wasn't nearly so restrained. He walked Dak a few yards away. "Hell, I would have bet money Alcea would hold on to you."

He was annoyed. "I didn't want to be held. That's no secret."

Jon had shook his head. "I don't think you know what you want, man. But it's all for the best. I sure don't think you're what Alcea needs."

Remembering that encounter, he wondered why so many people *expected* something from him. In the next moment, he was nettled that nobody really appeared to *need* him. Christ. No wonder nobody understood him. *Or do they?* a small voice whispered.

He rubbed a hand over his face. When and how had life become so complicated? Ending things with Alcea should have provided him with a clean break. Instead it seemed their parting had only made things more difficult.

Chapter 21

With the end of her relationship with Dak, Alcea's life hadn't become more difficult, but after spotting Monica Pratt on his porch step, it *had* become hectic as hell. Seeing the hard-nailed, blond evidence he'd leave soon, her unremitting buzz of anger toward him fueled a frenzy of work through the dog days of summer and into September. It also went a long way toward hiding her heartbreak.

She threw herself into her job and the daily rhythms of Cordelia. Peg O' My Heart now sported a new coat of paint, and she'd added apple tarts to her bakery menu after first testing their success at the diner's booth during the town's Apple Festival. When Paddy O'Neill went in for knee replacement surgery, she organized a mix of Peg's regulars and Kathleen's classmates to spell each other at his Emporium so it could stay open. And after the usual spate of rowdiness during the week before school started, she spearheaded a drive to scour the spray-painted stop signs, strip the toilet paper from trees, and rescue the cigar store Indian off the water tower. She hadn't been the country club benefit queen for nothing.

One evening a week, she watched Patsy Lee's kids; on another, she took accounting lessons from Florida. She experimented with recipes and acted as guinea pig for Rosemary's hairstyling experiments. She even volunteered to organize the O'Malley Fall Birthday

Celebration. She shanghaied her daughter, Melanie, and Daisy into helping with it all. On one memorable occasion, they'd hidden out, giggling, until Rosemary could get the antidote for a highlight that had turned the shade of Daisy's green eye shadow. On another they'd traipsed to the DMV. Kathleen had emerged with her learner's permit, but Alcea felt even more smug than her daughter. She'd thought of something for Kathleen that Serena had overlooked.

By the start of school, Kathleen still hadn't decided where she would live. Serena apparently had abandoned her plan to force the issue, probably afraid Alcea would scratch out her pretty green eyes. Through August, Alcea's hopes had risen her daughter would choose the Pink Palace. Then Serena had lavished Kathleen with a whole new school wardrobe, and Kathleen's allegiances had shifted again, although this time her reasons had nothing to do with her new Doc Marten shoes.

One of her new skirts had needed a hem, so she'd brought it to Alcea. When Alcea had learned it was one of a gazillion new garments, and that Kathleen was still waffling, she'd spouted something about bribery before she could bite off her words.

Instead of retreating into surliness, though, Kathleen had tried to explain. Hair curtaining her face, she'd fingered the skirt as Alcea had stitched. "It's not the things she buys me, Mom. It's . . . She's so *needy*. She wants children, in the worst way, and she can't have any."

Alcea remembered Kemp's remark when they'd encountered Stan and Serena at the country club last spring. "Something to do with a miscarriage?"

"Yes. And she was only in high school, not much older than me. "Isn't that *sad*?"

"It is, but these things happen." She tried to look sympathetic, but wasn't sure she succeeded. Material goods *and* emotional blackmail. Great. She stabbed the needle into the fabric with so much force she pricked her finger.

"And sometimes I think Serena will just die if I leave." Kathleen peeked out from behind her hair. "I don't know what to do."

Alcea put down the needle and thread. "So you'd like me to tell you? I think you know what I'd say."

Kathleen bit her lip and looked away.

"Sweetheart, Serena is not going to *die* if you leave, no matter what impression she's given you. You know how much I want you here with me, but if I started begging, wouldn't that be just as bad as what Serena is doing?"

Kathleen moved impatiently. "She's *not* doing anything bad, Mom."

Afraid arguing with her would just push Kathleen, into the very decision she didn't want, Alcea stifled her opinions on manipulative people. Instead she leaned over and brushed the hair back from Kathleen's face. "Well, you think about it. You're smart and you'll figure it out. Just remember, what's best for you may not be what other people want you to do." Oh, *God*. She couldn't believe she was parroting Dak's philosophy.

With a calmness she hadn't been feeling before, she'd picked up the needle again and had directed the conversation elsewhere, leaving Kathleen looking thoughtful.

And that had seemed to be the last real thought Kathleen gave the matter. Over the summer, the boys had grown taller and more mature. As she swept into her debut as a sophomore, Kathleen experienced a new popularity. Joey Beadlesworth had even called the trailer twice. Her Saturday nights were filled with parties and movie dates and giggling about boys with her cousins. Hating to spend Saturday nights alone, Alcea increasingly accepted Kemp's dinner invitations.

Kemp had darkened her doorway only a few days after she'd resisted the temptation to hurl Dak off the water tower. He'd picked up right where they'd left off, as though they'd never spent four months apart, and now they saw each other as often as twice a week. She went out with him because it was easier than coming up with excuses not to. And, with him, she could pretend those months had never happened.

While she'd avoided Dak for a while, it wasn't long before she'd decided avoiding him demanded more energy than he deserved. He was her landlord. He lived yards away. He was Florida's brother. Instead she adopted a formal tone whenever they encountered each other. And he responded likewise. She could act as though nothing had ever happened between them.

Unless her guard was down.

Occasionally, she'd glance out her window, and there he'd be. Working shirtless in the yard, clearing scrap or fixing a gutter or mending a screen. Mesmerized, she'd catch her knuckles against her mouth, wanting him so much she thought she would scream. And then she'd turn away, raging at herself for her stupidity. She'd bake something or clean something or run to the diner on an unnecessary errand.

By the time the O'Malley Fall Birthday Celebration had come and gone, she sported dark circles under her eyes, but she didn't care. The more she had to do, the happier she was. Or if not happy, at least too exhausted to lie awake missing the sound of Dak's breathing.

But as the last days of September passed, her remaining patience waned. The longer Kathleen lived with Stan, the more likely the arrangement would become status quo. And the longer Dak stayed, the more probable it was she'd end her days in a padded cell.

She wanted a decision from Kathleen. She wanted Dak to leave. Then she could quit feeling like a hamster on a treadmill and mold her life into some semblance of normally.

On the last Friday of September, Alcea locked the diner behind her and straightened from what she was afraid had become a permanent slump. She started toward home, reminding herself that tonight she had something to look forward to. Tomorrow she had a rare day off, and Kathleen was spending this weekend with her. She lifted her face to the sunshine splashing over the square. They had to attend parent-teacher conferences this evening, but tomorrow she'd give Kathleen those driving lessons she'd promised. Serena had yet to top that learner's permit.

The growl of an engine sounded behind her, and she turned just in time to see a big honker of an SUV hit the curb. Adrenaline had her flattened against the side of a building before she realized it had stopped. Heart hammering, she pried her fingernails out of the wall, stepped toward it, and gaped. Kathleen's pale face looked back from above the wheel.

The passenger's window purred down and Serena sparkled at her. Since that morning in the diner, Serena had retreated into charm as though the confrontation had never happened. "Hop in! We were on the way to your trailer." She leaned over and gave Kathleen a playful tap. "Naughty girl. I'd wanted to go to the conference, but she insisted you needed to be there."

Kathleen gave her a weak grin.

Miffed that Serena was giving her daughter the driving lessons she'd wanted to, Alcea allowed herself to be mollified by the idea that Kathleen had chosen her, not Serena, to talk to her teachers.

Alcea hoisted herself into a backseat as big as a theater, noting Kathleen's hands were clenched so tight on the wheel they'd need a crowbar to pry them off. "Isn't this a bit much for a new driver?"

Kathleen put the car in gear and eased off the curb using start-and-stop brakes. Alcea hastily wrapped the seat belt around herself.

"Oh, I hope not." Serena smiled over her shoulder. "When I found out Kathleen was learning to drive, Stan and I just couldn't wait to pick up this little honey. It's hers."

The words took a moment to sink in. "You've got to be kidding." Alcea would clench her teeth, but she was afraid with all the bucking they were doing, she'd bite off her tongue. "Off-roading be damned. You could go to war in this thing."

Serena frowned. "Stan says it's the best car on the market."

"Maybe it is, but—" Alcea looked up at the rear-view mirror and caught Kathleen's half-panicked, half-pleading glance. Alcea softened her tone. "But it's so big," she finished lamely. Obviously, Kathleen didn't want or need her mother and Serena having a show-down on Main.

"Isn't it?" Serena chattered away, ticking off the car's many features and the cost of each one. With each tick, Kathleen's face grew whiter. By the time she'd bumped into the drive at the Pink Palace, sweat had beaded on her forehead.

Out in the yard, Dak carted scrap over to a Dump-ster that had appeared last week. Seeing him, Alcea felt the usual pang. It did nothing to improve her mood. As they piled out, he shaded his eyes to look in their direction. When his gaze met hers, he dropped his hand and returned to his work.

"Kathleen, why don't you go tell Dak about your new car?" Alcea caught hold of the sleeve of Serena's pink sweater and steered her toward the trailer. "There's something I need to discuss with Serena."

With a grateful look at her mother, Kathleen made a beeline toward Dak.

"Ouch." Serena pulled out of Alcea's grip. "I'm not going anywhere. I have something I want to talk to you about, too."

In the trailer's living room, Alcea didn't wait to hear what Serena had to say. She pitched Kathleen's bag onto a chair, and turned with her hands on her hips. "What in the hell were you thinking buying a car like that for a fifteen-year-old who doesn't know how to drive?"

"Stan liked the idea." Serena's voice was tentative. She rubbed her arm. "And Kathleen adores it."

"Stan doesn't have a clue where kids are concerned, and Kathleen hates it."

"She said she loved it."

"Of course she did! She doesn't want to hurt your feelings." *You idiot.* "Did you see her face? It scares her to death."

A line furrowed between Serena's eyes. "I thought—"

"No, you didn't think. At least not beyond how you could sway Kathleen into staying with you. This is just like that absolutely insane school wardrobe. Quit trying to buy my daughter!"

"That's silly, Alcea." Serena's laugh was breathy. She avoided Alcea's gaze. "Maybe I overindulge her sometimes, but—"

"And quit loading her up with your sob stories."

"What are you talking about?"

"About how you got pregnant in high school and miscarried and all that rot. You're confusing her."

"Those aren't sob stories!"

Alcea tempered her tone. "Look, Serena. I'm sorry for your loss, I really am, but it's not right to use your past to manipulate my daughter. Do you really want her to stay with you just because she feels sorry for you?"

"She's happier with us!"

"No, she's not. Even if she doesn't know it yet, it takes more than a suite of rooms and designer labels and Cadillac Escalades to make someone happy. She needs a secure home with people who love her."

"We love her. *I* love her. You can't tell me I don't!" Serena's voice trembled.

"Not enough to put her needs over yours. This *car* just proves it."

"But I treat her like I would a—a sister."

"She doesn't need a sister. She needs a mother. And she already has one."

"I know that." Serena looked around wildly. "But—

but, one that's working all the time and lives in a stupid trailer and has a screwed-up love life." She licked her glossy pink lips. "And—and I'd bet a judge would agree with me."

Alcea stared at her.

Looking fearful, Serena poked her chin up. "I mean, if I tell Stan I want your custody arrangement changed, he'll do it."

Serena's voice had a ring of bravado, and Alcea wasn't sure the Pink Palace and her past relations with Dak were enough to sway judicial opinion—or Stan's, for that matter—but she damn well knew she couldn't marshal the funds to defend herself against a bevy of high-priced attorneys. "You—you . . ." She advanced on Serena, who retreated a step. "You just try it, and I'll bring up Stan's questionable moral record."

"That was all before my time."

"Then tell me why Florida Jones is carrying his child." As soon as she'd uttered the words, she wanted to call them back, but it was too late.

Serena looked stricken.

Alcea peered more closely.

But she didn't look enraged.

"There is that," Serena admitted. "Stan wouldn't want anyone to know, although I've tried to convince him he needs to take an interest in the baby." She looked at Alcea with chagrin. "I wanted him to adopt it, but he won't do it. He says he doesn't want to claim a relationship with an ext-ext-extortionist."

Mouth open, Alcea dropped onto a chair and stared at Serena.

Serena patted her hand. "But don't worry. I'll work him around so that he'll give Florida some money every month. We can afford it, and I know how hard it is to be a single mom." Her face looked sad. "Even though I never got the chance."

"You know about Florida?"

"Of course I know. He told me a month ago. And

now we're seeing my therapist. I think we'll get things all worked out."

A therapist? *Stan?* He really *did* love Serena. Another thought hit her. "If Stan told you Florida was trying to extort money from him—"

"Oh, no. Not Florida." Serena perched on the sofa. "Florida's mother."

"Tamara is extorting money from Stan?" She thought the woman was dead.

"Was that her name? No, not from Stan. She took money from Stan's father, S.R."

"Oh. That." Stan had said S.R. had shipped Tamara off to South Dakota. He must have paid for her expenses. "But that's not blackmail. Or extortion."

Serena's eyes rounded. "It most certainly is. Stan's parents paid her to give them Dak. She took the money and disappeared."

Alcea blinked. "Let me get this straight. After Dak was born, Ellen and S.R. planned to adopt him. So they paid Tamara for the baby, and then she took off?" She wasn't surprised at Ellen's role, or that she'd agreed to mother the boy. She would have done whatever S.R. wanted, and *she'd* always wanted more children.

Serena fluffed her pageboy and beamed at Alcea like she'd just aced a test. "Yes."

Alcea turned the knowledge over in her mind, wondering what this would mean to Dak and Florida. It was disturbing to know Tamara had denied Dak a normal childhood. Knowing Dak, though, he'd scoff at *normal.* And it sounded like when it had come right down to it, Tamara couldn't hand him over. At the time she was young, desperate, undoubtedly penniless, and maybe still in love with S.R. Addams. He'd probably broken her heart and then bullied her into agreeing to give him Dak. It sounded like one more reason for Dak to canonize his mother. It shouldn't bother either of them.

She brought Serena back on task. "About Kathleen . . ."

"Oh, I almost forgot what I wanted to talk to you about. Our therapist has suggested a long cruise to the Caribbean. We're leaving for three weeks on Sunday. So could Kathleen stay with you?" Serena squinted down a hallway. "I mean, if you have room."

Did the woman think Kathleen slept under the trailer on her overnight visits? "Of *course* there's room for Kathleen. Does she know?" What a great break.

"I didn't want to tell her until I was sure you did have a place for her. She has a lot of things." Serena still looked dubious. She turned and looked at Alcea. Something of Alcea's determination to make sure her daughter never left here must have shown in her face because Serena's eyes narrowed. "But when we get back . . ."

"When you get back, we'll let Kathleen decide." By then she should have Kathleen thoroughly brainwashed. "But until then, no more bribes. And no more talk of judges."

"Oh. Oh, of course not." Serena dipped to pick up her purse, her sweep of hair falling over her face, but not before Alcea saw the gears clanking away. Serena was likely trying to figure out how she could convince Stan to go to court. The woman had no honor. Her best hope of keeping Kathleen was convincing Kathleen this was where she belonged.

Serena straightened. "Um, you won't tell anyone else about all this while we're gone, will you? Stan wouldn't like it."

"I won't." Except for Florida. Florida could decide what to tell Dak. "As long as you keep your promise about extravagant gifts."

Serena bit her lip and the two women stared at each other. Stalemate.

When they went outside, they found Kathleen and Dak talking near the Escalade.

"Nice car," he commented, glancing at Alcea with his brows raised.

And without a warning to prepare for how his eyes could turn her insides to jelly, her defenses crumbled. She averted her head before he saw her longing. "Kathleen, looks like you'll be spending some time with me. Your dad and Serena are going on a trip." She wasn't going to waste a minute. "Why don't you hop on in the car and you can collect your things before we need to leave."

Kathleen's eyes narrowed. "I thought you said I could decide."

Dak leaned against a pole of the carport, hands pushed into his pockets.

"That hasn't changed, honeykins." Serena gave her an indulgent smile. "We'll be back in a few weeks, and then you can make up your mind whether you want to stay with us. By that time the house should be framed, so you'll have a better idea of what you can expect." She caught Alcea's glare and stammered. "Or you can stay here." She looked at the Pink Palace with an expression that said after three weeks here, Kathleen would beg to go back.

Kathleen nodded slowly. "Okay, then. We'll go get my stuff." She tugged the keys out of her pocket, looked at the car with a deep sigh, and sidled toward it as though it would bite. Alcea turned up the intensity of her glare.

Serena frowned, then her brow lightened as she caught her drift. "Why don't I drive?" With a look of relief, Kathleen passed her the keys.

When they'd pulled out of the drive, an awkward silence descended. Alcea crossed her arms. No time like the present. "She knows Stan's the father," she said bluntly.

"Did you tell her?" Dak asked.

"Yes. No." He arched a brow, and she sighed. "Okay, I did. But for a good reason," she added before he could berate her for spilling secrets. "She threatened to take me to court for custody of Kathleen. But she already knew." She drew a breath, prepared to tell him the rest, but he was already talking.

"If she'll go to that extreme with Kathleen, will she try to take Florida's child?"

"I don't know, but I don't think Stan—"

"Because if they do try, we'll fight them." The fierce light in his eyes and the word *we* surprised her. "They could never prove Florida wouldn't be a fit mother. She'd be better than—" He broke off.

Alcea hesitated. "Better than Tamara?" She braced herself for his reaction, but again he surprised her. Emotions struggled across his face, and she felt hope. Then his features smoothed. She wanted to swear.

"Not better . . . different. But a good mother." His voice turned firm. "Just *like* Tamara."

She didn't respond, wondering that he couldn't hear the defensiveness in his voice, feel the challenge in the look he directed at her. Even if Tamara had snatched Dak out from under S.R.'s nose, the woman had abandoned him later. She decided she wouldn't tell him what she'd learned from Serena. He'd twist it into further evidence of his mother's sainthood, and she didn't think she could stand to hear it. Both were busy with their own thoughts for a moment, Alcea staring at the fresh paint on Cowboy's house, Dak studying the clouds.

"Are you lea—?"

"I saw Kemp—"

They both spoke simultaneously. Alcea flushed. "You first."

"So you're dating Runyon again?"

She gave him a sideways glance. As usual, he looked for all the world like her answer didn't matter. But she recognized that stillness and felt a twinge of glee. The existence of Kemp Runyon back in her life bothered him. Good. "We go out, yes."

For a moment she thought he'd let the subject drop,

but he shifted a little, then said, "Maybe he'll be good for you."

Maybe he'll be . . . Alcea's temper flared, but she held herself as calm as him. "Maybe he will," she agreed.

She thought of her last date with Kemp. They'd exchanged a few kisses, apathetic, at least on her part. Kemp's breathing had grown heavy, but she'd broken off with a plea of indigestion. Which wasn't far off the mark. She knew Kemp was edging closer to expecting some kind of commitment, but she hadn't thought about it much. She was intentionally too worn out for much thinking, and it was easier to just let happen whatever happened. That sentiment sounded so much like Dak, it made her even more angry.

Dak stirred. "So what was your question?"

"When *exactly* are you leaving?"

He frowned at the exasperation in her voice. "I'm pretty close to getting things wrapped up, but—"

"But *what*?"

"But I'm thinking I'll stay until Florida's baby is born. It's only a little over a month."

Good God. Another month? She got to her feet. "Kathleen will be back soon. I need to start supper."

As she stalked into the trailer, she was conscious of his frown on her back. And it wasn't until she'd let herself in and slammed the door that she realized something. It was totally unlike Dak to postpone his departure. He was doing it for Florida.

Wow. For once he had thought of someone else's needs first instead of his own.

Chapter 22

On Saturday, Alcea wasn't thinking of fulfilling anyone else's needs besides Kathleen's. And those seemed to hinge on a suite of rooms. Rain drummed on the roof as mother and daughter stood side-by-side in Kathleen's bedroom at the Pink Palace.

"This place is so *small*," Kathleen groused, staring at her closet. Things were so packed in, the door wouldn't close. Out in the addition, the dryer churned, filled with more of Kathleen's clothes.

"You won't need your summer things for a while. I'm sure Florida will let you keep them over there." She bit her lip. Kathleen didn't see the love she'd put into decorating this room, only the size. Convincing Kathleen might not be the slam-dunk she'd thought it would be.

"And if I stayed here, then what? They're *moving*."

"And we'll have to, too. By then, the bakery will be turning more of a profit, and I'll be able to afford a bigger place." She hoped. There were still things the business needed, like that pesky interruption insurance Florida kept on about.

"It couldn't get any smaller." Kathleen pulled out a book and flopped on the bed.

Alcea watched her uncertainly. "Don't you want a driving lesson?"

"Not in this stuff." To punctuate her words, a grumble of thunder sounded. She opened the book and tossed aside the paper that had marked her page. It fluttered to the floor.

"Maybe later?" Alcea stooped to pick up the scrap, looked around for the wastebasket, and saw it buried under a pile of shoes. She sighed and stuffed the paper in her pocket.

"Later I'm going to Daisy's. Where they have real closets *and* two bathrooms."

Things were bad if Kathleen was envying the tumbledown farmhouse where Patsy Lee and her kids lived. Alcea folded her arms. "Don't you think you should ask me first?"

"Serena doesn't make me ask *her*. She says I can do what I want as long as I tell her where I'll be."

Alcea pressed her lips together. This first day was *not* going well. She tried to find another topic. "What are you reading?" God might give her a break and have it be something she'd read.

Kathleen flipped her book cover-side-up. Alcea started. "Where did you get that?"

"It was in the dryer." Kathleen's brows went up.

"I, uh, wonder how it got there." Every time she did the laundry, she took the book out, determined to pitch it, only to throw it back when she lost her resolve.

"I'd say my mother put it there because she thought maybe it was too old for me. I'm not a baby, you know." Kathleen went back to the page she was reading.

"I know you're not." Alcea perched on the side of the bed. "So what do you think of it?"

Kathleen heaved a sigh and rolled over, eying her mother. When she saw Alcea's interest was sincere, she relented. "It's good. But it's sad."

"Did you know . . ." Alcea hesitated, wondering if Dak would want Kathleen to know. Oh, hell. What did it matter what he wanted? "Dak wrote that book."

Kathleen's face lit. "He did? It doesn't sound like him. I mean, I've read a couple of those *One for the*

Road books, and they're boring. This is better." She looked alarmed. "You won't tell him I said that, will you?"

Alcea shook her head. "I thought the same thing. Not that they're boring, really, but that they just didn't have as much emotion as *Torn*. Kind of like the difference between *Canterbury Tales* and *Hamlet*." She might as well get some mileage out of all those hours spent reading.

"You've read *Chaucer*?" Kathleen propped herself up on an elbow. "Yeah. That's a good comparison. You know Dak's writing a book about Cordelia, don't you?"

Alcea nodded.

"Well, he's having problems because he has this other idea that's getting in the way. He should write it. I mean, I can't write at all if I'm not writing from here." Kathleen put a fist on her stomach.

"That's how I feel about my baking. If I think a recipe is going wrong, I lose all interest. And if I keep plodding on anyway, it never turns out right." Kathleen was looking at her with a new respect, and Alcea liked it. "So what's this new idea of Dak's?"

"A love story. Something about families. And regret and not appreciating what you have until it's too late." Kathleen frowned. "I can't remember everything he said." Her eyes widened. "Maybe he was thinking of you."

"Kathleen . . . Don't hold out hope that Dak and I will get back together. We just don't want the same things."

Kathleen dropped her head back. "I wish you did."

She wasn't the only one. The phone rang, and Kathleen bounded up to answer. Returning, she held out the cordless, looking like she'd swallowed something sour. "It's Kemp Runyon."

Undoubtedly calling to confirm their date tonight. Alcea took the phone, holding a hand over the receiver. "Are you spending the night at Daisy's?"

When Kathleen nodded, she spoke a few minutes to Kemp, conscious of the disgust on Kathleen's face, then handed back the phone. "What do you have against him? He's always nice to you."

"He is *so* not hot. Not like Dak. You aren't serious about him, are you?"

No, he wasn't hot, but hot hadn't gotten her much of anything except some jollies, she thought, dismissing everything else Dakota Jones had brought into her life. She picked up a shirt from a pile and started to fold it. "I don't know. It's too early to tell, but I *am* fond of him."

Kathleen gave her a long-suffering look and swiped up her book. "I'm gonna go read out in the addition." She paused in the doorway. "You know what?"

"What?" Alcea smoothed a sleeve.

"You don't need second best. You're doing fine without that loser."

Surprised at the dead seriousness in Kathleen's voice, Alcea looked up.

"I mean it. Do you know I told Joey Beadlesworth to go soak his head? You should do the same thing with Kemp Runyon. He's not right for you."

Before Alcea could untie her tongue, Kathleen had disappeared. She went back to folding. Turning her daughter's words over in her head, she put the pile of clothing on the dresser, then stopped at the sight of another shirt peeking out from under the bed. Picking it up, her heart squeezed. It was Dak's. Undoubtedly from those early days here, when he'd catch her by surprise, and they'd made love wherever they were. She wadded the shirt in her fist.

Maybe if she had Kathleen's youth and energy stretching out ahead of her instead of a lot of empty nights, she might feel the same way as her daughter. But right now—she hurled the shirt down the hallway—second best was looking better than nothing at all.

* * *

The next day Alcea pulled on the same jeans she'd worn yesterday, waited until she saw Dak's Jeep leave, then grabbed the damn shirt and went to see Florida. Overhead, the sun glinted through a leafy palette of orange and gold. She let herself in through the back door, and finding nobody inside, looked out front. Florida was raking leaves. She pushed open the screen door just in time to catch her hefting a stuffed plastic bag.

"What do you think you're doing?" Alcea dropped the shirt and hurried forward. "Do you *want* to have this baby early?" She hauled the bag to the alley, snatched up a couple of lawn chairs on her way back, and opened them up in a patch of sun on the lawn. "Now sit." She took the rake out of Florida's hand.

Florida sat, kicked off her canvas shoes, and wiggled her toes out in front of her. She watched Alcea rake. "Has Kemp recovered?" Her voice was amused.

"I think only his pride was injured."

And her dignity. After their date last night, Kemp had pulled up to the curb instead of driving through the mud-rutted alley to the Pink Palace. They'd been walking along the path to the trailer when, halfway there, he'd caught her up in such a fervent embrace, she'd squealed with surprise. Cowboy's back light had snapped on, and Dak and Florida had crowded the kitchen door. Kemp had been so startled, he'd pedaled backward and fallen on his rump.

"As was Dak's." Florida gave her a pointed look. "Or maybe more than his pride. He took off again this morning. He said he'd be back tomorrow."

Alcea pushed the leaves into a pile, tamped on them with the rake as though she could blot out the vision of Dak's silhouette in the doorway and how he'd immediately turned his back on the scene. "Kemp asked me to marry him last night." A few minutes after they'd left the country club, Kemp had swerved to a stop, turned to her, and blurted his proposal. Her shock had shown, and his expression had faded from determination to forlorn hope.

Florida hesitated. "That was fast."

"He said he was afraid if he waited, someone else would come along . . . again." And he'd said they'd be as happy as he and his first wife, Marjorie, had been. And that he'd take care of her, backtracking when she'd frowned at the mention she wouldn't have to work. Other than that, he'd painted a rosy picture. Traveling, entertaining, life of ease. What he hadn't said was that he loved her. Clearly, loneliness, not love, had inspired his proposal.

"You didn't tell him yes, did you?"

Alcea shook her head. "But I didn't tell him no, either." She almost had, but the refusal had died on her lips when he'd mentioned Kathleen. "I told him I'd think about it."

"What's to think about? Y'all don't love him."

Aye, there's the rub. Still raking, Alcea shot a look at Florida. "And love's so reliable? Kemp *is* reliable. I'd have a comfortable life with a good husband."

"And you're ready to settle for *comfortable*? He'd bore you out of your mind."

Maybe. But was the kind of partner she'd found in Dak likely to come along twice in a lifetime? Especially one that would stay put? "I have to think of Kathleen, too." Kemp had promised to raise Kathleen with as much love as he had his own daughter. "She's not happy with the Pink Palace. And in a few years, there will be college. Even on an upswing, our business isn't likely to bring in enough for me to do that for her."

"Stan would pay for that."

"Will he? If Kathleen doesn't move in with them permanently, do you still think Serena will still want to lavish all those gifts on her? She'll have a say in how he spends his money."

"Oh, pish. You're worrying too far ahead. There are loans and scholarships."

Alcea snorted. "And my credit's so good? Besides, I'm not just worrying about that. I'm worrying about what Kathleen will do *now*." And wondering where her obligation to her daughter began and ended. That "won't have to work" comment indicated Kemp's vision of their future together didn't include her orange uniform. Hell. The whole thing was a tangle. "Oh, balls, let's not argue. I haven't decided. And that's not what I came over here to talk to you about."

"I know." Florida sighed and tipped back her head so the sun bathed her face. "You want to talk about Serena's visit Friday."

"She knows about you and Stan and the baby."

"I know. Dak said Stan told her."

"Did Dak also tell you that I blurted it all out before I knew that?" Alcea stopped raking. "I am so sorry, Florida. I didn't even stop to think what it meant to you."

"Like after all I've done, I could hold it against you? That's not to say that last night I didn't think up a few ways to do y'all in, but this morning I decided to keep you around. I would have done the same thing if my child was threatened." Her hands splayed over her abdomen. "Do you think she'll try to get her hands on my baby, too?"

Alcea hesitated. "She's already tried that on Stan for size." Florida's eyes widened. "But don't worry. He said no."

"But what if he changes his mind?"

"He won't, believe me. Stan was the center of his mother's world, and he grew up thinking he should be the center of everyone else's. Kathleen doesn't make a blip in his life when she's there, but throw in diapers and bottles and car seats and . . . He hated all that. Mostly he hated the attention it took from him."

"Still. Serena might . . ."

"From what I heard, she's already given up on that front. Now, believe it or not, she's trying to convince him you deserve child support."

Florida sighed. "I said she was nice, damn her."

"Right. Nice like a fox."

Both women considered that a moment. No telling what Serena would do. Or what Stan would do *for* her. Alcea finally said, "Well, if it comes to that, Dak said he'd help you. You wouldn't lose." She went back to raking. She really didn't fear Stan would change his mind. And if he did, he'd be forced to deal with that light she'd seen in Dak's eyes. She grimaced. She wished Dak had shown the same willingness to fight for *her*.

"Dak told me the same thing." Florida said. "He's changed, hasn't he?"

"Not enough." Alcea dug a harsh furrow in the sod. "Not enough to get past the damage your mother did and learn love *does* come with strings, although they don't have to strangle him." She hesitated. She didn't know if Florida knew about S.R.'s short-circuited adoption plans. "Maybe he would have been better off with S.R. I guess he had that chance. Serena told me—"

"*What* did she tell you?"

At the alarm in Florida's voice, Alcea glanced over her shoulder. Florida's hands were white-knuckled on her chair arms. Gads. Any reference to Tamara and the Jones siblings had a panic attack. "It's nothing awful," she reassured her. "Just that S.R. gave money to Tamara in exchange for Dak, and then she ran off with both Dak and the cash. Which might have been the same thing I'd have done if I'd been young, broke, and thought someone was going to take my baby. Wouldn't you?" She frowned. "But I don't think Stan should call it extortion."

"Stan told Serena— Oh, God. Might as well post it on the Internet. Did you tell Dak?"

"No. But why should it bother him? It's only one more bit of proof of how much Tamara loved him."

"How she— You don't know the half of it." Florida's laugh was so rough, Alcea was startled. Florida gazed at her a long moment, then motioned to the other chair. "Maybe you'd better sit down."

Feeling a deep unease, Alcea dragged the rake over and sat. She didn't like the pasty look on Florida's face. "Maybe you'd better be careful what you tell me. Obviously, I'm crummy at keeping secrets." And she didn't want to know any more. Not about Tamara *or* her children.

"That's what I'm counting on." She took a breath. "There's more to what happened between Tamara and S.R. I'd hoped Dak would never have to know, but if Stan told Serena . . ."

Florida spilled the rest of the story while Alcea sat wide-eyed. Midway through Florida's recital, Alcea remembered the note she'd found in the trunk in Cowboy's cellar. She'd never had a chance to show it to Peg. After Peg had died, she'd simply stuck it between the pages of *Torn* and forgotten it. She felt in her pocket for the scrap of paper she'd picked up from Kathleen's floor yesterday. It was still there. *Thanks for the money, you fool. You'll never see the damn kid again.* It now made sense. Tamara had birthed the lies Dak believed about her and about himself, but the people closest to him had kept them alive. To Florida's credit, she hadn't known the truth very long, but the rest of them had. How much damage had they all caused in the name of love?

When Florida finished, they both sat silent. Finally, Alcea murmured. "This will knock the pins right out from under Dak. His whole self-concept is built around a bunch of lies. But, Florida, you have to tell him. If Stan told Serena all this—and he probably did—he'll find out from her or somebody she tells. It would be kinder coming from you."

Florida stayed silent, and a shadow of foreboding crept over Alcea. "What did you mean when you said you're counting on me not to keep secrets?" she asked slowly.

"I've tried, Alcea." Florida's eyes pleaded with her.

"But I can't tell him. He'd hate me. I—I'd never see him again."

"And it's okay if he hates me?" Alcea stared at her, and Florida stared back. Moving restlessly, Alcea averted her gaze. "All right, considering how things are between us, maybe it doesn't matter if he hates *me*, but . . ." How could she do it? That he'd hate her wasn't the only possibility; that he'd kill the messenger might be more likely. But he deserved the truth. If he could face what Tamara had done, he'd have a chance to heal.

She studied the jigsaw pattern of blue sky peeking through the fall foliage. Maybe he'd even learn how to love. Her mouth twisted. *The truth shall set you free.* She took a deep breath. "Okay. I'll do it."

Chapter 23

As she walked home from work on Monday, Alcea's heart felt as heavy as the quilt of clouds that lay over Cordelia. By contrast, Florida had been giddy all day, undoubtedly relieved at having shared the burden she'd carried. She'd remained behind to close up, giving Alcea time to talk to Dak alone. What a favor.

Immediately after Alcea had uttered her promise to Florida, she'd regretted it. Further thought hadn't helped any. Overnight, she'd wrestled with her sheets, and had realized two things. One, that she was stupid to think this might provide her and Dak with another chance. Two, that what she had to tell him could very well destroy him. But she'd promised.

When she arrived at Cowboy's, Dak was pulling his duffel out of his Jeep. She ignored the temptation to vanish down the path to the Pink Palace and instead paused near the rear bumper. "Good trip?"

"Yeah."

He gave her a curious glance as she followed him to the house, but at least he didn't shut the door in her face. She stepped inside and halted uncertainly, watching while he set down the duffel and straightened. Weariness lined his mouth, and a lock of hair dipped over his forehead. She tightened her grip on her purse strap before she could give in to the urge to brush it back.

He frowned. "Do you need something?"

"Um, just to talk to you."

They settled in the parlor, him sprawled on the horsehair sofa with an ankle on his knee; her in an opposite chair, bolt upright, purse at her feet and hands clasped in her lap.

Lazily, his gaze played over her, and heat rose in her face. "You look like a schoolgirl, waiting for the principal." His mouth quirked and she swallowed, unable to return the banter. His smile faded, and his eyes sharpened. "Are you pregnant?"

"No!"

He flexed his ankle. "Good. That would be a mess, wouldn't it? So, if not that—what?"

She took a deep breath. "I, uh, found out some things, that's all." *Yeah, that's all.* "And I thought you should know, even though . . . Well, it's about your mother. And Dak . . . Dak, you aren't going to like it, and it might hurt you." *Might? No question.*

"What about her?" He stopped flexing his ankle.

Keeping her eyes fixed on his face, she relayed everything she'd learned from Serena. About how S.R. and Ellen had wanted to pay Tamara for him, and how Tamara had taken their money and fled. When she was done, she paused while her pulse raced. That was the easy part.

Like she'd thought, he didn't think that was half bad. He even smiled. "Good for Tamara. She bested S.R. Addams." She noted he didn't refer to the man as his father.

"Yes, um— Yes, she did. But not *exactly* in the way you think."

He frowned, and she tried to find a gentle way to say what came next. "You're right—Tamara *did* take off because she didn't want S.R. to have you. But she—she did it because by then she hated S.R., not because"—It wouldn't be gentle at all to say, *Not because she loved* you. So she tacked in another direction, this time looking away. "You see, Tamara wasn't some kind of butterfly following her heart, Dak, not like you've always thought of her. S.R.—your father—kept looking for you. For—*years*. And Tamara ran—and kept running—because she didn't want him to find you." She glanced at him. His face was blank. Oh, cripes. He wasn't getting it. Or he didn't *want* to get it. She finally added, "It—it wasn't because she really wanted to keep you. It was . . . Well, keeping you away from him was a form of revenge."

"What are you talking about? She kept me with her for fifteen years."

"She kept you until she knew S.R. was dead. She'd won. And then she brought you here."

"That's not true." Each word was an ice chip.

"It *is* true. Stan told Florida." She explained why Ellen had told Stan. "And Florida asked Peg, and Peg verified everything." She took a breath. "Cowboy knew all of it, Dak. S.R.—your father—told Cowboy after Tamara ran off with S.R.'s money." His face had grown increasingly pale, his eyes increasingly cold. Alcea felt the chill, but she stumbled on. "In—in case Tamara got in touch with Cowboy, you see. Your father very much wanted you."

"Right." His eyes were as flat as concrete. "All these people knew, and nobody told me."

"They didn't tell you because they were worried about you. When Tamara left you here, you wouldn't let anyone get close. They didn't know what you'd do if you knew. They tried to *protect* you."

"And later?"

"Were they supposed to tell you by e-mail? By phone? You left. Life went on. Everyone thought you were happy, so why rock the boat? Stan wasn't going to tell you. He was afraid you'd make a claim on his money. Your father's money. Florida hasn't known for long, but she was afraid she'd never see you again if *she* told you."

"It's still nothing but different people's perception of the truth."

"No. No, it's not." The man was so entrenched in

his vision of Tamara, he wouldn't notice the truth until it slapped him in the face. "Do you remember that note I found?" She fumbled in her apron pocket and pulled out the note. She held it out to him, but he made no move to take it. "It *was* from Tamara, Dak. She'd written it to your father. Do you want me to read it?"

"I remember it. And I also remember it's not her handwriting. Do *you* remember the letters I told you she wrote me before she died?" He smiled, like a courtroom attorney who'd caught the key witness in a big fat lie.

She dropped her hand. "She didn't . . . She didn't die."

"Of course she did." She saw a muscle jerk in his neck. "That's why the letters stopped."

"The letters stopped because Julius hurt his hand," she whispered. "Tamara didn't write those letters, Dak. Or send you cards or gifts. Julius did. Because Cowboy asked him to."

For a moment he just stared at her. Then he shot to his feet so fast, she cringed back. "Leave." His body was no longer still, but so agitated it frightened her. He paced a few feet. When she didn't move, he whirled. "I said, leave! I don't know what everyone *thinks* happened, and I don't care. They might be right about some things but not—*not*—about Tamara's motivations. She kept me because she *wanted* me, not because she was warped by vengeance."

Alcea stayed where she was. Her heart bounced around erratically in her chest, but she didn't want to leave him like this. "You've always believed what you needed to believe, Dak. You were a *child*. You learned early on to protect yourself from your mother's indifference. You figured out what it would take to stay with her, so you did it. You asked nothing from her and convinced yourself that was the way it should be."

"You're wrong."

"I'm not wrong." Alcea pleaded with him, hoping he'd see. "You created this whole illusion of what Tamara was. Because you loved her. Every child loves his mother. Every child wants her approval. You didn't do anything wrong. You're not to blame. But *she is*. And Dak . . . *you* know it. *You wrote it all down in your book.*"

Dak turned and punched the wall with such force she was afraid he'd broken his hand. "Get out, Alcea. Go play your head games somewhere else." He advanced toward her, his face twisted.

She scrambled to her feet and backed toward the door. Her earlier thought about him killing the messenger might not be far off the mark. But anger surfaced along with fear. "So what now?" Reaching behind her, she fumbled at the door. "Will you run again? Or can you face the truth?"

"Get out!" The cords in his neck stood out. He took another step.

How dare he scare her? Alcea swooped, hooked his duffel in her hand and lobbed it. It landed at his feet. "No. *You* get out! You were never really here, anyway."

Without waiting for a reply, she turned, fled down the stairs, around the corner, and along the path to the Pink Palace. Her heart pounded. She'd expected anger and disbelief, but not that violence of emotion. She scrambled up the steps and inside, locking the door, relieved to find Kathleen was gone. The wall he'd built was so bricked by lies—his own and everyone else's—that he'd never see the truth. Fine! He could hide behind his damn barricade. She wouldn't try to knock it down again.

Will you run again? Alcea's words reverberated through Dak's brain.

He stared at the duffel. Battered and gray, it hunkered at his feet like a tired old mutt. Cowering. Cowardly. He kicked it aside, strode forward, and slammed the door Alcea had left gaping open. Turning, he prowled the empty house like an animal in search of prey. Up the stairs, down, through the hallway. Twice he stooped to pick up his duffel. Each time Alcea's taunt echoed again. He finally heaved the bag up the stairwell, where it landed like a sack of wet cement.

Finally, he sank onto the stairs and held his head, knotting his hands so tight in his hair, his scalp sang with pain. Every word she'd said was emblazoned across his brain in white-hot letters. When he raised his head, he realized his face was wet. Viciously, he scrubbed it dry with his shirt and took a deep breath. Then another. And at last his heart rate slowed. He rotated his head on his neck. Holding his hands out, he flexed and relaxed his fists, realizing for the first time that his right one ached where he'd smacked the wall. He examined it. Bruised, but nothing broken. Not like Julius's hand . . .

And not like his heart. He closed his eyes and thought, feeling a trickle, but only a trickle, of guilt for scaring Alcea so she'd run like hell. He had no doubt she'd only told him what she'd thought she needed to, and no doubt she was truthful in repeating everyone else's version of Tamara. And there *was* that note. But none of it matched what he remembered.

Or was it only what he'd allowed himself to remember? Images flitted in and out of his head, memories buried so deep he was no longer sure what was real and what wasn't. Tamara . . . what were the last words she'd ever uttered to him? He stretched his legs out in front of him and studied his boots, thinking hard. Her face popped into his brain. She was smiling, her hand gripped around a carpeted valise. *See you later, Dak.* But she never had. With a sound of disgust, he got to his feet. He was behaving like a child throwing a fit. He could face the truth, whatever it was, because it wouldn't matter. It wouldn't change his life. It wouldn't change him. Not in the long run. He knew himself, knew what made him happy. He *did*.

Wanting to banish all thought, he headed to the kitchen. Once there, he cracked open the bottle of Boone's Farm he'd found buried at the back of the refrigerator on the day he'd returned to Cordelia. It wouldn't have improved with age, but it would do. He took several long gulps. Then several more. The alcohol hit him hard. When he heard Florida's car rasp onto the drive, he strode up the steps to his bedroom, bottle neck swinging from two fingers, his duffel ignored. When he was inside, he closed and locked the door, then drank himself into unconsciousness.

The next morning, he woke to a splitting headache. Lying as still as he could, he heard Florida rise, the sounds of her shower, and finally the distant echo of a closing door. He hadn't wanted to see his sister last night, and he still didn't want to. Swinging his legs out of bed, he sat up and groaned, remembering why he rarely drank. A hangover banged against his brain. Yesterday's revelations flooded back, but he shoved them aside. He'd think about it all later. When he was back on the road.

Downstairs, a leaden morning glinted through the kitchen windows, matching the weight piled on his neck. He started coffee, then gingerly lowered himself onto a chair and held his head, trying to pretend nothing had changed. Florida banged through the back door, making him wince, and not just from the noise. She held a bag of groceries.

"Well, Lazarus has risen." She plopped the bag on the counter and started to unpack it. "Are you okay?"

"I thought you were at work," he mumbled. "It's Tuesday."

"Day off. Alcea and I take one occasionally." He suspected she'd stayed home because of him. He wished she hadn't. She stuck a carton of milk in the refrigerator and turned to look at him, her face concerned. "Let me fix you some eggs."

The thought turned his stomach. "No, thanks."

"You haven't eaten a decent meal—hell, a meal at all—for twenty-four hours. Unless you count that bottle of wine that was missing from the fridge."

He looked at her set chin and gave in. "Maybe some toast."

The coffee finished perking. She plunked a mug and a bottle of aspirin on the table. He reached for both, and she made no further comment until she'd slathered the toast with jam and slid it in front of him, along with a glass of juice. She pulled out a chair. "We have to talk."

"No, we don't." The coffee had hit his stomach with the jolt of a fist. He stuffed the toast in his mouth, effectively silencing at least himself.

But not Florida. "Look at you. You're a mess."

He looked down, just realizing he'd fallen asleep in his clothes. He swallowed and leaned back. "So what? I'll take a bath. Florida, I don't want to talk about—"

"I don't care what you want to talk about, Dak. You can't keep running." Her tone was half belligerent, half pleading. "I know what Alcea told you. I should have told you myself, but I was a coward. It's better now that the skeletons are out of the closet." She hesitated. "Isn't it?"

"Nothing's out!" The words burst through his lips before he could close them in.

"Dak, you have to face facts."

Anxiety crawled under his skin and skittered up his spine. It didn't help his nausea. He stood up. "Don't tell me what I have to do. I'm a man, for chrissakes. Not a little boy. I think I can figure things out for myself."

"But Dak . . ."

"That's enough, Florida! You and everyone bent the past into what they needed to believe. That's fine. But that's not what happened." He could almost believe that, if it wasn't for that damned note.

She leaned back, her eyes sad. "It *is* what happened, Dak. All of it."

"You always hated Tamara and you've let that hatred color everything."

"I didn't have enough time with her to fall in love with her, Dak. Not like you did." She paused. "And even if I had, Grandpa knew. You can't just make what he told Peg disappear."

"Stop it!" He realized his hands were shaking and put them in his pockets.

She watched him and then pushed back from the table. "Okay. I will. But if you have any courage left at all, go talk to Julius. Grandpa told him everything, just like he told Peg."

Determined to prove he wasn't falling apart, to defy Florida and Alcea, Dak showered and shaved. Then with Florida's challenge ringing in his ears, as well as Alcea's taunt—*Will you run?*—he went to find Julius.

The old man was in the garage, tinkering over an engine. He looked over his shoulder when Dak came in. "Hey, did I tell you Lil's rented me the two rooms over her bookstore? Looks like I'll have me a place to stay once you're outta here. Not only that, she wants me to do a storytelling hour every week. Shakespeare. Can you beat that?"

When Dak didn't respond, Julius's eyes narrowed. "You doing okay, boy?"

"Alcea told me. About Tamara." He looked at Julius's bent hand. "And about you."

Julius stilled. For one hopeful moment, Dak thought his face would pucker in confusion. Instead his shoulders slumped and he looked every inch his seventy-odd years. Dak's heart knotted. "Ah, boy. I figured one day it'd all catch up with us." He shook his head. "But mebbe it's for the best. I have some things to answer for, but I'd like it if you'd hear me out." He motioned to a metal folding chair and Dak sat, holding himself together by sheer will.

"Your mama . . ." Julius wiped his hands on an oily rag and shuffled over to join him. "Oh, she was somethin'. Curious, inquisitive. Beautiful, too. Florida's got the same look about her." He glanced sideways at Dak, who stared stone-faced toward the street. Julius cleared his throat. "But, you see, boy, she was headstrong. Too headstrong. Like a wild colt. Nothing seemed to settle her. And Cowboy. Well, he didn't know how to handle her. Let her have her head, mostly, once her mama ran off. Guess he felt bad. So she got spoilt." Julius gave him another look. "Do you get what I'm saying?"

He nodded. His fists had clenched and he slipped them into his pockets.

"By the time she was growed, she was selfish and willful. Wouldn't listen to nobody. And she was loose. Don't like saying it, but it's the truth. Cowboy was relieved when she took off for South Dakota. A 'course he didn't know the reason until a while later, when Addams brought him a note she'd left him."

The damn note. Dak wished he could plug his ears.

"Now, say what you will about S.R. Addams. He was a powerful man, and he threw his weight around some, but your granddaddy was convinced S.R. and his wife, that Ellen, would be the best thing for you. They wanted to raise you. And your granddaddy, he knew Tamara wasn't going to be no good as a mother. So he agreed to let S.R. know if he ever heard from Tamara. But he never heard a peep. Leastaways, not until you and Florida got dumped on his doorstep. And by then, S.R. was dead. She wouldna come back here otherwise."

An involuntary sound came out of Dak's throat.

Julius reached out and patted his knee with his gnarled, broken hand. "Know it hurts, boy, but that's the truth. Then she took off again, and we never saw no trace of her after."

"And the gifts, the letters?" His voice was hoarse. "Why did you write those letters?"

"I'm not proud of it, boy, but at the time, it seemed a kindness. You were lost without her, all wrapped up in yourself and silent as a tomb. Cowboy was beside himself, not knowing what to do. Ellen didn't want you anymore, not after S.R. was gone. Stan had become the center of her life by then. Cowboy, well, he knew I could turn a phrase, so he asked me to write those letters. Later on he planned to tell you, but he just never seemed to find the right time. And then you left for college and . . ." Julius spread his hands. "You got yourself a life. After I got into a tussle with that engine and couldn't write anymore, it just seemed better to let sleeping dogs lie, so to speak. So he told you Tamara was dead."

And he hadn't worried that Tamara would ever show up to prove him wrong. Dak closed his eyes and felt tears well up beneath his eyelids. Because he'd known she wouldn't.

"Here, boy."

He opened his eyes. Julius was hovering over him, holding out a rag. Suddenly, he was fifteen again, crouched against the side of the service garage, sobbing into his fists. A big fellow with red hair and a booming voice was holding out a hanky, his brows twisted with concern. "Here ya go, boy," he'd said. "You just go ahead and cry for your mama."

He'd forgotten that. Forgotten that Tamara had busted up his heart.

Just like then, he took the comfort Julius offered. And just like then, he wondered if the hurt would ever stop.

By the time Dak returned to Cowboy's, he no longer felt like crying. He no longer felt anything. He moved by rote up the stairs, picking up his duffel along the way, moving quietly past Florida's room. She was napping. Once inside his own room, he softly closed the door and dragged the empty boxes he'd come with out of his closet.

With stiff movements, he started with his clothes. Once his closet was empty, he moved to his dresser.

He hadn't collected much, so it only took a few minutes before his belongings were packed. He balanced his laptop on top of a box, then bent to gather the books from his bookcase. His hand fell on *Torn from My Arms*.

He stacked the rest of the books into a carton, then lowered himself to the edge of the mattress, holding his first novel. It was still in pristine condition. After he'd done the revisions, he'd never read it again, not even to proof the galleys. It had grown too . . . tiresome . . . for him to stomach. At least that was what he'd told himself then. He turned the book over in his hands. He remembered writing it. He'd scrawled the book with an exhilaration and abandon he'd never experienced before. And hadn't often felt since. Bending back the cover, he skimmed the first few pages. It was what he'd expected. Told from the first-person viewpoint of his protagonist, it was self-indulgent crap. Undisciplined. It was amazing that he'd sold it, let alone that it had reached the success it had. He was about to slap it shut when a line caught him right in the gut. *You see, my mother never loved me.*

A hundred images rushed in to choke him, ready to confirm the truth of the words, but he breathed deep until his head cleared, and read on. By the time he finished the first chapter, he'd crept up the bed and bundled a pillow under his head. By the time he was done with the second, his inner editor had fallen silent. He was captive to the words he'd written so long ago.

Toward the end of the fifth chapter, he lowered the book. Without doubt, his wife had provided the muse. Newly in love when he'd started the book, her belief in him had sparked a sense of security he realized now he'd never felt before then. But under the burden of their youth and her disapproving family, his confidence had fissured by the time he'd completed the book. When he'd read the script they'd concocted, the fissures had grown into gaping cracks. When the movie and the book became raging successes, the cracks had exploded wide open. And after his wife, bewildered and hurt by the demons that fed him, had left, he'd never written with such unfettered freedom until . . .

. . . Until he'd met Alcea. And the idea for the book he'd told Kathleen about had grabbed hold and wouldn't let go.

He pictured Alcea as she'd looked yesterday. Her burnished hair glinting in the low light of the parlor, her eyes, deep and fathomless, holding his. She had courage. More courage than he.

He picked the book back up, and, for the rest of the day, he read. Florida tapped on his door sometime during the evening, but when he only grunted, her footsteps faded back down the stairs. When he reached the final page somewhere after midnight, he felt shell-shocked. He dropped the book on the floor and squeezed his eyes shut against the pain that lanced through the numbness. Even with reality writ too large to fit back into the crannies where he'd hid it for so long, he still struggled to do it. Finally, he dozed off, his sleep racked by nightmares. When Wednesday's dawn broke against the windows, it found him on his back, his eyes wide open, unable to deny the truth of his past. It lay in and between every line of his own words.

Tamara hadn't loved him.

He'd denied it, but he'd known it all along. What it meant to the rest of his life still escaped him. He turned his head to face the windows. He hadn't closed the curtains, and a pastel tint melted against the panes. The next bend in the road whispered, sweetly seductive. A bird called, inviting him onward. But he was no longer sure if there was a vista big enough to fill up the hollow in his heart that, until last night, had held all the lies he'd told himself over the years.

Chapter 24

"I know he's in there, but I haven't seen him since yesterday morning. And he was a wreck then. Hungover." Florida thunked a refilled ketchup bottle on a table. Nearing closing time, the diner had emptied except for the two of them.

Alcea stood looking out the doorway. The first Wednesday in October had ushered in true fall. Against a bottomless blue sky, the brilliant splash of the maples hurt her eyes. Fallen leaves scurried into the gutters, chased by a crisp breeze that made gooseflesh rise on her arms. Or maybe it was Florida's words. She didn't want to care about Dak's turmoil, but she did. "He'll bounce back," she assured Florida, although she was none too sure herself. She hesitated. "I wish I hadn't told him." She moved to the counter and picked up several more bottles.

"He needed to know." Florida straightened with a hand on the small of her back. She stared out the window. "And he would have found out, anyway."

Alcea wished she could think of something to do to ease everything, but she was afraid if she tried to talk to Dak again, she'd only make things worse. Moving around the room, she replaced the ketchup and straightened condiment holders.

"So," Florida said, putting down another bottle. "Is tonight a date with Kemp?"

With some relief, Alcea accepted the change of subject. "No, he has some television shows he likes to watch Wednesday nights."

"Sounds like passion to me."

"At least I don't worry about where he is." Her voice was too sharp. She abandoned the condiments. "I think I'll get a head start on tomorrow and throw some brownies in the oven."

Florida's look was jaundiced, undoubtedly because she knew Alcea adhered to a strict fresh-from-the-oven policy. But she wisely kept her mouth shut as Alcea escaped to the bakery.

Safe in her domain, Alcea slammed the double boiler onto the stove, dumped in bittersweet chocolate and butter, then sifted other ingredients together. She didn't need Florida's sarcasm. Maybe Kemp wasn't *hot,* but she didn't need *hot.* Nor want it. Not if it came with the heartbreak she'd experienced with Dak. She whisked the chocolate mixture. Kemp would be no-risk, *easy*. She broke eggs into the mixer, followed by vanilla and sugar. She flipped on the machine, then the oven. Love would grow in time—into the stability she wanted. He'd provide for her, he'd be a good stepfather, he'd . . .

She jumped as a crash sounded. Flipping off the mixer, she hurried to the doorway. Not seeing Florida, she hurried to the back room. Clutching her abdomen, a grimace on her face, Florida leaned against the wall. A spilled crate of tomato cans rolled around the floor.

"How many times have I told you—" Alcea stopped, catching sight of the water pooled around Florida's feet. Her legs were wet. "Omigod. Looks like baby's on the way."

"But it's five weeks early!"

"I'm sure everything will be fine." Kicking some cans out of the way, Alcea grasped Florida's arm. "Does it hurt? Are you having pains?"

She got her answer when cords knotted on Florida's neck and she gasped.

"Let's get you to the hospital. Did you drive?"

Florida nodded. Because of her swollen feet, she'd bypassed the walk to the diner for the last week. "But I don't have my—my things."

"Forget the things. I'll fetch them later." At her last checkup, Florida's doctor hadn't said anything about an early delivery, and Cordelia's hospital didn't have a premier neonatal unit. But she smiled at Florida to cover her worry. "Come on, Hercules. Let's go have a baby."

After a breathless ride through Cordelia, Alcea mentally thanking Stan for Florida's speedy little Miata, she'd delivered Florida to the maternity ward. Florida's doctor decided to let nature proceed. By nine, Florida had delivered a baby girl, small at only four and a half pounds.

In the waiting room, already flocked with concerned well-wishers as the news of Florida's labor had traveled on Cordelia's grapevine, Alcea stretched in her chair, trying to get the kinks out of her spine and the low buzz of anger out of her head. Between bouts of pacing hallways, she'd gone to Cowboy's to pick up Florida's things. She'd both hoped and dreaded to find Dak there so she could deliver the news, but when she'd pushed open his bedroom door, it was empty. Her gaze had fallen on the stuffed duffel and packed boxes. For unfathomable reasons—what else had she expected—the sight had enraged her. She'd slammed the door shut, then tramped to the Pink Palace for Kathleen before remembering Patsy Lee had taken her and Daisy to Sedalia for a drill team event. She'd scribbled a note and had called Julius.

Julius had arrived on her heels back at the hospital, shaking his head when she'd asked if he'd seen Dak. "How's the baby? A mite early, ain't she?"

"The Apgars were okay, but she's in the nursery getting oxygen. Her lungs are a little underdeveloped." Julius looked bewildered, and Alcea patted his hand. "It's a precaution, mostly. I'm sure she'll be fine. They'll probably keep her for a week or so."

His face cleared. "Does she got a name?"

Alcea had smiled. "Missouri, of course."

Rosemary and Tansy had arrived soon after Julius, and not long behind them, Alcea's mother. Some of the diner regulars also appeared as the evening advanced. Glowing with excitement, Rosemary was now regaling them all with the story of Florida's sudden onset of labor. Zinnia shook her head with a long-suffering sigh, while Julius rubbed a callused finger down his nose, face amused. Somehow, Rosemary's version featured Rosemary in Alcea's role. Alcea looked around at their familiar faces, glad they were all sharing a joyous event, since the last time they'd gathered here had been such a sad one. Dak should be here, too. Damn the man for his infernal disappearing act. Couldn't he see what he was missing—what he *had* missed? There was nothing scary here. Thinking she should quit torturing herself over him, she laid her head back and closed her eyes. It was too late for them—his packed bags proved it. From now on, her gaze stayed firmly on her own future.

"Alcea!"

A hand jiggled her shoulder, and she jerked awake. A glance at the clock told her only minutes had passed since she'd drifted off. The room had gone quiet. Lil stood in front of her, eyes wide, face white. Jon and Zinnia hovered behind her. "Lands alive, honeybunch. The diner!"

Trying to recapture her wits, Alcea frowned at them. "What about it?"

"It's on fire!"

Lil and Jon were on her heels. Zinnia puffed along behind. Eyes smarting from the pall that hung in the air, Alcea pushed through the crowd that had gathered on the town square green and bumped up against a stripe of caution tape that cordoned off the area. Sparks swarmed like fireflies overhead. Uniformed policemen milled in front. She couldn't see. Reversing her steps, she forced her way back to the front of St. Andrew's and scrambled up the steps, disregarding the glares from the people she shoved aside. She heard Zinnia's muttered *'scuse me*. She didn't observe the niceties. This wasn't a spectator sport. It was her life.

Reaching the top, she pivoted and sucked in a breath. Spots from three fire engines bathed the brick of the bakery and diner in cold blue light, even as hot orange fire shot from the windows and licked their sides. Flames darted along the rooftop, chased by torrents of water. Backlit with gold, smoke plumed into the night sky.

"My God," Lil breathed from beside her, gaze transfixed. "What happened?"

Alcea knew what had happened. She'd left on the oven. She slumped against the arm she just realized her mother had tightened around her waist. Reaching from behind Lil, Jon squeezed her shoulder. She shut her eyes tight against the scene. When she opened them, Kemp had jostled between her and Lil. Like everyone else, his gaze was riveted on the fire.

"It will be all right, Alcea," he murmured, grasping her elbow. Unbelievably, she heard a suppressed note of hope in his voice. She knew his mind had already leaped into the future. If he no longer had to compete with the diner, she'd be more prone to say yes. She shook off his hand and squirmed through the crowd until she stood on the bottom step alone.

Silhouetted against the chiaroscuro of fire and water, helmets gleaming and faces obscured by masks, firemen worked in practiced precision. Certain she'd never be warm again, she hugged her arms and stood like stone, eyes transfixed, for what seemed like hours. But in less than one, the flames had died. The buildings still stood, but she knew little was left inside. An acrid stink hovered over it all, filling her mouth, her nostrils, and darkening her heart. Her dreams were shells of blistered paint and blackened brick.

The crowd had started to disperse. Behind her, Zinnia touched her shoulder. "Stay with us tonight, honeybunch. You don't want to be alone."

She stiffened. Yes, she did want to be alone. Grief was a private ordeal.

"Mom!" Kathleen pushed through the crowd. Her face was wet, eyes crazed. She sped toward Alcea like a bullet. Dak was behind her. He moved with equal speed, shoving people aside with a determined shoulder. Kathleen plowed into her and would have knocked her off her feet if Dak hadn't reached out and grabbed her arm. His grip was a vise.

She hugged Kathleen. "My God. Sweetheart!"

"I th-thought you were in there!"

"Oh, Kathleen." Alcea stroked her daughter's hair, breathed in her scent of floral shampoo, pained by the anguish her daughter must have experienced. "I'm fine, I'm fine. I left you a note. Didn't you get it?"

"But what if you'd forgotten something? What if you'd gone back?"

Alcea answered by clutching Kathleen tighter and raised her eyes to Dak's face, which was bathed with sweat despite the snap in the air. His hair was more disheveled than usual, and storms swirled in the transparent depths of his eyes. Relief mingled with fading panic.

Her mother took a step toward them, but Jon laid a restraining hand on her arm. Kemp hovered nearby, looking uncertainly from Dak's face to hers.

Dak licked his lips. "I— We thought . . . God, Alcea, if you'd . . ."

She wanted to fling herself into his arms, but the image of the packed duffel and cardboard boxes rose in her head. He'd never be there for her. He'd be gone, or a half step behind, but never beside her. "I thought you'd left." Her voice was flat. She pointedly looked at his hand on her arm, and he let it fall.

"He found me." Kathleen had pulled back. Her body hummed with hysteria. "Aunt Patsy Lee dropped me off, but I saw the smoke and ran to the square. And when I saw where the fire was coming from—" She broke off, her voice choking. "I didn't know what to do, and I was so afraid. I ran to Grandma's, but nobody was there. Dak saw me."

"I was taking a walk." Dak added. "And when I—"

"A last look around?" she asked coolly. "Before you skedaddled and left your pregnant sister to clean up your mess?"

Kathleen's face screwed up. "Don't *talk* to him like that. He *helped* me!"

"I'm sorry," Alcea murmured, more for her daughter's sake than Dak's. "Thank you," she added stiffly when Kathleen's face remained twisted.

Dak's lips had tightened. "Alcea . . ." He gave her family and Kemp a frustrated glance and closed his mouth.

"Florida's fine, by the way." Alcea couldn't keep her tongue still. While Florida was delivering a premature baby and their business was burning, he'd been out doing his solo routine. "You have a new niece."

"A girl?" A new level of excitement buzzed in Kathleen's voice.

Alcea pulled her closer, trying to still her shaking frame. She needed to get Kathleen home. She sent a pleading look at her mother. But her mother didn't step forward first; Kemp did.

He laid a hand on Alcea's shoulder, his eyes hard on Dak. "I think there will be time later for conversation. But right now . . ."

Her mother shrugged off Jon's hand and bustled up. "Yes. Right now, we need to get these two into a warm place and tuck some soup into their tummies." She shook her head. "Lord love a duck, what a night. C'mon, honeybunch. Let's get you both home."

Alcea was propelled forward. Lil wrapped a guiding arm around Kathleen. When she looked back, Dak stood isolated, silhouetted against the glare of the still-burning spotlights. For a second, she felt a pang of pity, then stiffened, reminding herself that was how he wanted to be.

"Have a good trip," she called over her shoulder. It was a cheap shot, but she felt no remorse when he took a step back as though she'd hit him.

Chapter 25

Dak's Jeep was still parked in the drive the next morning when she took Kathleen back to the trailer to get ready for school. Remembering her parting shot at him last night, she felt a pang of guilt, but shrugged it off. *What ifs* and *could haves* weren't important this morning. Survival was. Kathleen had clung to her all night and had wanted to stay home today, but Alcea was determined not to sit around and dwell over what had happened. Still shaken to her core by the fire, she'd had a sleepless night on the old sleigh bed in her parents' attic, but this morning she was full of restless energy. Activity would keep her sane.

Inside, she hustled Kathleen to her room, then stripped off her uniform. It puddled orange on her bedroom floor. She was right back to square one, she thought, scrubbing the smoke out of her hair in the kitchen sink while Kathleen claimed the shower. But she still had her life. And her daughter. And she could rebuild. At least she thought she could. Her mother had called a family meeting, of course, but after that, she'd go see Florida. They'd figure something out.

After she'd thrown on a pair of jeans and a fleece shirt, she carted Kathleen to school, gratified by the tight hug she got before her daughter slipped out of the car. Alcea then went back to the Pink Palace, taking a circuitous route around the square so she wouldn't have to see the burnt hulk of Peg's. Why push things? She was afraid the sight would shatter her spine. At the trailer, she called suppliers, canceling orders and making promises she'd contact them again when Peg's was back in business.

Next she paid a visit to the fire marshal. He was a crony of her father's and didn't harbor any suspicion of arson. There would be an investigation, of course, but he said it could have been the broken safety timer on the oven, or it could have been the old wiring in the building. She sagged with relief when he leaned toward faulty wiring, probably located in the second story. That would explain why the sprinkler system hadn't doused the blaze.

Two hours later, feeling optimistic after the sympathetic clucking of her suppliers and the fire marshal's belief she hadn't burned her own business down, she breezed into her parents' house. In the kitchen, looking cheerful in a cherry plaid shirt, Pop was hanging up the phone. Her mother was finishing up dishes from breakfast. The room held the heat and smell of bacon and cinnamon rolls. Alcea snatched a leftover piece of bacon and joined Lil and Pop at the kitchen table, wanting to get this over with quickly. She had a lot to do.

Zinnia moved to the table, toweling her hands on an apron covered with daisies. "Patsy Lee had to open Merry-Go-Read, and Jon had to leave for Nashville this morning, so we'll just see what the four of us can figure out here."

"There's nothing to figure out." Alcea tucked a leg underneath and munched. "I'll start over, that's all."

"With what?" Her mother asked, lowering herself into a chair.

"There will be insurance . . ." She faltered. If they had enough. "Or maybe we can get a loan . . ." She ground to a halt again. Her credit was lousy. She wasn't sure about Florida. "Well, really, I don't know exactly. But I will after I've talked with Florida."

Pop played with an unlit pipe. Zinnia fiddled with the hem of her apron. "Florida will be mighty caught up in that baby of hers for a while, now, you know."

"But she'll still . . ." Alcea looked at the three faces around the table. They all looked back in varying shades of sorrow. She put down the bacon. "Do you know something I don't?"

"Pop made some calls." Zinnia's eyes were troubled. "And things don't look too good."

Pop cleared his throat. "I thought you'd have your hands full today, so, uh, I hope you don't mind that."

She didn't. Pop never did anything without careful thought. "What did you find out?"

"I had a lengthy conversation with Florida. She's a smart gal, isn't she? Oh, and she said to tell you to come on over to the hospital later today so she can show off her baby."

Was that all Florida was thinking about? Of course, it was natural, but . . . She glanced at her mother, who had the intelligence not to say *I told you so.* "What else did Florida say?"

"She said you still have some debts to pay off on the bakery. Peg took care of the contractor, but you're still paying off that equipment of yours. Plus, there will be the wages you owe Rosemary and Tansy. Taxes. Bills." He faltered at the look of dread she felt creeping over her face. "Some other things."

"Go on."

He studied his pipe. "And you don't have enough insurance. She said Peg should have gotten an insurance reappraisal immediately after she added the bakery. But she didn't."

"And we were putting it off until we got back in the black and could afford higher premiums. I guess that wasn't smart." The energy was seeping out of her body. "Nor do we have . . ." She culled her brain for the right term. ". . . business interruption insurance, do we?"

Pop slowly shook his head. "I called your insurance company. They'll send someone down right away, but what you've got won't cover replacement."

The reality of it all slammed into her. Not enough insurance money. No nest egg left.

"And that's not all, honey." He reached across the table and squeezed her arm. "The way it works is . . . If the building owner can't rebuild, city codes still require you to make those buildings safe. Or tear them down."

"And probably," Alcea whispered. "That's about all we can afford."

His hand tightened. "There will be some left. But not much."

They all sat in silence.

Finally, Zinnia stirred. "And pretty soon, from what I hear, you'll be without a home, too."

Thanks for the reminder, Mother. Alcea dropped her head so they couldn't see her tears.

"Alcea, please let me . . ."

"No, Lil." Alcea dashed away her tears and looked up at her sister. "We've been over this before. Julius will move into your apartment, and I don't want your money. I'd never be able to repay you." Not that Lil would insist on repayment. Alcea knew that. It was a major reason why she couldn't accept. That and her own fear of that much debt. "I guess . . . I guess I'll go back to work at Sin-Sational or the Emporium or both." She looked down at her hands, knowing she'd have a hard time even with child support to stretch those wages for two people. "And we'll bunk with Lil or Patsy Lee until I can find someplace else." But she knew Kathleen wouldn't be happy sharing her sister-in-law's crowded farmhouse or playing the poor relative at Lil's. Serena's threat of a lawsuit loomed again. The Pink Palace was one thing. No home at all was another. "The only other way I can see out of all this is . . ." She sighed again and threw Kemp's proposal out on the table. Movement stilled and she was pinned by three pairs of eyes. "I hadn't told you about his proposal before because I'm not sure of my answer."

"Oh, Alcea." Lil touched her hand. "But what about—"

"You know he's a lost cause, Lil. I have to move on."

Pop harrumphed. "If you care about this fellow Kemp, he seems like a decent sort. Upstanding, able to support you and Kathleen. Maybe—"

"Maybe nothing." Zinnia patted Pop's hand in apology, then turned to Alcea. "Honeybunch, you'd be marrying him for all the wrong reasons. You say you aren't sure of your answer, but I think you were. At least before all this happened."

"No, Mother. I wasn't sure." She kept her voice even.

"Nope. You were sure, even if you didn't know it. You already settled once. You wouldn't do it again."

"Maybe settling is better than nothing," Alcea burst out. "I've tried my damndest over the last months to make something of my life. It hasn't worked out. What exactly do you *want* from me?" She clenched her jaw against the quaver in her voice.

Zinnia's eyes gleamed bright blue. "Why, just what I'd expect from any one of my daughters. I expect you to put up your chin and keep going." She reached across the table and grasped Alcea's hand. "I've been proud of you, Alcea. Real proud. But I hope you know that whatever you decide, I'll still always love you."

Alcea blinked, not knowing if she wanted to pinch her mother or hug her. Hug her, she decided. And much to her mother's surprise and her own, she stood up and did it. As she squeezed Zinnia against her, she thought how she made starting over sound like the easiest thing in the world. Maybe she was right. Maybe it *was* far easier than repeating old mistakes. Maybe.

That afternoon Alcea slipped out of Florida's hospital room, leaving the new mother scrambling into a robe as soon as a nurse had come to say she could sit in the nursery. Florida was determined to spend every second with Missouri. Her mother had called it right. Florida wasn't nearly as concerned about the fire as Alcea was. All her attention was on her new baby.

As well it should be. Alcea walked down the corridor, head bowed. There were still things to be thankful for. She just had to uncover them, no matter how bleak things looked. Florida had confirmed everything Pop had told her, so resurrecting her business looked hopeless. But she still had Kemp. In fact, Kemp had surfaced in her head with increasing frequency all day. She'd call him this evening. She wanted—needed—to talk to him.

She'd taken a few steps past the nurse's station when the elevator dinged open ahead. She looked up to see Dak emerge, holding a spray of flowers. She faltered but kept going, head now high. When he saw her, his eyes went smoky with wariness. They halted a couple feet apart.

"How is she?" he asked, although likely he knew.

"Missouri is still on oxygen, but they say she'll be fine. And Florida is in love. The fire has hardly fazed her at all."

Dak leaned a shoulder against the wall, as though reluctant to move on. "Maybe it just hasn't sunk in." The comment was banal; his gaze anything but. Still veiled, it pierced deep.

Alcea pretended not to notice. "She's so caught up in Missouri, I don't think there will be any aftershocks. She still wants to handle the insurance and everything. I think because she feels bad that she can't drum up the interest to feel as upset as I do." Before she could lock it in place, her chin trembled.

Dak touched her arm, and she stepped out of reach. A flicker of hurt crossed his features. She ignored it. "She's hoping Stan will take her back at the bank since Roberta Franks isn't working out. Or she might go to work for Kemp. PicNic needs a new accounting supervisor."

Dak went still at the mention of Kemp, but he only said, "She didn't love the place like you did. She enjoyed it, but what she loved was Peg." He paused and looked at the flowers in his hand. "When I saw the fire, it felt like some of my own history was burning up."

Good God. This wasn't about *him*.

He looked up, caught the expression on her face. "I'm saying this wrong. I just meant, well, if I'm feeling that way, then you must be—"

"Devastated." All her tears had dried up. "I am." She waited. She'd never heard him sound so uncertain. She kind of liked him that way.

"Yes." His gaze returned to the flowers. "So what will you do?"

"I don't know. Mari called. She checked Kansas City's ads, and there are jobs similar to what I did at Peg's. I'd earn a good wage, and Mari would let me room with her, but . . ."

"But you don't want to move."

"No." She appreciated Mari's offer, but even with the new footing they'd found after Peg's funeral, she couldn't see them getting along in tight quarters for more than ten minutes, although her sister had been sympathetic. That is, if you classified "You have guts, Hock," as sympathetic.

Dak's expression grew intense. *Come with me.* The unspoken words hung in the air.

"You still don't quite get it, do you?" She pretended all she was talking about was Mari's offer. "How could I do that to Kathleen? Ask her to move away from her friends, her family . . ." Or worse, have Kathleen insist on staying in Cordelia while she moved on alone. Kemp flitted through her mind again.

"I just— I thought you'd start over."

In his gaze, she saw he thought she had enough backbone to make a new beginning if she wanted to badly enough. The confidence he had in her moved her, and her anger dissolved as rapidly as it had jelled.

But success took more than a spine. "There isn't enough to just start over, and I'm fresh out of fortunes to blow." Again, she thought of Kemp.

Suddenly, he looked relieved, almost eager. "Hell, *I'll* loan you the money."

She started. She hadn't expected the offer, especially given with no apparent thought. She wavered on the verge of jumping on it with equal speed. But something stilled her tongue. She'd wanted a lot of things from him, but never his money. Maybe it wasn't fair to Florida to not even discuss it, but . . .

He saw the refusal on her face. "She's my sister. It's not odd that I'd do it, you know."

"No."

"Florida has options, but you—"

"—have choices, too. You taught me that. And I'm making one now. No," she repeated. His face looked so nakedly hurt, she tried to soften her words. "I already turned Lil and Jon down. I can't build my dreams on someone else's largesse. I tried to do that with Stan."

"But this is different. It's business."

"It's not business. It's a handout. And with you . . ." She took a deep breath. "I can't—won't—have that kind of connection with you."

"What's wrong with that kind of connection with me?"

"No matter what Florida does next, Missouri will be the center of her life for a while. She doesn't have the interest to rebuild like I do. I'd do most of the work. I don't mind that, not at all, but . . . I couldn't ever look at the books without seeing your money as a payoff."

"Shit, Alcea." Anger lay under the surface. "Do you honestly think I'd pay you off as some kind of a sop to my conscience?"

She studied him a moment. "I do."

He pushed off the wall, his jaw at a hard angle. "Then I guess we've got nothing left to talk about." He took a step down the corridor, then wheeled around. "I've thought a lot, Alcea. I've faced what you wanted me to face." Defiance stole across his features. "I've accepted the truth. I went to the library this morning to look up information on S.R. Ad—on my *father*. When Stan gets back, I'll have a talk with him. Maybe he doesn't want a half brother, but I'll try. And then we—you—can tell Kathleen."

"I'm glad about that, Dak. I really am."

He hardly seemed to register her words. He was talking faster than she'd ever heard him talk before, moving the bouquet from hand to hand. "I'd decided yesterday, before everything happened, that I wouldn't head out just yet. I'd stay for a while longer. Maybe we could, we could—"

"We could *what,* Dak? Repeat the past?"

"Yes. No! It would be different this time, because I—I . . ." He slapped the flowers against his thigh, and petals fluttered at their feet. "I think I love you, Alcea."

She sucked in a breath, and time stood still. Background noise receded until she could only hear the sound of her own breathing—and his. His words bounced around in her brain, finally pierced her heart. But . . . "You only *think* you love me?"

He sidestepped. "I—I want another chance." His eyes pleaded with her.

Her heart plummeted to her shoes as fast as it had shot into her throat. She took a step back, seeking the prop of the solid wall. "Another chance for what?"

"For us."

"And what would be *different* this time?"

Plowing a hand through his hair, he looked away. "You have to trust me."

She swallowed. "Tell me, Dak, have you unpacked your bag?"

"What?" His gaze returned to hers.

"Your duffel. I saw everything packed when I went to get Florida's suitcase. Have you unpacked it? Have you unpacked anything?"

"No." He looked down.

"I didn't think so." He still needed to see which way the wind blew before he'd make a commitment. She needed the commitment; damn the wind. "I can't do it, Dak. I can't live with *maybes* and *chances* and *a while longer*. Your love . . ." She dragged in a breath while her heart tore in two. ". . . it's not enough. I can't live with a man who still considers a duffel bag an option."

She turned her back and headed for the elevator before he could see her cry.

Although Friday was as autumn-cheerful as the previous day, Alcea wasn't feeling any jollier than she had after she'd left the hospital. Kathleen was at school. Florida was wrapped up in Missouri. She'd be discharged later today, although the baby would stay another week. Alcea had called her this morning, hoping to pick her up, but Dak had beat her to it. Her parents were busy. Lil was busy. Mari and Patsy Lee were at work. Everyone had a life except her.

She prowled the trailer, taking care of unnecessary chores. She tried to clean out her closet in preparation for moving God knew where, but left the clothes in a heap on her bed. She picked up a book, but couldn't concentrate. She pulled out some bakeware, then put it all back. She could go to Peg's to see what she could salvage, but didn't feel ready to face it. Finally, she stood stock-still in the kitchen, hands flat-palmed on the counter, and made herself think about the things she was avoiding.

Her thoughts tumbled through the events of the last thirty hours, finally bumping against Dak's words at the hospital. *I think I love you, Alcea.* No conviction. No promises. He didn't love her *enough*. She dropped her head, indulging in a bout of self-pity that might have lasted the rest of the day if a horn hadn't beeped in the driveway. Parting the curtain, she saw Kemp emerging from his Lincoln, his carefully combed hair glinting in the sun like light glancing off glass. She didn't know whether to be happy or irritated at the intrusion. Oh, balls. He'd be a distraction, and she wanted to talk to him, anyway. Hurriedly, she wiped her eyes and stepped outside.

His eyes lit up when he saw her, and he grasped her hands. "How are you feeling today?"

"Okay." Not okay. Her chin started to tremble again, but apparently he didn't notice. There was an odd glimmer of excitement behind his expression that made her uneasy.

"I got the message you left last night, but—hope you don't mind—I decided that instead of calling, I'd just come on over. There's something I want to show you, if you have time." Before she'd even answered, he was leading her to the car.

She slid inside without protest. What else did she have to do? "What's up?"

He settled in behind the wheel. "You'll see."

At least he had enough sensitivity not to take her past the diner as he headed the car into the countryside. She assumed they were going to the club. "Um, I don't have time for a meal." She had the time, just not the right clothes on, or the stomach for it.

He smiled, looking a lot like she'd imagined the Cheshire Cat would, and her disquiet increased. "Okay. No meal," he agreed. "In your message last night, you said you needed to talk to me about something?"

She squirmed around in her seat. With Dak's recent words addling her brain, she was hard-pressed to come up with a coherent way to express what she wanted to say. "Um, let's talk later."

"That's fine."

When she would have been happy just to lapse into silence, he started rambling. Like he was nervous. Maybe he'd construed her reluctance to talk into a refusal of his proposal. She let down her window. He mentioned he was flying out tonight to visit his daughter, Glory, in Texas. The wind ruffled her hair, blowing the cobwebs out of her brain. He'd be back Sunday night, and they could go to Discount Dinner Night on Monday. When she didn't respond, only taking a deep breath of the crystalline air, he stepped up his patter, moving on to his workday, the increase in prices at the dry cleaner's, and some mention of how his wife had once ironed his shirts to perfection. She sighed and let the breeze and the drone of his voice relax her.

Out here, there were no exhaust fumes, no waft of sausage grease from the grill or cinnamon from the oven. She studied the wildflowers bundled near the roadside. Her heart sighed. And none of Paddy O'Neill's cackle or Tansy's answering snort or the laughter, chatter, and twang of silverware that normally filled the diner. Only a buzz of locusts. Still, the silence settled her. But as they neared her former home, she tensed back up. "Where are we going?"

In answer, he pulled into the winding drive that led up to the colonnaded house.

The rest of her short-lived peacefulness fled. "I really don't want to visit anyone." Especially not the new occupants of her former home. She hadn't missed the house, but she'd rather not revisit the crime scene.

"Nobody's here." He stopped the car at the top of the drive.

Still puzzled but somewhat reassured, Alcea studied the house. Nothing had changed. The draperies she'd painstakingly chosen for the windows were still in place. The Mexican pottery urns she'd left behind still guarded the doorways. Even the grounds were tended. She wondered why she'd ever thought it was all so important. Still, it was a grand old place. She admired it for a moment. Then she turned to Kemp. "Why did you bring me here?"

He threw an arm over the seat back. His body almost thrummed. "It's mine."

She blinked. "Yours?"

"I bought it at auction."

She blinked again. "You did? But—but why didn't I hear about it?"

"I bought it through a middleman. I didn't want you to know."

"Ah." He must have thought she'd be upset that he'd taken advantage of a fire sale. Then her disquiet returned full force. "Why didn't you move in?"

His face turned pink. "I, uh, it wasn't for me. It was for you."

Alcea went mute.

"I know how much this house means to you. You talked about it all the time, and you struggled to keep it for so long. . . ."

"But I couldn't accept a gift like this." Nor could she afford its upkeep.

"It, uh, it isn't a gift." Kemp's face reddened more. He sighed. "I'm doing this badly. I bought it for *us*. To live in. After we're married."

"Oh, God." The words escaped her lips before she could stop them. He winced, and she touched his arm. "I'm sorry. I'm not ungrateful. I'm just . . . stunned." And appalled. How could he think she'd want to live here again? "I don't know what to say."

"Just say yes. We'll get married, and we'll live where you've always wanted to live, and Kathleen can have her old room back. It'll be a good life, Alcea, like the one I shared with Marjorie. You'll live the life you deserve to have, not scrambling to make the ends meet in some diner." His eyes shone. "I can't wait to tell Glory."

The reference to Marjorie didn't bother her. As far as he was concerned, comparing her to his wife was the ultimate compliment. But the implication that her business had somehow been a sentence in hell . . . The man certainly wasn't very perceptive.

She opened her mouth to refuse, then closed it. The plea in his face, the adoration in his eyes, how much he was willing to do for her . . . and for Kathleen. Like she had so many opportunities banging at her door, she could just carelessly toss this one aside? She thought hard, her gaze moving from him back to the house while Kemp sat silent, willing her with his eyes to give him the response he wanted. And it struck her. . . . It didn't really matter where you lived, did it? Suddenly, she knew her answer. Uncertainty was a fact of life. No matter how much you planned and wrung your hands, life's opportunities struck in different guises, and when they did, you had to grab hold with both hands despite your fears.

And walls weren't important. She turned to Kemp. Looking into his glowing face, she took both his hands in hers. What mattered was the life you built.

And build it she would.

Over the weekend, she pondered the long discussion she'd had with Kemp following the unveiling of his intended wedding gift. Her mind clicked away even as she chauffeured Kathleen and her friends to a soccer game in Sedalia; helped her mother and the Ladies' Auxiliary plan their Halloween Fright Night; checked in on Paddy, whose knee surgery had slowed *him,* but not his tongue, down; and let Rosemary trim her hair and bubble over her job at Up-in-the-Hair.

Her brain ran through her decision over and over as she helped Florida settle in and ferried her to the hospital to visit Missouri. True to his word, Dak had picked up his sister on Friday and installed her back at Cowboy's, but typically, he'd gone to ground immediately after. Florida said he was holed up in his bedroom, surfacing "like some damn groundhog" only when he needed to eat. Alcea supposed he was still stewing, but she forced herself not to consider them—or him—any of her concern.

By Sunday evening, as she browned hamburger for dinner and waited for Kathleen to get back from doing homework with Melanie, she was finally certain she was doing what she had to. Thinking of Kemp, her heart squeezed. He was a dear man. The best. He'd offered her a fresh start, and she'd repay him no matter what it took. She just wished she could love him the same way she loved Dak. He deserved that kind of love. But she couldn't provide it.

Turning down the heat, she leaned back against the counter and let her gaze wander around the kitchen, over the curtains she'd sewn and the dish towels she'd purchased to match the pink appliances. When she'd moved into the Palace, the bakery had been a bare glimmer in her imagination. And the trailer had been a pink tin can. But then she'd taken them both and with just the right ingredients she'd molded one into a home and one into a business. She hadn't loved these places as much as she'd *been* these places. Her mother's voice echoed. *I'm proud of you. Real proud.* And inevitably, Dak's voice rose, too. *Play the music you hear.* Her gaze settled on the pair of silly pig salt and pepper shakers Dak had bought that day in June. In his understated way, he'd urged her toward the choices that had made her so happy. She turned away from the pigs. Maybe, just maybe, she could be that happy again. . . .

A car sounded in the drive, and a moment later Kathleen shouldered open the door, her arms full of books. She glared at Alcea, said, "I ate at Daisy's," then stomped down the hallway. Her bedroom door slammed, and Alcea sighed. Back to square one. Kathleen had treated her to belligerence ever since Alcea had returned on Friday with Kemp. Her daughter did *not* approve of the man; that was obvious.

No longer hungry, Alcea switched off the stove. It would only take one long talk with Kathleen to turn her attitude around—she hoped—but she'd made the decision not to tell anyone her plans until she could present a done deal. Cowardly, she knew, but her convictions were still too unsteady to withstand her daughter's curled lip, her mother's wringing hands, or Lil's concerned gaze. Which might not be the reaction they'd have at all, but she wasn't about to take the chance that her new determination might crumble. She'd dodged phone calls from her mother and Lil all weekend. She'd also pledged Kemp to silence until after next Wednesday, when the deed was done. He didn't understand, but he'd promised.

She put the hamburger into the fridge, rinsed the skillet, and wandered into the living room, picking up a spiral notebook she was using to outline arrangements. Kemp had said he'd help her finish them tomorrow evening. But when she sat down, she just held the notebook in her lap.

On Friday evening, after she and Kemp had pulled back into the drive at the Pink Palace, Kathleen had been waiting outside to ask permission to visit the hospital with Florida later that night. Under her scornful eyes, Kemp had leaned over to give Alcea a chaste kiss on the cheek.

"I'll call you from Texas tomorrow," he said. "We'll go to Warsaw on Monday to get things going. I'm sure we can be ready on Wednesday like you want."

"I'll talk to you then." She laid a hand along his face. "Have a good visit with Glory. And Kemp? Thank you so much. For *everything*."

His smile was soft. "Warsaw wasn't exactly what I had in mind, but"—a glance at Kathleen and his smile faded. No wonder. Kathleen's scowl would frighten lesser men than he. "It's probably for the best."

She got out and stood by Kathleen, who glared after Kemp as he pulled out of the drive. As they walked toward the trailer, Alcea tried an arm around her daughter's shoulders. Without telling Kathleen anything, she wanted to get some idea of how she would react to her decision. "Do you know what that sweet man did? He bought our old house."

"And I bet he wants to marry you and move us in there." Kathleen shrugged off Alcea's arm. "You'd do anything for that dumb place."

"Dumb place?" Alcea followed her into the trailer,

feeling rather cheerful despite Kathleen's surliness. "I thought you wanted bigger closets."

Kathleen whirled. "You can't go home again," she announced dramatically.

Alcea would have laughed if Kathleen hadn't looked so serious. "Huh?"

"It's a *saying*. It means, like, things can never be the way they were. *You* shouldn't even want them to be the same, not after you've done so much. I was *proud* of you."

"Proud of me? If I remember right, you hated that I moved here, hated that I worked at Peg's. You pretty much hated everything. Aren't you the one who moved in with your dad?"

"But I moved back, didn't I?"

Alcea had held her breath. "You mean, you'd stay? Even if it was here?"

"Well, yeah. But it can't *be* here, can it?"

Kathleen hadn't waited for Alcea's reply. Just like tonight, she'd trounced down the hall and slammed her door. But despite the theatrics, she'd left Alcea with a warm glow. Kathleen planned to stay.

Alcea opened the notebook. Or Kathleen *had* planned to. It remained to be seen if Alcea could convince her to accept their new living arrangements. She shrugged. Kathleen would approve; she knew it. At least eventually. But Alcea wouldn't even try to convince her until she'd made it through Wednesday. When the ink was dry and it was too late to turn back.

For a while, she jotted notes. Kathleen prepared for bed and snapped off her lights without a good night. As the clock inched toward midnight, Alcea finally laid the notebook aside and followed suit. But once in bed, she couldn't sleep. Her brain refused to still. It wandered through her memories of Peg O' My Heart, finally halting on her bakery. She hadn't returned since the fire. She still avoided Main.

Swinging out of bed, she yanked her clothes back

on. It was time. It was time to say farewell to the old so she could welcome the new.

Alcea loitered for a moment outside the brick husk of Peg O' My Heart Cafe. A stiff breeze kicked up small cyclones of ash. The square was deserted, but she took a last long look around before she ducked under the flapping caution tape and switched on the beam of a powerful flashlight she'd unearthed in a foray to the service garage a few minutes ago. If anyone saw her, they'd undoubtedly stop her.

Pulling in her stomach against her nerves, she stepped over some charred timbers and entered the gaping doorway. The stench of smoke filled her nostrils. Through the gaping holes where the plate glass windows had exploded, moonglow glimmered, its blue cast dancing eerily with the yellow beam she played over the space. Dust motes were thick. Only the chrome features remained of the tables and chairs, melted and stroked with the black paintbrush of flames. Beneath her feet, the linoleum curled like a choppy lake, windswept and freeze-dried. She took a step forward, trying to identify the lumps in front of her—a few booths, looking like reflections of themselves in a fun house mirror, their color no longer red.

Some fun house. Her heart had plummeted somewhere into her stomach and pumped sluggishly, as though trying to hide from the shock of seeing her beloved business reduced to shadows and soot and waterlogged blackened timbers. The grill still stood. Coated with gunk, but possibly salvageable. The safety features had worked, even though the fire hadn't started there. Thick retardant had poured from the hood, like it had belched up an inedible slop. Turning away, she flashed her light toward the bakery doorway, studying it for safety before she ventured through. The weight-bearing beams that supported the brick wall above were chewed by the fire, and it looked risky. Still, she took a step forward.

Then halted abruptly when a muffled clunk sounded from the bakery. She sucked in air heavy with ash, triggering a fit of coughing. When she stopped, there was silence. Raccoons, she assured herself, or a stray dog. Maybe something falling. But what if it was a looter?

Resisting the urge to flee, she listened intently. All she heard was the wind funneling through the windows. Then somebody sneezed, and her temper flared. How dare anyone intrude on this place? Oblivious of the broken glass crunching under her footfalls, she marched toward the doorway, shooting the flashlight beam into the bakery. The sight of the ruin almost made her gag. "Who's there? I have a gun." She didn't, but what the heck.

Silence at first, and then a shuffle. "Don't shoot," Dak said dryly, and rose from behind the hull of what remained of the display case. His face floated before her, his dark hair and dark shirt blending into the flame-licked brick of the walls behind him. His expression held a sheepish look, his arm several soot-covered stainless steel mixing bowls.

"Why didn't you call out or something?" She looked from the bowls back to his face. "What are you doing here?"

"I, um— I didn't know who it was. Thought it might be a looter." He took a step out from behind the counter, dragging something behind him. A board snapped under his tread. He stumbled and pitched forward, barely keeping on his feet. Above him a timber groaned in a sudden gust of wind, showering them with ash.

She glanced up, felt a smidgen of fear. "It's dangerous in here. You shouldn't be here." The combination of surprise and relief made her voice sharp.

"You shouldn't, either."

"I needed to come. I needed to see it to say goodbye." Her gaze dropped back to the bowls. "Why are you stealing my bowls?"

"I wasn't *stealing* them. I was salvaging them." He motioned behind him with his head. "The oven's gone. But I think you could save that." Another motion at her prep table. "That is, if you want to. Salvage anything. Maybe sell it?" His flash of white teeth was briefer than ever before. The self-assurance he'd always carried so lightly was threadbare, just like when she'd seen him at the hospital.

"Maybe. Maybe I'll want to." She didn't plan to give him the satisfaction of knowing anything she intended.

"Well, I thought if you didn't, Florida might."

"And you thought you'd do this salvage operation at midnight?"

"Would you get that thing out of my eyes?" was his only reply. Before she lowered the beam, she saw him flush. A flashlight went on from his side and shafted across the floor, joining hers in the waterlogged debris. "I couldn't sleep, and I just thought of it, and I wanted to see what I was up against. Before I came over here in the daylight, that is."

"Mmm."

Another gust, and a piece of scrap fell, narrowly missing his head. He jumped a foot forward. "I've been dodging that stuff for the last hour." Hour? Timbers groaned again under the wind's onslaught. He glanced up. "I think that one is ready to give. We'd better get out of here."

Alcea took a last look around, the sight burning its image on her brain, then turned and picked her way back through the diner. Outside, she gulped in a great mouthful of air. She heard Dak follow, and a muttered curse as he bumped up against something. Then a large crack as something split and crashed to the ground. To her relief, Dak lunged out the doorway just a moment later, still dragging the salvage.

"Are you okay?" Her heart was in her throat.

"Fine. But that's the end of the prep table." Stopping beside her, he righted the chair.

No, not a chair. With something akin to awe, she reached out and touched it. Peg's stool. My God, the stool had survived. The upholstery looked like a bubbled marshmallow that had been held too long to the campfire, but the chrome stand was intact. She looked at Dak, suddenly feeling like laughing and crying all at the same time. The wind caught his hair, blowing it back from his forehead, revealing a harsh scrape beaded with blood. She touched the side of his forehead. "You're hurt."

"A board glanced off me. It's nothing."

She took the mixing bowls from his hands. "No. It's something." She wasn't talking about the scrape. She waited for more, but all he did was heft the stool and set off in the direction of Cowboy's. She followed a couple of steps behind. They didn't talk. His stride was stiff, and she knew he didn't know what to say. Her mind was too busy to say anything coherent at all.

When they finally reached the concrete block patio of the Pink Palace, he stopped and set down the stool. "Can you manage to get it inside?"

That was it. She sighed and nodded. "Thanks."

"Okay. You're welcome."

Without a backward glance, he stuffed his hands in his pockets and ambled down the path. She watched him go, shook her head again, and turned to Peg's stool. Despite her roiling thoughts and her anxiety over everything she'd set in motion with Kemp, she felt a sudden elation. She gave the poor misshapen thing a pat. When she looked back up, Dak was disappearing into the house. The door shut softly behind him.

Hugging the bowls with one arm, she slid the other under the stool and lugged it into the Pink Palace. It wasn't much, but it *was* something. She balanced the bowls on its bubbled upholstery, plopped onto the sofa, and stared at it with wonder. *Really* something.

Chapter 26

All that work last night scrambling through the remains of Peg O' My Heart Cafe, and all he had to show for it was a scraped head, some worthless junk, and injured dignity. Dak touched the bandage he'd put on his forehead, then concentrated once more on his phone conversation. It was nearing noon and he'd been talking rapidly—and, he hoped, convincingly—for the last hour.

Florida had already left for another day at the hospital with Missouri, full of cheer because Missouri could come home in a few days. No apnea, no jaundice. She'd landed a kiss on top of his head before she'd flown out the door, happy with him, as well.

Last night, before that reckless visit he'd made to Peg's diner, he'd accompanied Florida to the hospital. While Florida had talked to the nurse, he'd placed his hands on the cool surface of the nursery window and studied his niece. Or rather, he'd studied the oxygen tent around her. Like on Thursday, he could barely make her out. Then a tiny fist had popped up and flailed. A tiny, defiant cry pierced the glass. "You just give 'em hell, honey." He'd whispered. "Uncle Dak's right here." Florida had broken off her conversation and looked at him with surprise. When she'd returned to the nurse, she'd worn a satisfied smile. Feeling sheepish, he'd shrugged. Who could resist a baby?

He hung up the phone and splayed his fingers on

the table, thinking of Missouri, Florida, Alcea, Kathleen . . . and the events he'd just set in motion. Last night's wind had faded to a whisper that eddied through the open back door. Somewhere nearby, he heard a car pull off.

The conference call he'd arranged early this morning had gone about as well as he could hope. Both his agent and editor were excited, but he still had work ahead of him before his publisher would commit. And if they did . . . he curled his fingers until his nails bit his palms . . . he'd open himself to a firestorm of publicity and speculation with a sequel to *Torn.*

During the call, he'd heard the drool in his agent's voice and the buzz of excitement under his editor's feigned caution. Feigned because Dak was certain his editor was only wondering how much of an advance he'd demand; there was no doubt the interest was there. He was doing what they'd hoped he'd do for years: capitalizing on the success of *Torn,* revealing his identity, and submitting to a publicity tour where interviewers would probe for parallels between his life and his protagonist's. The idea made his palms wet.

The new book he'd pitched had taken shape over the weekend, when he'd holed up in his bedroom, laptop on his knees, and pounded out his emotions into the bits of the story Alcea had provoked. He'd returned only grunts to Florida's tentative queries from the other side of his locked door. Formed from the pieces he'd revealed to Kathleen and fueled by events of the past week, a dam had burst and surged through his fingertips. This time his protagonist wouldn't succumb to the weight of his past, though. This time he'd triumph. Maybe. The ending had yet to be written.

Before he'd even finished talking, his agent had been exploring the possibilities of rereleasing the first novel, timed to prime sales for the second. By the end of the call, even his editor was talking media blitz. They had only one reservation. After all of the *Road* books, they weren't sure he was still capable of the pull-out-the-stops writing he'd done for *Torn*.

He'd made such a botch of the conversation in the hospital with Alcea—what kind of a wimp said *I think I love you?*—nothing less than a grand gesture would convince Alcea he'd changed. He'd seen the intractable doubt on her fact.

His gut clenched as his own doubt rose. This might *not* convince her. And he might not be able to stomach the obliteration of his deep-seated need for a measure of solitude. He now knew he wanted to participate in life, not just play narrator with a mouthful of pithy observations. But putting himself at center stage rubbed his psyche the wrong way. Irritated at the seesaw his thoughts had become, he shoved them away. For Alcea, he'd do what he had to. And if this didn't work, there was always a new town, a new horizon. . . . The idea exhausted him.

Using his fists, he pushed himself up from his chair. One thing at a time. He'd promised a written proposal within the week, but perhaps his time would be better spent polishing the first few chapters. The raw emotion he'd felt when writing them would surely convince his editor like no proposal would.

"Dak!" Kathleen's voice sounded.

He went to the door, begrudging the interruption. "What are you doing out of school?"

"Lunch hour. I have to talk to you and it's important, so, like, don't tell me I shouldn't be off the school grounds." Clutching her backpack, she shoved her way past him. "I would have told you this weekend, but Florida wouldn't let me *bother* you."

Kathleen's seeming certainty she could never be a bother normally would have amused him, but feelings of uncertainty had made him edgy. "Can't it wait? You *could* get in trouble."

"That is *so* not important. Not compared to this."

He glanced at his watch. "If you hurry, you'll be able to—"

"Mom is marrying Kemp!"

He halted, momentarily staggered, but it really wasn't something he hadn't expected. And wedding plans would take time. "That's nice. Now, why don't you go on back—"

"That's *nice*? Are you *listening*? He took her to Warsaw this morning. The *county seat*. Do you know what that means?"

"A marriage license, probably. Look, you need to be in school. I have things to do."

"Don't you care?" She slapped her backpack on the table.

"Kathleen." His temper ratcheted up a notch. "Go back to school."

"Quit telling me what to do. You are *not* my dad."

Flashing eyes, hands on hips, chin in the air. At that moment, her likeness to Alcea was so unbelievable he almost burst out laughing. Suddenly, Missouri's tiny fist flashed through his mind. The mulish set of Florida's jaw. He thought of Jon describing Lil's sweet determination. And Serena's velvet-shod iron hand dealing with Stan. By God, they had a bunch of stubborn women to contend with in this . . .

Family.

His knees went weak. Tenuous as some of the connections were, they were *his* family.

His anger evaporated. With all their attendant kinks and knots—and strengths. Tamara had denied him these kind of bonds throughout his childhood, and then he'd denied them himself. Now he stood at the threshold of another choice. He suddenly knew why Alcea had shunned his half-assed declaration of love. It wasn't enough to *consider* staying; he had to *commit*. Not for Alcea. Or not only for Alcea. For himself. Without a word, he stalked to the front door, flung it open, and took the steps in a bound.

"Where are you going?" Behind him, Kathleen hurried to keep up.

Out in the yard, he stopped next to the FOR SALE—

THREE ACRES—TWO BUILDINGS sign. Grasping it with both hands, he tore it from the earth and threw it aside.

Kathleen watched, openmouthed. "You're not leaving." She breathed.

"I'm not going anywhere." Regardless of Alcea, he had two nieces, a half sister, a half brother, friends, and ties to this community, whether he'd ever wanted any of them or not. To re-coin the old adage, loving people could lead to heartache, but heartache was better than never experiencing love at all. "You're right. I'm *not* your father." Confusion joined the excitement on her face. He put his hands on her shoulders, and gazed steadily into her eyes. "But I *am* your uncle."

He watched as the words penetrated, then shock widened her eyes. "Oh. My. God. Does that mean my mom is your sister?"

"No!" He laughed, feeling immeasurable relief to not just admit their relationship, but to *embrace* it. He hugged her tight, then led her back into the house.

In the kitchen, he motioned her to a chair, then straddled another, briefly sketching out his history. "But don't tell anyone. At least not until I've talked with your dad, when he gets back."

She looked fascinated. And thrilled. She made a zip-my-lips gesture. "I won't say a *word,* I promise. But, omigod, this is *so* awesome." She beamed at him. "We're related. And if you're staying, then you and my mom . . . God, I almost *forgot* why I came here."

"Because your mom plans to marry Kemp. Well, I have some plans of my own where she's concerned."

"You'd better be fast, because they're going to *elope. Secretly.* On *Wednesday.*"

Wednesday? His flush of excitement faded as a bolt of panic hit his chest. "If it's a secret, how do you know?"

"Because they talked about it right in front of me. He says to her, like, 'Be ready on Wednesday to go back to Warsaw.' Dak, there are *judges* in Warsaw.

They thought I was too dumb to figure it out, but I knew. And then Mom said he'd bought our old house. He wants us to *move* there. He's picking her up at ten. Wednesday, I mean. I looked at her calendar, and she has it written in big letters with underlines and everything."

"Ten?" His voice was weak. Less than forty-eight hours from now.

"It's the worst thing *ever*."

He understood the feeling. "Why the rush?"

He was talking to himself, but Kathleen answered. "I don't know. Maybe she wants his money really fast so she can rebuild Peg's. She needs money—everyone knows that."

And she'd sell herself to Runyon rather than take what he'd offered? He shook his head. That was the old Alcea, not the Alcea he knew. More likely she was doing it for reasons involving Kathleen—quickly and quietly, before Kathleen could mount World War III. But that wasn't something he'd share with her daughter. "Where is your mom now?"

"At the library. This morning, she said she had to make lots of plans, and she couldn't get any peace and quiet at home. I think because Grandma and Aunt Lil keep calling."

Zinnia. He got to his feet. "Call your grandmother. And your Aunt Lil. I'm calling an O'Malley Family Meeting. At your grandma's house, today at three."

Kathleen raised her brows. "Have you ever been to one of those things?"

He didn't answer. He was already heading into the dining room, where he'd left his laptop. He had only a few hours to pound out a proposal. If he hurried, maybe, just maybe, he could get his publisher's agreement before Wednesday. No more quibbling over what horrors the publicity would be. The alternative was worse. His footsteps faltered. Wasn't it?

He glanced back. Kathleen still sat at the table staring after him. "Get a move on." He smiled, covering the sick feeling in his stomach whenever he thought of his past laid bare in a *media blitz*. But it was hardly anything compared to the nausea he felt when he thought about Alcea and Runyon married. "And then get yourself back to school."

She curled her lip. "And miss all this? No way!"

Chapter 27

When Wednesday morning dawned, Alcea woke feeling decidedly miffed.

After the fire at Peg's, everyone had been so solicitous, checking on her so frequently that their kindness had become a source of aggravation. But since Sunday, none of her family had called, Florida had been wrapped up in Missouri, she hadn't heard a peep from Rosemary, and even Julius and his cronies had been AWOL from the garage's stoop all week. It seemed they'd all but forgotten her and her plight. Perversely, that aggravated her more.

As for Dak . . . whatever he was doing, it hadn't been at Cowboy's. His Jeep had been more gone than there for the last forty-eight hours. And he wasn't the only thing missing. So was the sign from Cowboy's yard. She assumed he'd finally sold the place, but she hadn't asked anyone. She hadn't wanted to know. Fingers clutching at her sheets, her gaze moved to the newly polished stool that stood in the corner of her bedroom like some kind of shrine. She'd been so *sure* . . .

Oh, balls. She swung her legs over the side of the bed and sat up, leaning over to part the curtains. Except for some early falling leaves tumbling across the yard Dak had cleared of debris, nothing moved under gray skies. She grimaced and dropped the curtain, refusing to speculate. She wouldn't worry about Dak. Not today.

She glanced at the clock. She'd slept longer than normal. Understandable since she hadn't fallen asleep until near dawn, wrestling with the anxiety that hit her every time she thought about what today would bring. But now she had only just over an hour before she was scheduled to meet Kemp at Stan's bank. He wanted to pick up some papers there before they traveled to Warsaw.

Shrugging into a robe, she poked her head in Kathleen's room. Piles of discarded clothing, a rumpled bedspread, no backpack. She'd mentioned last night that Patsy Lee would give her a lift to school, so there had been no reason for her to wake Alcea before she'd left. But Alcea wished she had. Even a sullen good-bye was better than none at all. Especially today.

Except Kathleen hadn't been sullen since Sunday night, Alcea thought, swerving into the bathroom. Nor had she said another word about Kemp. She threw a handful of vanilla-scented salts into her bath, turned on the spigots, then hustled to her room to lay out a cream-colored silk pantsuit, one of several she hadn't worn at all for the last six months except on her dates with Kemp. Kathleen's cold-shoulder treatment was gone, but her behavior was . . . odd. She'd scurried around, avoiding her mother's eyes, a secret glint in her own. Maybe some boy had turned her head. Or maybe her daughter was scheming how to move back to her dad's. She shook her head. Those thoughts weren't fair to Kathleen. They were her own guilt talking; if anyone was acting secretive, it was Kathleen's mother. *She* was out of sorts because she was scared.

Thinking of Kemp, she felt anxiety bubble up faster than her bath. On Monday when he'd picked her up to go to Warsaw, he'd done his best to reassure her that she'd made the right decision. He hadn't helped. On the way there, fortunately after he'd stopped the Lincoln and she'd hurried to the back of the car, she—

who had never been carsick in her life—had upchucked. Lowering herself into the bathtub, she wished her stomach would quit doing somersaults. God, she hoped what she was doing was *right*. But at least she was doing *something*.

Glancing at the clock again, she rushed to dry her hair, smoothed it into a knot, then shrugged into her clothes. Finally, she hunted through her closet for a pair of heels. On her dates, she wore flats so she wouldn't tower over Kemp, but today *confidence* was her buzzword. She found a pair of stilettos buried in the back and pulled them out. Marc Jacobs. She smiled dryly. Actually, she now preferred Adidas. She slid them on and headed to Kathleen's room, where she rummaged in her jewelry box until she found a pair of pearl earrings. Something borrowed . . . She remembered when she'd worn her mother's pearls for her wedding to Stan. Pearls for every beginning. Thinking how different this occasion was from that lavish affair, she would have laughed if she wasn't sure anxiety would choke her if she tried.

Finally ready, she took a deep breath, a last look around, and headed for her car. In the rearview mirror, her face was a death mask. She looked away and prayed she wouldn't whoops all over her suit, pleased when she negotiated the drive and alley without even a burp. She turned onto Main. Then halted abruptly and swore. A half a block ahead, a crowd milled across the road, effectively blocking her route.

She'd just turned to look over her shoulder in preparation for backing up when someone tapped on the passenger's window. She jumped and hit the brakes. Lil peered in. Oh, balls. Had her sister somehow found out and come to talk her out of it?

When a line began furrowing between Lil's eyes, Alcea finally lowered the window. "What's going on?" She nodded her head toward the crowd.

Lil didn't answer. Expression holding suppressed . . . something . . . she just opened the door and got in.

Alcea watched her suspiciously. She was dressed in blue denim from one end to the other. "Kemp asked me to watch for you. He wants to meet you up there." She waved a vague hand up Main.

"You know?"

Lil nodded. "He told me."

"And you've come to talk me out of it. Well, it's not going to work."

Lil shook her head. "You know I'd always stand behind you, Alcea, no matter what I thought." Lil's voice was firm, but without censure. "Come on, he's waiting." She moved to buckle her seat belt.

Having steeled herself against Lil's arguments, Alcea felt churlish. She put a hand on Lil's wrist. "Just a minute. I'm sorry. And I want to say thank you. You *have* always been there for me."

Lil shrugged. "That's what sisters are for. Let's go."

Why was serene Lil in such a gol-darned hurry all of the sudden? "But I wasn't always there for you. I do love you, Lil."

"And I love you. Except . . ." Lil twisted to look at her. "You know, last spring you said some things that bothered me."

"What a surprise," Alcea said dryly. "I apologize for all of them."

"No, it's not me you need to apologize to. It's Mother. She was hurt when you said she played favorites between us. She doesn't. She never has."

"I know." Alcea sat back, stared out the windshield. "At least, I know that *now*. It wasn't that she loved you more, I was just always a pain in the patootie." Alcea gave Lil a quick smile, forestalling the objection she saw rise on Lil's face. "It's true. But it didn't mean she loved me less because of it. I think it was easier for me for a long time to blame my circumstances on everyone else but myself. And I'll talk to Mother, I promise."

"Good. Now get a move on."

Alcea frowned. Did she think Kemp would evaporate or something? "And Lil, I'm going into this with clear eyes. If things don't work out, I'll only have myself to blame."

"Oh, I have a feeling everything will work out just fine." She pointed ahead. "If you ever get there."

"Okay, okay." She put the car in gear. Lil. The infernal optimist, God love her. She wished she could be as certain.

"Pull the car clear up, just short of the crowd." Lil instructed.

"And then what?" Alcea put the car in gear. "Why isn't Kemp just meeting me at the bank? And what's going on here, some kind of hoedown?" She studied the people ahead of them as she edged up close. Most were in work clothes. Serious work clothes. Denim and Dickies and heavy leather boots. "Or is it a barn-raising?" She stopped the car, and Lil hopped out.

"Wait a minute. Where's Kemp?" Alcea leaned out. "Lil! Where are you going?"

"We have to walk," Lil called back without breaking her stride.

"Walk?" Alcea looked at her shoes. "In these?" Her protest went unanswered.

Grumbling, she swung out her legs. By the time she traversed the sidewalk along the square, she'd have blisters the size of balloons. When she straightened, Lil had disappeared. Alcea shaded her eyes and finally caught sight of Lil's cap of curls. But Lil wasn't following the sidewalk. Instead she was cutting across the church green. Grabbing her clutch purse, Alcea followed, grimacing as wet earth sucked at her shoes. After all her preparations, she'd look just like she had when she'd stormed into Stan's bank in her muddy bare feet. The grimace turned to a scowl.

Which must have been effective. As she marched forward, the crowd parted to let her through until she felt like Moses at the Red Sea. Her eyes darted left and right. Geez, almost everyone she knew was there. The air was festive. She caught sight of Rosemary and

Tansy. For some odd reason, they were dressed in their diner uniforms, Rosemary bouncing like she had to pee, Tansy flashing her a huge smile. Her frown deepened. She'd never seen Tansy do more than cackle.

Grins splitting their faces, the Steeplemier twins and Paddy stepped back to let her pass, Paddy after a hearty slap on the shoulder. She stumbled forward, her chignon slipping. When she braked to poke up the pins, someone plowed into her, almost pitching her onto her face. She whipped around, choice words on her lips, but she faltered midglare. People had filled in the path behind her. They'd all stopped when she did. In the front, Old Ben beamed, Erik Olausson flashed a shy smile, and Julius winked hugely. Under their gazes, she flushed, her mind scrambling for an explanation. Then Florida pushed through the crowd. Like almost everyone else, Florida wore attire suitable for mucking a barn, along with a smile that outstripped the glow of her sunbeam-yellow sweatshirt. She grasped Alcea's arm and pulled her along.

"What is all this?" Alcea called over excited voices, hoping she'd get more of an answer than she had from Lil. Mud slopped up her heels after the first steps, then one shoe stuck in the mire, and she stepped right out of it. "Florida! My shoe!" Twisting, she tried to spot it between pairs of legs. She tugged at Florida's grip. "I've got to—"

"C'mon." Florida was relentless. "Everyone's waiting."

"Everyone?" Alcea would have dug in her heels, had she any heels left to dig in with. But both shoes were now somewhere behind. Mud oozed between her toes, her hose were ruined, and the hems of her pants wouldn't bear looking at. She didn't object again. Somehow she didn't think Florida would care. "What do you mean everyone?"

The crowd had grown thicker. She bumped into

shoulders. The chignon finally gave way completely, and her hair spilled over her shoulders. "Florida!"

"Your family is waiting. And Kathleen. And—"

"Kathleen? She should be in school!"

Florida glanced over her shoulder, still smiling. "Not today. Don't worry—your mother got permission."

Her mother? "Florida, I've got an appointment! An *important* appointment. I can't—" Her voice dried up as Florida yanked her to a halt.

"Look, Alcea!" Her eyes were as wide as Peg's pancakes.

Alcea looked. They'd stopped in a clearing in front of St. Andrew's. Three long tables had been set up and dressed in red-and-black checkered tablecloths. One table held water jugs, coffeepots, and stacks of foam cups; another was laden with food. And on the third was an odd assortment of containers. Behind the tables, she recognized some faces from the Ladies' Auxiliary. Every last one of them was dressed in orange, her mother looking like a grinning pumpkin in one of Pop's eye-numbing flannel shirts. Off to the side, she saw Pop, an orange striped scarf wrapped around his neck. He was helping some men stack lumber.

Florida poked her. "Julius salvaged some of that from Cowboy's backyard."

"But what—?" Alcea's gaze swept up. A banner fluttered over the church steps. Handmade, it proclaimed, SAVE OUR DINER!

Her jaw dropped. Around her a smattering of applause grew to a cheer. "Save our diner! Save our diner!"

Florida grabbed her arm again. "Isn't this just plain exciting?" She led Alcea forward. "I could have just fainted when Julius fetched me early this morning."

They halted in front of the table with the containers—a cheese crock, an oversized plastic jar with an UTZ PRETZELS label, and every last one of the stainless steel mixing bowls Dak had salvaged. Emptied of their original contents, they were all—all—stuffed with money.

"My God." She stared at the bounty, then looked up. And into Kemp's face.

He smiled, almost sadly. "When I got to the bank, I wandered over to see what was up. And when I found out . . . well, I cancelled our appointment. It looks like you don't need me."

"But I—" She was too bewildered to form a sentence.

"No, you don't need him. You never did." Beside him, Zinnia hit a button on a calculator.

"Mother!" Embarrassed, Alcea darted a look at Kemp.

He spread his hands, his smile still gentle. "I tried to tell her."

"With the mayor's contribution, that makes $6,434." Florida and Alcea gasped. Zinnia smiled in satisfaction, then patted Kemp's hand. "It's not that I don't think you're a nice boy, Kemp. It's just that you're not quite right for our Alcea."

Omigod. "Mother, you don't know what you're talking about."

Kemp folded a piece of paper and dropped it into a jug. "Make that $11,434."

She abandoned her mother and stared at him. "Oh, Kemp. You can't. I—I—"

Florida elbowed her. "Don't be a goose."

When Alcea clamped her jaw shut, Julius turned toward the crowd. "She's overcome! She's thrilled! *To business that we love we rise betime!*" When the crowd stared at him dumbly, he shook his head and sighed. "Let's get to work!" Motioning with his arms, he waved them all toward the diner. In moments, orders were shouted. The buzz of saws and the whines of drills filled the air.

While everyone surged to their appointed tasks, Jon

sidled forward and deposited another scrap of paper. When Zinnia picked it up, her eyes popped behind her glasses. Alcea could only imagine the amount Jon and Lil had contributed.

Jon smiled at her and Florida. "Go get 'em, kids."

"I'll never be able to repay you." Alcea held her hands to her heated cheeks, her mind in turmoil. Had Jon and Lil organized everything? Was this Lil's way of running an endgame around her? Or maybe it had been her mother's scheme. "I have to— I'd planned—"

"Plans change." Jon held her gaze with his tiger eyes. "Lil told me, Alcea. You couldn't have—"

"I'll say she couldn't." Zinnia nudged her way in front of Alcea. Her face beamed. "Why, when Kathleen told me what you intended to do today, I was about fit to be tied."

Kathleen? She'd told nobody. "What *exactly* did Kathleen tell you?"

"That you were marrying Kemp Runyon, of course."

With a knowing grin, Jon sidled off. Smart man.

Zinnia pulled her off to one side. "I know you don't like any interference, but you know sometimes when you see somebody you love about to make the biggest mistake of her life, you just don't have much choice except to step in and put your foot down." Her voice was emphatic, but her eyes were wary. Alcea knew her mother was just waiting for her daughter to blow. "I mean, it's just no good telling me that I shouldn'ta stuck my nose in where it wasn't wanted because—"

"I know," Alcea said quietly. Before Kathleen had started leaning toward staying with her at the Pink Palace, she'd decided she would have to put her foot down, too, no matter what her daughter wanted. Or how much Kathleen might have hated her for it. Or how hard she might have had to fight Serena and Stan. Just like her plans for today, sometimes you just had to do what your gut told you was right, reason be damned.

"—no matter what you said, I would've moved heaven and earth— What did you say?"

Alcea reached out and drew Zinnia into a hug. "I love you," she whispered. "Even though you drive me nuts." Keeping an arm around her mother's shoulders, she turned and looked toward the diner. People swarmed over the structure. Beside her, Zinnia sniffed and swiped a finger under her glasses. "So you did all this," Alcea said. "Unbelievable. And the money you've collected . . . astounding."

"The money? That was easy," Zinnia said. "Here you've been so busy refusing help, you didn't realize you've been dishing out your own right and left. A lot of these folks feel they owe you. And Peg's . . . well, Peg's was an institution. And now it's a memorial to a fine woman. They're not about to let it go belly-up if they can help it."

Alcea's heart squeezed in gratitude. Kathleen came running up. Lil followed her.

"Isn't this *awesome,* Mom? Now you don't have to get married."

Oh, she still wanted to get married. But there would be time to explain that to Kathleen later.

Lil linked arms with their mother. "So, Alcea, what do you think?"

"It's amazing. How did you pull this whole thing together?" Alcea asked them.

Her mother and sister exchanged an odd look.

"*They* didn't do it." Kathleen interrupted, pointing to the roof of the diner. "*He* did."

Alcea followed Kathleen's finger. Silhouetted against the blue expanse of the sky, Dak stood with his legs planted wide, his thumbs hooked in the tool belt slung on his hips. Under a hard hat, his hair blew away from his face. He looked like a conquering Viking. "Dak did this?"

Lil put an arm around her shoulders. "He actually called an O'Malley Family Meeting on Monday afternoon." Lil giggled. "He's much braver than I gave him credit for. He summoned Mari here, too."

"And I think I really like the guy." Mari pushed through the crowd and threw her arms around her two sisters. "Sorry I'm late, but the traffic out of K.C. this morning . . ." She shook her head and the gigantic earrings that drooped from her ears hit the side of Alcea's face. She bent her dark head—today black with purple streaks—to Alcea's gold and Lil's pale yellow. "Way to go, Hock."

For once the nickname was endearing rather than grating. Alcea drew back and smiled at her sisters. Lil glowed. And Mari looked happy, her face clear of the worries that had wreathed it after Peg's funeral. Alcea could only assume she'd dumped her boyfriend. "All for one, eh?"

Both of them nodded. Then Lil turned her around. "I think someone's waiting for you."

Dak still stood on the rooftop. Even at this distance she could feel the pierce of those clear, bottomless eyes.

Mari snatched her purse from her hands and gave her a push. "What're you waiting for? If I had a hunk like that drooling over me, I wouldn't be standing here with my *sisters*."

Her gaze fixed on Dak, Alcea moved toward the diner. Like before, the crowd parted, but this time as she passed, voices fell to a hush. When she reached the blackened hull of the building, the work site had fallen silent. Someone handed her a pair of too-large work boots and a bright yellow hard hat. With trembling hands, she slipped them on. Then other hands reached out to help her clamber up to the roof. Her silk suit would be ruined, but she couldn't care less.

The roof of Peg's diner was blackened, nothing much left in the middle, but intact around the edges. Dak had paid an exorbitant amount to get a crew in here yesterday morning to clear out some of the garbage and reinforce the walls. They'd even worked under lights after dark. This morning, an inspector had deemed it safe enough for the work planned today.

He leaned his hips against a concrete parapet and watched Alcea's progress through the crowd. She watched back, her face a pale oval, her eyes unreadable at this distance. Despite the casual pose, his body was taut as barbed wire. When she reached the base of the building, she disappeared, and Dak knew willing hands were helping her up. Heart hammering, he pushed off the parapet and checked to be sure that the sheaf of papers he'd brought were still stuffed in his back pocket. He wasn't sure they'd do any good, but he'd brought them, anyway. He moved to the top of the ladder and waited. Alcea's yellow hard hat appeared, but her gaze was fixed on her feet. She finally glanced up, but only to grasp the hand he held out. Below her, other hands let go. When she'd straightened to his level, they stared at each other. Her gaze was guarded.

The pressure from her hand increased. "I don't know how to thank—"

He put his fingertips to her mouth, then moved his hand along her cheek to tuck back a wisp of hair that had blown across her face. "I don't want thanks. Just don't marry Runyon."

Something leaped in her eyes, then went still. She let go of his hand. "You're here under false pretenses, you know."

He didn't understand. "I have the truest intentions I've ever had in my life."

A brow raised. "And those are?"

"Let's talk." He led her along the edge of the building and they settled side by side near the parapet. Below his dangling work boots faces turned upward, and the crowd held its collective breath. Alcea didn't even glance at them; her eyes were on him. He reached for the papers and handed them over.

She unfurled them, read a moment, then looked back at him. "What is this?"

"The proposal I did for a new book. It's a love story. About how a man finds his place in the world through the love of a woman. I thought you'd see parallels. . . ." He stumbled. Under her gaze, he couldn't recall the speech he'd prepared. "It's also a sequel to *Torn*." Rapidly, and not too coherently, he outlined the plans he'd made on Monday, the revealing of his name, the publicity tour—all of it. "If my editor accepted it before you married Runyon, I thought I could show you a contract that would prove I was no longer hiding from my past. That I no longer needed to run. That I was willing to stand up and shout the whole mess to the world."

She frowned. "You'd hate that."

"I know. It'd kill me. And so I"—he swallowed hard. "Alcea, I don't just *think* I love you. I do love you. But I can't follow through. Not even for you. I'll write the book—I can't *not* write the book—but I don't want the publicity. It's enough for me to know I've come to terms with my past and—" He stopped, flabbergasted.

Without a change of expression, she'd flipped her wrist and cast the papers over the side. The breeze caught them, and they danced above the crowd.

He stared at her, feeling defeated. "You don't believe me." He gathered himself, then launched in again. "Alcea, I love you, and I want to stay with you. Right here in Cordelia." He faltered under her even gaze. "At least most of the time. I know I'll still want to travel. Maybe sometimes alone. But I promise you I'll never sneak away in anger or in hurt or because I'm avoiding you or anything else I don't want to face. And I want you to come with me. But only whenever you feel you can leave your business and Kathleen." He ran out of breath, stopped, and waited.

"Those are just words, Dak." She motioned at the

papers she'd tossed. "All words. And not necessary because—"

"All I have are words!" He burst out, so frustrated he thought he'd explode. "I don't know what else I can say to convince you. I'm trying to be honest."

"—because I already knew you weren't going anywhere."

"And—" He stopped as her words caught up to him. "What?"

She smiled and touched his face. The crowd sighed. "When I saw you at the diner Friday night, I knew you weren't leaving. You'd risked your neck for some sooty bowls and a mangled chair." She smiled. "What else could I think? You did that for me. For me and for Florida . . . For Kathleen and for Missouri. Also for Peg. You cared about those things more than you cared that you could get brained trying to rescue them. Because all of *us* are important to you." She laughed. "Don't look so surprised. *You* taught me all about metaphor."

He frowned, thinking of that night. He'd acted on sheer impulse, but she was right. His subconscious must have prodded him. "Why didn't you say something then?"

"I could tell you hadn't realized it yet. If I'd told you what I thought—no, what I *knew*—you probably would have gone into your stubborn act or packed your duffel or something just to prove I was wrong."

"*I'm* stubborn?"

"Uh-huh." She patted his hand. "But you're pretty smart, too. I was sure you'd figure it out sooner or later."

He took off his hat, swept a hand through his hair. "You minx."

"But you're still here under false pretenses." Her expression was stern, and he couldn't tell if it was mock or real. "You assumed I was marrying Kemp Runyon for his money." There was a how-could-you note in her voice.

"Not really. But Kathleen said, and I didn't know what to think. I knew you didn't love him, so I—" He halted, suddenly alarmed again. "You don't love him, do you?"

"Kiss her!" An impatient voice called out and was immediately shushed.

"So you did all this." She swept an arm out. "It wasn't any more necessary than your book proposal. I'd made plans, you know. I had an appointment today—"

"You're not still planning to go through with that, are you?" She hadn't answered his question. Did she love Kemp Runyon?

She flashed him a disgruntled look. "Would you let me finish?"

Mute, he nodded.

"I'd made an appointment today—at a bank."

"A bank?"

"A *bank*. Not a wedding chapel. The bank PicNic uses in Warsaw was going to loan me the money to rebuild, provided Kemp would cosign. And I probably would have been in debt up to my wazoo for the rest of my life. But I had to try."

"I thought you were planning—"

"I know what you thought. I told Kemp last Friday I couldn't marry him. It never would have worked. I didn't love him, and Kemp was in love with the idea of marriage, not with me. He had to admit I was right. And then— I can't believe I had the gall—"

"I can," Dak said, and when she frowned at him, he shut up.

"I asked him if he'd help me get a loan. A real one. Not a handout from Lil or you." She stared off. "I was scared but I planned to work like a dog to pay it off, make a home for Kathleen, and wait for the idiot I love to come to his senses. And when he finally did . . . Well, I'd also realized it didn't take walls to make a home." She hesitated. "I really would like to go with you sometimes. But I won't mind if you go alone. Because I'm sure now that you'll always come back."

"Well, I'll be . . ."

She looked out over the crowd. "So you see, all this wasn't necessary, but I love you for it." Her voice grew soft. "In fact, I love you all for a lot of things."

He followed her gaze. From here, he could see a swatch of Cordelia, including the narrow roof of Cowboy's home. No, *their* home. His, Kathleen's, and Alcea's. Through a patch of trees, Alcea's trailer gleamed in all its pink splendor. He'd paint the Pink Palace a different color for Florida and Missouri, if Florida wanted him to. But he hoped she didn't. His eyes lingered over it all, thinking of the future, then he studied Alcea's profile. Elegant brow, delicate nose, strong chin . . . all etched against the horizon. "I always liked the view from the water tower, but you know what?"

"What?" She turned her head and their eyes met.

"I like the view better from here."

"Kiss her!" The heckler yelled again.

So Dak did.

Chapter 28

Held back by a wide ribbon Lil and Zinnia had stretched across the entrance, an excited crowd milled in front of Peg O' My Heart Cafe *and* Bakery. Across the building's brick facade, scoured clean of its charred past, an orange-and-red striped awning ruffled in the mild June breeze.

Reconstruction had taken eight months. Record time, considering the interruptions caused by the holiday season, some harsh winter weather, and some almost-as-harsh arguments between bastions of the old and proponents of the new over the diner's interior design.

Retaining the name of the business had been a no-brainer. Deciding on the color scheme, though, had been a topic of debate hotter than whether or not Tansy Eppelwaite had been insane when she'd allowed Rosemary Butz to dye her gray curls a brassy blond last October. (Alcea leaned toward a padded room, but kept her mouth shut. Tansy was happy.)

At Dak's suggestion, Alcea and Florida, who had maintained carefully neutral positions, had launched a "Design O' My Heart" contest last fall. In November, with more turnout than the last presidential election, the town had voted. Mari had won with a scheme she called "Retro Peg," and was now entitled to the first Dark Cocoa Buttermilk cake to emerge from Alcea's new oven, and a lifetime of free coffee.

Mari was now somewhere in the crowd behind her. Wearing a new striped uniform that matched the awning, Alcea stood up front between Dak and Kathleen, her arms around their waists. On Dak's other side, dressed in the same outfit, Florida held Missouri. The baby stared around wide-eyed at the fuss, momentarily forgetting to fret at the strings that tied a red tam topped by an orange pom-pom to her headful of dark curls. Serena had spotted the hat in a Kansas City boutique during one of Missouri's bimonthly outings with Stan.

Yesterday, Alcea and Florida had made a final inspection in preparation for today's grand reopening. Black and red squares—real tile this time, not linoleum—still hopscotched across the floor, interrupted at intervals by small inlaid orange tiles in the shape of butterflies. Just like the ones Peg had worn in her hair. The same lively colors, melded this time into a cohesive whole, continued through the rest of the decor. The dining area remained largely unchanged, although Mari's design had opened up the wall between diner and bakery to expand seating. Chrome chairs and tabletops in orange mixed with red booths that would have exactly matched the old ones if the duct tape hadn't been missing. The back room, the kitchen, and the bakery space had been reorganized so waitstaff and cook staff would no longer bump hips trying to serve customers. (And a space had been left so no shoe vaulting was required for the waitstaff to catch Tansy's trademark flings of food down the counter.)

They needed the efficiency. If the fund drive that had continued through the winter was an indication, they'd be swamped in the coming months. They'd hired two waitresses, one to replace Rosemary and another to move between the bakery and diner as needed. Alcea had also latched on to a new assistant who could take over the bakery when she traveled with Dak. Besides fresh paint and the Cordelia artifacts Mari had scrounged from O'Neill's Emporium, the walls held Peg's reupholstered stool, bolted into place by Julius, and a plaque that commemorated Peg's life, the date of the fire, and all the contributors that had made the business's rebirth possible. It was a big plaque.

And the results looked like a dream come true. For Alcea, it was.

On the other side of the ribbon, Cordelia's mayor, a plump woman with severely cropped salt-and-pepper hair, stepped onto a makeshift dais Julius had hammered out yesterday. She settled half-glasses on her nose and launched into a ponderous speech about traditions and community cooperation and entrepreneurial spirit. The fund-raiser Dak had instigated had attracted the attention not only of the *Cordelia Daily Sun,* but of other regional papers, as well. Politicians had picked up on the drive. And money had poured forth—from the town, from suppliers, from their summer tourist trade, and even from PicNic Poultry Processing Plant before Kemp Runyon had transferred himself back to Texas to be near his daughter.

Alcea and Florida had scrambled to make sure no names were omitted from the plaque, and Alcea had made sure one name headed the rest. Knowing her eyes brimmed with gratitude, Alcea tipped her head to look at Dak. He leaned toward her and they shared a soft kiss, breaking apart only when the crowd politely applauded the mayor off the dais. It was time.

Handing Missouri to Kathleen, who cooed into the baby's face, earning a gurgle, Florida grasped Alcea's arm and they stepped forward together. They cut the ribbon, and the crowd cheered. Over the noise, Alcea heard Peg's voice in her ear. "That's the way, sweetness." Noting the tears filming Florida's eyes, she knew Florida heard Peg, too.

With a smile that tore at her cheeks, Alcea turned to face the crowd. Pop beamed from a face as red as his suspenders. Her mother applauded wildly. Patsy

Lee hoisted her youngest daughter, Lily, so she could see. As she stood next to Jon, Lil's eyes glowed. And Mari stuck two fingers in her mouth and let out a piercing whistle. Feeling her heart well with love, Alcea swept with her gaze all the familiar, dear faces and finally settled on Dak. His piercing eyes held her soul.

But even in the sweet-savory warmth of the moment, Alcea felt a thrum of impatience to get going. She had a business to run, and more things to move from the Pink Palace—that Florida and Missouri would soon inhabit—into Cowboy's newly remodeled house, now complete with a full-service kitchen, a ruffled bedroom for Kathleen, and an office for Dak, where he would put the finishing touches on his novel. It would be published next year. Under his pen name.

She also had a September wedding to finish planning. The wedding would be a snap compared to figuring out what she could stuff in the duffel bag Dak had given her for Christmas. Soon her bag would sport the same scuff marks and ground-in dirt of his own. They'd decided on a long honeymoon with no clear destination. They'd meander to their hearts' content, and explore new horizons.

Then they'd come home.

Dear Reader,

I sincerely hope you've enjoyed *Follow Me Home*, the second in a series of novels all based in and around the fictional small town of Cordelia, Missouri. Which begs a question I'm often asked: "Why Cordelia?" My answer: I couldn't envision anywhere more special.

Having spent many summers in the Missouri Ozarks, I'm in love with its small towns, seasonal rhythms, lakeland beauty, and people. Like in most places, the area and residents shape each other. The two are intertwined, inseparable . . . and not just a matter of hard geography. I didn't choose to create this fictional town, its surroundings, and its characters, as much as they chose me.

Cordelia, Missouri—and all that it encompasses—is the *home of my heart*.

Just as it is for Lil O'Malley in *Sing Me Home* and Alcea O'Malley in *Follow Me Home*. While both women learn they can, and sometimes should, make choices that range beyond the boundaries of Cordelia, each has always known that *home*—whether held in their hearts or firmly under their feet—represents what matters most in all of our lives: roots, family, friends . . . love.

Ahhh, but in the upcoming *Hurry Home*, Mari

O'Malley doesn't yet understand this. But when an emergency summons her back to Cordelia, she, too, will have the opportunity to learn something about *home*. Not just from her family, but from her former best friend, Andy Eppelwaite.

In the following excerpt, Mari and Andy encounter each other for the first time since her return to Cordelia. Having lost touch with him in her late teens, when Andy's drinking and carousing earned him the moniker No-Account, Mari is unaware of the changes Andy has made in his life, even though he's realizing one thing has remained constant . . . his love for his childhood chum.

I hope you'll enjoy spending more time in Cordelia. . . . Welcome back home!

Jerri

Hurry Home

On Monday, Peg O' My Heart Cafe and Bakery, on the corner of Main and Oak Haven Road in the old town square of Cordelia, was in its usual state of bedlam. Waitresses flew across its red and black tiles, crockery clanked, the grill sizzled, and conversation mounted as the old-timers settled into the red vinyl booths for a good jaw, just like they did every morning.

Andrew Eppelwaite gave up trying to catch his grandmother's attention. Tansy stood at the grill, as she had for the last half century, shoulder blades moving like scissors under her thin frame as she alternately flipped pancakes and handed off plates to a couple of buxom twins who gave him a twitch of their apron bows whenever they passed his stool at the counter.

With an inward grin, he touched the brim of his baseball cap, but didn't otherwise answer the come-on. At thirty, he had about a decade on them both. They were too young to know him—he hadn't been back except for a few days at a time for over four years—but you could bet their parents did. If No-Account Andy showed up on their doorstep, Mom and Dad would give him the old heave-ho. And they'd be justified. He'd been a hide-the-good-silver and lock-up-your-daughters kind of guy back then. If he hadn't been lifting a skirt or launching a brawl, he'd been guzzling beer at the Rooster Bar & Grill.

He tossed some change on the counter and eased off the stool, stomping a boot to get too-tight faded jeans back into place over his long legs. He hadn't had the time or interest—or the money, for that matter—to do much with a wardrobe since he'd gotten out of the hoosegow a few years back. "See you later, Gran," he called out.

She turned and nodded a birdlike chin. Her near-white sausage curls—a vast improvement over the gold dye job she'd had a few years back—bobbed. "Don't you go gettin' yerself up to no good, Andy." But she cackled as she said the words. What was once a worry was now a joke between them, bless her loyal little heart.

Andy grinned back and sidled over to the cash register. From the stool behind it, the proprietor, Alcea O'Malley Jones, gave him a smile that could make a man's heart melt. She was a looker—always had been—but of course, from her almost-eleven-years-older perspective, she'd never noticed the lanky kid with the too-long hair who had hung out with her littlest sister, Mari.

"Glad to see you're back, Andy," Alcea said, reaching out to take the check he laid on the counter. "Tansy's pretty proud of you."

"So Gran tells me about, oh, twenty times a day. It's about time I gave her something to be proud of."

"Mari's in town. As of Saturday night." Alcea handed him his change. "You should look her up."

He fumbled, and a quarter rolled onto the floor. Blood rushed to his head, and not just because he'd stooped to pick it up. "Might do that."

He tipped his cap and pushed through the screen door with studied casualness. He wouldn't mind seeing Mari O'Malley; in fact, he'd like nothing better. But he wasn't so sure Mari would want to see him. They'd once been best buds, but after a trip into the back of his pickup at sixteen, things had changed. His fault—and something else he could live to regret.

Outside, he squinted at a robin's egg sky, tugged down his cap against a blustery May wind until just a hint of blond curly hair stuck out underneath, then started toward the east edge of town, walking along the row of brick-fronted shops, taking in the sun-kissed green of the Ozark hills off in the distance. Once was nobody thought he'd amount to much, but just like they'd shaken their heads over him when he was a whelp, now the folks of Cordelia had rallied behind him. You'd think that by landing a job—and not just any job, but one that had taken hard work to pull off—he'd roped in the moon.

Pushing regrets to the back of his brain, enjoying the sunshine, enjoying the feeling of well-being that, except for a couple of blips, was several years old and still too new to be taken for granted—if he was lucky, he would *never* take it for granted—he passed Rusty's Hardware and neared Merry-Go-Read, one of the three children's bookstores Mari's middle sister Lil had started after she'd flummoxed the town by getting hitched to a country music superstar almost nine years back. Mari had been in college then, only visiting Cordelia now and again, and never once looking him up. Much to his chagrin. She'd—

Like he'd conjured her up, the bookstore door snapped open on a jangle of bells and Mari strode out, nearly knocking him down.

His heart jumped, but he acted like their first real encounter in fourteen years wasn't that big a deal. "Whoa. Hang on there, Mar." He locked onto her arm to keep her from falling.

Mari steadied herself and shrugged out of his grasp. "I swear if I ever get out—" She glanced up. Blue eyes locked on blue, and her jaw dropped. "*No-Account Andy.*"

He gave her a one-sided grin. "I prefer just plain Andy, but good to see you anyway." And it was. More than good. Same generous mouth. Same sprinkle of freckles. Same perpetual exasperation. Same . . .

Looking at her hair, he frowned. "What's up with the do? Looks like a kid outlined your hair with Magic Marker."

She flushed as red as her hair, one of her hands flying up to pull at a black tip. "I just haven't had time to get it cut." She glanced at his faded jeans, up to his faded plaid shirt, and into his eyes, her color returning to normal, her hand dropping, disdain lurking behind her gaze. "*Some* of us are busy."

He started back down the walk, feeling a grin hiding behind his lips. They'd picked up squabbling almost right where they'd left off. "Oh, I've got places to go, people to see," he assured her.

They passed the cigar store Indian sitting out front of O'Neill's Emporium, and the grin surfaced big-time. He remembered when the two of them had roped it up and tied it to the belfry of St. Andrew's Church.

"Yeah, I'll bet." She'd fallen in beside him, her steps matching his stride for stride, a long peasant-type dress in some silky material slapping around her calves above cork-heeled shoes two stories tall. With the doodads on her ears, she looked the part of an artist. Or, at least, she looked like she wanted to look the part of an artist. That was Mari. Trying to be anything the town wasn't. In your face. Honest to a fault. Things that had maddened him; things he'd admired. "That's why you're headed in the direction of the Rooster?"

"Which is also"—he pointed out—"the direction of Beadler's Feed." The Rooster Bar & Grill lay next door to the farmers' supply store. "You going that way?"

"I'm going that way." Her voice was grim. "My sister Alcea lives next to Cowboy's." Cowboy's Tow and Service was across from Beadler's.

"She's not there. I just saw her at the diner." It felt good, just swinging along beside Mari.

"I know, but Dak—her husband—*is* home. And I need to pick up an edition of Mother Goose and Lil s he probably has one. Which *she* didn't, although you'd think a children's bookstore would have a frigging nursery rhyme book, but, *nooo*, and now I'm hotfooting it down there and will probably spend the next hour searching through shelves—Dak has a ton of damn books and you can bet neither he nor Alcea has put them in any kind of order. Alcea and Dak don't *do* order. They say they're too busy."

He almost laughed, remembering the mess in Mari's room, her backpack, and her school locker. Open it up, and chances were that you'd get buried alive. "Why a Mother Goose emergency?"

"Because Mom has it in her head that she needs to know the exact words of Humpty Dumpty—because she and Pop were arguing whether it was 'couldn't put him together again' or 'couldn't put him *back* together again,' and *this* after I'd just dropped an egg on the floor and got a royal reaming over how hard she's always worked to keep those floors clean. Which is nothing compared to the earful I got yesterday after she asked me to weed her garden and I pulled up some—some . . ." She frowned.

"Perennials?" he offered.

"Yes. What do I know? They look like weeds to me. But it's not my job to say no to anything she asks me, even if she knows I have a brown thumb. It's my job—bestowed on me by my two *wonderful* sisters—to play Steppen Fetchit for the next God-knows-how-long." She paused for a breath. "And wouldn't you know Pop's computer is broken and I don't have my Mac set up yet, because it would have been a snap to look it up on the Internet."

Ah, Mari was in fine form. He realized just how much he'd missed her chatter. They passed under the green awning of Sin-Sational Ice Cream where they'd shared many a soda—no romance there, just lack of funds to buy two—and stepped off the curb onto Maple Woods Drive. Beadler's Feed was on the opposite corner.

He motioned up the street. "Your folks still live that way?"

"They won't move out of there until they die." She threw a black look where he'd gestured. "Which might not be too many hours from now."

"I thought you all got along." As a kid, he'd envied Mari her family. He'd had Gran, but nobody else except for an absent sister. His mood momentarily dipped at the thought of Anna.

They stepped up on the opposite curb.

"We do get along." Mari sounded unconvinced. She drew a deep breath as they paused on the corner. "But Mom just had bypass surgery. The doctor warned us she might have some emotional issues—or some temporary personality changes. I guess it does that to some people."

"Gran told me about the surgery." Without thinking, he brushed a short lock of hair back from her forehead like he used to do, but she didn't react. If she was harboring any long-held yearnings where he was concerned, she certainly hid them well. He let his hand fall. "So she's not herself."

"No. She's short-tempered and has all these *unreasonable* demands, and Pop's not used to dealing with her like that, and me . . ." Her gaze flew up to his, and he could see the worry behind her frustration. "I'm just not used to seeing her like this, Andy. She needs help with *everything*, and she looks so pale and so *small*."

The intervening years had just fallen away. She was just as confiding, and he was just as willing to listen.

"It'll get better, Mar."

"I hope so." She looked around as though just remembering where they were. Her gaze fell on his truck. "*Omigod*, you still have that old thing?"

He laughed. "Hard to believe, isn't it?"

They scraped over the graveled parking lot to his Ford pickup sitting next to a pallet stacked with bags of sand and black soil. Once a shade of apple red, the ck was now an oxidized pink where it wasn't pure rust. She peeked into the bed, apparently not seeing the assortment of shovels and spades and gardening tools, but only the past, because when she turned around, her face matched the truck.

And when their eyes locked, he knew they were both reliving the same scene. Moonlight. Tanned hands on milk-white skin. A lot of fumbling and cursing and grunting.

He refused to let the number of times he'd thought about that night show in his face, and grinned at her instead. "I had bruises on my knees for a week. Always wondered what it had done to your backside."

"Gee, how chivalrous." Mari punched his arm. Hard enough that he wanted to wince, but he didn't. "My backside was just fine, thanks."

He lowered the gate, stooped to pick up a bag, settled it into the bed, and went after another. She watched him. When he glanced up, her gaze was full of speculation.

"This all yours?" She motioned at the bags and tools. When he nodded, she nodded, too. "Doing some work for old Erik, are you?"

Erik Olausson owned a lawn business. In high school, even after, the old Swede had handed Andy some odd jobs, knowing Andy would be good for them until the next paycheck. Which Andy drank away before he got back to work.

He started to answer her, but as usual she already thought she had it all figured out and was off at a run. He let her go, hoping for an opportunity to rein her in later.

"You don't suppose you have time to do some work over at the folks' house, do you?" she asked. When his brows drew together, she added, "I'd ask Erik, but Mom already said she doesn't want to spend the money on—"

She broke off, but hardly looked abashed at the gaffe she'd been about to make. He knew her—her brain was just spinning with how to weasel what s[illegible] wanted out of him in a politically correct way.

"On someone's *professional* help?" he asked mildly, heaving another bag up.

"Well, yes. But they'd pay you . . . something. I think."

Behind her, a Mercedes pulled up in front of the Rooster. He glanced over, then at his watch.

Mari snorted, apparently misinterpreting the gesture as a need for libation. He didn't wonder at it. Time was, he'd be knocking back brews before noon.

"Seamus doesn't open up the bar until eleven." Her tone held derision.

He hid another grin. Let her have her delusions for now. "I have an appointment at the Rooster." He bent for another bag.

"With who? Jim Beam?" She didn't wait for an answer, but rushed on. "So, will you? Help out Mom? It would mean a lot to her to know her gardens were taken care of, and by someone who knows at least something about what he's doing. Puh-lease?"

He straightened and looked down at her. She raised her eyes, looking miffed at having to do so. At almost five-ten, she was no shrimp and she'd liked looking over everyone's heads. She'd always hated that he'd grown to six foot four by the time they were fifteen.

"Since when have I ever said no to anything you ever asked?" He gave a pointed nod at the pickup bed.

Her face fired up again, and memories wafted between them.

"A TREASURE."
—SUSAN WIGGS

Sing Me Home

by Jerri Corgiat

Lilac O'Malley Ryan doesn't even recognize country music star Jonathan Van Castle when he bursts into her store. She just wants to make the sale and get him out the door. But after he's gone, she can't get his to-die-for smile out of her mind...

Jon and Lil are about to discover what happens when two unlikely lovers hit the perfect note.

"A DELIGHFUL BOOK, A MASTERFUL BLEND OF NASHVILLE GLITZ AND DOWN-HOME SIMPLICITY THAT WILL TOUCH ANY ROMANCE READER'S HEART."
—CATHERINE ANDERSON

0-451-41128-5

Available wherever books are sold or at www.penguin.com

o556